ALASKA
A RICK SPEARS ADVENTURE

Robert P. Long

iUniverse LLC
Bloomington

ALASKA
A RICK SPEARS ADVENTURE

iUniverse books may be ordered through booksellers or by contacting:

iUniverse LLC
1663 Liberty Drive
Bloomington, IN 47403
www.iuniverse.com
1-800-Authors (1-800-288-4677)

ISBN: 978-1-4917-3145-1 (sc)
ISBN: 978-1-4917-3147-5 (hc)
ISBN: 978-1-4917-3146-8 (e)

Library of Congress Control Number: 2014906997

Printed in the United States of America.

iUniverse rev. date: 05/28/2014

This book is dedicated to
Miriam Long

Cover art credit to
Linda Zick

CONTENTS

PROLOGUE

Rick had been trying desperately to find a comfortable position so that he could sleep. This was the first night after having been attacked by a huge grizzly bear. The pain killer had helped, but he could not find a way to lay his head without putting pressure on an injury. The doctor had used more than seventy stitches. Rick's brave dog Bart had incurred a concussion defending him. He lay on the floor by the bed.

Rick's head, chest and back were bandaged. The doctor was concerned about infection from the deep bites on his head and the cuts on his back from the bear's filthy claws. The bear had drawn Rick's head into its massive jaws. He could still smell the foul breath from the grizzly's mouth.

Being unable to sleep, he diverted his attention from the attack and his injuries to reviewing in his mind how his Alaska adventure brought him to this point.

It all started like this:

PART ONE

CHAPTER I

Rick was nearing the end of his trip from North Dakota to a remote area of Alaska. He was a writer of short stories about fishing and hunting small game. He had camped out hundreds of times, usually for a few days at a time. He was frequently accompanied by his photographer and a member or two from a hunting club. There had been little danger. On occasion they might see a black bear, but these bears steered clear of humans.

Now he would be entering the wilderness where the predators were aggressive. The grizzly was huge and afraid of nothing. The wolves hunted in packs and would attack animals much larger than themselves, including man. He would be alone, and there would be no answer to a 911 call.

This trip had been planned for a long time. He wanted to write a book about the experience of living alone in the wilderness without electricity, as the old timers had done. Only then could the book be written from firsthand knowledge.

He was driving his pick-up and was accompanied by his large Malamute dog, Bart. In the back of the truck Rick had his woodworking tools, his axe, guns, fishing gear, and supplies. He was towing a flatbed trailer with a canoe and a combination cart and sled. He had made the cart so that he could use it on dry land with wheels, or as a sled on snow and ice with runners. The cart could be pulled by Rick or by the dog. Bart was very strong and could pull the cart fully loaded with ease.

Forty miles north, after leaving the last town, the road grew narrow and then stopped in front of a log building with the sign "TRADING POST". A moose head was hung above the sign. Rick parked the truck and he and Bart went into the store. There they met "Joel" the proprietor who was in the center, in front of a huge potbellied stove. To the right of Joel was the hardware section with saws, traps, guns, knives, to the left were blankets, sleeping bags, parkas, scarves, boots, socks, gloves and mittens. Behind the stove were food items, mostly nonperishables canned goods, dry beans and rice, hardtack, and various kinds of jerky.

Rick and Joel introduced themselves, and Joel `motioned for Rick to have a seat.

Joel said, "I have been in Alaska for over twenty years. I did some gold mining and some hunting. I was a Bush Pilot, and now I have been the proprietor of the Trading Post for about ten years."

Rick saw that Joel appeared to be in his late sixties or early seventies. He was about five foot ten inches tall. He had put on a few pounds around the middle, but was not fat. He wore suspenders and dungarees. His hair was turning grey.

"Tell me a bit about yourself Rick."

"I just drove here from North Dakota. I am a writer of short stories for a sports magazine. The stories are about fishing and small game hunting."

Joel asked, "What is your last name?"

"My last name is Spears."

"I have read some of your articles and they were great. Why are you coming up to this remote part of Alaska?"

"I want to write a book about living alone in the wilderness. Any suggestions that you can give me to help me get started will be welcome."

"Let me ask you a few questions? How much time do you intend to spend on this project? Do you have the finances to see it through? Do you have supplies and food?"

"Finances are not a problem. My intention is to learn as I go, along. I want to live subsistence style. I want to experience both summer and winter seasons. As to tools and equipment, I have a canoe, a cart, and wood working tools not requiring electricity, guns and knives. I have cold weather clothing. As for food, I have brought some staples, and of course, I intend to fish and hunt for small game."

"Where do you intend to stay?"

"I have camping equipment, until I can find or build a more substantial dwelling."

"I can help you there. There is a vacant cabin, fifteen or so miles north of here. You can move right in. No one will bother you. The last person who used it left about a year ago. He couldn't stand the isolation and had a close call with a grizzly. It is by the river and has a very nice view."

"That sounds great. Thanks."

"It will take some work to get it back to a livable condition, but it will be better than a tent. You are starting late you know. It is now August and the winter starts up here in October. You will need lots of wood to keep you warm this winter. Trees will need to be felled, cut into stove size lengths, hauled to the cabin, and then stacked, and covered to keep the rain and snow off. Once it snows it will be one hundred times harder than it is now. Your fishing and small game hunting will be helpful, but in addition a large volume of meat will be needed to last the winter. You might consider building a smoke house to preserve your meat. A deer would be enough considering that you will have small game and fish. Beginning in October the bears want to hibernate and the other animals become scarce, except for wolves and wolverines. Next, what do you plan to do about water?"

"I will carry it from a stream or river. Do you have any suggestions?"

"Just that one must assume that it is polluted. Of course you will be boiling the water, but I also have pills to purify it. Let's go and gather up the things that you will need initially. You can come back in a month or so to get the rest that we missed today."

They made a list of the needed items then collected them.

"You have had a long day. I have a bunk room that I have for customers who are unable to make it home before dark. You and Bart can sleep here tonight, and get an early start in the morning."

"Thanks, that would be great. I am very tired from all of those hours driving. I was just about to leave and find a place to set up my tent."

"Come; let me show you to the bunk room. The bathroom is in the next room. We will have dinner in about one half hour. I'll come by your room to show you the way to dinner."

Rick and Bart went to the truck and got a few things. Then Rick took Bart for a ten minute walk. Bart was glad for the walk and scampered around like a puppy, retrieving sticks that Rick threw for him. Rick had spent considerable time training Bart to always come when called no matter what. Even when Bart was chasing a small animal, he would stop and return to Rick when called. They returned to the room and got ready for dinner.

Joel came by and showed Rick his living quarters. It was spacious and had a large and beautiful fireplace. Joel introduced Rick to his wife Jane.

Jane said, "Welcome Rick. What a beautiful dog you have. Tell me what kind of a dog it is."

"Thanks. I'm glad to meet you. My dogs name is Bart. He is a bit reserved with those he doesn't know. He is of a breed called "Malamute". It serves much the same purpose as a Husky, which most people are familiar with, but it is larger and stronger. These dogs are well known as powerful sled dogs. This breed was selected by Admiral Perry to go to the Pole."

They sat down to dinner. Bart acquainted himself with the room and then lay down by Rick's feet.

Jane said, "Joel caught this beautiful salmon early this morning. This is the time of the year when they are plentiful and we do enjoy them so much."

Joel told Rick, "That reminds me to tell you. On your way to the cabin you will see the river. It runs close to the trail at that point. The bottom of the river is hard, and the water is shallow, probably only one to two feet deep. The bears like to fish for salmon there. The river is called, Bear Creek. I wonder if the bears will be bothered by the sight of your dog. I suggest going by as quietly and inconspicuously as possible."

"Thanks for warning me about the bears. We will be careful. The salmon is delicious. This is the first that I have had fresh salmon for quite a while."

Jane asked, "Rick, are you, or have you been married, or have someone special?"

"I was married once, briefly, it just didn't work out. We parted amicably, and there were no children. I have several beautiful girlfriends, but marriage is not in my mind."

Joel said "Northeast of the cabin there are two brothers who trap animals for their fur. They live some eight or so miles from the cabin, but they are your closest neighbors. They come here in the spring to sell their furs, and in the fall to replenish their supplies. They have lived there a long time. They are ok. If you have time you might enjoy meeting them. There is a Native Village north west of the Brothers. There is also a small lake east of your cabin. I have seen it from the air but I haven't been there."

They talked some more, then Rick decided to write a few letters to friends and business associates, letting them know that they could write to him care of the Trading Post, and said good night. Later he and Bart went for a walk before going to bed.

In the morning Joel knocked on Rick's door and invited him to breakfast. Rick asked Joel if he could let his truck at the Post and Joel agreed. Rick settled up his bill with Joel, he then packed up, including a good sized cabbage that Jane had given to him. Bart was in his harness ready to pull the cart. Rick had his Smith and Wesson 500 revolver in a holster on his right hip. This revolver is well known and used by Alaska Outfitters and Guides as it is a powerful last line of defense. On his left hip was a scabbard with a combination knife and machete. It was shorter than a machete, being only 18 inches long, but even stronger.

They all said goodbye, and Rick gave the signal to Bart to go and they were on their way to the cabin.

CHAPTER II

Rick started off at a nice easy trot beside Bart and the cart. He was thinking of his running and long distance skiing in North Dakota.

Back at the Trading Post Jane was saying what a nice man Rick was and she said, "Do you think he will be ok?"

Joel answered, "He has a lot of outdoor experience, and he is used to the cold. Our summer season only lasts four months, and he is arriving late with only two months left. He will not have time to have a vegetable garden."

Rick continued to jog, remembering that Joel had told him about the bears feeding in the river. He hoped that the bears would not bother him as long as they were eating. The exception would be if a cub came near the trail and Rick. He saw some small game, but no bears or wolves. After several miles he saw the river at a distance. As he got closer it looked like there were bears in the river. Rick noticed something moving off to his right in the woods, but then it stopped. After a bit, there it was again. There were three wolves. Bart uttered a deep growl, but Rick told him that it was ok and the growling ceased. He looked again, and the wolves were coming towards him. They were baring their teeth. They were ready to charge.

At that point Bart whirred to meet their attack baring his teeth and snarling visciously. Rick pulled his 30-06 rifle from the cart, and took aim on the leader of the pack. Just then the wolves turned and ran into the woods. Rick put his rifle back into the cart and hugged Bart, telling him what a great dog he was. Bart wagged and gave Rick a kiss. Rick got Bart and the cart back on the trail. When he looked up he saw a bear at a distance of not more than twenty feet, eating a salmon. The bear had scared the wolves away.

Rick exclaimed, "Let's get out of here."

They walked quietly until they were past the bears. Although Bart wanted to express his displeasure at the bears Rick told him it was ok and he was quiet.

A mile or so further, the grass was high between the trail and the woods. It was four to six feet tall. An area of about twelve by fourteen feet had been trampled down. Rick could see it rising slowly. A bear had been there just minutes ago. The nearby trees were clawed at a height of twelve or more feet. That was no black bear. That was a grizzly! As he looked deep into the woods he saw the back of a grizzly walking away.

A number of miles later they saw the river appearing on the left, and then the cabin. They hurried on and parked the cart in front. Rick released Bart from the harness. He shook himself and then ran around the cabin before coming back to Rick. Rick examined the outside and saw that the door was partly off its hinges, caulking was missing from between some of the logs, and the smoke stack was askew. Walking around the cabin he saw a stack of boards, and wondered what the previous resident had intended to do with it. At the back he found an "Out House". It appeared to be in good condition.

Returning to the front he noted that most of the trees between the cabin and the river had been removed. It was a beautiful view. The land sloped down from the cabin to the river, dropping several feet over the length of about two hundred feet, and then it dropped more sharply for the last several feet to the river. Rick saw that this would be an ideal place for a dock for the canoe.

He went into the cabin and was surprised at what he saw. In the center of the room was a very nice cast iron stove suitable for cooking, baking and heating the cabin. Joel had told him that there was a jewel in the cabin but would not elaborate. The stove could make the difference between success and failure of his stay. Looking around he saw a single cot, a table with three chairs and a kerosene lamp on it. In the corner he saw a snow shovel, a broom and a wash tub. On the wall there were wooden boxes, three wide and three high, with the open ends facing the center of the room. They could be used as cupboards without doors. There was a small window in the front of the cabin that was approximately two feet wide and two feet high. As he looked at the walls he could see daylight through the holes between the logs. Large hooks hung from the rafters. Although there was work to be done, the condition of the cabin and the items that had been left by the previous tenant was encouraging. Things were looking up.

Now it was time to empty the cart. First he took the canoe inside and hung it from the rafters. He completed bringing items from the cart.

Rick selected some fishing gear and went to the river. After a few casts he had a nice salmon for dinner. The cabin stove could not be used until he repaired the smoke stack so he got his camping gear out and cooked the salmon on it.

After eating he decided to get some firewood for use in the morning. He got his cart, axe, and saw and went to the woods. A lot of dead branches had fallen to the ground. These were ideal for kindling, and were brought to the front of the cabin.

Rick gathered his writing materials and began the project of writing his book. It was the reason that he had come to Alaska. The words came easily, but before he knew it, he was almost nodding off. It had been a busy day. Running, unloading and sorting the contents of the cart, gathering wood, fishing and writing, had taken their toll. He was tired. He took Bart for a walk. They returned to the cabin and went to bed.

Early the next morning they took a walk around the cabin. Rick took in the beautiful view, looking across the river. Near the river, the evergreens blanketed the land which sloped upward. In the distance the trees had stopped growing and the mountain side revealed cracks and crevices. The colors varied from dark shading to the sparkle on a rocky seam. Above, he saw the magnificent mountains with their white robes of snow. He carried water from the river, and added a tablet to purify it. He made some instant coffee and ate a power bar, and went to work. First he repaired the door, then the smokestack. He found that the mud from the river had a clay-like quality that he could use for caulking. Using a trowel he caulked both the outside and the inside of the logs. The windows were also treated.

Now it was time to get to the big job of cutting wood. He got the cart, saw, axe, and his armament and went to the edge of the woods. He left them there while he searched for the trees that he wanted. He was looking for dead trees that were dry that could be used for firewood. They would be easier to handle and cut. He found three within an area of a couple acres and felled them. The limbs were cut off. Next he sawed the trees into smaller sizes. The trees were too heavy to drag to the cabin.

The project was continued in the following days. Before stacking the wood, he built an overhanging roof on the front of the cabin, to protect the wood from rain and snow. The roof ran from the door (which was on the left facing the cabin) to the end of the cabin. Each piece was then cut to the appropriate length for the stove. It was then neatly stacked. The stacked wood was about four feet high, four foot deep, and eight feet in width. This was approximately one cord of wood. He was not certain how much he would need. He heaved a sigh of relief when it was finished.

It was time for dinner, so after taking a break he made a fire in the stove and put water on to boil. He then went fishing. His first catch was a small nondescript fish that he gave to Bart. Bart was delighted. He picked it up and tossed it around, playing with it before he began to chew at the head. Rick knew that an uncooked fish would not harm Bart even if he ate the bones. His next cast provided a beautiful salmon. They returned to the cabin and Rick prepared a meal for himself of carrots, potatoes and salmon. For Bart he mixed some salmon with premium dry dog food. Although salmon was plentiful now, he did not want to spoil Bart from the staple dry dog food. It had been a full day and Rick was tired. They went outside and saw the beautiful clear evening overlooked by thousands of glittering stars.

In the morning he looked over the work that he had done and realized that two weeks had already passed since he arrived at the Trading Post. This day seemed like a good one to take off from chores and to spend time with his good friend and to do a bit of hunting or fishing. He played with Bart and although Bart was not great on retrieving he did bring a few items back. Rick had breakfast and gave Bart a biscuit. They walked around and gravitated toward the river. Walking north he saw animal footprints on the soft ground by the water. Further on he saw a log that had run aground. This might be easier than cutting down a tree. He pulled the log further onto the land and went back to the cabin to get some line. He had brought with him one hundred feet of three eights inch strong nylon rope. He put a harness on Bart, connected the line to the harness and to himself. With both pulling together they got the log fully up on the land. He would let it lay and dry out before cutting it up.

After removing the harness and returning it and the line, Rick got the canoe out. Bart jumped in readily and they shoved off. Going along the river he saw another log and decided he would get it the next day ¬ or so. But today was goof off day. On the far bank he saw a moose. It would be great to have all that meat for the winter, but he didn't have a way to preserve it. He would have to think more about the idea of having a smoke house. Then the idea occurred to him of going to see the Brothers. Yes, he would go.

CHAPTER III

The next morning they had breakfast. Then he caught two salmon for the Brothers. They were each two and one half feet long. He removed the heads and tails and gutted the fish. Then placed them in a large plastic bag, and then in his backpack. He took his tent and other camping gear. In addition, he took food for Bart and himself. He also took his armament. He slung on the backpack and attached the rifle to it. Bart was eagerly waiting, and so it began. Rick started off with his usual ground covering trot.

Joel had told him to go North on the trail a number of miles until he came to a large split tree. It may have been hit by lightning. Then he was to go northeast until he reached his destination. They found the split tree. Rick consulted his compass and got on the new course. The trail here was more overgrown than the main trail, but wasn't a problem. He did slow from his trot. He saw small game, lots of squirrels, some birds and a rabbit now and then. And then he saw a deer. He was tempted, but this was not the time to kill a deer. As he walked along he wondered if the Brothers had dogs. Bart would get along well within a pack of sled dogs, but would be aggressive to others. Rick had spent a good deal of time teaching Bart to stand still, and let the others sniff. The other dogs usually sniffed, and then guardedly withdrew realizing the strength and steadfast gaze of Bart. Rick kept his fingers crossed. The trail was now fairly clear and Rick resumed his trot. After a mile, it was time for a break and they stopped for a few minutes. Rick had a power bar and a drink of water. Bart had a dog biscuit and some water. They resumed their running, and in a few miles, he saw smoke rising in the distance. Very soon they came into a clearing and saw the large cabin. Two hunting dogs came bounding out, baying as some hunting dogs do. Rick cautioned Bart to be on his good behavior and they stopped. The hounds came up, sniffed, and gingerly backed down.

Rick hollered, "Hello", and sae two men walking toward them. Both men called hello at once and came to greet Rick. Introductions were made and George and Phil invited Rick and Bart into their cabin. Rick gave them the fish. The Brothers were delighted since they did not live near the water. Fish was a rare treat. The cabin was spacious, having several rooms. The main room had a large stone fireplace which was burning brightly. Outside it was about 40 degrees, and the fire took the chill out of the room. Heads of various animals hung on the walls. They all sat down and George asked Rick to tell them how he happened to be visiting them.

Rick told them essentially what he had told Joel and Jane. He also told them of his work on the cabin. He said, "I am not sure how much wood that I need, I have just about a cord stacked."

Phil said, "For an average winter, if you don't keep the cabin too hot, you might get by. If we have a cold winter you will be short. On the safe side you need to double what you have."

"That is quite a dog you have," said George. "He plumb bamboozled the hounds—they didn't know what to make of him."

"Oh, they knew." said Phil, "They were afraid of him."

"Now that they have met I am sure that they will be fine," said Rick. "Let's take you on a tour."

Each man had a bedroom with its own wood stove. There was a large room with a big table in the center that was used to process the furs. The kitchen was large and had a stove like the one in Rick's cabin.

Phil explained that the stoves had been delivered at the same time to each cabin.

There was a large pantry. The room was 8 by 10 and the shelves were filled with vegetables that the Brothers had canned. It almost looked like a grocery store. Then attached to the rear of the cabin was another room. It was a chicken coup.

They explained that each spring they got 24 hens. These chickens were dual purpose birds. They laid some eggs, but they were excellent meat birds. The breed was called "Bahamas". They were gentle and could become pets. They were of a light buff color. The Brothers fed them well, and when winter came, one hen became a dinner each

Sunday. The outer door opened to a large fenced area where the hens could hunt and peck.

Now that they were outside Rick saw that they had a large vegetable garden. He also saw that they had a Jeep and a flatbed trailer. Next to the Jeep was an enormous amount of wood. It had been cut for either the fireplace or for the stoves.

Rick commented on the quantity of wood.

George explained, "Our primary source of income is from our trapping and selling furs. Every year is not a good year for furs however and we supplement our income in various ways. One way is to sell wood cut to the customer's specifications."

Rick said, "I would like to buy a cord from you, but my objective is to do all I can by myself in order to experience each task."

Rick was impressed with what he saw and asked if they would mind if he took photos.

They were pleased with his interest and asked if he would send to them copies of the pictures.

"Of course," Rick agreed. He thought that he might write an article for a magazine.

They went back inside and the brothers invited Rick to have dinner with them.

He thanked them.

Phil told Rick, "You have your choice of dinner tonight. George and I are going to enjoy your fish, and you may have fish, or our pot roast."

Rick said without hesitation, "I would like to have the pot roast."

"I'll have it ready in a jiffy. Come out in the kitchen with me so that we can continue to talk. We don't have much opportunity to talk to anyone other than ourselves."

Rick asked, "Tell me about your trapping."

"Well, our trap line runs to the north from here about thirty miles. We can't walk that far carrying animals, so we use snowmobiles. We always take two because of the potential volume of animals, and then for safety. If we are twenty miles from here and one breaks down, we can't walk our way out. We tow a small trailer behind each snowmobile."

"Do you ever have problems other than mechanical?"

"Yes, there is a problem, and you need to watch out for it too. It is a man called 'Krazy Joe'. We believe that he has been robbing our traps. He has also been bothering the girls at the Native Village. Then he came down here and tried to push me around. When he saw George coming out of the cabin, and knew that there were two of us he backed off a bit. We finally had to give him a chicken to get rid of him. How big are you Rick?"

Rick answered, "I am six foot-one and I weigh 190."

"Well, that is big, and you look to be strong, but Krazy Joe is 6-4 and is about 250 pounds. Of course, you have that dog of yours and I imagine he would be a help."

"Yes, whether it would be a man, a bear or a wolf, I know that Bart would defend me to the death."

Upon hearing his name Bart looked up at Rick and wagged his tail. Rick petted him.

"I guess that you are about 35 years old Rick."

"Thanks, for the compliment, but I am 45."

"We are in our mid 60's, but we keep active, and healthy."

Rick said that he would like to feed Bart first. He got the food out of his backpack and put it in Bart's dish.

Phil put a large spoon full of the beef stew on top and Bart dove in.

Dinner was on the table.

George said "Grace", and for a bit the conversation stopped.

Then Rick said, "Tell me please, what kind of meat this delicious pot roast contains."

"That is black bear meat," said Phil, "We think it is as good as cow meat any day."

"I couldn't agree more," said Rick.

After dinner they talked for an hour or so, and Rick was invited to stay over. They showed Rick to his room. Rick took Bart for a walk, and the hounds followed. Upon returning to the cabin they all said good night and went to bed.

In the morning they had breakfast.

Rick asked about the lake.

The Brothers told him where it was and said they had gone there once for a half a day to fish but did not have a single bite so they left and haven't been back.

Rick invited them to visit him and said that he would get fish for them if it was available when they arrived.

The Brothers said that they might be able to visit in about two weeks, just before winter was to begin. They gave Rick some fresh vegetables. They talked a bit more and said their good byes.

Rick slung on his backpack and waving, trotted down the trail homeward bound.

Only two hundred yards from the cabin, Rick made a change in plans. He thought, I am near the lake and I might not get up this way before winter. I better go now. He looked at his compass and turned due south. He called Bart. Now they were no longer on a trail and he would have to walk, dodging limbs, and jumping over downed trees. This would take time. The Brothers had told him that it was five or six miles. At the rate he was going it would probably take him three to four hours. He was determined to find why there had been no fish in the lake. He saw small game, but he had sufficient food for Bart and himself. He arrived at the lake without having to alter his course.

The lake was small. He took off his backpack and walked around. There was a small waterfall, perhaps four feet wide with a drop of three or four feet. Looking for the source of the water he found a spring bubbling up from the ground with some force. The spring was about 25 yards from the waterfall. Going to the other end of the lake he saw some runoff. It was no wonder that there weren't any fish. They would not have had access to the water.

Rick decided to sit and rest a bit before returning to his cabin. He got out his lunch and biscuits for Bart. After eating he walked around again. He enjoyed looking at the small waterfall. The spring water would not be polluted so he had a nice cool drink. As he looked down at the base of the fall, he saw something shiny. Kneeling down he saw other shiny objects. He carefully picked them up, one at a time and examined them. Were they gold? Or were they "Fools Gold?" It had a kind of brassy look. He didn't know, but he would ask Joel about them when he went to the Trading Post. He put them in the button down pocket of his shirt. He slung on his backpack. This time he looked at his compass and chose a course going west. He and Bart continued and in due time arrived at the cabin.

Early the next morning Rick carried water from the river. He put kindling in the stove and when the fire was ready he put the water in a pot to boil. The water was then put in the rain barrel. After breakfast he took his cart, axe, saw and wedges to the log that he had brought on land from the river. He sawed, chopped and brought wood in the cart to the cabin. It took numerous trips till the work on the log was completed. Next he went to look for the other log he had seen on the edge of the river. It was intact so he went to the cabin to get Bart's harness and his rope. They pulled the log on to the bank and Rick stripped it of its limbs with his axe. First, it would have to dry out. He put the limbs in the cart and took them to the cabin. He cut the limbs to size for kindling in his stove.

The next morning work began on the second log. Getting the logs from the river had saved a good deal of time and effort as opposed to cutting a tree from the woods. Work continued on the log until it was all cut to the proper size and brought to the cabin.

A shelter was needed for the wood so he built another lean to on the side of the cabin. He now had about one and one half cords. He needed another half cord.

Rick had been thinking about a new project. He took his tools into the cabin, selected a location and built a box in front of it. It measured four feet wide, three feet deep, and two feet high. The box had three sections on the inside running from front to back. One was in the center (two feet from either side), and one was on the left side, one foot from the left of the box. The lid for the box was divided in two, and each slid towards the front. On the front of the box were two handles. Next he removed portions of logs from the side of the wall. The space was large enough for the box plus room to reinforce the remaining logs. It was also large enough to provide space for the supports the box would sit on. The box was installed in the opening. Rick tested it by moving the box toward the outside, and pulling it by the handles to the inside. One foot of the box would be on the inside of the cabin. The remaining two feet would be on the outside. The front, on the inside, had an extra layer of wood for insulation. The insides of the box were lined with heavy plastic that he took from his 100 foot roll. This was Rick's version of a freezer for meat. He reasoned that the meat in the box would freeze with the cold weather. He had built a roof over the area on the outside of the cabin to protect the freezer from rain and snow. He hoped his idea would work. He kept his fingers crossed. Joel had suggested using a smoke house, but Rick didn't want the scent to attract bears and wolves.

He was tired from the wood work. It was now the second week in September and he wanted to go to the Trading Post. He decided to take the next day off however to rest and enjoy some fun time with Bart. A canoe ride was also a good possibility.

Later Rick caught some salmon and he and Bart ate.

Rick worked a bit on his book but realized that chores and traveling had cut into his time and energy for writing. But there was a cold winter ahead with lots of time for writing. He was tired and turned in early.

CHAPTER IV

Early the next morning Rick and Bart went for their usual walk. The weather was a chilly 35 degrees. They had breakfast and Rick got the canoe down. He got the paddles, the anchor and life jacket. He decided to look for another log. Not to prepare it today for firewood, but to get it on land to dry it out. He took the canoe and gear to the riverside, and launched it. Bart was in the front. First he checked the cabin side of the river for a half mile in each direction. Then he went to the other side and repeated the search. No logs were spotted. He started back to his side of the river when Bart looked north and barked. Rick saw a log floating towards them but it was still some distance off. He thought to himself, "That's real luck, I come looking for a log and one comes drifting down to me."

Bart barked again and this time Rick looked closer. He thought he saw a motion just above the log. It looked like someone waving. He paddled towards the log and then he saw someone holding onto the log. He saw a feeble wave and a faint cry of help. As they got closer he saw that it was a small person hanging on to the back end of the log. He maneuvered the canoe to intercept the log bringing the port side of the canoe alongside of the log.

He called to the person, "It is ok. I'm going to bring you into land. Just hang onto the log."

He paddled with his right paddle and came up to his usual launching place. He and Bart got out. He beached the canoe and then secured the log to the land. He then lifted the person from the log and found it to be a young girl, probably 14 or 15 years old. She was so cold and shivering so violently that she could not stand up or talk. Rick picked her up and carried her into the cabin.

He told her, "I'm going to help you. You are so cold I am going to

20

take your wet clothes off, dry you and put warm clothing on you. Don't be afraid. I'm going to help you."

He did as he said, and put one of his warm shirts on her. It reached down past her knees, and of course her hands were not visible in the sleeves. All this time he was holding her to keep her from falling. He picked her up and put her in his bed, covering her with another blanket. He put an additional log. On the fire, and hung her wet clothes up by the stove to dry.

He said, "I must go bring the canoe in. I'll be right back."

Rick and Bart went out and brought the canoe into the cabin. He hung it from the rafters. He looked at the girl and she was sleeping. Rick and Bart went back out and brought the log further up on the bank. Returning to the cabin, the girl was now awake, but she was still shivering. Rick told her his name and asked for hers.

She said, "Dawn".

"Just stay there and rest. Can you tell me what happened?"

She said "Krazy Joe," he took me away, but I ran and jumped in the water. Krazy Joe can't swim. I found the log to hold on to but it was so cold I almost couldn't hold on anymore until I saw you."

"Everything is going to be alright now, Dawn. Don't be afraid, Krazy Joe can't hurt you now."

Rick went to the stove and made vegetable soup. He took it to her and fed her with a spoon. She was looking better and thanked him for saving her. He asked where she had come from and she said from the Native Village.

Krazy Joe had taken her the day before and it was only today that she had been able to get away.

Rick told Bart to guard her and then he excused himself and went out to get some meat to add to the vegetable soup for dinner. This time he took his 22 magnum rifle with the 4X scope. It was extremely accurate. Of course he also took his revolver and his knife. He told Dawn what he was going to do and asked her to just rest. Bart sat down by Dawn as Rick left.

An hour later Rick returned with two squirrels. He had skinned and gutted them outside and washed them off. Now he separated the parts and tossed them into the soup. He added more carrots and another potato. Now he had a stew. When the meat fell off the bones it was time to eat.

Rick told Dawn that he and Bart were going outside and suggested that her clothes were dry and she could dress while they were out. Upon their return Rick prepared Bart's dinner then he and Dawn sat at the table and had their stew with "Triscuits," the cracker that Rick had found to hold up best on his hunting trips.

Dawn told him that there were over fifty inhabitants at the Native Village.

Rick told her that he would take her home the next morning.

She said that it would be a long walk, perhaps twenty or so miles.

Rick told her to sleep in his bed. After a walk with Bart he put his sleeping bag on the floor, put another log on the fire and said good night to Dawn. He got into the sleeping bag. Bart curled up by his side.

The next morning they had breakfast and Rick made preparations to go. He put food in his knapsack, got his revolver, his knife, and his rifle. He let Dawn wear the shirt that she had worn before. He rolled up he sleeves, and they were ready to go. Just then the door was knocked open with a BANG! Dawn screamed and Bart jumped towards the door barring his teeth and snarling at the huge man in the doorway.

Dawn yelled, "That's Krazy Joe don't let him hurt me!"

Krazy Joe said, pointing to Dawn, "My girl."

Rick said, "No it isn't. Stop right where you are. I don't want to hurt you, but the dog and I will if you do not do as I say."

Krazy Joe said, "I'll tear that dog to pieces with my bare hands."

Rick said, "Right now the dog is ready to get you if I give it the signal. You will be hurt badly. Listen. I have the dog, a revolver and a great knife. Now, get against the wall facing it. Put your hands behind your back with your wrists together."

As Rick approached him Krazy Joe swung around with a roundhouse right at Rick's head. Rick ducked and Bart charged tearing into Krazy Joe's leg. Krazy Joe screamed and swung at the dog. Rick used the butt of the revolver on Krazy Joe's head and he crashed to the floor.

Rick told Bart to back off and to guard. Rick pulled Krazy Joe's hands behind him and tied them with a snare he used to trap small animals.

When she saw that it was now safe, Dawn stopped crying. Rick pulled him outside by the scruff of the neck and dumped him unceremoniously on the cold ground.

"Now," said Rick, "what should I do with him? I could take him to the Trading Post, or I could take Dawn home and take him along for the Native Village to deal with him as they see fit. That is what we will do. We'll go to the Village."

Rick got his knapsack, and his rifle. He jerked Krazy Joe to his feet and slapped his face until he opened his eyes. He told him where they were going. Pointing to the trail, he told him to march. The trip was long and tedious. Dawn showed the way when the trail broke down. They stopped to rest several times. Bart kept close watch on Krazy. They finally arrived at the Village.

As they approached, the local dogs set up a cry and came aggressively at Bart. Rick cautioned him to be good so he stood to be examined by the local dogs. When they had sniffed him and saw his demeanor they respectfully backed off. Then children came out followed by the adults. They were crying and laughing at the same time, so happy to see Dawn.

The leaders of the group welcomed Rick when Dawn told them what had happened. Krazy was handed over to what Rick assumed was their "Medicine Man" and Rick was relieved of that responsibility.

It was close to sundown and Rick was invited to join them for dinner. They all gathered in a large hut. Rick, as the guest of honor, was seated with the elders of the tribe. After they had eaten Dawn was asked to address the group and tell in detail what had happened.

Dawn told the whole story about how Krazy Joe had abducted her, and how she had escaped. She told how Rick had saved her and had brought her back to health. She also told the details of the fight Rick had with Krazy and how Bart had attacked Krazy in defense of Rick.

When she had finished, the elders withdrew and after a bit returned to the gathering. The Chief addressed Rick and thanked him for his courage. He said that they had not known how to deal with Krazy Joe but they knew now. They said that they would like Rick to be an honorary member of their Village and that he could call on them at any time that he needed their help.

Rick thanked them and accepted their offer.

The Chief told the group that they would be dealing with Krazy Joe in the morning, and asked Rick to stay with them over night. Rick accepted and he and Bart were shown to a small hut. Dawn came by, and returned his shirt and thanked him again.

In the morning they all gathered in the main hut for breakfast. It was a kind of stew. The leader announced that they were to meet behind the hut where preparations had been made to deal with Krazy. Behind the hut was a line of red embers about four feet wide and thirty-five feet long. Natives with sticks lined up on each side of the length of the embers. Krazy was led to one end without his shoes, socks, or shirt. His clothing was placed at the other end. He was instructed to go down the middle of the column, walking barefoot over the burning embers. At the end he could get his clothing and leave, never to return.

Krazy needed an incentive to start so they gave him a strong shove on to the embers. Then he ran and as he passed, each person switched him. He picked up his clothing, shook a fist at Rick and said "I'll get you." Then he ran away being chased by the native dogs.

Smiles and laughter filled the faces of the natives, especially Dawn. Rick had much to do. So he gathered up his belongings, and said goodbye to the elders, and to Dawn's parents.

Dawn came to him, gave him a hug and a kiss. Then she said, "I would like to visit you."

Rick said, "It is too dangerous to come alone. Perhaps your Father may bring you with him when he goes to the Trading Post and you both could stop by to say hello."

Rick called to Bart and they began the trek to the cabin.

Upon returning to the cabin Rick got water from the river and made a fire in the stove. Then he split the log using his wedges, cut the log into manageable pieces and carted it to a location near the cabin. He didn't have the energy to finish the job this evening, but at least it was now a manageable project even if it snowed before he got to it. Rick decided that he would go to the Trading Post the next day.

After dinner he made a list of the things he wanted to accomplish at the Trading Post. First, he wanted to pick up the items that he had ordered, second look through any mail he may have received third, to get information from Joel about the types of people in the area for his book and fourth, to ask Joel about the shiny objects he had found.

Now that he had visited the Brothers, seen the lake, and had been to the Native Village, he made a map to indicate their relative locations.

He made notes regarding the experiences with Dawn and Krazy Joe as well as the Native Village. The writing of this data for the book would come later when he was not so tired. He took Bart for his evening walk and went to bed.

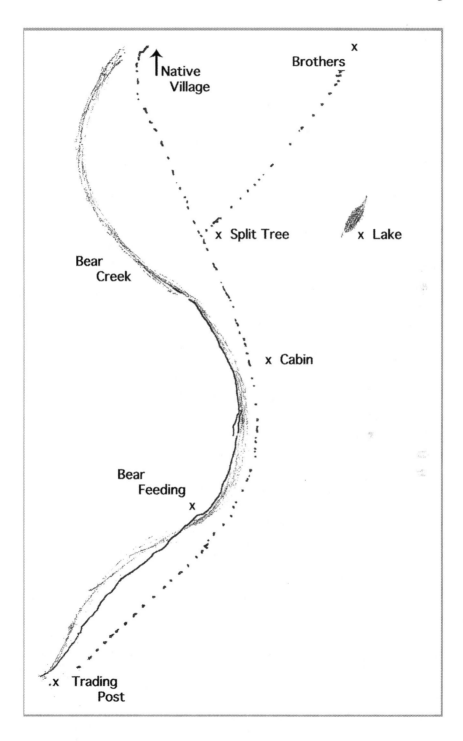

CHAPTER V

He was returning to the Trading Post several weeks after his intended visit. The lake trip, the incident with Dawn, and the wood cutting had put him behind. There was also the need to find a deer or an elk for his winter meat.

Rick had his cart, the harness for Bart, and his defense equipment. He also had the shiny objects from the lake.

He started off trotting. Bart was pulling the empty cart. Rick was wondering if he would have mail, and if the items that he had ordered would have arrived. He saw small game, and when he reached the bears feeding area he saw two, where there had been a dozen when he left the Trading Post. Arriving at the Post, he parked the cart near his truck, released Bart from the harness and went into the store. Joel was there, they shook hands and Joel said "Congratulations on your handling of the Krazy Joe kidnapping. You are a hero to those in the Native Village, and to us also."

Rick said, "How did you hear about it so fast, I just came from there two days ago?"

"Two of the men from the Village came to get supplies, and you were all they could talk about. Have a seat Rick and let's talk a bit."

"Well," Rick said, "I have cut a lot of wood, made a few repairs to the cabin, and visited the Brothers. Time has gone by so fast, and I haven't had time to get meat in for the winter. I needed to come and get some supplies and to see if I got any mail. What is new with you?"

"My daughter has come to visit for a couple of weeks before winter starts in earnest. Mary is a nurse. She is 37, about your age I guess. You know, Jane and I are in our early 70's and we think of you and Mary as kids."

Rick said, "I need to tell you that I am not quite as young as you think, I am 45."

"Well, that's great, you do look younger, and the way you run, it does you credit."

Just then, Jane and Mary came into the store.

Jane said, "Oh there is Rick. Mary, come meet the hero. Rick, this is our daughter Mary. She has come for a visit."

Jane gave Rick a hug.

Rick said hello to Mary. As he shook her hand and looked into her eyes something passed between them that they both felt.

Jane said, "Mary and I are going to get lunch ready, we will call you."

In the kitchen Jane said to Mary, "I saw that glance between you two. What happened?"

"I don't know," said Mary, "He is an unusual man."

Joel said to Rick, "I have some mail for you." He produced a packet of more than a dozen letters. A couple of them have a nice scent."

Jane called, and they went to lunch.

Rick said, "Mary, would you tell me what kind of nursing you do?"

"I am the Head Nurse of the emergency room of a large hospital on the coast about 100 miles from here. Each day we have incidents ranging from nose bleeds to serious shootings."

Rick said, "That sounds very interesting but very hectic."

"It is very busy, but I enjoy each day."

Rick said, "These sandwiches are delicious, tell me what kind of meat this is."

"That is an elk burger. We don't have elk that often and it has a little different taste than deer."

Joel said, "The men from the Village had a message to me from the Chief. He asked that I contact the legal authorities to advise them of the assault and kidnapping by Krazy Joe. I have done that and they will no doubt ask you for your input when they are next up this way."

After lunch Joel and Rick returned to the store to talk.

Rick said "I have something to show to you but I must ask that you keep what we talk about confidential. Would you agree to that?"

"Of course, that is no problem."

"I am not sure what I have, but I found these items, and I would like your opinion as to what they are."

Rick showed Joel the bright items.

Joel said, "These are gold. Where did you get them?"

"Right now I need to know more about them so that I know what to do."

"Well, you have about a thousand dollars worth of nuggets here. If you think there is a lot more there, you will need to stake a claim. There will be paper work, a survey, a search to see if anyone owns the land, and it will cost some money and time. If you feel that there is not much there you might check it out a bit further by yourself. Get what you can and forget about it. Of course after checking it out again, you could also get a partner to do the paper work, title search and share the costs and the profit."

"Since there is so much to do before winter I believe I will wait until spring to check it out again. If I then find it worthwhile I will consult you again as to the best way to go. If there is reason to follow through I would like to ask you to be thinking about being my partner."

"Thank you for thinking of me on this venture. When we have more facts I will consider it, if that is the direction you would like to go."

"There are a few things that you will need when you next check it out. Since you may wish to do that before you come back here you can get them now. You will need a garden spade, a special metal pan, and a miniature sluice box. In commercial gold mining the sluice box may be fourteen feet wide and fifty or more feet long. I am thinking that you need a small portable one that you and I can build while you are here. It will be in two sections of four feet in length each, and about two feet in width. Depth wise probably five inches."

"The top is louvered like louvered shutters for a window. The sluice box is slanted and the dirt you choose is hosed down. The heavy gold drops through the louvers into the box below. The lighter dirt and rocks too large to go in the louvers is washed off. When you are finished with the dirt, you remove the louvers. Then you place the residue in the special pan I told you about. You add water, rotate the pan. The water along with the dirt is thrown off, and the gold is left in the pan. You are panning for gold."

"Thanks Joel for the course '101 in Panning for Gold'. It will be fun to make the sluice box."

"The "Bunny Boots" came in. What are they?"

"They are fairly new," said Rick, "They will keep one's feet from freezing at 30 degrees or more below zero."

"The rain barrel also came in. What do you plan to do with it?"

"It will be used to hold water. I'll use it differently than usual however. It will be kept in the cabin so that it won't freeze. I won't have to go to the river for water on a really nasty day. I also want freezer bags of all sizes."

"I have those Rick, what will you do with them?"

"I will use them to protect meat. I have made a freezer that I am interested in using. It will hold 24 cubic feet of meat, and it doesn't use electricity. I would like to show it to you along with some other changes I have made to the cabin. Come visit me."

"By golly," said Joel, "I believe I will. Let's gather up the things you want, and materials for the sluice box."

When they finished Joel said, "Let me show you to your room and I'll call you for dinner in about one half hour. We'll have more time to talk then."

"Thanks. I'll take Bart for a walk and be right back."

Joel called Rick for dinner. When they went into the dining room Bart went right over to Mary who squatted down and took his head on her lap and petted him. Bart wagged his tail and showed his pleasure.

Rick said, "That is so unusual. I don't recall him ever going over to a stranger like that before."

Mary said, "I love dogs and I wish I could have one. With my hours it would not be fair to the dog."

Bart backed up, walked over to Rick, looked up at him and wagged his tail. He was asking for Rick's approval. Rick reached down, petted him, and told him he was a good dog.

They had a pleasant time at dinner, and then they all went into the living room.

Rick asked Joel, "I need more information for my book. I would like to know more about the kinds of work that people in the area do."

Joel explained, "Most of them are very self-sufficient. They come to the Post from a radius of 75 miles. Some use snow mobiles and other machines using gas and oil. Some use dogs to pull their sleds. But gasoline is six dollars a gallon, and each dog eats one fish per day. If they have twelve dogs, that is a lot of fish to catch for each and every day. Some have fur traps, some sell lumber or fire wood, some sell fish.

Some have cattle or chickens. Those with animals have to raise feed for them and have predators to deal with. These people enjoy being on their own and dealing with nature and the challenges of not having a steady income. Somehow most of them get by."

They talked about other items then Rick said that he would like to take Bart for a walk.

Mary said "I would like to go for a walk too. I'll go with you.

"On the walk there was little discussion, but then Rick said, "I will be leaving in the morning, I have much to do. I invited your dad to visit me, and I would like to ask you to come with him."

Mary said, "I am sorry you are leaving so soon, but I do want to see you again and I will come to see you."

On the way back their hands touched and they then held hands the rest of the way.

They parted then and Rick went to his room to look at the mail.

First was a letter from Art Pines, the sports magazine editor. It told that his check had been mailed to his bank and that they were giving him more space in upcoming issues due to reader response. His checks would be growing accordingly. Next was a letter from his photographer saying he had completed one of the assignments that Rick had given to him. He also asked that Rick take pictures of any scenes that he wanted to send to the magazine. There was a letter from Jean, one of his girlfriends. Jean said in part "Hey you big hunk I miss you already. Let me know and I can be there in a week ready to go skiing and fishing." There was a letter from another girlfriend Gail. She said, in part, "Our last night together before you left was one that I will always remember. The flowers, the fabulous restaurant, the wine, and then the pheasant that they served was one that you had shot." Rick wrote a few replies and then turned in.

Rick took Bart for a walk and when he returned, Joel was waiting to take him to breakfast. It was a pleasant time and Mary was there also. Jane had prepared bacon and eggs, a breakfast that Rick would not have for a while.

They gathered up Rick's merchandise and loaded it on to the cart. The rain barrel took up a good bit of space so they put it on first, and then put many items in it. All was loaded. Bart was in his harness and ready to go. Rick shook hands with Joel and thanked him for all his advice and help. He hugged Jane and then Mary. The spark was still there. Rick reminded them to visit soon, and began trotting beside Bart and the cart up the trail.

It had been harder to leave this time because of Mary. It gave Rick much to think about. There was Jean. There were no secrets from her. They discussed almost everything. They ran and enjoyed skiing together. Jean was a senior factory rep for "Jeep". She helped dealers and individual buyers with their problems.

There was Gail, a lovely, bright bank executive. Gail had the most problems in that she missed Rick so much when he was away. There were other girls, but not as significant as Jean and Gail.

Now there was this attraction with Mary. He really didn't know Mary, but there was something there. Things were getting a bit too complicated in this area. He loved them all, but no one enough at this point to marry.

He reached the point in the trail where the bears fished in the river, but there were no bears. This bothered him for two reasons. First had all the bears hibernated as a sign of an early winter? Here he was without meat in the freezer. And second, did it mean that the salmon had stopped running? And of course, he had not stockpiled salmon.

He continued on the trail seeing only some birds and a squirrel or rabbit now and then.

Arriving at the cabin, he released Bart from the harness and began unloading the cart. The skis, snow shoes, and boots came out first, and then the remainder of the items from the rain barrel. He took the rain barrel inside and placed it on the stand that he had previously built for it. He completed the unloading, and rested for moment before getting some lunch.

It had been freezing for perhaps a week now. It was another indication of an early winter. His freezer could be used now if he had the meat to fill it. It gave him an idea. Before hunting for big game he would try to get some salmon by gill fishing. With gill fishing one uses a net, similar to a tennis net, but larger and without posts. His net was designed specifically for salmon in that the holes were the right size for the fish to attempt to swim through, but their gills would be caught by the nylon filament. The top of the net had floats along its length. The bottom of the net had lead weights to hold it down. The net was 100 feet long, and four feet deep. The end closest to shore had a line leading to the shore. The other end had an extra weight at the bottom to keep the net from floating down stream. The net would be put in the water running across the river. It would be placed there just before dusk and retrieved in the morning, hopefully with fish. Rick carefully examined each foot of the net to ensure that there were no snags, or missing floats or weights.

That evening he got his canoe and then loaded the net and cast off, leaving Bart to wait on the bank. He carefully dropped it off, a couple of feet at a time, on his port side. He now dropped off a weight to hold the net in place. Now there was nothing to do until the next morning. He rowed around the net back to his landing and beached the canoe. Bart was glad to have him back. Rick gave him a hug. He pulled the canoe up to the cabin and left it there for use in the morning.

Rick was eager to see what the gill net had brought for him, so breakfast was a hurried affair. He gave Bart a biscuit, put on his coat and went out. It was cold. He took the canoe and the paddles to the river, launched the canoe and jumped in. Bart remained on shore. Rick went to the far end first and began pulling the net into the canoe. After a few yards he came up with a fish, then another. Then there was nothing for several yards. Finally, he got another fish and then two more. This was not going to be a bonanza. Ten yards later he got another, and that was it. It was a disappointment, but better than nothing.

He took it all ashore, cut the heads and tails off and gutted them. He tossed one of the heads to Bart. Bart played with it first, tossing it around, and then chewed on it. Next he filleted the fish, put them in large plastic bags and took them to the cabin. Now the freezer bags that he had bought from Joel could be used. The pieces were cut to portion size and placed in the bags. Rick pulled the handles on the freezer box and put them on the left side. There was lots of room left for the red meat he hoped to get.

Now the clean-up portion of the project started with cleaning and then examining the net for tares, or missing floats or weights. The net was then let to dry, folded and put away.

CHAPTER VI

The lack of a really good catch of fish put the pressure on to get some red meat. After lunch he gathered up his knapsack, and his armament. He put Bart "on guard", and left. He decided to first look where the bears fed, but came up without sighting a bear again. He now went into the woods using all of his skills as a hunter to look and listen for clues in finding game. He saw small game tracks and the longhairs of a wolf caught on branches. He was always careful of not stepping on a twig that would reveal his presence. He pressed on going deeper into the woods, but generally heading in the direction of the cabin. He saw no sign of bears, moose, or deer. It was getting close to sunset.

He returned to the cabin to exchange the rifle for his 22 magnum, and put his attention to small game. Before long he had a squirrel and a rabbit. He skinned and gutted each animal. Inside the cabin he cut them into pieces and prepared one for freezing. He must begin to stock pile red meat.

Rick and Bart had their dinner then Rick put Bart on guard while he went outside and set some snares. These were set where he had seen tracks. Later, he made notes for the book. It wasn't long before Bart and he took their evening walk, and turned in. Before he drifted off, he mulled over the prospects of getting a good supply of meat for the winter.

After breakfast, Rick put Bart on guard and went to check the snares. They were empty. He decided to check again in the evening. He returned to the cabin and got his equipment ready for a day of hunting. This time he took Bart with him. He decided to hunt to the north since he had already hunted to the south. They went deep into the woods. Again he saw small animal signs, but nothing that he was looking for. Noon time came without a sighting.

Rick took a break and he and Bart had something to eat.

They had gone as far as the split tree and now they started back walking sometimes near the trail, and sometimes deep in the woods. They arrived back at the cabin empty handed.

Rick decided to set the gill net again on the chance that he would get better results in the morning. After setting the net he brought the canoe up by the cabin.

He checked the snares again but had no luck.

After dinner he wrote in his journal that he had found that living alone in the wilderness had its share of problems.

They went for an evening walk, admiring the stars in the sky and then retired.

He was thinking, 'I have to do something different to get big game."

The snares yielded three large rabbits. He collected all the snares and the rabbits. The rabbits were skinned and prepared for freezing as were the others. The snares were put away.

Rick got the canoe and once again hauled the net in. The results were slightly better with eight fish. They were plump and in good condition. Rick returned to shore, prepared the fish for freezing and turned his attention to the net. It was cleaned, inspected and dried before returning it to storage.

Rick had lunch and contemplated on his next move to get a volume of red meat. Joel had told him that it would be one hundred times harder once winter snows came. Rick was familiar with snow and realized how a three foot snowfall would make the hunting he had done in the last few days very difficult. And of course, if the meat was hard to find now, what would it be like once the snows came? He decided that tomorrow he would explore the area across the river. That of course, would require using the canoe and taking Bart along as well. There was no certainty that he would be able to return to the cabin each evening as he had done on his side of the river. The tent and camping equipment would be required, as would be food for Bart and himself. He got everything he could think of that was needed and placed it near the door. He planned to get an early start.

After dinner they went for a walk, enjoying the quiet and the beautiful scenery. Rick wondered if the cabin and the surrounding land belonged to anyone. He also had the thought of buying the property but immediately dismissed the idea since his goal was only to experience the seasons and not to become a land owner. Yet, somehow the thought was intriguing.

Rick made notes in his journal and then took Bart for the last walk for this day.

CHAPTER VII

All was ready for an early start. First a good sized breakfast with buckwheat pancakes, sausage and coffee. Rick was ready for a strenuous day. The canoe was taken to the riverside, and the gear was brought down and placed in the center. Bart got in the bow and Rick jumped in the stern. On the other side of the river, the canoe was beached. Rick swung on his backpack, including the tent and his rifle. He also had food for them both.

They went through the woods, always going towards the mountain. There were no signs of big game. They stopped about noon for something to eat. Then they continued upward until they could see ahead some distance where the tree growth was thinning out. Rick had a great view of the bare portion of the mountain. No game was sighted.

It was near sunset and he selected a fairly level area for their campsite for the night. He removed his backpack and went back in the trees to pick up wood for the campfire. This was something he had done hundreds of times on his trips hunting and fishing. He set up the tent. It was a three person tent since Bart was usually with him, and Bart took up a lot of room. They had dinner, and they listened, but it was quiet. It had been a strenuous climb, and it wasn't long before Rick rolled out his sleeping bag and called it a day.

In the morning after breakfast and coffee, Rick closed up the camp. He put out the fire, and slung on his backpack. They started back down the mountain. He used a zig zag pattern, skipping the areas they had covered yesterday. The weather was cloudy and it looked like it might snow. After about an hour he saw an area that had been disturbed. On closer examination he saw signs of a bear. Then there was a hole in the side of the mountain that looked like a cave. Rick looked closer and saw more signs leading to the cave. He thought there just might be a bear in there. Already he had covered almost a five mile radius from his cabin and this was the first positive sign. But, what to do if the bear was hibernating in there? It was dangerously risky, but if he didn't try to entice it to come out, what other opportunity for meat would he have? And, it did look like it might snow.

He decided to try to get the bear to come out, if in fact there was one in there. He removed his back pack and looked for a tall slender tree. One was found to be about twenty five feet tall. He cut it down near the base, and removed the limbs. It was straight and strong. It was about four inches across at the base. He thought it over and reasoned that the 30-06 rifle would not be powerful enough to stop the bear in the short distance from the entrance of the cave to him. The Smith and Wesson revolver with its more powerful charge would have to be his weapon of choice. This revolver was so powerful in its recoil that it must be held with two hands. Of course, one hand at least would have to guide the tree into the cave. He drew his revolver, checked to be sure that it was fully loaded and that the safety was off. He returned it to his holster. Now he lifted the tree and put the top end in the cave. He called Bart to him and told Bart to sit and stay. Then he began to poke the tree into the cave. No response came so he became more aggressive and pushed harder. He heard a grunt and with that he used only his left hand on the tree. He took the revolver in his right hand. He pushed harder and a growl came from the cave. It was too late to stop now so he pushed hard again and with a ROAR a huge bear came out charging. Bart dropped his stay and charged the bear, biting it in the leg. The bear concentrated on Bart which gave Rick a bit of time. Bart ducked out of the way. The bear then went for Rick. Rick had dropped the tree and grabbed the revolver with both hands. He fired three shots as fast as he could while stepping backward. The bear was almost on him when Rick tripped and fell backwards. He woke in a minute or two with Bart licking his face. The bear lay still on the spot where Rick had stood a few moments ago. Rick was dazed and rubbed the back of his head. Already a lump was forming. He got up and kicked the bear just to make sure it was dead.

It was a huge grizzly. It was at least ten feet tall, and probably weighed over one thousand pounds. The revolver was returned to its holster. With a great effort, Rick turned the bear over on its back. It had beautiful fur. The bear was plump and in prime condition. Rick got his knives and began the task of skinning the bear. He wanted to keep the head and hide so he cut carefully to remove the hide from the body. He saved the heart and liver but discarded the guts and the ribs. He removed the meat from the legs. He had brought plastic sheets and bags with him. This took a great deal of time. He was concerned that animals would get the smell and converge on him before he was finished. The meat was packed in plastic bags.

He took the tree that he had used to get the bear out and found another just like it. He shortened them both to about twenty feet, tied the small ends together and used the short pieces he had cut off as cross members to join and strengthen the long pieces. The cross members also provided a platform to hold the hide with the meat inside plastic bags. All was tied down to the platform.

Rick put Bart in his harness and secured it to the poles. He also had a line from the poles to himself.

They pulled the makeshift sled down the mountain. Rick wanted to get away from the bear remains as soon as possible. Wolves would soon be after the remains. He didn't want the wolves to be following him. He just wanted to get back to the cabin as soon as possible. They were making good time. Then Rick went on one side of a tree and Bart went around the other side. They had to stop to get untangled. Fortunately there was no sign or sound of wolves until they were nearing the river. But now he could hear the wolves growling and fighting over the bear.

Rick and Bart were now within one hundred yards of the river when they realized they were being followed. Rick heard them behind, and then off on each side.

He took his 30-06 from his backpack, checked the ammunition and took off the safety. The wolves were getting nearer and he and Bart increased their speed. He didn't want to have the wolves surrounding him. The wolves on the right looked like they were ready to get in front so he took his rifle and fired at the first one. It yelped and fell. The others backed off. The ones in the rear were moving closer. He didn't want to stop his forward motion, for then they would certainly surround him. He paused momentarily and fired at the leader of the group. It was hit and the others backed off. There were still wolves on the left. Rick continued on, but it was slower since he had to handle the gun and stop now and then. He put the sling of the rifle over his shoulder, reached in the hide and pulled out a plastic bag of meat. He threw it back over his shoulder. The wolves converged on the meat.

Rick and Bart redoubled their race for the river. The wolves were coming again. He threw the meat on the canoe, Bart and Rick jumped in as the wolves snapped at Rick's heels. The wolves stopped at the water's edge.

He paddled rapidly in the safety of the river. They got to the other side and beached the canoe. He heaved a sigh of relief.

At the cabin the meat was cut into portion size, placed in freezer bags and stacked in the freezer.

Rick now had his meat for the winter. What a relief it was.

The canoe was hung from the rafters.

They had enough excitement for now.

In the morning Rick made an outdoor table. He needed one to work on the bear hide, but it would also serve as a table to sit at, picnic style, for eating out in nice weather. He got his sharp knives for removing each small piece of fat or skin that adhered to the hide. He didn't know how to preserve the hide, or what to do with the head. He had no experience in taxidermy, but he felt that as long as it remained frozen it wouldn't deteriorate very much. The Brothers or Joel would know what to do and they were due any time for a visit. He completed his work scraping the hide and stretched it out, and tacking it to the table.

Late that afternoon he decided to try once again with the gill net. Everything was ready an hour before sundown. Within an hour the net had been set.

That evening Rick wrote in his journal.

The next morning, after breakfast, he got his canoe, and leaving Bart on the bank, began to bring in the net. Luck was with him this time; he more than doubled his previous haul. He got eighteen beautiful salmon. So, the salmon had not stopped running. He returned to shore, prepared the fish for freezer bags and put them in the freezer.

He felt pretty good that, as a first timer, he had the wood and meat that he needed. He could always get small game for a change in diet. His food needs were assured.

CHAPTER VIII

It was mid-morning when they heard the sound of a motorcycle approaching. Bart barked. There were two people on the cycle and someone waved. Rick now saw that it was Joel and Mary. He told Bart that it was ok. Rick waved and went to greet them. Joel and Mary got off the cycle. Rick and Joel shook hands and Rick and Mary hugged. The spark was still there. Bart went over to Mary. She hugged him and he wagged his tail.

Rick said, "I didn't know that you had a motorcycle or that one could be used on the trail."

Joel said, "This is a BMW motorcycle. It's especially designed for on, or off road use. With this cycle I can jump over a small log or a curb. Small brush is not a problem. What is this I see on your table?"

"We needed some meat and this bear obliged. Come into the cabin. We'll have a seat and talk."

In the cabin they looked around. Joel said, "I see that you have made some improvements, but I don't see the freezer."

"Well, it is right here," Rick said as he pulled open the door of the freezer.

"Well, I'll be darned. You count on the freezing cold outside to freeze your meat."

"Yes, since I did not have electricity I needed to come up with another solution. You can see that the meat is frozen. You can see the outside later."

They sat at the table, and Mary asked, "Tell me about getting the bear."

Rick told the whole story including his search for large game before finding the cave. He ended telling about the final run to the boat."

"Wow!" said Joel, "That was a real dangerous thing to do." You could have easily been killed."

Mary said, "You are very brave Rick."

"Well, I had Bart with me and he got a good bite on the bear's leg. I cleaned and stretched the hide, but I don't know what to do about the head."

Joel offered, "If you wish, I can take the hide back with me. I have a taxidermist who is skilled with bear hides."

"That would be great. Could you put the charge on a running bill for me?"

"Yes, that would not be a problem. By the way, I have some mail for you. Also, your sports magazine sent me a card saying that you had ordered a year's subscription for me. Thank you."

"I am always pleased to get mail and you are very welcome for the issues. I am getting to like the cabin and this area. I would like to make further changes and possibly an addition to the cabin, but I don't want to go to the trouble if some owner will come by someday and take over. Would you be able to contact a realtor or someone to determine ownership and some information on the size and boundaries of the land?"

"I'll be glad to do that, The FBI and the local sheriff came by the Trading Post two days ago. They said that they would come to see you in a few days regarding Krazy Joe."

Rick asked Joel to tell him more about his motorcycle.

Joel said that with the motorcycle it had only taken about 45 minutes to get to the cabin.

It had taken Rick a bit under three hours to make the trip.

Mary said, "Rick, I see your canoe and I have never had a ride in a canoe. Do you think you could take me for a ride?"

"Of course."

Rick got the canoe down from the rafters, and gave Mary a life jacket. He picked up the paddles and took the canoe to the river. He instructed Mary to get in front. Bart was told to stay with Joel. Rick shoved the canoe off, and jumped in. Although cold, it was a nice bright day. First he paddled north. Then he turned around and drifted with the current.

He asked if she liked to fish. She said that she did. She had fished with her Dad from the shore. He gave her a rod and reel, with a lure attached. Mary was pleased and cast the line. After several casts, she caught a nice salmon. She was thrilled at her success. She pulled in the fish and removed the hook from its mouth. Rick was pleased. Mary admired the view of the mountain, woods, the river, and the cabin. She said it was all so beautiful and peaceful, she believed she would enjoy living in this type of an environment.

They then returned to the landing and went ashore.

Rick asked Joel if he would like to canoe a bit, but Joel declined.

The canoe was returned to the rafters. Then it was time for lunch.

Mary said that she would like to eat the salmon that she had caught.

Rick took the salmon outside, and prepared it for cooking.

Mary asked if she could prepare lunch.

Rick welcomed that offer. He and Joel talked about the motorcycle. Rick asked if there was a possibility that the trail could be smoothed out and slightly enlarged to accommodate a car or a truck.

Joel said he knew a man who had the proper equipment to do the job but it would be costly.

They had lunch and Mary said that she would be going back to work in a few days. She enjoyed her vacation with her folks and coming to visit Rick.

After lunch Joel said that they would need to leave.

Rick took the tacks out from the hide and folded it so that it could be packed on the cycle. Rick thanked them for the visit and said that if weather was good he would like to come back to the Trading Post in two or three weeks.

Rick and Joel shook hands, and Rick and Mary hugged. They said goodbye.

Joel and Mary got on the cycle, waved and drove off.

After they left Rick thought about the cycle and other transportation options such as a helicopter. Then he said to himself. "Why am I thinking like this? I am on a short term project." He also thought about Mary. He had purposely not done anything to make the spark into a flame since she was here only on vacation. It was not likely that he would see her again. Yet, the spark was there. He didn't really know her but she was obviously a respected professional. She seemed to like the outdoors. She was very pretty, and Bart liked her, and she liked him.

Rick leafed through his mail. He found a letter from Jean and one from Gail. He also found a five thousand dollar check for an exotic carving he had made of a Balinese girl.

That afternoon a motor boat with official markings on it pulled up and beached at his landing. Rick told Bart that it was ok and he went to meet the men. One was from the FBI, the other was a local sheriff. After introductions were made, Rick invited them into the cabin. The FBI man stated that they were investigating the alleged kidnapping and assault by a man going by the moniker of "Krazy Joe." They asked Rick to tell what he saw and what he knew for a fact. Rick told them the whole story in detail. He also told of Bart's role in the matter. They asked if he knew the whereabouts of Krazy Joe. Rick said he had no idea. The men told Rick that he may be called to testify when and if there was a trial. They left going further north to the Native Village.

Two days later Rick saw the boat with the Sheriff and the FBI agent heading back towards the Trading Post. He had wanted more salmon, but he didn't want to run the risk of the boat running over his net. He got all the gear and rowed out in the river dropping the net as usual. Now he would wait for the results in the morning. He brought the canoe up by the cabin. He still had time before dinner so he set the snares again for small game.

After dinner he wrote in his journal. The weather had been great; the early winter had not materialized. He had his meat and firewood. The wall freezer was working perfectly, and he had made good friends. He felt good.

Later, he and Bart took a long walk, admiring the night sky. The next day the first project was to pull in the gill net. Bart remained on shore while Rick went to the far end of the net and began to reel it in. This was exciting. On his first attempt to get salmon he got only a few. Now this time he had hit a bonanza. The last time he used the net he got eighteen and now he had sixteen and more net to pull up. He continued and got a great catch of twenty one beautiful fish. He paddled ashore grounded the canoe and began the task of cutting off their heads and tails and gutting them.

He had just finished this first part when he heard someone calling, and Bart barking. Here came the Brothers. Rick told Bart that it was ok, and he welcomed George and Phil.

"I told you that when you visited I would get salmon for you if they were available, and today they were available. I have twenty one for you, with heads and tails off. What a remarkable coincidence that you came here today. I am very happy that it worked out that way."

Phil and George were excited about the fish and thanked Rick.

George said, "We brought some fresh vegetables for you."

Rick said "Thanks. That is always welcome. Let's take the fish in the cabin and put them in the freezer."

"What freezer are you talking about?" said Phil, "You don't have electricity."

Rick replied, "Well before we go in let me show something to you on the side of the cabin."

Rick showed them the outside of the freezer without explanation. Then he took them into the cabin, and pulled the drawer open to see the frozen fish and bear meat.

The Brothers couldn't get over the simplicity of the freezer and congratulated Rick.

George said, "Would you help us build a freezer in our kitchen?"

Rick said that he would be glad to.

The fish were placed in plastic bags, and then in the freezer.

They sat down at the table. George said, "We offer our congratulations to the hero of the Native Village. When we saw some of the natives you were the prime topic."

"Well, I had Bart to help me. An FBI agent and a Sheriff were here. Did they come to see you also?"

Phil replied, "They did, and no one seems to know where Krazy Joe is, or where he lives."

"I was very impressed with your cabin, and your lifestyle. As you recall, I took some photos. I would like to come back after you have resumed your trapping and have some furs. I could use more photos and to learn more about the furs. Would you consider letting me write an article about you both for the sports magazine?"

Both agreed immediately and said it would be an honor.

They had something to eat, and talked a bit more before saying they would have to leave.

Rick got the fish and the Brothers put them in their backpacks. They invited Rick to visit in a couple of months. The delay would give them time to get some furs.

They shook hands and were off.

CHAPTER IX

It was morning, and there were dark storm clouds. The temperature was sixteen degrees. It was now October fifteen, and winter had not yet appeared except for the cold and the dark clouds. He felt that a storm was coming so he began to prepare. He got wood from the side of the house and brought it into the cabin and put it beside the stove. He got water from the river, put it on the stove to boil and returned to get more water in another pail. As the one finished boiling he poured it in the rain barrel. Then got more water and continued until he had a good supply. During this time Bart had accompanied him while he completed his chores.

The wind was picking up and it got darker.

They went into the cabin. It began to snow. It was so thick it was a "white out". The wind was howling. It was his first Alaska blizzard. He put another log on the fire. He was prepared for this experience. It was a good day to write in his journal.

It was still snowing the next morning. The accumulation was over two feet at this point and no telling how deep it might get. For three days and three nights the wind continued to shriek and the snow to fall. As the snow abated he put on his parka with the hood. He had previously made a ladder. He went up on the roof and shoveled the snow off. Heavy snow could cause a roof collapse. Bart was jumping around enjoying the snow and trying to catch each shovel full that Rick threw off the roof.

Rick had sufficient wood and water inside so his chores were minimal.

Returning to the inside, he put wood on the fire and had breakfast. He loved the beauty of the new fallen snow. He would now be able to see tracks in the snow more easily. This would give him good information as to where to put his snares. Once again he put on his parka and this time he decided to try out his new "Bunny Boots" and snow shoes. He found tracks easily enough and reset the snares. They walked to the river and found that ice had formed on the edges by the shore. One day the river would be totally frozen over. They went back to the cabin for another day of writing the book, and writing letters. This was also a good time for him to resume reading a book by "Kira Salak." The book is a true story about her traveling alone, paddling an inflatable canoe for 600 miles to "Timbuktu," on the "Niger River" in Africa. Rick was awed by her courage in her dangerous mission.

In the days that followed he used his skis and snow shoes to get around. He got some rabbits in his snares, and fished with rod and reel for salmon. The time for gill net fishing was over. He thought about an addition that he might make to the cabin along with some changes to the current cabin. Of course, this was just day dreaming. He didn't own the cabin and thus his speculation was merely an entertaining exercise. It did remind him however, that he had asked Joel to have a realtor find out who owned the property and to find out the size and boundaries of the land. He had told Joel that he would be coming to the Trading Post in a week or two, and two weeks had passed. He had letters to mail, and the check from his wood work to deposit in his bank. He prepared to go.

CHAPTER X

Today he used his snow shoes. He took his usual armament, his letters and his check. The fire was banked in the stove to keep the cabin warm as long as possible. They were ready to go.

The snow was two to three feet deep, except where the wind had formed drifts. They were five or six feet in height. Bart's large feet served him well as Rick's snow shoes served him.

He thought of Joel, Jane and Mary. They all made him seem so at home. It had been a long time since he had a relationship with a family. He and Joel had hit it off, and he could envision a close long term relationship if it weren't for his short term goals.

It was still snowing, but it was not as hard or windy. The snow felt good on his face. It was slow going with the deep snow and snow shoes. He passed the area where bears had fed in the river in the summer. Of course, they had all hibernated by this time. It really was isolated out here, and he could imagine that some people would have a hard time without daily contact with others. Finally he saw the Trading Post.

Joel welcomed him into the store. They sat down to have a cup of coffee. Rick gave Joel the letters that he wanted to be mailed.

Joel asked, "How long did it take you to get here today?"

"With the deep snow, and using snowshoes, it was slow. It took me nearly six hours."

Joel exclaimed, "You must be exhausted. Let's just sit and talk while you rest."

Joel had some incoming letters for Rick. "We certainly enjoyed our visit with you. Mary was thrilled at the canoe ride and catching her salmon."

"I also enjoyed your visit, but it was so short. I really need more room to accommodate guests. The Brothers also came to visit. I had salmon to give to them. They are very likeable. I was wondering what work they did before fur trapping."

Joel replied, "They don't talk about that. I don't know for a fact, but it is rumored that they were involved in a moonshine deal that nearly put them in prison. They cleaned up their act and have been law abiding citizens ever since."

"I am thinking of writing an article about their place for the sports magazine."

"I checked into the land and the cabin that you live in. I found that the original owner has been gone for many years. They have not been able to find him. The property can be taken over by anyone who pays the taxes. The property is four acres more or less with 200 feet of water front. The property is like a rectangle. One good thing about it is that the deed states that the land extends into the river. That means that one may build a dock or a pier, and it will be perfectly legal. The cabin would of course be included."

Rick commented, "That sounds pretty good, but how much are the taxes?"

"It would come close to eleven thousand dollars."

"What would one need to do to close the deal?"

"I believe it could be handled pretty much by phone and by mail. The realtor that I contacted said that he could handle it for you."

"That sounds like a real bargain to me, but I value your knowledge and I would like to have your opinion."

"If you like the area and that specific site, even if you used it only in the summers it seems to me that you would have an inexpensive "get away". There is one thing to keep in mind. The trail goes over the property near the river and it has been used for many years by many people. You would not be able to prevent them from using the trail in any way."

"It sounds good to me. I would like to proceed with the purchase. Please tell the realtor that I would like to have a title search and a survey. Also, I would like to have the cabin insured for fifteen thousand dollars. This will be a cash transaction. I have a check here now for five thousand dollars that I will endorse over for the down payment. I will give to you an additional check large enough to handle the balance and any unforeseen expenses to be used at closing. I am sure that the realtor will receive his fee from the seller, but I want to give you something, for all of your help and counsel."

"That really is not necessary, but thanks."

Jane came in, welcomed Rick with a hug and told them that dinner was almost ready.

Rick went to wash up. Then he glanced at the mail. He saw that he had a card from Mary, two letters from his girlfriends, and the photos from the Brothers' property. He also had the photos he had taken of the bear skin and the cabin. He opened the card from Mary and felt a rise in his pulse. She said in part that she had enjoyed the visit to his cabin and that she had the choice of being off from work either on Thanksgiving or Christmas and had chosen Thanksgiving. She invited him to come to the Trading Post for two or three days to help them celebrate the holiday. He returned the card to the envelope to read the rest later.

At dinner Jane and Joel invited Rick to visit them for Thanksgiving. He said he was delighted to accept and asked what he might bring. They said that was not necessary. Rick was determined however to bring something. The question was what could he bring? Rick showed his photos to them. They asked if they could have copies and Rick agreed.

After lunch Joel said, "Come to the living room, I have something to show to you."

As Rick entered the room he saw his bear hide lying on the floor in front of the fireplace. The bear had his mouth open in a snarl. The long nails from each paw were shiny black.

Rick said, "That is magnificent. I didn't know it would be done so fast and so well. I am very impressed. It is so big. I didn't bring my cart this time. Would you mind if I left it here until Thanksgiving?"

Jane said, "That is not a problem I would like for Mary to see it as well. It is so beautiful."

Joel and Rick went back to the store. Rick made his purchases and settled his account with Joel. They talked about the bear skin and the proposed land purchase.

Joel told Rick that the FBI and the Sheriff had concluded their investigation regarding the "Krazy Joe" incident. They didn't know where he lived or where he was.

Joel warned, "He will turn up one of these days. Be on your guard Rick. When he threw up his fist and told you that he would get you he probably will carry out his threat when one would least expect it."

"Let's hope the law gets him first, but I will be on my guard."

That evening Rick answered his letters, and sent a note to Mary thanking her for the invitation.

The next morning Rick filled his backpack with his purchases, said thanks and good bye and with Bart began to snow shoe home.

Rick's thought turned to the cabin and the land. He had some ideas about building an addition on to the cabin. It would probably be a bedroom with a window or two. He thought about having the room divided by a partition so that it could be used by two people. He also thought that he should buy a chain saw. When weather permitted he could cut down some trees to be used as logs for the addition. He would also need a stove for the room like the Brothers had. Time went by swiftly since his mind was so busy. He also thought fondly of Mary and looked forward to seeing her again.

At the cabin Rick decided to make a meat stew. He would use, for the first time, some bear meat. He decided to make a fair amount since he could freeze what he didn't eat right away. The stew was started, first the onions, then the meat, and later the vegetables. He wanted the meat to be tender so he counted on letting it cook for quite a while. He didn't know how long bear meat would take.

While the stew was cooking he decided to see if he could catch a fish. The ice was beginning to form out from the banks of the river for about three feet. With these freezing temperatures it would not be long before the river was completely covered. Rick made a few casts and caught a small fish which he threw back. Another half hour of casting and he had two good size fish; which he prepared for freezing.

The fish were placed in the freezer and the stew was checked. Rick went outside again and placed the snares where he had success the last time. He could see that it was a never ending task to get prepared for the cold winter ahead.

The stew was very good, but was missing something that the brother's stew had.

Rick spent the evenings working on his book. He certainly was getting lots of material from meeting with others and observing nature. The storm came and went and he could anticipate that the weather he was experiencing was mild compared to what the winter would be after the first of the year.

CHAPTER XI

Rick arrived at the Trading Post about eleven a.m. on the day before Thanksgiving. Bart had been pulling the empty sled. Rick had removed the wheels and installed the runners for use in snow or ice. Bart was unhitched from the harness and the two of them entered the store. Joel welcomed them, showed Rick to a seat and gave him a cup of coffee. Rick said that they had an uneventful trip, and asked what Joel could tell him that was new.

Joel said that all was well with the land purchase and all that they needed was the survey. It was to be done right after Thanksgiving.

Rick mentioned that he would like to cut down some trees to provide logs for an addition to the cabin. He would like Joel's opinion regarding the choice of a chain saw.

They walked over to the hardware section and Joel selected one that he could recommend.

Rick agreed and Joel moved it off to one side where he would place other items that Rick wanted.

Rick indicated that he would like to have fresh vegetables, particularly those that would last as long as possible.

Joel asked if Rick wanted nails. Rick said that he could use a box for other purposes, but he would use pegs instead for the log cabin.

Jane and Mary came into the room and each welcomed Rick with a hug. Mary's hug lingered a bit, and Rick was pleased. Jane said that lunch was almost ready.

Joel and Rick left to wash up. After lunch they went to the living room and Mary told Rick how beautiful she thought the bear was.

Jane also commented that she loved the look of it by the fireplace.

Joel added that he wished that he had shot one.

Rick responded, saying that he was pleased that they liked it because the bear skin was his gift to them for all that Joel had done for him and for the warm hospitality that Jane had given to him.

They all exclaimed their pleasure and their thanks.

Mary said that her father had told her of Rick's decision to buy the cabin and the land. She said that she loved the area.

"Do you have any plans for the land or the cabin," asked Mary.

"Only tentative plans at this time. I have thought about adding a bedroom. When I return, I plan to cut down some trees to be used as logs for the addition."

Rick asked Joel about his customers.

"They are still coming in, but most of them have picked up their supplies for the winter. Those trapping for furs have already started setting their traps. They all have a hard life, just barely making ends meet. The important thing above all else for them is the independence of living without others telling them what to do. The most intrusive thing that bothers them is paying their taxes. In this remote area that is not really expensive. It seems like a lot to them when their annual income may be only four to eight thousand dollars."

Mary asked, "Rick would you take me fishing?"

"Sure would you all excuse us?"

Rick watched Mary cast and gave her a few tips.

She was successful in no time.

He helped her prepare the fish for cooking. He thanked Mary for inviting him to celebrate Thanksgiving with them. He then invited Mary to visit him again when she had time and the weather was fair.

They returned to the cabin. Mary gave Jane the fish and Rick returned to the store to be with Joel. A trapper by the name of Peter came in to get supplies for the winter. Joel introduced them.

Peter said that he had heard of Rick's handling of Krazy Joe. He said that he had set his traps and now had to wait for the animals to cooperate. He collected his supplies and said he wanted to be home before dark. They all said good bye.

Mary called them to dinner and they gathered around the table filled with the turkey and all the fixings. The wonderful aroma of the dinner added to the beautiful visual display. They all sat, joined hands and Joel said grace as they bowed their heads. Then they all said "Happy Thanksgiving." Each one had reason to be thankful and each expressed them.

Rick told them how much he enjoyed being with their family on this day.

After dinner Rick fed Bart and took him outside for a walk. Upon his return he joined Joel in the living room. Jane and Mary joined them and Mary snuggled up to Rick on the couch.

Jane smiled with a look of approval.

Rick felt very much a part of the family.

Later Rick said that he would like to take Bart for a walk and Mary said she would go along. On the walk Mary put her arm in Rick's. The spark was still there.

Rick said to Mary, "I am fond of you Mary. With your working far away and visiting occasionally, and my short term goals, it is difficult to see where our relationship might go."

Mary said, "I see what you are saying. Let's just go with the flow and see what develops for us."

Rick gave her a hug and they kissed.

"It has been a wonderful Thanksgiving, Mary."

After breakfast the next morning Rick and Joel gathered up the things that Rick had purchased and loaded them on the sled. Bart was harnessed and was waiting to be on the trail.

Goodbyes were said and with thanks and an extra hug for Mary, they were on their way.

When they arrived at the cabin, Rick released Bart from the harness. He took the contents of the sled into the cabin. Inside, on the floor, He saw a note. The note was from the Brothers and it said, "Please come visit with us for a few days over the Christmas holiday." Both brothers signed the note.

"That is wonderful", he said to himself. "To be invited out on the two most important holidays is really great. What can I take to them?"

In the days that followed Rick cut down trees that would make good logs for his cabin addition. It took a lot of time since he also cut away the branches so that they would have a smooth even surface. He then decided on the length for each log and where it would be used. He etched an identifying mark on each so that he would know where it was to be placed. Taking the logs from the woods to an area near the cabin took both Bart and Rick to pull together. One by one the pile of new logs grew. Rick began to make shingles for the roof. Before he realized the time it took, it was within a week of the time to visit the Brothers.

On the morning that he would leave, he would see if he could catch some fish. But he also decided to use his wood carving skills to carve a present for each. He carved a wolf and also a bobcat. The wolf was about six inches tall and eight inches in length. The bobcat was smaller, but in relative proportion to the wolf. With as many chores done as possible, he spent time writing in his journal.

He took his sled to see the Brothers. He wanted to ask the Brothers for hints in using his new chain saw. He took his tent camping gear, and his journal. He thought that weather permitting that he might go by the lake on his way back to the cabin. The sled was packed but he wanted to get fish first. It took longer than usual but he finally caught two good sized fish. He cut off the heads and tails, gutted them before placing them in plastic bags, and then in his backpack. They were ready to go. Bart, in his harness, was secured to the sled and they began their journey. They went up to the split tree, then northeast. It was slow going with the sled. He had to move some limbs and brush out of the way from time to time. Then he saw the clearing, and heard the baying of the hound dogs.

The Brothers appeared at the door waving to him. They all shook hands. Rick gave them the fish. This time the dogs knew each other and there was no trouble. Bart was released from his harness and they went into the cabin.

The fireplace had a nice fire going and Rick walked over to warm his hands. The Brothers had set their traps and were waiting over Christmas for the animals to get caught.

George got a cup of coffee for Rick and Phil said that lunch was almost ready.

Rick told them of his visit to the Trading Post and of his pending purchase of the land and the cabin. They were enthusiastic about his purchase and about his being a more permanent neighbor.

He told them about his plan to enlarge the cabin. He asked them to look at his chain saw and give him some tips. They talked about the chain saw and its uses. They made suggestions, and approved the one that Rick had bought.

For lunch they had a hearty soup and homemade biscuits.

The Brothers said that in the spring they were going to build a greenhouse in order to extend their growing season.

At dinner Rick had the bear stew that he had enjoyed so much last time. He told them that he had made bear stew but that it seemed to be lacking something. They asked what was in the stew and Rick told them.

The Brothers noted that he did not include rutabagas, and thought that might have made the difference. The Brothers had the fish for dinner. Rick fed Bart and took him for a walk. Upon his return they all sat in the living room, enjoying the heat from the fireplace.

Rick told them that he had been working on the article about their place, but couldn't complete it until they had some furs for him to photograph. He also wanted to know more about the process of getting and preparing the furs for market.

Phil said, "Rick, just extend your visit a bit and go with us right after Christmas to see what results we got from our traps."

George said, "That is a great idea. Rick how about it?"

"That does sound like a great idea, but how long would you be out there?"

"Probably just for a couple of days."

"Great, that will give me the first-hand knowledge that I need for the article and for my book."

George asked, "Did you bring a tent?"

"Yes, the tent and my camping gear just in case."

They talked about the weather, the Trading Post, Rick's cabin and many other items until the Brothers saw that Rick was tired and nodding off. They took pity on him and said it was time to go to bed.

Rick took Bart for a walk and then retired for the night.

In the morning the Brothers served sausage and eggs, with homemade biscuits. This was a treat for Rick. It was Christmas morning and Rick gave the Brothers the wood carvings that he had made. They were delighted and very impressed with Rick's skill in producing professional carvings.

The Brothers said that they had something for Rick. It was a good sized bag of vegetables and a carton of eggs. They said he would receive it just before going home.

Rick appreciated their judgment in giving him what he needed most.

That afternoon they went out and selected a small three foot tree which they brought in for Christmas. They hung acorns and pine cones on the tree for decoration.

For Christmas dinner they had one of their hens rather than a turkey. They had leaves and pine cones on the table for decoration. After dinner Phil played Christmas songs on his harmonica, and they all sang along.

Rick told them how much he enjoyed being with them and thanked them for their hospitality and friendship.

George suggested that they plan ongoing on the trap route the first thing in the morning.

After a hearty breakfast they got ready to go. Rick left his sled and chain saw, put on his backpack and armament and was ready. The Brothers were using their snowmobiles. Rick rode on the back of one.

They stopped frequently to check a trap. Near one they saw the long hairs of a wolf, but he had avoided the trap. At the next trap there was a wolverine. It was caught by the foot and been attempting to chew the foot off so that it could get away. In order not to damage the fur they hit the animal on the head with a large stick, then severed its main artery while it was dazed from the blow. The animal was removed from the trap and the snow brushed out of its fur.

Phil said that the fur would be worth about five hundred dollars. The animal was bled out and gutted and placed on the trailer. The next few traps had nothing and then the next one had a fox. It was dead so they prepared it as they had the wolverine and put it on the trailer. Later, after finding empty traps they came upon a Marten. It was also dead. They processed it and moved on. After about twenty miles they had six animals.

George elected to return to the cabin to process the six animals while Phil continued on to the end of the trap line. He would return the next day.

Rick went with George on the return trip. On the way back no other animals had been found so they returned fairly quickly to the cabin. Rick was interested in the processing of the furs and took photos, and made notes in his journal that would help him complete his article.

It was dark when George completed his work on the furs. They had leftover bear stew, and talked the evening away.

In the morning Rick prepared for his trip to the cabin. Bart was in his harness and ready to go. Rick thanked George for the wonderful Christmas and invited them to visit when they had time and good weather.

Since Rick had the cart with the chain saw and the large bag of vegetables and eggs, he decided not to go to the lake on this trip.

The return trip to the cabin was uneventful until he was within one mile of the cabin. Then it looked like smoke from a fire. Perhaps someone was camping out. As he drew closer he could smell the smoke. It now looked like it was near his place. He hurried on, running now until he saw smoke coming up from the embers of his cabin. He was shocked, but he had the good sense not to rush into the immediate area of the cabin. He released Bart and then they circled looking for tracks. He saw nothing until he got to the back and then he saw tracks leading to and from the cabin. He immediately set out to follow, remaining to one side of them to avoid destroying them. They followed for about a mile and then lost the tracks. He returned to the cabin to see that nothing really was left. Only the stove still remained, charred and debris laden. The fuel used to set the fire must have been spread all around, for such a complete burning.

Now what should he do? He decided to return to the Brothers. They could notify the Native Village who could send a boat swiftly to the Trading Post. They would notify the law and perhaps get tracking dogs on the trail. Of course, Rick suspected Krazy Joe. He immediately returned to the Brothers' cabin. Both brothers were there. Phil left to go to the Native Village using the snowmobile, and George returned with Rick to Rick's cabin. They looked around but nothing new came to their attention. George asked Rick to return with him but Rick opted to await the law, and to answer questions. He thanked George for his support.

George left, wishing Rick good luck and offering to help in any way that he could.

Rick selected a site closer to the river than where the cabin had been, and set up his tent. He gathered wood for a fire and then went fishing. There was nothing he could do about the cabin so he didn't mind waiting for a nice fish to take his bait. In time he got his fish and with the vegetables that the Brothers gave him, he had dinner.

Rick and Bart sat in front of the tent by the fire. It was dark now and getting colder. Rick and Bart had been camping like this many times before, but this time it was different. His cabin, his food, his firewood and most of his belongings were gone. This was a big loss, and he was very depressed. There was nothing to do but wait for the law. He had his data for his book. He had experienced both summer and winter seasons. He had made friends and one enemy. And his relationship with Mary was important to him, but had no resolution in sight. He made notes of the events in his journal.

Rick's tent had been chosen for very cold temperatures and very strong winds. His sleeping bag would maintain his proper body temperature even if the outside temperature went to more than twenty below zero. Rick and Bart were very tired so they turned in. He tried to clear his mind of his cabin problem so that he could go to sleep.

In the morning he had breakfast of the remaining fish. Although he had all the original goals accomplished, he had grown to like this country and its people. He wondered if the purchase of the property had been completed. He had cut the trees and prepared logs for the addition. Of course, he had only cut logs for three sides of the room, assuming that the one cabin wall would be there to complete the bedroom. He had time on his hands so he decided to cut more trees and to prepare more logs.

Three days later the law arrived by boat. The officer brought a helper and bloodhounds with him. He also brought a letter for Rick from Joel. He questioned Rick. Rick showed him the tracks to and from the cabin. The officer and the helper took the dogs to the tracks and began their search for the culprit.

He read Joel's letter. It said in part, "I am sorry for this to happen to you. Please feel free to come to the Post and stay as long as you like. I have good news for you. The purchase on the property went through. It is all complete with no problems. I am holding your paper documentation until I see you. The insurance that you requested on the cabin was also approved and was in affect before the cabin burned."

Several hours later the officer and his helper returned. They had gone somewhat further than Rick had due to the dogs' sensitive noses, but eventually they lost the trail. They got in their boat and sped off.

Rick continued to work on the logs for the next two days while he thought things over. He then decided to go to the Trading Post the next morning. There was not much to do to get ready to go. Rick struck the tent and rolled up the sleeping bag. The fire had gone out. The tent and sleeping bag were placed on the sled. Before putting the harness on Bart, they walked around the cabin site one more time. In the back

Rick saw a movement in the woods. It was a big man. Rick called to him and the man ran.

"BART, GO GET HIM!" yelled Rick.

Bart took off like a bullet after the man, with Rick chasing after. Bart hit the man hard and the man fell as Bart grabbed his arm in his teeth. Rick arrived to see that it was Krazy Joe. He had come back to see his dirty work. Rick leveled his revolver at Krazy, and called off Bart. He ordered Krazy to get up, and put his hands on his head. Rick told him to walk towards the river and then to the sled. Rick tied Krazy to the sled instead of Bart. Bart watched him closely, just waiting for the order to bite Krazy again. Now they were ready and followed the trail to the Trading Post.

Joel notified the sheriff to come to get Krazy Joe, which they did without delay. They questioned Rick and had him sign a statement.

Joel gave the property documents to Rick.

At dinner Rick announced that he would be leaving in the morning for North Dakota.

Joel said that he understood. The snows would be coming, and trying to rebuild in the winter was impossible.

Jane said, "In the short time that you have been here, you have saved a young girl's life, you have captured a kidnapper, and now you have captured an arsonist. You will always be our hero. Please come back to us."

Rick said that he would be back in April or May, and that he intended to build a larger cabin. He didn't mention it to Joel, but he also intended to check out the gold prospects at the lake. He wrote a note to Mary giving his North Dakota address and phone number. He told her what his plans were. He also notified friends and business associates of his return to North Dakota.

After breakfast he loaded the pick-up, and put the sled on the trailer. He told Joel and Jane how much he appreciated what they had done for him. They all hugged and said good bye. Rick and Bart drove off for North Dakota.

PART TWO

CHAPTER XII

Rick arrived at his house. It was a modest three bedroom two bath, with a living room, dining room, and kitchen. He used one of the bedrooms as his office. There was also a large two car garage with room for the two cars, his cart and canoe. It was a comfortable house and it provided what he needed.

Upon arrival he walked around the house, and then through all the rooms, just checking to see that all was as he had left it. He especially checked to see that his Porsche, his pride and joy, was ok. Financially, he lived well below his income, but this car was his one extravagance.

Rick unloaded the pick-up, and brought his notes for the book to his office. It was about five p.m. He poured a glass of wine and sat down to reminisce about the last five months in Alaska. Now that he was over the disappointment of the cabin burning, he had a good feeling about what he had learned, what friends he had made, and what he had accomplished. He thought about Mary, and realized that he was going back to Alaska, and that he would see her again. He also looked forward to seeing Jean and Gail. Business-wise, he would need to contact the sports magazine editor, Art Pines, and his photographer.

The wine glass was empty and it was close to dinner time. He fed Bart, and then took him for a walk. Upon their return he took the Porsche, and drove to a local deli for a corned beef on rye sandwich. He drove around after eating, looking at all the familiar places. He had lived here for quite some time, but was frequently leaving to do some research for an article, to give a lecture, or to attend some business function. In the course of a year, he was probably gone about half of the time. Sometimes, Jean went with him for a few days. Gail was not able to get off work as easily and rarely went with him. On the way home he stopped at a grocery store to pick up a few things for breakfast.

Tomorrow he would need to do some real shopping, but he wasn't up to it tonight.

When he got home, he made a fire in the fireplace, put on some good music and made detailed notes about his last visit with Joel and Jane, and the trip home.

It had been a tiring day and he turned in for the night.

When he returned from shopping the next day, he decided to call his photographer. They met and finalized the photos for the Brothers' article. Next he made a luncheon appointment with Art Pines. He submitted the Brothers article, and was assured that it would be in the next issue. Two other articles were pending, but the Brothers article got priority. Art asked him to give a talk to a hunting and fishing club in Colorado in February. The magazine paid his fee and all expenses.

Business attended to, he called Jean and invited her to dinner. She accepted and was delighted that he had returned. That evening was great. It was like a homecoming party. They knew each other so well, and their relationship was so comfortable.

Rick took them to a nice restaurant that they had been to before. She asked about Alaska. He told the story in brief. He told her that he would be going back in April. She asked if she could go along but he told her that he didn't have accommodations for her. He also said that he would be very busy. He did tell her about the trip to Colorado and said that she could go along if she could get time off from work. They decided to go skiing when she had a day off in the next week or so.

Rick told Jean that he was thinking of trading in his pick-up and buying an SUV with four wheel drive. He asked for her suggestions. Since she worked for, and was very familiar with Jeep, her suggestion was to buy the Grand Cherokee. He said that he wanted it to have a hitch on the back so that he could tow his flatbed trailer. He also wanted winter tires all around. It was to be silver in color. It was to have a fine sound system, and a navigation system.

Jean said that she could get him a nice discount on the Cherokee, and a good price on his trade.

Rick said, "Go ahead get what I asked for and add anything else that you think is important for me to have."

After dinner they went dancing, but Jean had an early flight to Chicago so they left early, and Rick took her home.

In the next days, he began pulling all of his journal notes together and the book began to take shape.

Rick received letters from Joel and Mary. Joel enclosed Rick's check from the insurance on the cabin. He said that although the law had ample evidence on Krazy Joe for the kidnapping and assault, they didn't seem to have enough evidence on the arson charge. Joel said that he had found a man that he could recommend, to assist Rick in the log cabin building.

He sent a letter to Joel, thanking him and asking him if he had someone who could recondition his stove. He reasoned that if fire wouldn't hurt the inside, perhaps it wouldn't ruin the outside. He told Joel about what he was doing and the upcoming business trip to Colorado.

Mary's letter told Rick how sorry she was about the cabin. She was pleased that Rick would be returning and rebuilding. She told him how fond she was of him and that she missed him.

Rick began to design the new cabin. He wanted a large living room with a fireplace. There would be two bedrooms, each with its own stove. He also planned to have one or more bathrooms. This time he would use the new improved port-a-potty versions. There would be a kitchen and a dining room. He hoped to use the stove from the old cabin in his new kitchen. He planned to have a shed for the cart, the canoe, and tools like the chain saw. He thought that he might build the new cabin on the location where he had set up the tent after he discovered that the cabin had burned.

Each day he spent many hours on the book. He was making good progress. He looked forward to sending it to Ted, the publisher, for review.

Rick called Gail. She was happy to hear from him and invited him to come to her place for dinner on Friday. Gail was a good cook. He looked forward to seeing her again.

He arrived on Friday about four p.m. He had brought Bart for he knew how Gail liked him. He also brought a nice bottle of wine.

They embraced, and Gail took him by the hand leading him to the kitchen where she had been cooking. Gail asked him to open the wine. When it was poured they intertwined their arms, toasted their reunion and then kissed. It was a long kiss and it reminded them how much they had missed each other.

They took the wine to the living room and Gail asked him to tell her about Alaska. He did as he had done with Jean. She told him that all was going well at the bank. She enjoyed her new status and the work that she was doing.

They went to the dining room. Rick was put to work carrying their dinner. He also was asked to pour another glass of wine. The dinner was splendid and was comparable to one from a fine restaurant.

After dinner he helped take the dishes to the kitchen. They returned to the living room. Gail snuggled up beside him. They talked, and hugged and kissed. Gail invited him to stay for the weekend. He accepted with pleasure.

Later they took Bart for a walk and then called it a night.

Days later, he finished his book and took it to Ted, the publisher. It was entitled "WILDERNESS". Ted was well known for the adventure books that he handled. He also knew of Rick's short stories in the sports magazine. Ted read the first few CHAPTERs and told Rick that it looked like a winner. He said he would call him in the near future.

Rick saw the girls an average of once a week each. The new Grand Cherokee had come in. Rick and Jean picked it up. It was just what he wanted. Jean accompanied him to Colorado. He completed several short stories for the magazine that he had been holding.

Time went by and before he knew it, it was the end of March. He began planning to go to Alaska near the end of April. He wrote to Joel, Mary, and the Brothers, telling of his plans. Then it came time for shopping for supplies, and for arranging for his mail to be forwarded. This time he packed his battery powered tools. He purchased a good sized generator. Since his canoe had burned, a new one was purchased. It was slightly larger than the old one in length, and would be a bit faster. He arranged to have a farewell dinner each, with Gail and Jean. It was a difficult parting for each of them.

Ted, the book publisher, called and accepted the book for publication.

The day came. He had packed up the night before. After breakfast he hitched the trailer to the SUV. He put the cart, his new canoe, chain saw, and generator on it. Rick and Bart started the trip to Alaska.

CHAPTER XIII

Rick parked in his usual place and let Bart run for a minute or two before they went into the store. Joel was there with a big smile and an outreached hand, welcoming them back. He was pleased to be with Joel again, and to think of the good times they would have together. They sat and Rick told him that the book was finished and he could move on to building the new cabin. He inquired about Jane and Mary and was assured that all was well. Joel said that he had found a man to refinish the stove and that he would start as soon as Rick told him to go ahead.

Jane came into the room and welcomed Rick with a hug. She had been hoping he would arrive soon since she was waiting to hear all about his experiences in North Dakota. She said that dinner would be ready in about an hour and suggested that they have a glass of wine while they talked. Joel poured the wine.

Rick told them that he had completed his book and about his new car. Jane wanted to see it right now, so they went outside. Jane was vocal with her Oh's and Ah's. She said to Joel, "Why don't we get a nice car like this?"

They returned to the cabin and Rick told of his plans for the cabin. Joel was interested in the new toilets that Rick described. Rick had brought a catalog and said they could look at the various makes once he unpacked. Rick asked if Joel thought the man who would help build the cabin could be available in the near future. Joel thought that he would. Joel would call him in the morning. They talked about fishing and then Jane said that she was going to make dinner.

Joel and Rick began making a list of the supplies that Rick would need. Rick asked Joel to pick out a small outboard that he could use with his new canoe. The canoe had a square stern to accommodate a two horse gasoline engine. They looked over Rick's catalog to determine which toilet to order. Two of them had good features and they couldn't decide which one to choose so Rick ordered one of each. Time will tell which will be better. They had just about finished the list when Jane called them to dinner.

Joel said grace and then poured them, each another glass of wine. Jane said that all was doing well with Mary, and that she had said she might visit them but had not given a date. Jane asked Rick when he might return to the Post. Rick said that he needed to get the cabin assistant started on cutting trees first. He assumed that it would be about two to two and a half weeks.

After dinner they sat in the living room and talked until Rick remembered that he had to unpack. Rick let Bart roam about while he took necessary items into the bedroom. He called Bart to come in, said goodnight to Joel and Jane and turned in.

In the morning, after breakfast, Joel called Pete, the cabin helper, who agreed to come to see Rick in a couple of hours. When Pete arrived Rick observed a strong man about 40 hears of age. Pete appeared to be about six feet tall. His nose had been broken at some point that gave him a rugged appearance. Rick asked him if he would bring his own tools, and Pete said that he would. Rick asked if he had a tent and the supplies he would need. Pete answered in the affirmative. Rick further questioned him about his experience in building log cabins and was satisfied. Rick told him that the first priority was to find and fell the proper trees, then to prepare them for use as logs. They agreed on a daily wage, and decided to meet at the cabin in two days. Rick gave him directions how to get there. They shook hands and parted.

Joel and Rick gathered up the items and loaded them onto the sled. There was still enough snow on the trail, but it would be just about a week until wheels would be needed instead of runners.

The next morning, after breakfast and saying good bye, Rick hitched Bart to the sled and they started up the trail.

The trip to the property was uneventful, although black bears had gathered to fish at the usual place. Bart pulled the sled effortlessly, while Rick trotted beside.

It looked just as he had left it; the burned residue littering the location of the cabin and the stove standing in the middle. He released Bart and they walked about a bit, taking in the beautiful scenery toward and beyond the river. Thoughts of the best location for the new cabin occupied his mind, while he selected a site for his tent. He pitched the tent and gathered wood for a fire. They walked around the property, finding the corners where the surveyor had placed posts to mark the corners. Somehow, seeing them made him feel more like the owner now. Jane had given him a large box of vegetables and a loaf of fresh bread. With the fish and game being in abundance at this time of the year, having enough food was not a problem. Towards evening he caught a nice fish and they had dinner. After dinner they sat in front of the tent and watched the constantly changing flames in the fire. It was a beautiful night and with the array of stars to watch he was in no hurry to go to bed. He looked forward to getting Pete started on the log project. He decided to work with Pete in the morning to get a good start and then, he and Bart would leave to go to the lake for a day or two.

About 9 a.m. the next morning, they heard the sound of a motorcycle coming up the trail. It was Pete, towing a small trailer with his tent, tools and supplies. They greeted each other and Rick said that he was glad to see that Pete had arrived. Rick suggested that Pete select a site for his tent and offered to help him unpack. Pete thanked him but said he didn't have that much and could handle it ok. Rick had made some coffee and gave Pete a cup when his tent had been set up. After coffee they walked around and Pete saw what logs Rick had accumulated, and the quality that Rick wanted. They then began selecting the trees to be felled. Each time, Rick let Pete give his opinion first, and was pleased with what he heard and saw. They worked together for about four hours and then Rick announced that he had a task to perform and that he would be back in about two days. They shook hands, Rick told him to carry on. After loading the sled and harnessing Bart, they took off for the lake.

Rick and Bart made their way north to the split tree and then turned east toward the lake. After the split tree, the going was slow with limbs and brush that had fallen during the winter. There was no trail here, and he needed to use either his axe or his knife almost constantly. Sometimes the sled became entangled. They arrived at the lake however and it looked very pretty and peaceful. Bart was released from his harness, and he bounded around. Rick set up his tent in a clearing near the waterfall. There were still icicles, but the water was coming over the falls. He walked to the source of the spring and saw the water gushing up. He then walked down to the lake and found that the level had risen since he had last been there. It was now somewhat after four p.m. and it was time to get firewood and have some dinner. He had brought along sandwiches for this evening, and a bowl of soup was sufficient. Bart had dry dog food, and there was an ample supply of water. Both enjoyed the cool clear liquid. He had the fire for mostly aesthetic reasons, but if felt good on chilly hands. Tomorrow in the light he would examine the gravel at the base of the falls. He would collect some of the gravel, run it through the sluice box and see what he had found. Hopefully it would be gold.

After a quick breakfast he was excited and gathered his materials. He had his sluice box. It was made as Joel had directed except that Rick had added a two inch edge, running the length of the sluice box, and on either side. This edge extended up above the box to keep the water from running off over the side. He also had the garden spade, a five gallon plastic bucket and the special pan. In addition he had a very thin carpet that was cut to the exact dimensions of the bottom of the box. This was to help catch the small slivers of gold that might otherwise escape.

He made a trough to be used to divert some of the water from falling where he would be digging. He set the sluice box up close to the falls. It was set at an angle so that the gravel and the water would flow down the box. The lower end was placed on the edge of the stream. He had also made a chute or lip to be attached to the top of the box to help guide the gravel to the box. The angle of the box would probably have to be adjusted but he started off with about a 10% grade. The chute was adjusted and he began to dig the gravel from beneath the falls. He placed a few shovels full on the chute and poured water over it. The shoveling continued for several hours. A few times he took a brief break to rest his back. He decided that he had done enough to find if he had found any gold. Here moved the trough and let the water go over the falls as before. He placed the box in a horizontal position, and removed the top portion revealing the box itself with the residue. He filled the plastic can half way full of water. Then he carefully rolled the thin carpet, with the residue, and put it in the bucket. He shook it to get the residue off the carpet and into the water. Having done that it was now getting close to finding if he had any gold. He now poured some of the water from the bucket to the pan. He swirled it around.

The water and light weight particles went off the sides of the pan. He was now "Panning for Gold".

Unfortunately he didn't see any gold. He took more water and continued to pan. He did get some specks that looked like gold, and a few small nuggets. When he had finished the water in the bucket it looked like he had only about half a thimble full of what he thought was gold. The carpet was placed in the bucket for Joel to examine. The small vial of gold was placed in the button down pocket of his shirt along with the nuggets. All in all, he was disappointed in the amount he got. But it did prove that there was gold there. He would get Joel's opinion.

He carefully cleared the site, leaving it as he had found it, with no trace of what he had done.

He packed up his gear. He and Bart had lunch and then they started back to the property.

Pete greeted Rick and took him to see what he had done. Rick was impressed and complimented Pete. Rick set up his tent and got fire wood. He was hungry and decided to fish. He told Pete that he could join him for dinner if the fish took the bait. Pete readily agreed and went to get his plate and utensils. Pete then went to the river to watch Rick fish. Within a few minutes a nice salmon took the bait. Rick prepared it for dinner and soon they were eating.

Rick asked Pete if he had any trouble with the trail being difficult for the motorcycle. Pete said that the trail could be cleared some. He thought that if they both worked at it, that Rick might be able to bring his SUV to the property. Rick said that he would be going to the Trading Post in about a week or so and that they could be clearing it on the way down. Pete could continue clearing on the way back. Rick would continue his business at the Post.

After breakfast, Pete resumed his work on the logs and Rick marked out the corners of the new cabin location with wood stakes. He put in additional stakes for the fireplace location.

In the week that followed, they both worked on the logs.

They took their tools and went down the trail, removing brush and tree limbs. The SUV had a slightly higher ground clearance than a regular car so it was not necessary to clear the trail down to the ground. They worked well together and made good progress. It did look to Rick as though he would be able to bring the Cherokee to the property.

It took most of the day until they arrived at the Trading Post.

They went into the store and Rick told Joel what they had done. Joel complemented them and said they must be tired and hungry. There was no disagreement. Joel invited them to dinner and said that Pete could stay overnight. Jane came into the store and welcomed them. She said she would add two plates for dinner and that they would eat in about a half an hour. Joel suggested that they all wash up and meet in the living room.

Pete admired the bear skin and ran his hands through the fur.

Jane called them to dinner. "We are having elk burgers, French fries and soup tonight."

Rick said, "That is a real treat. I recall when you made them before how good they were."

Rick had admired their fireplace before and he asked if the person who built it was still available. Joel replied that he had passed away, but that his son had taken over and was doing quality work. He asked Joel for his phone number so that he could call him. He reasoned that it would be easier to build the fireplace first, and then add the logs than the reverse. Rick asked about Mary and Jane said that Mary was well, but needed a break from the hectic schedule of the emergency room. Jane said she would call her.

After dinner they talked in the living room enjoying the fire in the fireplace. Pete decided to turn in for the evening. Jane left to call Mary and to go to bed.

Rick said, "I have something to show to you."

"Let's go into the store Rick."

"I'll get some things from my room and be with you in a minute."

In the store Rick showed the vial and the bucket and carpet. He said that he was disappointed in the amount of gold that he got, and perhaps it was his inexperience that was the problem. Joel got out his scale to weigh the gold from the vial. It came to half an ounce. Then Rick remembered the small nuggets and gave them to Joel.

Joel asked, "How long did you dig?"

"About three hours."

"I don't believe that you have reason to be disappointed. With gold at $1500 an ounce, you have earned nearly eight hundred dollars, and it only took you three or four hours of work. I see that you brought a bucket and a carpet with you. Let us take a look at it."

Joel looked at the carpet and said, "I believe there may be a bit more in the carpet. Let's take it outside and hose it down."

The pressure of the hose did loosen more small granules of gold, adding perhaps fifty dollars in value.

Rick asked Joel, "What do you think, is it worth staking a claim?"

"It seems that it would be, but I have more questions that I am not sure you want to answer them at this point."

"Now is the time that I want to tell you everything. I just ask that you keep what I tell you between the two of us. Would you agree to that?"

Joel said that he could, and Rick told him about the lake and the spring and the water fall. Rick said that he would like for Joel to join him on this venture as a partner. He also asked Joel to come with him to see for himself.

Joel agreed and asked his questions. "Where did he dig? Was Rick prepared to invest, time and money in the venture?"

Rick told him where he had dug and said that he was willing to invest money but time was a problem since he was building a cabin. Joel said that he was in the same situation, being willing to invest money, but that he could not spend much time at the site since he had to run the Trading Post.

"It looks then, that if your visit to the lake confirms that further effort will be worthwhile, that we will need to hire someone to manage the site, while we finance it and generally guide the work from arm's length."

"That sounds good to me. I believe that I know just the man to do it if he is willing. In the meantime, I will see if the site is for sale, or who owns it, and if claims have been made on the property."

"There is one other thing we should discuss. We need to know how to divide the expenses and the potential profits. I suggest that we go 60% to you and 40% to me, after all, you found the site."

"I'll have none of that. We'll be equal partners 50-50, and let us shake on that."

Joel thanked him and they shook hands.

"Let's go back to the living room and have a drink to our new venture," said Joel.

In the morning they all had breakfast and Pete took his leave to go back up the trail. Jane reported that Mary was not able to get away from work since the one who would fill in for her was sick. Joel made his calls to the realtor to check on the ownership of the lake property and to see if any claims had been filed. Rick made contact with Earl who agreed to start the fireplace within the week. He also ordered rafters, plywood, tar paper and other roofing materials, as well as windows.

Rick and Joel discussed what they would need to take along. Joel decided that they needed a small pump a generator (which Rick had), a garden hose with a nozzle that could produce a forceful stream. The sluice box, bucket and thin carpet were needed. In addition, Joel wanted a hand drill of at least three inches in diameter to test the soil. Joel gave Rick a packet of mail that had arrived. Rick answered letters and spent the rest of the day with Joel and Jane.

In the morning he packed up his supplies and said good bye. He and Bart left to see how the SUV was on the trail. Joel said he would be coming up in about a week. At that time perhaps he would know about ownership on the lake property. He would bring the pump and drill and other necessary items with him. They all waved as the SUV started up the trail.

CHAPTER XIV

Driving up the trail in his new Cherokee gave Rick a whole new perspective of his surroundings. He wasn't going fast, but it was faster than his usual trot. The trail had a covering of vegetation several inches thick that would prove to be of value as the ground thawed and turned to mud. Before long he saw the river appearing and the black bears feeding.

One had a whole different feeling while passing the bears while in the car as opposed to being on foot. He saw some small game along the way, but no more bears or wolves. The trail had been cleared and was no problem. Now Earl, the fireplace man, and the delivery of roofing materials would not be problem. The time passed quickly. It took just about forty five minutes for the trip. It was about the same time it had taken Joel on his motorcycle.

Arriving at the property he saw Pete and they both waved. He parked near his tent site, let Bart out to run, and proceeded to unload only the items he would need at his property. Items needed for the lake he left in the car.

Rick and Pete shook hands and Rick complimented Pete on the trail clearing. He also saw, and commented on, the good work that Pete had done on the logs. It seemed that they now had enough logs for the main cabin and enough for the shed. Since Earl was coming to make the fireplace, Rick decided to have Pete help him begin the shed first. Rick decided on the location and put stakes at the corners. Selection of logs, and then notching them began. In the next two days the walls were completed to the height of eight feet. The back wall had an opening for a window. Rick decided to have two doors swinging out from the center. Building the doors was started.

Earl drove up in his pick-up and said that he approved the good condition of the trail.

They all shook hands and then Rick showed him the stakes marking the location for the fireplace. Earl said that he would get started and would probably finish the next day. Rick wished him well, and returned to work with Pete.

The next day the roofing materials arrived, and the following day the fireplace was finished. Rick and Pete completed the shed, installing the rafters, the roof, the window and the doors. The cart, canoe, outboard and other items were placed in the shed. One project was completed.

Attention was now fixed on the main cabin. It seemed logical to start on the fireplace wall, and then extend the side walls. Work progressed, and after the first log was set all around the cabin, the flooring was started. Once the flooring was completed the stove could be brought in.

Joel drove up the trail in his truck.

Greetings were made all around and Rick and Pete showed Joel the progress they had made. Rick explained to Pete that he and Joel would be working on a separate task and that Pete should continue on the cabin. Rick called Gene, the stove repair man, and asked him to begin work as soon as possible. He got an affirmative on that.

Rick got the cart, the generator, spade, sluice box, plastic bucket and pan out of the shed. He attached Bart's harness, and then connected it to the cart. They went to Joel's pick-up and got his auger, pump and hose. At Rick's car they got the remainder of the items and, some food for Bart.

Bart pulled the cart north on the trail. Rick, in deference to Joel's age, walked beside him instead of his usual jog. The trail was good until they reached the split tree and turned east. Rick went this way last time with the sled and had to chop through the brush and the limbs most of the way. His work then was a help this time, but the knife and axe were still frequently used.

They arrived at the lake site and Joel was impressed with the view. Rick untied Bart. Before they began to work, Rick took a number of pictures of the spring, the waterfall and the lake, so that he could always remember it in its natural state.

Joel and Rick first walked all around the property, beginning with the gushing spring. They walked beside the stream to the waterfall. Here Joel stopped, and stood beside it for a few minutes. They followed the stream to the lake, and circled it. They returned to the spring. Joel got his auger and asked Rick to bring the bucket. He went north of the spring about six feet and began screwing the auger into the ground. This became hard work for Joel and Rick took over. As he got deeper it became more difficult.

Joel said, "The problem is the permafrost. The ground is still frozen at that depth."

They carefully removed the auger and pulled the dirt into the bucket. It was examined for gold particles. There were none to be seen. The dirt was returned to the hole. Joel made a note in his book about the date, the depth and the results. Then another sample was made just two feet below the spring. This time some particles were found. The dirt was retained in the bucket. The next one was made at the base of the waterfall. More particles of gold were found. Again the dirt was retained to the bucket. Notations were made. A fourth drilling was made just inside the north lip of the lake. Here, more evidence of gold was found. The dirt was retained and data recorded.

Joel now asked Rick to set up the sluice box while Joel set up the pump. Rick got the generator out and got it started. Joel connected the hose to the pump and the generator to the pump. They were ready to start. Rick put the dirt, one shovel full at a time, of the chute while Joel sprayed a stream of water on it. This continued until the bucket was empty. It was now half filled with water. The top of the sluice box was removed and the thin carpet was carefully rolled up with the residue intact, and then placed in the bucket with the water. At this point Rick asked Joel to take over. Joel unrolled the mat and gently shook it to loosen the residue. He then used the hose to dislodge the rest. The mat came out clean. Rick poured some water into the pan and Joel swirled it letting water and residue run off. The heavier gold particles remained. There were only a few.

Joel said, "What we are looking for is mostly on the bottom. As we continue, we will get it all."

The gold panning continued, and as Joel had said, the results were improved as they got lower in the bucket. They finally finished and Joel weighed the results on his scale.

"We got about three quarters of an ounce today. There was gold from all drillings except from the first one. In addition, we were never able to dig down more than two feet except at the waterfall and at the lake."

"Well, what do you think?" said Rick.

"It looks good to me. I have been holding out on you with some good news. The land is for sale and no claims have been filed. It is a nineteen and a half acre tract and the owner wants twenty thousand dollars for it. I wanted to see the results today before I told you. What do you think we should do?"

Rick said, "Let's call the realtor now and tell him that we will purchase it for twenty thousand, cash. Also, tell him to have the property surveyed, and put both our names on the deed."

"That sounds good to me."

He got his cell phone out and called the realtor.

"We should celebrate our first joint gold mining and our prospective purchase of the site."

Joel said, "I have got that covered."

He brought out a bottle of Pinch from his knapsack.

Rick smiled and said, "You really came prepared."

They toasted the new venture and shook hands to seal the toast.

Rick said, "Let's pack up our gear and then sit down and talk about what we should do next."

Joel was agreeable so they put it all in the cart and sat down. Jane had sent some sandwiches along for them so they ate and talked. Rick asked that nothing be said about their new business at least until the sale went through and the survey was completed. He asked Joel to tell him about the man that could possibly oversee the operation.

"His name is Seth. He is about 70 years of age and has lots of gold mining experience. He is level headed and tells you straight off what he thinks. He is as honest as the day is long. This man is set in his ways. He is not one for socializing. I will have to find out, after we own the land and the survey is completed, if he is interested."

Rick said, "I'll look forward to hearing what he has to say."

"What shall we do about establishing a bank account Joel?"

"Well, I'll suggest something and you tell me how it sounds to you."

"Let's each put twenty thousand in a checking account, with both our names, plus the nine hundred dollars from the gold we got today. That would give us a start. Remember, with equipment and a manager, this first amount will be the tip of the iceberg."

"I know that, and I am ready to go for it."

Joel continued, "The purchase and the survey will take half of what we are putting up at the start."

They had finished their lunch, and Rick said, "By the way, now that I have my car at the property I can charge my cell phone on the cigarette lighter and we can keep in touch by phone."

They double checked their packing and then began their way back to the split tree. On the way they did additional clearing of the brush and limbs, realizing that motorized equipment would have to come this way. They reached the split tree and started south. They had only gone about one half mile when they were hailed from the rear. They stopped until the four men caught up with them. It was Dawn's father and three other men from the Native Village.

They all shook hands and Dawn's father said, "We come visit you Rick. We hear that you are back and building. We come to help."

Rick thanked them, and said, "I really don't know what to say. I am overwhelmed by your generosity."

They said, "What you do for us, this is nothing. You are one of us."

Rick did of course remember that he had been made an honorary member of the Native Village.

"Well," said Rick, "you have arrived at a very opportune time. The logs have been cut and are ready to be placed to make the walls. Your visit is most welcome."

They proceeded together to the property. They found Gene working on the stove, and Pete notching logs. Introductions were made all around. Joel told Rick that he would be going, and that they would keep in touch by phone. Rick told the native men that Pete had done most of the log work and that he would ask them to follow Pete's lead on raising the logs in the proper order. Pete took over and the natives willing hands made a great difference in the speed in which the walls went up.

Rick talked with Gene about the stove. Gene said that there was no permanent damage and he expected to finish the job today. Rick remarked that it already looked almost like new. He took the cart to the shed and unloaded it. He put the cart away.

Dawn's father spoke to Rick and said, "We stay here tonight. Work tomorrow and then we leave."

Rick thanked him, and said that he would catch some fish for dinner.

Rick got his fishing gear. He and Bart went to the river. He felt good about the results at the lake, and about the good will of the natives. It also felt good to be fishing for them. Rick caught three large fish. They were beautiful salmon. He prepared them for dinner, cutting them into generous portions. There were lots of vegetables. He got out his camping equipment and began to cook them.

Before long dinner was ready and he called for them all to come and eat. Rick had made a fire and they all sat around it in a circle. It was great fun, eating and feeling good about what they had accomplished. There was also the good fellowship. The natives asked Rick to tell them about Krazy Joe breaking into his cabin and the fight he and Rick had. Rick repeated the story leaving nothing out. The natives yelled and cheered him on as he related the story.

It was a late dinner and with the story telling it had become dark. The natives rolled up in their blankets, Gene left and Pete and Rick went to their respective tents.

Morning came, Rick caught more fish. They ate, and got to work. It all went so smoothly and so fast that by noon the logs were up to the height of the eves. They had a last meal together. They joked and laughed. Rick thanked them all and the natives returned to their village.

Rick and Pete took a short break and then made ladders so that they could put in the rafters and then the roof. This work continued for several days. Finally the roof was on. Now it was time for windows and doors. The fireplace looked great, as did the stove. Rick was very pleased with the progress to date. After the doors and windows, they began caulking the area where the logs met. The stove, looking new, was fired up and it worked fine. Rick was surprised to see that the cast iron pots and pans had also been cleaned, and looked like new.

Rick called Joel and told him what had been accomplished. Joel said that he had contacted Seth; the man he felt could manage the mining. Seth was willing to meet with the two of them. Rick said that he could come to the Trading Post in three days if that would be ok. Joel said that would be fine and he would ask Seth to meet them then. Rick gave Joel a list of things he would need to pick up. Among them were a rain barrel, a broom, a table and chairs, a kerosene lamp, a single size mattress, blankets, sheets, pillows, and dishes. Rick said that he would make the bed frame.

Rick realized that he would need a garage for his SUV and the flatbed trailer. He staked out the edges for the garage adjacent to the shed. Using one joint wall he told Pete that they would enlarge the cabin at a later date, but that the garage would be the next project. Pete and Rick knew that they would have to fell more trees and prepare the logs. They agreed on the dimensions and began selecting and felling trees. Working together they made good progress. In two days they had moved the logs down near the shed.

Rick turned the garage project over to Pete and hitched the flatbed to the SUV. Rick and Bart drove to the Trading Post.

Now that Rick could use the SUV to go to the Trading Post, much time was saved, as was energy. He parked in his usual place and they went into the store. Joel was waiting and greeted them warmly. They had a cup of coffee. Joel said that the property purchase had gone through. Joel had already set up the checking account, and had sent the check to the realtor. The survey was done and they would get a copy in the next day or two. Rick said that was good news. Joel said that Seth was due to arrive in about an hour. He said that he had picked out some of the things that Rick wanted and after Seth left they could see what else was available. Jane came into the store and welcomed Rick, giving him a hug. Jane asked Rick if he could stay for a while, but Rick said he would have to get back probably tomorrow or the next day. He explained that he still had much to do and he would need to help Pete with the garage. Rick said that while he was at the Post he wanted to get pictures made of the photos he had taken of the gold site. He said he would get a set for Joel and Jane also. They heard a car drive up and Jane excused herself, believing that this was Seth and she did not need to be there for the business meeting.

Seth came into the store and Joel introduced Rick and Seth. From the start, Seth was all business and they got right down to it.

Joel said, "Rick and I are equal partners in this business."

Joel had drawn a rough map of the area for Seth showing the physical relationship of the three parts.

"Rick discovered the site and he and I hand drilled four holes. The maximum depth that we drilled was two feet because of the permafrost. Only one drill, just above the spring, did not yield any gold. From this drilling, we got three quarters of an ounce. Neither of us have the time to manage the mining. We would like to know if you would be interested in the job."

Seth paused a minute and then he said, "At my age I no longer am interested in gambling. You may find a few thousand dollars' worth of gold or maybe five hundred thousand, but the amount is unknown. If I were to take the job it would be for a salary, for the project regardless of the results of the digging."

Rick observed Seth. He did not see a physically impressive man. Seth was slightly built and about 5'10", but Rick saw a strong inner self that he could relate to.

"I will tell you what you will need, said Seth. You will need good quality machinery, and you will need a good mechanic. Initially you will need a sluice box, a dump truck, a large generator, a large pump and an excavator. All of these need to be first rate commercial items. You may be able to rent some, the rest you will need to buy, and they are expensive. It could easily cost you five hundred thousand to a million. If you don't get gold you may be stuck with the equipment. If there is a mechanical problem and the mechanic can't fix it quickly you can locate me in my home. I am not going to stand in the cold waiting for equipment to be fixed. If you want me to do the job, and I don't know if I want it, you two would pay me twenty thousand dollars beginning at the time we agree until the first hard snow. Do you have anything you want to ask me?"

Rick said, "Could you help us find the equipment? I don't know anything about commercial equipment and I would not know if I was getting a good deal or was being taken."

Seth said, "I like your honesty, and I can help."

Rick said, "You have already been a good help to us. Let us absorb what you have said and get back to you within twenty four hours."

Seth got up, shook their hands, and said "That's fine." Then he left.

Rick said to Joel, "You described him well. I like him."

"His salary of course, is just part of it though, said Rick, "Two big killers will be the equipment and the rest of the payroll. Included will be the manager, the mechanic, the driver for the excavator, and the dump truck. Joel, if we must buy the equipment, what kind of ball park figure would you suggest for the three major items?"

"Just as a guess, I would think maybe thirty five thousand for each."

Rick said, "My guess is that the total salaries for the six month period would be close to eighty thousand. What about fuel costs, Joel?"

"That could easily run five hundred per day. If we worked five days per week, it could cost us sixty thousand for the six months."

"So in summary, our guesstimates add up like this: property purchase twenty thousand, salaries, eighty thousand, equipment one hundred and five thousand, and sixty thousand for fuel, for a total of two hundred and sixty five thousand dollars."

"So far, we have invested forty thousand nine hundred. That means we each have to come up with an additional one hundred and twelve thousand and fifty dollars." said Rick.

"We are guessing at these numbers, but even if they prove to be fairly accurate we must remember that there will always be unexpected items," said Joel.

"That means we would have to get over 156 ounces of gold to break even," said Rick.

"Of course there is another option to consider. We could spend a day a week up there ourselves; improving our equipment and our technique with the goal of making enough to get our initial investment back. From then on it would be gravy. If the gold stopped coming we would not have much to lose and we would still own the property."

Rick said, "That is a good option to consider, and our estimates may be low. Seth suggested five hundred thousand as a minimum. I don't believe that we included the costs of the generator and the pump. I suggest that we use Seth's lower figure as our estimate."

Jane came into the room and asked if she was intruding at a bad time.

Joel said, "No, this is a good time. Rick and I need a break and time to consider what we have learned."

Rick agreed.

"In that case I have some cheese and crackers and you can get us all a drink Joel."

Joel poured the wine and they talked about Seth and the money that would be needed, but they came to no conclusion.

Finally Rick said, "We are interested in the search for gold probably as much as for the gold itself. We know that working with Seth and getting all that is needed is a huge gamble. We really don't know if there is enough gold there to justify the five hundred thousand expenditure. It seems to me that your suggestion would be more enjoyable than letting Seth do the work, and we worrying about the finances. I like your idea of spending one day per week together and making some money. We can at any time at a later date, when we know more, resurrect the manager idea. In the meantime we can research equipment prices and educate ourselves."

Joel said, "I think we are agreed then. That takes a load of thinking off our shoulders. If you are willing, let's shake on the new plan."

Rick agreed. They shook hands.

Joel said, "I will call Seth in the morning and tell him of our decision."

Rick said, "Let's all go out for a while. I want to get two sets of the photos made, and while we are out let's go to a nice restaurant."

Jane said, "That sounds exciting. Give me a few minutes to get ready."

Joel said, "Your car is still hooked up to the trailer, I'll get my car and meet you outside in about ten minutes."

Rick took Bart out for a short walk and then freshened up before going out to meet them. Bart was told to wait and guard.

They had a great dinner and had the photos made of which Joel and Jane received a set. Upon returning to the Post Rick and Joel reviewed the list of what Rick needed and gathered it all together to be loaded in the morning. It was late and they turned in.

After breakfast there was a knock on the door and the survey copies were delivered. It was quite detailed, not only showing the borders, but showing the lake and the stream locations.

Rick loaded the trailer and said good bye, agreeing to keep in touch by phone. Rick and Bart went up the trail to the cabin.

CHAPTER XV

They drove up the trail, seeing the black bears again. There were more this time, probably about fifteen of them. He wondered to himself whether he would be hunting bears this year for food, or if he would be back in North Dakota.

The time passed swiftly and soon he saw his cabin, and Pete working on the garage. He pulled up near the garage. He and Bart got out. Pete came to greet them. Rick was pleased with what Pete had accomplished and told him so.

He took some items to the cabin and some to the shed.

Rick joined Pete in building the garage. It took several days to complete it. It looked good to Rick.

He said to Pete, "You have done a great job. Would you like to take a few days off to rest and to be with your family before we begin on the bedrooms?"

Pete said that he welcomed a break and two or three days would be just about perfect.

Rick said, "I want to pay you what we agreed for each day of work, but in addition, I want to give you a bonus. I am very pleased with your work, and your ability to take over completely when I need to leave on other business."

Pete didn't expect a bonus but he accepted it with thanks.

Pete struck his tent and loaded up the trailer behind his motorcycle. They shook hands and Pete went down the trail.

Rick went to his cabin and put things away. He had been thinking about going to see the Brothers. He remembered his cell phone and called. George say hello.

"Hi George, this is Rick."

George put his hand over the phone and yelled, "Phil, its Rick on the phone."

Phil replied, "Tell him to come visit."

George came back on the phone and told Rick what Phil had said.

"That's why I'm calling, I have a couple days free and if it would be ok with you I could come up tomorrow,"

We're looking forward to your visit. We'll have a lot to talk about."

"I'm practically on my way. I'll see you tomorrow."

Then he called Joel. "I have a change of plans. Rather than ordering a mattress and table and chairs, and building the bed frame myself, I want to come down and go shopping. I'll get all those things delivered. With building a cabin and chasing after gold I need to limit what I do. Do you think you could help me do the shopping?"

"I'll do better than that. I'll bring Jane along and you won't have to worry about a thing. When were you planning to do this?"

"Tomorrow I'm going to the Brothers for two days. When I get back I'm going to get Pete started on the bedrooms. Then it will be time for you and me to have our day of gold mining. I'm free after that."

"Ok, that sounds good. I'll see you in five days for our digging, and I will alert Jane about the shopping, she will be delighted."

"Thanks, I'll see you then."

Rick spent the rest of the day, busy in the cabin and then went fishing for dinner. Later he and Bart took a nice long walk by the river. When they returned he unrolled his sleeping bag and turned in for the night.

Everything was ready for the trip to see the Brothers except for the fish. He was at the river casting for the second one. Just then a fish took his bait. He took off the head and tails and gutted then. He put them in plastic bags before placing them in his knapsack. He was ready, including his armament and Bart's food.

They went up the trail as usual to the split tree, and then NorthEast to the brother's cabin. He called, and their dogs came out baying. Phil and George were right behind them. There were handshakes all around, and then Rick handed over the fish. They were happy to get them and thanked him. The dogs wagged at each other, and they got along fine.

Rick put his things in the room. Then Phil and George took Rick to see their new greenhouse. Already it was loaded with new planting of all kinds of vegetables. George said that they believed they got an extra month of growing time by having the green house. They took Rick into the living room and gave him a mug of apple cider.

"This is delicious, are you growing apple trees now?"

They replied that they had them shipped in.

George said, "Tell us what has gone on since we saw you last."

"I finished my book; bought a new car and Pete and I cleared the trail from the Post to my property. Now I can drive there. My main cabin has been completed. Dawn's father and three other men from the Native Village came and helped raise the logs. I had a nice fireplace built, and had the original stove reconditioned. Oh, and one more thing, the article on your endeavors should reach you in about a week. Except for that, not much has happened."

"Wow", the Brothers both said at once. "That's enough for a whole season."

"In two more days Pete and I are going to start building the bedrooms."

"Tell me about what has been going on with you."

"Well, we had a good fur season. You have seen the greenhouse. We hope to sell firewood and vegetables this winter."

Rick said, "I have not decided whether I will spend the winter here. If I do, I will order two cords of wood and as many green vegetables as I can eat."

"Speaking of eating," said George, "let's rustle up some lunch."

They went to the kitchen where the Brothers heated up some stew and homemade biscuits. They had another mug of apple cider.

After lunch Rick said, "If you would still like for me to help you build a freezer we can get a start now and finish it up by tomorrow."

They did want the freezer and had already picked out a wall for it. Rick told them what tools he would need. He examined the wall where they wanted it.

"The one I built was four feet wide, two feet high, and three feet deep. That gave me twenty four cubic feet of freezer capacity. The top of the drawer came out to waist high. That way I didn't have to stoop over to see what I had in the drawer. How would you like yours positioned?"

The Brothers agreed that the way Rick had his was the way they wanted theirs. The Brothers got the materials that Rick wanted, and the work began.

Rick began making the box to exact measurements. He partitioned it as he had done for his freezer. The Brothers were making supports for the box to rest on.

Phil told them that it was soon time for dinner. Rick used chalk to mark which logs would be cut and then he washed up. The Brothers had fish and Rick had venison. Rick fed Bart and took him for a walk.

The box was partitioned. Half of the space could be used for deer or other large animal meat and the remainder partitioned for fish and small game. A lid was made. The box was lined with thick plastic in such a way that moisture could not reach the wood. Rick began work on the logs he had outlined in chalk. The log portions were removed and the bracing installed. The Brothers helped place the supports for the box. Then they lifted the box into place. Two handles had been made and attached to the front of the box. Rick pulled it out and pushed it back in. It had a firm, but smooth motion. Extra wood insulation had been placed on the portion of the box that would extend into the room to prevent the cabin heat from defrosting the meat. The Brothers were enthusiastic about their new freezer and looked forward to cold weather when they could use it.

During the rest of the day they talked, and walked around the property. The Brothers had purchased a new flock of hens that were doing well, and had started to lay eggs.

After dinner they gathered in the living room by the fire place. They talked and sang to the accompaniment of the harmonica. Rick asked them to visit him, and they said they planned to come to see him in two or three weeks. Before long it was time to go to bed.

After a delicious breakfast Rick gathered up his things and prepared to leave. The Brothers gave Rick a good sized bag of vegetables and a carton of eggs. They all said goodbye and Rick and Bart began their journey home.

CHAPTER XVI

Arriving at his cabin, Rick looked things over and liked what he saw. The cabin, shed and garage looked great. He put his vegetables in the cabin and went out to place stakes in the ground to mark the corners of the bedrooms. His plan was to have the building in the form of an H. The main cabin with the fireplace would become the living room. To the right facing the cabin would be the bedrooms, with a bathroom between them. To the left would be the kitchen a bath and the dining room. He placed the stakes, measuring carefully, and stepped back to see how it looked. The front bedroom extended forward of the cabin and the second bedroom extended back of the main cabin, forming the right side of the H.

He heard a motorcycle coming up the trail. It was Pete pulling his trailer behind with his gear. Rick and Pete shook hands and commented on their good timing. Rick said that he would make coffee for them and be back. Pete began to unload the trailer and put up his tent. Rick returned with a mug of coffee for each of them. They walked around the stakes and Rick explained the H and the bathroom locations. Their first task was to fell trees and get logs. After the coffee and a bit more conversation they gathered their tools and got to work. They felled trees and cut and shaped the logs. They moved them to the cabin. Rick had told Pete that he would be leaving with Joel but would work with him until then.

During the next month Rick alternated working on the cabin and mining with Joe. They also alternated between the waterfall and the lake. Joel suggested that they get an excavator to get more gold and to reduce the heavy work that Rick had been doing. The excavator enabled them to double their gold that they got from the lake. They also extended the length of the sluice box, believing that some gold had been lost due to the short length of the box. Profits increased as a result. Gold now brought $1700 per ounce.

Rick said, "Before too long the water will be too high as we dig deeper. I have been thinking that we need to dig a hole near the lake so that we could send some of the water from the lake to the hole."

"We would need a dozer for that, said Joel. "Then we could dig a trench using the excavator, from the lake to the hole. It looks to me as though we have maybe two or three weeks before our digging will get us too low. We better get the dozer now. What do you think?"

"I agree, do you think that you could rent one from the same dealer?"

"Yes. I'll get started on that."

Rick received a phone call from the Brothers.

Phil said, "We would like to visit you and give you a hand with the cabin. Will you be home today, and would that be ok?"

Rick said, "Yes on all counts, I look forward to seeing you. I will also catch some fish for you."

"We are on our way. Goodbye for now."

Joel ordered the dozer, and took care of the banking.

Rick told Pete about the help they would be getting from the Brothers. Rick and Pete redoubled their efforts to get everything ready.

The Brothers arrived and Pete was introduced to Phil and George. The Brothers brought some eggs and vegetables for Rick which he thankfully accepted.

Rick said to the Brothers, "You have come at a most opportune time. Pete and I have need of help to get the top logs on and the rafters up so that we can start the roof."

The Brothers said they were more than happy to return the work that Rick put into their freezer.

Rick said, "Let us forget about working more today. It is almost five p.m., and I need to get some fishing done pronto."

Rick invited the Brothers to look around while he got his fishing gear. Rick told Pete to knock off work and to join them for dinner. Rick went to the river and began to cast. The Brothers and Pete came to watch him fish. Phil asked Rick if he wanted him to cook some vegetables while Rick fished. Rick was glad to have the help. Pete offered to build a fire near the picnic table.

George said, "I'll just keep you company while you fish Rick."

Rick felt good about the company and the good natured spirit of all. He finally caught a nice fish. It was probably enough for four people, but with hard work comes good appetites. He fished for another and soon he had it. He prepared the fish for cooking and joined Phil in the kitchen.

George said, "Here Rick I need to do something, let me cook the fish."

So they all were in the kitchen looking forward to a nice meal and talking with each other. Phil soon announced that the vegetables were about ready and George chimed in that the fish were almost ready also. They took the food outside and sat at the table to eat. This hungry crew had no trouble eating both fish.

Then they gathered around the fire. Today this didn't seem at all like a wilderness to Rick. He knew that in the winter, by oneself, with several feet of snow and the wind howling that it would again become a wilderness. Pete asked where the Brothers lived and what they did. The Brothers told him about the greenhouse, the hens and their fur trapping business. Rick told them that this issue in the Sports magazine contained the article that he had written about them. They said that they had not been to the Trading Post to pick it up. They sang some, accompanied by the harmonica. They also told a few far-fetched stories. They admired the weather and the stars that were now brightly shining. It was now time to turn in.

Pete went to his tent and Rick and the Brothers went to the cabin unrolling their sleeping bags on the floor. Rick put a couple of logs on the fire and they got in their beds. Bart curled up beside Rick. They all said goodnight.

In the morning they had an egg breakfast and then got to work. With four of them, it was a fun day and they got the rest of the logs and the rafters up. The Brothers said they would stay overnight and work till about two p.m. the next day. They had so much fun during dinner the previous day that they repeated the tasks, each taking on the same duties as before. They also repeated the after dinner scene, enjoying it all.

Rick took time out to call Joel to see if he got a dozer. Joel said it would be delivered the day before he would come out. Rick asked if those who delivered the dozer could give him a lesson in operating it. Then he could help with the work. Joel said he would check and call Rick back.

After talking and spinning yarns they got ready for bed. In the morning Rick got the call that the instruction on the dozer was on. Then they all got to work. They worked until lunch time, ate, and after a short break got back to work until 2 p.m. They had accomplished a great deal and Rick told them how much he appreciated it. Rick fished while they were getting ready and had two fish for them to take home. There were goodbyes and handshakes all around. Then they were gone.

Rick and Pete got back to work and at the end of the day they were tired but pleased at the progress the last two days had made.

Rick again fished, and he and Pete had dinner together. It was getting to be a habit.

They had all the materials for the roof, and the windows. Work continued the next day, but Rick knew that the dozer would be coming. He told Pete that he would be going for the rest of the day.

Rick got his knapsack, food for himself and for Bart and started up the trail.

He arrived at the lake and waited for them to arrive. The dozer was delivered on a flatbed trailer and was pulled by a large truck. The driver asked if he was Rick. Rick assured him that he was, and the driver said he had heard of him. The driver unloaded the dozer and said that he had been asked to give Rick instructions.

"I know how to drive a car, but I know nothing about heavy machinery."

The driver showed him how to operate the controls, and demonstrated digging up the ground to begin making a hole. He turned the machine, lifting the blade, and backing up.

The driver said, "That's all there is to it."

He shook Rick's hand and drove off in the truck. Rick practiced for about an hour, feeling that he knew the basic moves, and left for the cabin.

Rick helped Pete the rest of the day, and the next morning.

Joel arrived in his truck. They loaded up, said goodbye to Pete and went to the lake. Together they marked off the outline of the hole and then Joel began pushing the dirt. After about an hour he turned it over to Rick. Rick was glad for the opportunity to do it himself. He did see how Joel maneuvered the equipment so easily. Joel gave him a few tips and Rick got started. He worked for about an hour and then turned to Joel.

Joel said, "We need to go deep enough for the water to flow down by gravity and we also need to have it deep enough to hold a good quantity of water. We may even want to divert the stream to this hole. You seem to be doing well with the dozer, why don't you continue with it, while I use the excavator to begin digging the trench for the water to flow to the hole. I won't break the side of the lake until the hole is deep enough."

Rick agreed and continued on the dozer.

An hour later Rick stopped, leaving the dozer where it sat and suggested to Joel that they begin their four hours of digging for gold. Joel agreed and they set up the sluice box and other equipment. They worked for four hours, cleaned the sluice box and weighed the gold. This time it came to a bit more than an ounce. Joel recorded the data. Once again they had earned over $1700. They packed their gear in Joel's truck, had lunch and returned to the cabin.

The schedule continued for two weeks, working on the cabin and one day on the gold site. This day they arrived at the gold site and it seemed that it wasn't as they had left it. The excavator had been moved a bit and there were new tracks around the lake. Joel got in the cab of the excavator and noticed that the fuel level was down from where it was last week. Rick examined the edge of the lake where they had been digging, and saw that further digging had taken place. They came to the conclusion that someone was jumping their claim, and using their equipment.

Rick said, "What can we do about this Joel?"

Joel said, "Somehow we have to catch them in action or somehow confirm that it is going on."

Rick said, "What if we get pictures of them working? They have no need to use the dozer; at least they did not use it last time. What if we place the dozer in a good spot and attach a camera to it?"

"That's a good idea. There is a shop I know of that can fix us up with what we need."

They were not about to skip digging for gold so they got started and worked the four hours. The results were as before. Joel made his notes including what they had observed of the claim jumpers. The result of their digging was almost identical to the last digging. They packed their gear, had their lunch and departed. Joel said that he would check out the camera. Perhaps they could install it tomorrow. He would call Rick.

Rick began working with Pete the next morning but then received a call from Joel.

Joel had the camera and was on his way to Rick's cabin. Rick told Pete that he would have to leave with Joel, but would be back later in the day.

Joel arrived and Rick and Bart jumped in the truck. Joel told Rick that the set up would be rather simple, and effective. They arrived at the lake. Joel repositioned the dozer but did it in a way that it was not obvious as to the reason, and attached the camera. They got in the truck and Joel dropped Rick off at the cabin.

Joel arrived at the Trading Post and called the police. He told them of the trespassing and the claim jumping. Also, he told them about the camera. He asked if a helicopter would be able to come to the lake if warned in time that the thieves were there. They said that they would do their best.

Rick called Joel and said that he would go to the lake each day sometime between the hours of 11 a.m. and 1 p.m., to see if he could see them in action.

Joel said, "Rick, please don't get personally involved. Let the police handle it. I have already called them."

"I'll be very careful," said Rick, "but I can't agree not to get involved. The circumstances will make the determination. I will agree to call you each day when I get there to let you know what is or is not going on."

Rick joined Pete working on the cabin. The next day he went to the lake site at 11am. He stayed in the woods at a point where he was hidden from anyone at the spring, waterfall, or lake. With his rifle scope he had excellent vision. He called Joel as he had promised. After an hour of no activity he returned to the cabin and resumed work. The next day was a repetition of work on the cabin and a visit to the lake at 12 noon. Again there was no activity. He called Joel with his report. The next day he arrived at the lake at one pm. There was a dump truck backed up to the north end of the lake near the excavator. One man was in the cab of the excavator just ready to drop a bucket load of dirt into the dump truck. The other man was standing beside the rear of the truck. Rick saw all this clearly with his rifle scope. He told Bart to stay and to be quiet. He immediately called Joel.

Joel answered, and Rick said, "They are here." And then his phone went dead.

"What a time for my phone to go dead," Rick said to himself, "Perhaps Joel heard enough to send help."

Rick was concerned though when the dump truck was almost full and they appeared ready to leave.

"I have to do something," Rick said to himself, "I just can't let them go."

The driver of the excavator got out of the cab. Rick aimed his rifle at the front tire of the truck and shot. The tire exploded. The crooks were shaken but began to run to the dump truck. Rick showed himself and told them to stop and put their hands up. He had them covered and on camera. The man nearest to the driver's door of the truck started toward it. Rick shot again and hit the back tire of the truck. It was a loud bang as it exploded. This explosion was very near the man, and it shocked him into submission. Rick told both men to walk with their hands on their head toward the dozer.

When they were within a dozen feet of it, he had them face the dozer and said, "You just had a close up picture taken of you both."

"Now, one at a time, walk toward me until I tell you to stop, then turn around and put your hands behind your back. I hope you noticed that I have a dog. He will attack you if I give him the signal. You do not want to be bitten by this dog."

The first man did as instructed and Rick put the animal snares on his wrists. Then the second man followed the instructions, and was handcuffed with the snares. Just then a helicopter was heard. They watched it land.

The officers got out and Rick introduced himself and told them what had happened. The officer said he knew of Rick's rescue of the girl and the capture of the kidnapper. He said he was not surprised that Rick had pulled this capture off. They examined the snares and said that they were doing the job and would do until the men were in jail. The officers took down a detailed statement from Rick, beginning with the first clues that claim jumpers were there, and ending with the capture. The officers asked if the dump truck belonged to Rick, and Rick said no. They then said that it would be confiscated in a couple of days. They said the exploded tires would be a problem.

Just then Joel drove up. Rick introduced him to the officers. The officers told Joel that Rick had done all of their work for them. Rick told them about the posed photo in front of the dozer. The officers said they would like to have a copy for their files.

Rick said, "No problem."

The officers took the two men in the helicopter and left.

Joel said, "You didn't talk very long on the phone."

"Sorry about that, my phone went dead."

Joel asked Rick to tell him what happened. And he said, "Don't leave anything out."

Rick told the whole story leaving nothing out.

"You see, I didn't have any choice. They were ready to leave with our dirt, and I couldn't let them go."

Joel remarked, "I am glad that you were not hurt and that the claim jumpers will be in jail."

"We don't know when they will come for the dump truck, and we don't want them to take our dirt. Would you dump the dirt where it would be most convenient for you when we do our digging tomorrow?"

Joel agreed, started up the truck and positioned it before dumping the load. Joel took the camera off the dozer and said, "We can all enjoy looking at this film when you come to the Post next. I'll get a copy of the photo of the men to the police."

They got in Joel's car and went to the cabin.

Joel continued on to the Trading Post. When he got home he said to Jane, "Rick caught the claim jumpers by himself, and hadthem handcuffed before the police arrived."

Jane said, "Yes, knowing Rick, I am not surprised."

Rick joined Pete working on the roof. By four p.m. they had also finished the bedrooms except for removing the temporary door from the living room to the hallway. With that done, they sat and talked a bit about the next project; the kitchen and dining room. More trees would need to be felled and made into logs.

Then Rick said, "You know that Joel and I have been busy with a project."

He told him about the gold mining and the problems they had with the claim jumpers. Pete said he didn't want to ask although he was curious. Rick thanked him for his patience. Rick asked Pete if he would like to take a couple days off before starting the new project. Pete said he would.

"Take a good rest Pete, you have earned it. If you need three days rather than two, that will be ok. I want to pay you now for what you have earned. As usual you have done a fine job."

Pete thanked him, then struck his tent, put his gear on the trailer and rode his cycle home.

Rick wanted something different than fish for dinner so he got his 22 magnum and went to look for small game. The hunting was good and he got a rabbit. He saw a squirrel also, but he didn't need both for dinner tonight.

After dinner he retired early, it had been a busy and exciting day.

It was hard for him to realize that it was mid August already. He had only a month and a half until winter started. He hoped to finish the outside of the cabin and then make his decision whether to stay for the winter.

Rick met with Pete and showed him the stakes he had put in the ground to indicate where the kitchen, bath and dining room would be. He told Pete that he would help him as much as he could but that he had other things that he needed to do. He told Pete that he had every confidence in his ability to carry on without him when necessary. He asked Pete if he knew of an experienced man who could work with him from time to time as needed, when Rick was not able to help. Pete said his brother Al might be able to help. Rick asked him to sound him out. Once again they needed to fell more trees to get new logs. Each time they had to go deeper into the forest. They got started and worked for several days when Joel called and said that he would be out the next day for their weekly digging.

Joel arrived in his truck, they packed up, said goodbye to Pete and drove off. Rick asked Joel if he would teach him how to operate the excavator. Joel was agreeable. When they arrived, Joel spent time demonstrating, and then having Rick do the same things. Within an hour Joel pronounced him to have passed course 101. They proceeded to enlarge the hole and to complete the ditch from the lake to the hole.

Rick said, "Do you think the hole is deep enough?"

Joel said, "It is hard to tell, we don't know how deep the lake is we will just have to dig a deep hole and hope for the best.

Let's get some gold."

This time they used the dirt that the claim jumpers had dug. They didn't check the time, but worked until the supply of dirt was used up. They processed the dirt. They got about two ounces. Their take for today was almost three thousand, four hundred dollars.

"You know," said Rick, "they probably took away about that much when they were here before. Wouldn't it be something if we could get that dirt back or the equivalent in dollars?"

Joel laughed, and said, "Slim chance, but yes, it would be nice."

Joel made his journal notes and said that he would put the money in their account. They noticed that the truck was gone. They packed up, ate their lunch and drove off. On the way back Rick talked about visiting the Post and going shopping as they had discussed previously.

Joel said, "Fine, let's take a few days off work, do the shopping and have some fun. I know Jane would love it."

Rick asked Joel to talk it over with Jane and let him know when it would fit into their schedule.

Joel dropped Rick off at the cabin and proceeded on to the Trading Post.

Rick and Pete talked some and Rick said he wanted something other than salmon for dinner tonight. He got his 22 rifle. Rick told Pete that he could join him for dinner if he had any luck getting some game. He spotted some squirrels, and that became the meat for dinner. He had lots of fresh vegetables so they had a good dinner.

Rick had charged his cell phone so he called Mary. He said he was sorry that she had not been able to visit last time. He told her of the upcoming three day visit to the Post and wondered if she would be able to join them. Mary asked when it would be. He told her that Joel would be talking with Jane to see when it might be. She decided to call Jane. He asked Mary to reserve one evening for him to take her to dinner. She was enthused about the whole thing and thanked him for the call.

Rick took Bart for his evening walk and then turned in.

CHAPTER XVII

Pete said that his brother would like to work with him. Rick asked that Al come out to meet him tomorrow morning with Pete. He should bring his tools, and be prepared to work. Rick and Pete got to work.

Joel called. He said that Rick should come whenever he was ready, and that Mary would be arriving also on the day after tomorrow. Rick thanked him and said that he would come down in two days.

For this day, and the next Rick worked with Pete. Al arrived and Rick and he talked. Rick asked Al to follow Pete's lead since he knew what Rick wanted. They agreed on a daily wage and got to work.

The next morning he and Bart left in the SUV for the Trading Post.

On the way he saw quite a few black bears, and a deer that was on the other side of the river.

He parked in his usual place, let Bart run for a few minutes, and then they went into the store. Joel welcomed them and gave Rick a cup of coffee. Joel said that Mary would be arriving about noon. Jane came in and welcomed Rick with a hug.

She said, "Each time I see you, you have become a hero again; this time capturing the claim jumpers."

"There really wasn't much to it Jane."

"I hear that your cabin is coming along, getting bigger and better. I am looking forward to going shopping with you. There is nothing I like better."

"I can certainly use your help. I want furniture that will blend in with a log cabin."

"Joel, I hired Al, Pete's brother to help on the cabin work. I plan to have him work when I am involved with other things. Do you know him?"

"Yes, he is a good man and needs work."

Jane said, "I'm going to see what we will have for lunch."

Rick said, "I better bring my things in from the car. Shall I put them in the room I usually use Joel?"

"Sure, that will be fine. I'll go along and help you."

Bart went along also and walked around the area while they carried things into the room. Just then Mary drove up and parked. They all greeted her with a hug. And Bart, not wanting to be left out, came up to her wagging his tail and looking for some petting.

"It is so good to see you all," said Mary. "Will you help me take my things inside please?"

They all carried something to her room and then Joel and Rick went to the living room. Rick felt the fur of the grizzly and admired the good work that the taxidermist had done. They talked until Jane called them for lunch.

Mary said, "Tell me Rick, what will we be shopping for?"

Rick said, "For the spare bedroom I want two single beds and a chest or bureau. With single beds the Brothers will be able to stay over when they visit. For my room, I want a queen size bed, end tables, a battery powered lamp, and a bureau. I will also need sheets, blankets, pillows, and towels. In the living room I need a couch, and a reclining chair. I was thinking of leather."

Jane said, "Leather feels very cold here in Alaska, Rick."

"I imagine you are right, considering that I will not have a good central heat system. Also, I will need a table large enough for about six, and chairs. The table and chairs will go to the dining room once the kitchen and dining room have been built. I'm sure that you ladies will think of more things that I need."

Jane and Mary, both at the same time said, "Oh yes."

Joel said, "Do you have a schedule for these three days Rick?"

He said, "I was thinking we could shop tomorrow. I would like to take everyone out to a nice restaurant tonight; one that you and Jane choose. Tomorrow I would like to take Mary out to dinner. I would leave the last evening for you to decide. How does that sound to you?"

"That sounds good to me." said Jane, and the rest echoed her.

Joel said, "Good, then we can goof off this afternoon."

Mary said, "Rick, tell me about your latest capture."

"Mary, it wasn't much of anything, really."

Mary said, "Oh no, you don't brush it off that easily. I really want to know, so tell me."

Rick then gave in and described in detail how it all had evolved including the police report, and Bart's part.

Joel added, "The police specifically said that Rick had done their work for them and that they were not surprised, knowing of him, that he had pulled it off alone."

"Thank you, I wanted to know the whole story." said Mary, "once again we have our hero in our midst. Well done."

"Let's talk about something else." said Rick. "Mary, how is the work at the hospital going?"

"It is hectic, but I like it. I really need more three day breaks like this one, otherwise, one gets burned out."

Joel said, "They set a trial date for Krazy Joe for some time next year on the kidnapping and assault charge. I haven't heard anything more about the arson case."

"Well, hopefully one day we will hear that he has been sentenced to life," said Jane.

They talked some more, and then Jane excused herself, followed by Mary to get ready to go to dinner.

Joel said, "Relax Rick, it will take them at least a half hour to get ready."

"Well, I'll wash up now. Then I'll be right back and wait with you," said Rick.

He took Bart out for a walk, washed up, and then waited with Joel.

"Where are we going this evening?"

"There is a nice Italian restaurant. It is quiet, has good food and good music."

"That sounds great. One thing I do not want is salmon. It is so easy for me to get, and so little trouble to prepare, that when I am tired, I have salmon. The alternatives of squirrel or rabbit are not much better."

As Jane and Mary came out Rick exclaimed that the wait was certainly worthwhile. They looked beautiful. Rick told Bart to wait and guard.

They took Rick's car and Mary commented that it looked really nice. Joel directed Rick to the restaurant and they found a nice quiet table. The background music was just right. Joel and Jane had been here before and told Rick and Mary what some of their favorites were.

Their meals were ordered and before long they were served along with fine wine. Conversation continued, but it took second priority to the delicious meal. They had dessert and coffee. Rick asked how far the restaurant and other shopping were from the Trading Post.

Joel said, "Most shopping is about fourty miles from the Post. It is no problem when the weather is good, like today, but when the snow comes and the roads are not cleared we may be snowbound for several weeks or more. The road to the Post is not a priority to be cleared."

When they returned they sat in the living room. Jane put some classical music on and they talked. Bart came to Mary, put his head on her lap and wagged. She talked to him and petted him. Rick again commented on how unusual it was. Bart lay down by Rick's feet.

When it was time for bed Rick took Bart outside for a walk and then said good night to everyone and went to bed.

Shopping day had come; but first Jane made a breakfast that Rick loved. They had sausage, eggs, toast and coffee. They lingered over breakfast enjoying it and realized they had to wait for the stores to open. When the time came they got in Rick's car and Joel directed him to a store they were familiar with. Rick suggested that they all look around and tell him if they saw something that they thought would be appropriate. Now that the leather idea had not been seen to be practical, Rick really didn't know where to go from there. He just looked around and waited to hear what Jane or Mary thought might be good. Before long they had his bedroom furniture picked out. Rick did see single beds that might be alright for the spare bedroom. They had masculine headboards. He asked their opinion and got a 'Well maybe,' comment. He waited awhile and they came back with a new spare bedroom set to look at. He looked at it, and it did look better. Now Jane and Mary started out for the sheets, etc.

Joel said to Rick, "Let's go look for the dining room table and chairs."

They saw two that they thought would be good, but reserved their decision for the ladies opinion. It turned out that Jane and Mary found one that suited Rick that was better. Rick and Joel had to laugh about it, but they were happy with these choices and told Jane and Mary so. Rick and Joel were ready to go, but the feminine group needed to look a bit more.

Rick arranged to have the items delivered to the cabin sometime next week.

Rick thanked Jane and Mary for their good work in choosing better items than he could.

They stopped for lunch at a deli and then Rick took them back to the Post.

Bart was glad to see them and Rick took him for a nice long walk. He threw a few sticks for him, but Bart wasn't much of a retriever and gave up on the chasing after a few throws.

Back in the living room Rick found Joel in the recliner chair, and the women had gone to their rooms for a nap. Rick stretched out on the couch and before long he had dozed off.

They awoke about the same time, and after stretching and yawning, Rick said, "This is so different from the hectic seven days a week schedule I have been on. I am really enjoying this break."

Rick asked Joel if he knew if there was a restaurant that cooked French style in the area. Joel said he didn't know of one, but there was another nice restaurant comparable to the Italian one, that served good food and had a nice quiet atmosphere. Joel told him where it was. Rick decided to take a shower and change clothes. Joel said he would see him later.

Rick came back to the living room to find that the ladies were there. Everyone was rested. Rick told Bart to wait. They said good-bye, and Rick and Mary went to the restaurant.

They were seated at a corner table that was quiet where they could talk. The background music was just right. Rick ordered a good bottle of wine. He and Mary toasted their being together again after such a long time. They studied the menu and placed their orders. Mary asked if he planned to stay over the winter. Rick replied that he had not decided. Right now he had the cabin to build and the mining operation that he and Joel shared. Mary talked about her work and her apartment. Then their meals arrived. They both said that their meals were delicious. When they finished their meals they ordered dessert and coffee.

Rick said, "Mary I want to talk to you. I believe you know that I am fond of you. Ever since we met I have been drawn to you. I also have become good friends with your parents. For these reasons, at the start of our relationship, I want to tell you up front a bit about me. When I first met your parents, Jane asked me about my romantic relationships.

I told them that I had been married once for a short time. It did not work out and we parted as friends. There were no children. I have lived in North Dakota for a long time and I have girlfriends there. Two of them are very special and I have had them for a long time. They are both aware however that the relationships are not exclusive. I wanted you to know this before our relationship developed further. At some time I will probably invite them, one at a time to visit me here for a few days or a week if they can get time off from their work. If our relationship continued I would invite you also. I felt that in all fairness that I should explain this to you. Do you have any questions for me?"

Mary said, "I really don't have questions for you. Mother had told me that she had asked you and she told me what you had said. I also date, so I understand your situation. I thank you for telling me up front. I don't know either where our relationship will go from here, we'll just take it a day at a time."

Rick said, "Thank you Mary.

The check arrived, Rick paid the waiter and they left the restaurant.

When they parked at the Post, Rick said he would take Bart for a walk. Rick opened the door and called Bart. He told Joel that he was taking Bart for a walk. When he returned, Rick told Joel that the restaurant had proved to be a success. They all talked for a while and then decided to call it a day.

After breakfast Rick and Joel went to the store and talked about the mining business. Joel reported that they had already earned about half of the cost of the land. He expected that they would earn enough to have paid for the land with the gold they had mined by the end of the season, maybe even a bit more.

Rick said, "It looks to me as though we made the right decision to go it alone. Next season, if not later this season, we will actually make a profit above expenses."

Joel said, "I am thinking that perhaps next season we should have a larger sluice box. I am not sure how much gold is washing off the end of our short box. We might get a more efficient screen for the top of the box.

Rick said, "Those suggestions sound good, but we may have a problem in transporting a larger sluice box. I hate to leave it at the site for someone to come along again and use our equipment for their gain."

"That is a good point Rick, we will have to give that some thought.

Jane came in and called them to lunch. Mary announced that she would be preparing dinner this evening, and that they should be available to help.

After lunch Rick prepared a list of what he needed in the way of supplies. Rick and Joel looked through some mining catalogs and found a thin carpet, or mat, that looked better than what they had been using in the sluice box. They agreed to order it.

Before dinner Mary called them to help. The work turned out to be mainly chopping vegetables. But with all working together it turned out to be fun. Rick and Joel were then temporarily dismissed while the cook took over.

Rick asked Joel to go along for a walk with him and Bart. On the walk Rick told Joel much of what he had told Mary. Rick explained why he had told Mary and Joel understood. Rick explained that he valued the friendship that he had with Joel and Jane and didn't want a lack of information to inadvertently cause a problem.

Joel said, "Not to worry, Rick had done the right thing."

They were called back inside and given more chores. They carried dishes and then food to the table. It was soon time to eat. Joel said grace and poured them each a glass of wine. Pot roast delighted Rick. He was so glad that it wasn't salmon. The meal was declared to be delicious by all.

Later they all gathered in the living room, Mary sat with Rick and they talked about various topics. Time went by and they decided to call it an evening. Rick took Bart out and when he returned they all said good night.

Rick went to his room and prepared for bed. As he was drifting off to sleep he thought to himself that it wasn't quite the same now with Mary. Somehow she seemed cooler to him.

After breakfast in the morning Rick packed up his supplies and gear from the bedroom. They all hugged and said goodbye and Rick and Bart drove up the trail.

CHAPTER XVIII

Arriving at the cabin, Rick first went to say hello to Pete and Al. They had made good progress, and Rick complimented them. Al was expecting to be sent home upon Rick's return, but Rick told them both to continue what they were doing.

He unloaded the car and called Joel. "I am confused as to which day you will be coming this week."

"It is tomorrow. Our three day vacation mixed me up a bit too."

Rick said, "When I was using the spade to dig, we stopped at four hours, and then we continued that schedule after we got the excavator. I was wondering if you would consider working six or eight hours so that we would definitely get a profit this season. We could alternate running the excavator and hosing the dirt. What do you think?"

"You are right. We just continued the schedule we had started. Yes, I'll go along with that. I'll come a little early tomorrow, probably about eight thirty."

Rick agreed and they said goodbye.

He looked around his cabin trying to decide where his new furniture would be best placed. It would be a bit crowded until the dining room was completed and the table and chairs could be moved in there.

Joel arrived as planned, and they loaded up the truck and drove up the trail.

"I don't know what I did, but Mary seemed to withdraw after I talked with her."

Joel laughed and said, "Yes, Jane and I noticed it too. We asked her about it and she finally said that she didn't like the idea of your having your girlfriends using the furniture that she had helped pick out. We told her that she was nuts. It was your cabin and your furniture and as far as her picking it out you asked me to help you, and I asked Jane to help. It was just coincidence that Mary was along on the shopping trip. Don't worry about it. I think she finally saw it in a different light."

Rick said, "Thanks Joel, the last thing I wanted to do was to alienate Mary; or you or Jane."

They arrived at the lake and got gear ready.

Joel said, "Let's angle the sluice box so that the run off goes back to the lake. That way if any gold has been getting away because of a short sluice box, we will be having another chance to get it later."

"OK."

Joel took the first sift with the excavator. They worked until noon when it was time for lunch.

Joel said, "The most gold will probably be at the deeper part of the lake, and we need to gradually head in that direction. We are getting mostly dirt now, but later we may get more gravel and rocks. When we begin to get rocks we may have to strengthen the sluice box and beef up the under supports."

"I am sure glad I have a partner that knows what he is doing. Without you I would just stumble along."

They ate their lunch and Rick took over with the excavator. After a few hours they stopped and hosed off the mat, in two parts. After panning both parts they measured the gold and they got two ounces. That had a value of three thousand and four hundred dollars. They were very pleased. If it continued like this they would make a profit in their first season.

They drove back to Rick's cabin and Joel stopped for a minute to see how they were progressing. Joel hadn't seen Al for a while and made it a point to talk with him.

Joel left for the Trading Post.

Rick told the men that it was time to quit for the day and they could both take up in the morning where they left off today.

Jane had given some pot roast to Rick and he invited the men to join him at the picnic table in about a half hour. They arrived with their plates and utensils. It was a good dinner, and they appreciated the change in menu.

The next morning Rick worked with the men. Pete said that he believed they could start on the flooring the next day. About noon they heard a truck. It was Rick's new furniture arriving. The driver and his helper unloaded the truck and placed the furniture at Rick's direction.

After they left he put the sheets, pillows and blankets on the beds. He liked the battery powered lamp on the bed side table. He looked over the living room and thought, 'Why didn't I get a couple of lamps for here? Well, I can get them later.'

It was time for the men to quit work for the day and Rick told them that it was back to salmon for dinner. They all liked salmon, but eating it almost every day was too much. Rick told them that they could join him and he went to the river. Before long he had a nice fish. During dinner they talked about having to go deeper into the forest to get the trees. Bringing the logs back was the hardest part. Rick asked if they could get the kitchen and the dining room completed before winter and they said they could. Rick still didn't know if he would stay or not, but if he did stay he would have to order fire wood from the Brothers and to get in a supply of meat. That reminded him that he would need to build the freezer that would go in the kitchen wall. They talked a while and then the Brothers turned in.

Later at dusk, Rick heard a light knock on the door. Bart barked. Rick went to the door and there was a young lady. She asked to come in and then Rick recognized her.

"Dawn," he said, "Is that you?"

"Yes," she said.

Rick couldn't believe what he was seeing; she was so different from the little girl that he had pulled out of the water a year ago. She was beautiful. He knew that she would only be about sixteen, but she looked like she was eighteen.

Rick said, "Dawn, what are you doing here, are you in trouble?"

"I came to visit you. I want to stay with you."

"Dawn, you can't do that, your parents will be worried about you. Did you walk all the way down here?"

"Yes, but they will not worry. I am grown up now."

"I will take you home in the morning; it is dark out now. Have you eaten today?"

She said that she had not, so Rick prepared something for her. They sat at Rick's new table while she ate. Rick got her to talk about the Native Village and her parents in order to get some reality back into the conversation. She asked to look around the cabin so Rick took her on a brief tour. He asked if she had boyfriends and she said they were all too much like children. Rick kept her talking but he could see that she was tired after walking more than twenty miles. He finally saw that she was nodding off and steered her to the spare bedroom. He told her to use one of the beds. She said that she liked the other room with the big bed. He had to physically restrain her from going there. Eventually she gave in to her need for sleep and lay down on one of the single beds. Rick covered her up, and heaved a sigh of relief. He went to his new queen size bed.

Rick got up early and let her sleep. When she awoke they had breakfast. Rick said that he would take her in his new boat with the outboard motor. It would be faster than walking. She protested, but he put her in the front of the boat, with Bart in the middle. This was the first he had used the new boat with the outboard and he liked the performance. They arrived at the Native Village and Rick took Dawn to her parents. Rick explained what had happened. Dawn's father did not seem concerned.

He said, "You are one of us. She is grown now."

Rick said, "I have my own girlfriends, and she will need to find someone more her age. Please tell her not to come to my cabin again, unless you have her with you and stop by to say hello."

Dawn's father said, "I tell her."

Rick said goodbye to them and got in his boat to head down river to his cabin.

CHAPTER XIX

In the morning Rick worked with the Brothers until about noon, when he received a phone call from his book publisher. He said that sales were good and that he wanted Rick to go to New York for a book signing. All expenses would be paid and an advance would be given to Rick. Rick explained that this was not a good time for him to go but the publisher was insistent. He told Rick that this would be a big deal, and it would include photographers. The publisher said it would be in two weeks and Rick should go first class and take a friend along if he wished. Rick was to make his own travel arrangements, but the publisher would make the hotel arrangements in the hotel where the signing would take place. Rick agreed, and they said goodbye.

Rick thought to himself that he would have to go by his house in North Dakota to pick up appropriate clothing. He had lunch in the cabin, thinking about the work that needed to be done here, and what he needed to do regarding transportation. He decided to drive home, and then fly to New York. He would need to put Bart in a kennel. He knew of a good one where Bart had stayed before.

He called Gail and told her of the signing, and asked if she would like to go with him. He told her that he planned to be in New York for three days and then return to North Dakota. Gail was enthused and said she would see if she could get away. She said she would call him back within twenty four hours.

Rick called Joel and told him about the New York trip and that they would only have their digging this week because he would be gone the following week. Rick asked if they could do the digging tomorrow since he would have to drive first to North Dakota.

Joel agreed and said, "Congratulations, it is great that your book is selling so well. It is also good that we went to six to eight hours of digging last week."

Rick worked the rest of the day with the Brothers. They had dinner together. Nothing was said about Dawn being there.

That evening Gail called and said that she was able to get off work and she loved the thought of going to New York, especially since it was with Rick. He said he would call her as soon as he arrived at his home. They talked a bit more and then said goodbye.

The phone rang and it was Mary on the line.

She said, "I am sorry Rick, I got off on a tangent. I am back to thinking more rationally now. It took courage to tell me the facts of life, and I thank you. I am very fond of you and I want our relationship to continue to develop."

"Thank you Mary, I was concerned that I had offended you."

"All is well Rick. I hope that we will get together again soon."

They said goodbye.

Joel arrived early the next day. They packed the gear in the truck and took off up the trail.

Rick said, "While I am away, I would like to ask you to keep an eye on the cabin work. I will let Pete make cabin decisions, but if any other type problems come, up I would ask you to make those decisions. Would you be willing to do that?"

"No problem, glad to do it."

Rick said that Mary had called and all was well on that account once again.

They arrived at the lake and set up their gear. This time the excavator was placed totally in the lake bed, facing the deep end. They put the sluice box nearby. Joel took the first shift with the excavator, and Rick handled the rest. About twelve thirty they stopped for lunch. They then exchanged duties until they stopped digging for the day. The cleanup was almost a duplicate of the one from the previous week, with a bit over two ounces of gold. They were very pleased. They packed up their gear in the truck and drove to the cabin.

At the cabin they talked with Pete and Al. Rick told them that he would be going to New York for a book signing. They were to continue with their work, with Pete in charge, and that Joel would have the decision making authority in all other matters. Rick told them to feel free to call Joel at any time if a problem came up.

Joel then continued to the Trading Post. Rick began to sort out what he needed to take along.

That evening they had dinner together. They asked Rick about the book signing. He told them that he would prefer not to go, but he really didn't have a choice. This was an opportunity to publicize the book and get additional sales.

Rick turned in early, leaving the packing till the morning.

He was up early. After eating breakfast he packed what he needed and put the things in his car. He fed Bart and then the Brothers came out of their tents. They shook hands and Rick told them that he had confidence in them. They wished him success in New York.

Rick and Bart got in the car and drove to the Trading Post. Rick stopped there just for a minute to say goodbye and then he drove off to North Dakota.

CHAPTER XX

At his home he immediately called Gail. They set an early morning time for Rick to pick her up. Rick called the kennel and made arrangements to board Bart for a few days. He then selected clothing that he wished to take along and repacked his suitcase on wheels. He reluctantly took Bart to the kennel. He called the airline and arranged for two round trip, first class tickets to New York, for the next morning. He called the publisher's office and left the information about his arrival. They gave him the hotel information.

In the morning Rick called Gail and said he was on his way. He called a cab and they picked Gail up on the way to the airport. Gail was excited. Rick told her that she looked great. The flight was smooth and uneventful. They enjoyed being together again. The excellent hotel had fine accommodations. They relaxed that afternoon and then went to dinner. He ordered a nice wine and they studied the menu. Rick wanted something entirely different so he ordered leg of lamb. Gail ordered lobster. They enjoyed the dinner and brought each other up to date on recent happenings. After dinner they went dancing before returning to the hotel. There was a message from the publisher stating that the signing would begin at ten a.m. in the blue room.

They had breakfast in the hotel dining room. On the way to breakfast they saw signs in the lobby advertising the book signing. They lingered over coffee until just before ten o'clock. Rick was surprised to see that quite a few people were there. He was met by a representative of the publisher who introduced him to the group, holding up a book so they could see the cover with the title "WILDERNESS". A reporter with his photographer also introduced himself. As Rick began signing books the reporter asked Rick questions.

Then he said to Rick, "I saw an article in an Alaska newspaper regarding the rescue of a young girl who was drifting on a log in the river. Are you by any chance the man who rescued her?"

"Yes."

The reporter said, "Did you also catch the kidnapper?"

Rick said, "Yes."

The publisher's representative immediately called the publisher and told him about Rick.

The publisher said, "Bring him to my office immediately after the signing."

Rick continued to sign, but those who had heard the reporter asked Rick for more details about the rescue and the capture of the kidnapper. The crowd grew as others heard portions of the story. The signing continued long after the scheduled time.

The reporter asked for an interview, but Rick said, "I can't do it at this time, but I will be glad to talk with you later. I have a meeting now with my publisher."

The publisher's representative told Rick that he was to go with him. When they met, Ted, the publisher said, "Rick, why didn't you tell me that you were a hero? This changes the whole thing. I want to have you on television telling your story. It will double or triple the sales on your book."

"I would really rather not dothat." Rick said, "I have much to do in Alaska. It is almost winter there."

"I'm not asking you to stay here for a week or two, just an additional day or two. I promise you that it will be done quickly and we'll set it up so that it is satisfactory to you."

Rick said, "The reporter at the signing asked for an interview."

"By all means, meet with him. All the publicity you can get is beneficial. Let me take you and your friend out to dinner. I know that you will enjoy the restaurant that we will go to."

Rick agreed, the dinner sounded like a good idea, and if it only added one more day he thought he could go along.

The restaurant the publisher chose was "The Four Seasons." The publisher said for Rick to call him Ted. Ted ordered champagne while they studied the menu. Ted recommended shrimp cocktail as the appetizer.

For the main course, Rick ordered Baby Pheasant in golden sauce, with nutted wild rice. Gail ordered crisped duckling with peaches, sauce oasis. Ted ordered Roast Sirloin of Beef. He told them that the menu changes four times a year at the Four Seasons.

As they waited for dinner, Ted asked Rick to tell him briefly of the rescue and the capture. He told an abbreviated version knowing that it would all come out in detail in the TV filming and in the newspaper.

Dinner arrived and they enjoyed the excellent food. They had dessert and coffee. Ted then suggested that they sit in a quiet corner of a lounge and talk.

Ted said, "I know that you are concerned about getting back to Alaska as soon as possible. I have an idea. Is there a TV station close to where you live in North Dakota?"

"Yes".

Ted said, "I can arrange for the filming to be done there. I will send one of my men to conduct the interview. Now, I would like for you to be wearing the clothing that you had on when you rescued her. Also, have your guns with you. Your dog also was a big help and he needs to be by your side at the filming."

Rick said, "What a great idea, my clothing, guns and the dog are in North Dakota. Not having to bring them here will save a lot of time. Thank you."

Ted said, "I will see that you get a tape or a disc of the interview. You have tomorrow to enjoy New York, what would you like to do?"

Gail said, "We planned to go to see a Broadway show."

Ted said, "Fine, I'll see what is available and get tickets for you. I have to run now. My secretary will be calling you."

They shook hands and Rick thanked him, and said how much he appreciated his help.

Rick and Gail went dancing in the ballroom, enjoying being with each other, and listening to the beautiful music.

In the morning after breakfast at the hotel they decided to walk along the street to see the buildings, the people and the traffic. They stopped at a deli for lunch and then returned to the hotel. At the desk there was an envelope from Ted's secretary with information about the show. Tickets were included along with a note from Ted to have a good time. There was also a message from the reporter asking him to call to arrange a meeting for the interview. Rick called and they set a time of eight a.m. The next morning, Rick asked the desk to call him one hour before they would have to leave.

They decided to take it easy before showering and dressing for the show. They would get a quick dinner in the dining room just before leaving.

The cab took them to the theater. The show was "Cat on a Hot Tin Roof." by Tennessee Williams. It was an enjoyable evening.

At eight am the reporter arrived and he interviewed Rick for his paper. Rick told him of the filming for TV and the reporter said he would follow up on that with the publisher, he also said that he would send a copy of the article to Rick. They thanked each other and the reporter left.

They took the plane to North Dakota. Rick got a cab and took Gail home first. She told Rick that she loved every minute and sincerely expressed her thanks. Rick asked the driver if he could pick up his dog at the kennel. The cabbie said he wasn't permitted to carry dogs except for Seeing Eye Dogs. He took Rick home.

Rick carried his things in and then took his car for Bart. The kennel said that there had not been any problems and that they had bathed Bart in accordance with Rick's orders. Both Rick and Bart were excited about being together again. On the way home Bart nuzzled him. Rick drove with his left hand while petting Bart.

That afternoon he received a call frontend's office with details on the filming which would be tomorrow morning at nine AM. Harry would be interviewing him. Rick got his Alaska clothes ready as well as his armament. They were as ready as could be. Rick called Joel and told him what had happened in New York. He said that he would be delayed one day due to the filming for TV.

Harry interviewed Rick with Bart at his left side. He held his rifle in his right hand. His knife, in a sheath, and his revolver in a holster, were on his belt. Harry asked Rick why he was living in Alaska, Rick told him about living alone in the wilderness so that he could write a book with knowledge from firsthand experience. In plain view was Rick's book, WILDERNESS. Harry asked him to describe the area around the cabin and the river. He also asked him to describe Krazy Joe and Dawn. Rick described each of them. Then he was asked how he happened to be in a canoe on the river. Rick told of the need to get a large amount of firewood before the snow and the freezing cold set in. Harry then asked him to tell what happened on the river. Rick did this and brought the story up to the next morning when he was about to take Dawn to the Native Village. Rick then told in detail how Krazy Joe had kicked open his door and the fight, and Bart's attack on Krazy. Rick then described the twenty plus mile hike to take Dawn back to her parents. He also described the Native Village and the punishment given to Krazy by the villagers. He ended by telling them of Krazy Joe's threat. The interview was concluded. Theyy shook hands. Harry said that he would get a copy of the interview to Rick.

Rick returned home with Bart and made preparations to go once again to Alaska.

He arrived at the Trading Post. He let Bart walk around and then they entered the store. Joel was there to greet him. Joel said it was good to have him back, and Rick said it was good to be back.

Jane came into the store and welcomed him with a hug. She said, "I want to hear all about New York. You know, you are just in time for dinner.

"I am tired from driving and I would love to have dinner with you. Thank you."

Joel said, "I didn't realize it was this late. Let's go in the living room and we'll all have a nice glass of wine."

"Now," Jane said, "tell us all about New York."

Rick explained what happened at the book signing and the subsequent interview with the reporter and then the TV interview. He also told them of the dinner at "The Four Seasons", and the Broadway show "Cat on a Hot Tin Roof." He told them that he would be getting a copy of the newspaper article and of the TV interview.

Joel said, "That is a lot to accomplish in just three days."

Jane said, "I am envious of the dinner and the show."

Rick asked what had gone on here. Joel told him that all was well. He had gone out to the cabin once and talked with Pete and Al. They were doing good work. Jane excused herself to make dinner. Rick asked if tomorrow was a digging day and Joel said that it was. Joel said that next week would surely produce enough so that they would have earned the cost of the land and expenses.

Jane called them to dinner. Rick told them that he hadn't seen Phil and George for a while and wondered how they were doing. Joel hadn't seen them either and assumed that they had been busy.

Rick told them about the new greenhouse that the Brothers had built.

Rick received a phone call and excused himself for a minute. It was Ted, the publisher. He told Rick that the TV interview would be broadcast one week from today at nine p.m. on channel 204. Rick thanked him. He relayed the news to Joel and Jane. Joel invited Rick to come back and see the show with them. Rick accepted with thanks.

After dinner they went to the living room. Joel invited Rick to stay over and drive home in the morning. Rick was glad to stay over. He was tired. After talking for some time Joel noticed that Rick was beginning to nod off and said it was time to go to bed. Rick took Bart out for a walk, said good night and thanks, and turned in.

After breakfast they took off for the cabin with Rick leading and Joel following in his truck. Rick noticed only a couple of bears at the feeding area. At the cabin Rick unloaded his car and changed clothing. Joel loaded up the rest of the mining gear in the truck. Rick talked briefly to Pete and Al and told them that they would talk more when he returned.

They drove up the trail and arrived at the lake. It looked as it had when they left. They wasted no time setting things up and Joel began to dig. About one p.m. Rick took over digging and they finished about four thirty. They were now old hands at this and it didn't take long until they were weighing the gold. All was recorded including the date, and time. Joel would add it to their account in the morning.

On the way back Joel asked, "Are you any closer to making a decision about staying for the winter?"

"No, I haven't. I have been busy enough that my mind was fixed on other things. I realize that if I do stay I have a lot to do to get ready. The firewood I can buy from the Brothers, but the meat I would have to get, and the freezer has yet to be built."

"If there is any way that I can help you Rick, just let me know."

"Thanks."

Joel dropped Rick off with some of the gear and then proceeded to the Post. Rick put things away and then talked to Pete and Al. They had made good progress and Rick complimented them. He saw that the walls were going up and he explained to Pete where the freezer would be placed on the outer kitchen wall. He explained that he would begin working on the box tomorrow. It was time to quit work for the day. Rick hadn't had fish for a while so he told the men that they could join him if the fish took his bait. Rick got a nice fish and with the vegetables from Jane they had a nice dinner. Rick asked if they had enough logs to complete the two rooms and Pete said they needed to get one or two more trees. They asked Rick about New York and Rick told them as he had told Joel and Jane. They talked some more, then Rick took Bart for a nice long walk before turning in.

Rick started to build the freezer box after having breakfast. It was identical to the ones he had made for the original cabin and the one he made for the Brothers.

In the meantime, Pete and Al were in the forest cutting trees. Rick made the supports for the freezer and framed out the area where the box would be placed. Pete and Al came back and Rick showed the box, and where it would be placed. They completed the logs around that location. This was easier than having to take existing logs out first to make a space for the box. They all worked well together placing the supports and installing the box. Rick took hold of the handles and pulled the box toward the kitchen. He slid the lid back which revealed the spaces for the meat. It had been freezing weather for some time now so the freezer was ready for use when meat was available. The freezer door moved back and forth freely.

The Brothers expressed their appreciation of the simplicity and the practical aspects of freezing meat without electricity. They took a short break for lunch and continued work on the logs. Working together the three of them made good progress for the next several days.

Joel arrived and he and Rick headed for the lake.

On the way Rick said, "I hope this digging today will earn us enough to break even for our first season. Would you be willing to let it be the last digging session for this season? I still have much to do on the cabin and winter will be closing in on us."

"That will be fine. I will call the dealer tomorrow and tell them to pick up the excavator and the dozer. Isn't it nice that we didn't have to buy them and let them sit there all winter?"

"Yes, it worked out fine."

They arrived at the lake and proceeded to dig. After a couple of hours Joe pointed out to Rick that he was beginning to get some gravel rather than just dirt. He saw this as a good sign. After lunch Rick began digging. After a while he mentioned that he was getting more gravel. Rick finished his turn on the excavator, and backed it out of the lake. Joel brought the dozer up beside it. They processed the mat with the dirt in two segments and Joel weighed the gold. Joel would deposit the amount in their account. He made his journal entries.

They packed up and drove to the cabin. Joel reminded Rick about the TV show that would be on tomorrow night. Rick said that he would come in before noon.

Rick got his 22 magnum and went looking for dinner. He didn't want salmon tonight, and he wasn't too keen on squirrel or rabbit so he kept his eyes open for something else. After hunting quietly for a while he spotted something that he had not expected to see. It was a bird of Alaska by the name of Ptarmigan. It was about the size of a small chicken. It was brown in color in the summer and white in the winter. This particular bird was in the process of changing color. Rick didn't have his shot gun with him and he didn't want to destroy them eat so he decided to try a more difficult shot by aiming just below the head. He was successful. The bird was neatly decapitated. It wasn't much meat for three people, but with vegetables, they would make do. It turned out to be very tasty.

CHAPTER XXI

In the morning he met with Pete and Al. He told them that he would be at the Trading Post for two or three days. When he returned he would work with them. He packed the car, and called Bart. He waved to the Brothers and then drove to the Post. He saw what looked like Mary's car.

They went into the store and found Joel who gave Rick a mug of coffee.

Joel said, "Have a seat. I have something to tell you. We balanced out on our gold mining venture with a little over twenty thousand dollars spent for the land and legal items. We earned over twenty one thousand in gold sales. We own the land free and clear. We still have the partnership and money in the bank."

"That is terrific for our first season."

Rick said, "As we dig deeper the rewards will be so much greater. Just imagine what we could achieve if we worked full time on it as others would do."

Joel added, "We have all winter to think about it."

Jane and Mary came into the store. They both hugged Rick and patted Bart.

Rick said, "I'm glad that you are here Mary."

"When Mom called and told me about the TV show and that you would be here I checked and I have quite a bit of vacation time accrued. So I am taking a week off."

Rick said, "I am glad to hear it."

Rick's phone rang. He excused himself to take the call. It was the TV channel that would be airing the film this evening. The TV executive introduced himself as Steve.

He said, "Rick, we have already viewed the film and have also come to know of your short stories in the sports magazine. We like what we see and hear. We would like for you to come to meet with us next week. We would like to have you on TV for one half hour each week telling one of your hunting or fishing stories. We already have a willing sponsor. I can assure you that the money you get will be first rate. Can you come to meet with us next week?"

"No, but thank you. It is the end of the summer season, winter is about to begin. The first that I would be able to see you would be in three or four weeks."

"All right, I understand that I didn't give you sufficient notice. Please make it as early as you can. We are excited about the kind of program you will have. Please take down my phone, name and address and call me as soon as possible."

Rick took down the information and then said good bye.

Joel said, "We heard some of that can you tell us what is going on?"

Rick told them what Steve, an executive of the TV station, had said.

Mary said, "That is quite a compliment to you, and quite an offer that might come up once in a life time, to one in a million people."

Jane said, "I am really impressed."

"Well, Rick said, they just really invited me to come and talk. There was no offer other than he said the money would be first rate."

Joel asked, "Will you go to see them?"

"Yes I will go talk to them, but I need to concentrate on the cabin first."

Jane asked to be excused to make lunch and took Mary with her.

Jane said, "He is going to be a very wealthy man someday."

Mary said, "I don't think it will change him, he will still be an honest caring man."

Rick went to wash up and Joel went to the kitchen. Mary asked Joel if he thought that Rick would change as a result of money and publicity.

Joel said, "No, and I'll give to you an example. Rick hired Al to fill in only when Rick was away. I told Rick that Al was a good man and needed the money. Rick has kept him on full time since then even when Rick was there."

Rick was called to lunch. Again they thought about the Brothers since they had not heard from them.

Joel said, "They usually come for their winter supplies before this."

Rick asked if Joel had their phone number. Joel said he must have it written in their account and he would check after lunch. They all enjoyed the chicken salad, and the strawberry short cake for desert. Jane said that she had the strawberries shipped in.

Joel got the phone number and Rick called. Phil answered and Rick asked how things were going. Phil said that they had been busy but were going to the Trading Post tomorrow and would stop by to see Rick on the way home. Rick told them where he was and that he would see them at the Post tomorrow. They chatted a bit and said good bye until tomorrow. Rick told them what Phil had said.

Joel exclaimed, "That's a relief, I was worried about them."

Rick said, "Before we do anything else, I need to take Bart for a walk."

Mary decided to go along. Outside as they walked, Rick told her, "I'm glad that you are here. This near the end of the season I need to finish the cabin. The furniture arrived and I would like for you to see it all before winter."

Mary said, "I'll see what can be worked out."

They walked and on the way back Mary took Rick's hand. Rick thought, "The spark is still there."

In the afternoon they played Rummikub and then Scrabble. There was no one winner, but they all had a good time. Jane and Mary went to take a nap.

Joel stretched out on the recliner and Rick ended up on the sofa. Jane came into the room waking them and telling them that she was starting dinner and that she needed a few things from the store. Rick said that he would go with Joel and that they could use his car. At the store they picked up what Jane wanted. Rick picked out a few bottles of wine that he liked and asked what Joel and Jane liked. Joel told him that they liked, "Frontera" a wine rated highly by Consumers Report. The wine is from Chile. Rick bought them a red and a white wine.

Back at the Post they made their delivery and were advised that dinner would be ready in one half hour. Rick took Bart for a walk and then washed up. He met Joel back in the living room. They were called to dinner. Joel said the blessing and then announced that Rick had provided the wine. Tonight they had spaghetti and meatballs with a chef's salad. Mary asked how the gold mining was coming along.

Rick said, "We have finished mining for the season, but your dad can tell you how we made out."

Joel said, "We worked once a week. We earned enough to pay for the land and all expenses in the first season."

Mary said, "Wow, it sounds like the mine has a great potential."

They lingered over the dinner, and then the men carried the dishes to the kitchen.

Later they all met in the living room. It was now eight thirty and the show was to start at nine. They talked, but kept watching the clock. At last nine o'clock came and Joel turned on the TV. After the commercial the scene appeared with a background of an Alaska river. Rick was sitting by a tent with Bart on his left and he was holding the rifle in his right hand. In clear view on his lap was his book, "WILDERNESS." The publisher's rep set the background and then asked Rick to explain why he was in Alaska. Rick told of his desire to live alone in the wilderness to experience what it was like so that he could write a book factually about the experience." He was asked why he happened to be canoeing in the river with his dog. Rick replied that he was looking for a log to use for fire wood. He went on to describe the rescue of Dawn, and her physical recovery. He was asked to describe the man who kidnapped her and then to tell what happened next. Rick told the story in detail including Bart's attack on Krazy Joe, and Rick s fight with Krazy. He later told of the twenty mile hike to return Dawn to her parents and the punishment that the natives took on Krazy. The interview concluded with Rick telling of Krazy's threat to him.

They were all very excited about the film, and complimentary to Rick.

Joel said, "You are very photogenic Rick and your voice is good. It is no wonder that they want you to have your own TV show."

Mary said, "I want to watch each episode."

Jane said, "Do you have copies of your book yet?"

"Thank you. That reminds me that I have one for you and Joel, and one for Mary. Wait a minute and I'll get them for you."

He returned with the books and they wanted them signed. They were signed.

Conversation went to several other topics and then Rick said it was time to take Bart out. Mary came along and asked how long Rick was staying at the Post.

"I'll probably stay here tomorrow, but it will depend a bit on the

Brothers. I will need their help to move the stove to the kitchen. I really should leave here when they do."

They walked hand in hand and shortly returned to the cabin. They talked in the living room. Mary had snuggled up beside Rick. Later they all said goodnight and went to bed.

Rick loved the breakfast of ham, eggs, hash browns, toast and coffee. There was no hurry today. They were waiting for the Brothers and enjoying being together. They lingered over the coffee and Rick thought to himself that it felt like he was a member of the family, at least they seemed to treat him that way. Being with a family gave him a warm feeling. He and Joel and Jane had become very good friends. In addition, there was the attraction to Mary. He wanted to know her better. He needed more time alone with her. If she visited at his cabin that might help, but he would be so busy working.

Jane and Mary decided to go shopping by themselves leaving Rick and Joel to decide what Rick needed to take along to the cabin. They made a list and then gathered up the items in one spot ready to be loaded when the time came.

Rick realized that if Mary would be visiting he would need some cereal, milk, eggs, bacon, bread, and something other than salmon to eat. Joel agreed to go with him. They went in Rick's car and returned about the same time that Jane and Mary did. Rick's things were placed in the refrigerator, in the store bags so they didn't get them mixed up.

It was noon time, so they had lunch.

About one o'clock Rick received a call. It was from Ted, the book publisher.

He said, "Rick I am so excited about the results of the TV show. You were a real hit. I have had reports from all over and the book sales have sky rocketed."

Rick thanked him and then told him of the call from the TV executive.

Ted said, "Go for it, and call me when you come to New York. We'll get together. I have some ideas that I believe will interest you."

They chatted a little more and then said goodbye.

Rick told them of Teds call.

Just then the Brothers arrived. Joel and Rick went to the store to meet them. There were handshakes and greetings all around. Joel asked them to sit and talk some before getting to their supplies.

Rick commented, "I have not seen you for such a long time, and much has happened. I first want to tell you why you didn't find any fish in the lake. There was no access for fish to get in since the water came from a spring. There was no way for them to get out either. While I was there I spotted bright items that Joel identified as gold. Joel and I bought the land and have been part time mining it."

The Brothers exclaimed, "That is some story, did you find more gold?"

Joel said that they had, but working part time. The yield had not been high.

"But that's not all," said Joel, "Rick has been on TV and his book is selling like hot cakes."

George said, "Do we get a copy of the book Rick?"

Rick said, "Indeed you do and I'll get one for you right now. By the way, did you get the copy of my article on your place?"

Joel interrupted, and said, "I have it right here."

Rick signed the book for them.

Joel asked, "What do you fellows need?"

Phil said, "Nothing perishable, mostly the usual beans, rice, flour, and some canned goods. We also need some trap parts and some ammunition. They walked around selecting items they needed and others that they just wanted.

It took quite a while and Joel said, "You fellows may as well stay overnight. I have the bunk house room that you can use. I will see if I can arrange an outside cookout of hamburgers and hot dogs for dinner."

"It is a long haul home, and it is getting late. Most of all, the cookout sounds great. Let's stay Phil," said George."

"Right on," replied Phil. "I see that you are making good progress on your new cabin Rick."

"I'm glad that you came today, and we can leave together tomorrow. I would like to ask your help in moving my stove to the new kitchen."

"No problem," said Phil, "we were planning to stop and help you with the cabin anyhow. We won't have any perishables with us so we will have some time, and no problems."

"Thanks that will mean a lot."

They continued to collect more items.

Joel invited them into the living room, and asked what they would like to drink. For Phil it was beer, George wanted bourbon, and Rick chose beer. Joel went along with the beer also thinking it would go good with the cook out food.

Jane and Mary came in and they both asked for wine. Joel told them that he was thinking of cooking hamburgers, and hotdogs outside. He wanted baked beans and coleslaw also. Rick volunteered to cook the baked beans, if they were available in a can. Mary offered to take care of the cold slaw.

Jane said, "Thank you, since I don't have to cook I'll just relax and enjoy it."

After dinner they all went to the living room. The Brothers admired the bear skin. They talked about a variety of items. Mary sat close to Rick and the Brothers noticed. Later Rick decided to take Bart for a walk, Mary went with him.

Rick said, "I'll be leaving with the Brothers in the morning. You are very welcome to come with me but you must realize that in the daytime I will be busy helping to build the cabin."

Mary said, "I'll go with you. My dad has agreed to come to get me when I call him."

"That sounds great; I was hoping it might work out that way. I was concerned that I couldn't be with you to take you to the lake and for canoe rides."

"It will be ok Rick, we'll manage."

He gave her a hug and a kiss. They walked hand in hand as they returned to the cabin.

The cook out was a big success. They kidded Rick about his big job of heating the canned beans. The Brothers asked more about the mining operation, and how much land they purchased. They also wanted to know what kinds of equipment they used. Rick's phone rang and the Sports magazine editor, Art Pines, was on the line. He reminded Rick that he only had two episodes ready and that he wanted Rick to speak to a hunting and fishing club in Virginia in one month. Rick got the date, time and place written down. They talked some and then said goodbye.

Rick told them about the call.

After dinner they talked. Rick told them that Mary would be coming along to visit. She hadn't seen the new cabin but had been there once before the arson. Phil said winter would arrive in about two or so weeks and they were in the process of getting ready for trapping. They asked if Rick was staying for the winter and he said he hadn't made up his mind yet. The Brothers said that they would turn in.

Rick and Mary took Bart for a walk. Rick said he was glad Mary was going with him to the cabin. They hugged and kissed when they returned to the cabin and said goodnight.

After breakfast they all packed their vehicles. Goodbyes were said and Rick led the way followed by the two Brothers in their pickup.

CHAPTER XXII

Arriving at the cabin Rick took everyone for a tour of the shed and garage, and then the cabin. There were handshakes with Pete and Al. Rick told them how pleased he was with the work that Pete and Al had done. Rick excused himself to unload the car and Mary helped. He put Mary's things in his bedroom telling her that the two Brothers might stay over and if so would use the spare bedroom. He said that he would sleep on the couch. He apologized that he didn't have doors on the bedrooms yet, but there was one for the bathroom. Mary began unpacking and Rick joined the men.

"I would like to ask that all hands help move the stove to the new kitchen. We will have to go out the front door and around coming in through the dining room since the walls are getting high in the kitchen."

The stove was moved successfully after the smokestack was carefully removed. Rick then asked Pete to direct operations of raising logs in the appropriate sequence. They all worked together following Petes directions. They worked until close to dinner time.

Rick said he would catch some fish. He got three nice salmon and prepared them for cooking. Mary asked if the stove was available and he said that it was not, but he would build a fire. They could cook outside. While Rick and Mary began dinner preparations work on the log walls continued. Mary got vegetables from the cabin. Rick built a support over the fire for the vegetables to cook. He waited until Mary said they were about ready. He then began to cook the fish. The men were called. They brought their dishes and their knives and forks. Dinner was served. The Brothers were happy about having salmon.

After dinner they gathered around the fire. They talked about the log raising, and Pete asked the Brothers to tell about their fur trapping. They also wanted to know more about the gold mining. All these subjects were discussed and then they sang, accompanied by the harmonica. It was a fun time and was enjoyed by all.

It had been a busy day so Pete and Al said goodnight and went to their tents.

Shortly thereafter they went into the cabin. Rick explained the sleeping arrangements, and apologized for not having doors on the bedrooms. He said they had their choice of the outhouse or the port-a-potty in the bathroom. Rick and Mary took a walk with Bart along the river bank. Mary said the evening had been fun, especially talking and singing around the fire. When they returned the Brothers had gone to bed. Rick and Mary sat together on the sofa. Later, Mary said she was going to bed.

Rick prepared his bed on the sofa and turned in also. Bart curled up on the floor beside him.

After breakfast work began again. The Brothers told Rick that they would work until about two o'clock and then leave. Rick worked with them and the logs that Pete and Al had prepared went up quickly. After lunch they started work again and by two o'clock the walls were raised and it was ready for the rafters.

Rick had stopped about one thirty and caught two good sized salmon for them to take with them. He put them in plastic bags and they put them in their pickup. Thanks and goodbyes were said. The Brothers headed north on the trail.

Rick resumed work and they made good progress. Rick told them that he would work the next day, but the following day he would take off to show Mary around. He also told them that they were on their own for meals until she left.

In the evenings he and Mary had dinner, and took walks, and talked. They were getting to know each other.

In the daytime Mary played with Bart, took short walks and took over meal preparations. She made a list of things that she thought Rick might need, like additional lamps. They got along well. Respect and admiration grew for both of them along with increased affection.

Rick worked the next day, but on the following day he took Mary for a hike to the lake. He showed her the spring, the waterfall, and the lake. He explained the reason for the hole beside the lake. When they returned they had lunch and then a canoe ride. Bart was with them throughout the day. Evening came, they had dinner. Mary called Joel and asked him to pick her up at his convenience the next morning. They were both sorry that she had to leave, but she had to get back to nursing and Rick needed to work on the roof. They agreed to keep in touch by phone and by writing. They kissed goodnight. Mary now had the spare room and Rick had his bed back.

After breakfast they walked to the river while waiting for Joel. Rick got his camera and took a number of pictures. He agreed to give Mary a set.

Before long Joel drove up the trail and parked. Mary gave him a hug and the men shook hands. Joel saw the great progress that had been made on the cabin. They talked for a little while and then Mary got her things and prepared to leave. It was a difficult parting for both of them. They hugged and kissed and then Joel and Mary were gone.

Joel asked Mary how it went.

She said, "I loved every minute. He was a perfect gentleman, and the men looked up to him."

Rick returned to work. Within a few days the roof was completed. The temporary door between the living room and the hall to the kitchen bath and dining room was removed. The windows were set, and the caulking began. The kitchen had one window in front, and a small one over the freezer. The bathroom had a small window. The dining room had two, one on the side and one in the rear.

When they finished they took a tour admiring their work. Rick said that he was very pleased with their work. He paid them as he had agreed and gave Pete an extra bonus for taking charge while he was gone, and for supervising when others came to help.

Al said, "You don't know how much the work you gave to me helped. I will always be ready to help you when needed."

Pete said, "The bonus is very generous, but I really enjoyed working for you. Thank you."

Pete and Al left.

Rick and Bart went for a long walk to think things over. Now that the cabin was done and the mining was finished for the season he had to make his mind up. He walked for about an hour seeing pros and cons on each side.

He went into the living room and when he looked up he saw a hole in the roof that the smoke stack had gone through. He got a ladder and completed the job on the inside, and then went on the roof to complete the outside.

In the morning he believed he had the answer to his question as to where would he be in the winter. He began packing his things. He left the sled and the mining equipment, but took the flatbed trailer, the canoe and outboard. He called Joel and told him he was on the way to the Post. He also said that he had come to a decision. He locked up the shed and the cabin, and drove to the Trading Post.

CHAPTER XXIII

As he passed the part of the river were the bears normally fed he noticed that there were no bears. They probably hibernated. He parked in front of the Post. He let Bart run before going into the store. Joel was there with a smile and a hand shake greeting. He asked Rick to have a seat and got coffee for him.

Joel said, "Mary enjoyed her visit with you."

"I wish I would have had more time, but we did go to the lake and she had one canoe ride. She was very helpful with meals and she made a list of the things that she thought I needed. I was sorry to see her go."

Joel brought out a packet of mail that had arrived for Rick.

"We finished the cabin exterior thanks to the Brothers' help and the good work of Pete and Al. The stove needs to be connected to the smoke stack, and there is a lot of interior work to be done, but it is locked up. By the way, I would like to ask you to hold on to a set of keys for me. You know by now that I will not be staying here this winter. I would like to talk to both you and Jane about that after lunch."

"Of course that will be fine," said Joel, "Pete and Al stopped here after they finished at your cabin and had good things to say about you."

"They turned out to be excellent at their trade, and were good workers. I wouldn't hesitate to hire them again."

Jane came in and welcomed Rick with a hug. She said, "Mary enjoyed visiting you. She has returned to work."

Joel said, "Rick is going to stay with us today. He said that he will tell us about his decision."

"That's fine." said Jane, "You men talk and I'll let you know when lunch is ready."

Joel showed Rick some new items that had come in for him to sell.

He also had a new catalog that showed an electric powered toilet. That reminded Rick to tell Joel what he had left in the shed and garage.

Jane called them to lunch. Joel told them that the weather report predicted a very cold and snowy winter. Rick told them that he had built a steeper pitch to the roof of his cabin than usual since he would not always be there to shovel it off if the snow was too deep. He also told them that there were no bears feeding at the usual spot on the river.

Jane asked if he had taken pictures of the new cabin. He said that he had, including some of Mary. They talked about the two Brothers and the natives, and other topics.

Rick told them that he would be going to North Dakota in the morning. He could find lots of logical reasons for going, including the fact that he was not writing a book this year. He had lots of work to do with the sports magazine and the TV station. His big problem was in leaving this area and the two of them and Mary. In any event, he planned to return in the spring. I look forward to being with you again, working on the cabin and gold mining."

After lunch Rick took Bart for a long walk. They then returned to the store. Joel always had things to show to Rick. Joel had a catalog of mining equipment and showed him a metal perforated sheet that could be used on the sluice box to filter out the gold from the dirt and rocks. They thought it might be an improvement over the wooden louvered top that they had been using. They ordered a sheet that they could cut to the size that they needed. They played checkers and told some stories. Jane came and got them to help her with dinner preparations.

After dinner they had coffee, and Rick said, "Regarding the gold mining, I have an idea that I would like to ask you to consider. We earned more than twenty thousand dollars. This was with homemade equipment. I believe that with commercial equipment professional men could increase the return. I would like to ask you to consider putting the claim up for sale in the spring. We can keep on digging, one day per week and see what happens. Do you think there is any merit to the idea?"

Joel said, "What do you think we could sell it for?"

"I would suggest asking for one million."

"Whew," Jane said, "That is a heady figure."

Rick said, "If we just projected our take, and not even considering commercial equipment or first rate professional know how, their take, working six days a week would be about eight hundred thousand for the first year. Add if the commercial equipment and first rate know how was included, it would not be much of a stretch to see them earn one million the first year."

Joel said, "How do we know there is that much gold there?"

"We don't. But they are the professionals. They can dig for samples, and we have our records to show them. Then it is up to them."

"That's a lot to think about, said Joel."

"We have all winter to think about it. Nothing need be decided or done until next spring."

"For an initial investment of just over twenty thousand dollars, that's a big step up to one million. In response to your question though, your idea is definitely worth merit,"

They talked some more, but here was no conclusion. They turned to other topics, but kept going back to the mining one.

Rick said, "I think I need to clear my head, and a walk will do that for me."

"A walk would do me good also. I'll go with you."

Bart of course came along. Conversation continued on and off during the evening till it was time for bed.

After breakfast Rick called the Brothers and Mary, and then the business associates, as well as Gail and Jean. He packed his things in the car, thanked them and said goodbye.

He smiled and then said, "Imagine what you could do with half a million dollars." He waved, and left to begin his new adventure.

PART THREE

CHAPTER XXIV

Rick arrived at his house in North Dakota and made his usual security inspection. All was well, so he unhitched the trailer and unloaded both the SUV and the trailer. Rick fed Bart and then had a glass of wine while he unwound from the road trip from Alaska to his home. He thought about his cabin and Joel, Jane, and Mary. It reminded him to have photos made to send to them.

He got his Porsche and went to the deli for dinner. Then to the drug store to have photos made from his digital camera cartridge. He got multiple copies of the cabin. Compared to the original cabin, this one was huge. He returned to the house, took Bart for a walk and went to bed. It had been a tiring day.

In the morning he made his usual business calls. Appointments were made for one each day starting tomorrow. He called Gail and Jean. Gail invited him to dinner at a restaurant for that evening. He would take Jean to dinner on Friday.

He picked Gail up and they went to the restaurant. They ordered dinner and had a nice glass of wine. Gail wanted to know all about his stay in Alaska. He showed her pictures of the new cabin and of the gold mine area. He told her that he would be returning to Alaska again in April.

After dinner he took her home and she invited him to come in for coffee. When they sat in the living room with the coffee, Gail asked, "Do you intend to always spend five months or so in Alaska?"

Rick said that he wasn't certain, but he did have work to do there both on the cabin and on the gold mine.

Gail said, "You know that I love you and would like for us to be together, but even when you are back from Alaska you are frequently away on business."

Rick said, "I have to admit that you are right about that. It is the nature of my writing business to be out by a stream, fishing or in the woods hunting, or talking to a club somewhere".

Gail said, "I do wish that we could work something out, but it seems that your work will continue to keep us apart."

Rick replied, "I knew that. Although we have been seeing each other with this kind of a schedule for several years, and that we both would have preferred more time together. You seem to be more concerned this time than in the past."

"That is true. As you know I have been seeing other men as you have been seeing other women. Now I need to make a decision. I don't want to continue to date different men at this point in my life. If you can see a way for us to be together we will have something to talk about."

"This is a big decision, Gail, and I don't want to say something now, without proper thought. May I see you later in the week so that we will have time to give this decision the serious attention that it deserves?"

"Yes, leave now and call me in a few days."

They kissed and Rick left. He got in the car and shook his head. He felt like he had been hit by a ball bat. It was so unexpected. He did love her, but he also loved Jean and Mary. If he married one, he would lose the others. He thought of how wonderful a homemaker Gail would be. Then he thought how Jean and he had so much in common, skiing and running and loving the outdoors. And then there was Mary. She loved his cabin, and the fishing and canoeing. She said she would love to live there. If she could live there, after being a nurse in a big hospital she could adapt to any situation. He thought, "They are all career women, and I am a career man, why can't they let well enough alone?"

Rick went home and continued to review the situation. This was stressful. He had a drink and paced the floor. No easy solution was developing. The pacing continued. He thought to himself, 'If this could happen with Gail, it could in time happen to Jean and Mary.' One piece of the puzzle was clear. He intended to continue writing stories about the outdoors no matter where it took him.

He met with his photographer in the morning putting the finishing touches on three articles. In the afternoon he met with Art, the Editor of the Sports magazine.

The editor complemented him on the success of his book and accepted the three articles. Rick told him about the interest that the

TV station had in a series of half hour TV shows with Rick telling stories of hunting and fishing.

The editor responded immediately, saying, "That is a conflict of interest Rick. We pay you to write articles for the magazine and then you tell the stories on TV for another fee. That is totally unacceptable."

Rick was shaken by this response.

"I had not thought that a conflict would exist, the last thing that I would want to do would cause a problem in our relationship."

"Let us just forget about the TV show and we will not have a problem," said Art.

"I will meet with Steve, the TV executive, and tell him that I hadn't realized that a conflict of interest would exist and therefor I cannot do the show."

"Fine now that that is settled I have a talk that I would like for you to give to a club in Indiana. The usual fee and expenses will remain as before. We have received a ton of favorable response to your article regarding the Brothers' fur trapping story. See if you can pull another one like that out of your hat."

They talked some more then shook hands and Rick left.

He was bothered by the conflict of interest issue. Why hadn't he seen the problem himself? Perhaps it was the idea of being on TV with the extra money it would bring in.

That evening after dinner he sat in his office and began to take stock of where he was at this time in his life regarding relationships and finances. He was now forty seven years of age. Financially he was doing well. He must remember to see a financial advisor to invest the money he had let sit in his checking account. He owned outright his house in North Dakota, the cabin and land in Alaska and he owned half of the gold mine claim. He didn't owe anyone. Relationship-wise he had received awake up call. Gail's surprise announcement had told him that his life as a carefree bachelor could probably not continue with his current girlfriends. Unless he could change his goals he would be changing girlfriends frequently. There was time to work things out, but he wasn't looking forward to the meeting with Gail. This was going to take some serious thinking.

Rick got something to eat for dinner, fed Bart, took him for a walk, and then went to his office to review the situation with Gail. He knew that Gail loved him and might marry him if he asked her. He knew that he loved her. She would be a marvelous homemaker. She was beautiful and very intelligent. With these last two assets alone, she would be a great help when social and business interests mixed. But, he could see the problems that would arise almost immediately. He would need to go to Alaska, or to speak to some club somewhere, and Gail would want him to be at home. He did not believe that she could give up her bank position and travel with him sometimes in rough country. If he had a nine-to-five job locally, all would be well with Gail, but in no way would it be well with him. He loved her, but their life styles did not mix. He needed to think about this some more, and decide how to talk to Gail without hurting her. But then a new thought occurred to him. Perhaps it would be less hurtful on her, if she were to tell me that it wouldn't work than for me to tell her. He thought, I'll sleep on that thought and then play it by ear.

CHAPTER XXV

The next morning he prepared to meet Steve, the TV Executive. He had been looking forward to this meeting until Art Pines had pointed out the conflict of interest issue. There was nothing to do except to admit his error and make the best of a bad situation.

Steve met him with a big smile and a hearty hand shake, saying, "We have great plans for you Rick. Please sit down."

Rick said, "I very much appreciate your interest in the TV appearance that I made, and your ideas as to what we could do, but I have made a very big mistake. I didn't think through things enough. If we were to make half hour segments of my telling stories, it would create a conflict of interest with the sports magazine that I write for. I therefore cannot accept your kind invitation."

Steve said, "I appreciate your being straight forward about this, but let us think about this. These kinds of stories are good indefinitely. What if we used stories that you wrote five or six years ago?"

"They would still be stories that the magazine paid me to write."

Steve said, "Let us think of a legal and ethical way to avoid the conflict of interest entirely. Wait, I've got it. We'll ask Art to join us as a sponsor. That will eliminate all conflict."

"That would be great," said Rick, "How do we accomplish that?"

Steve picked up the phone and asked for Art's number. Rick gave him one of Arts cards. Steve dialed the number, told them who he was, and asked to speak to Mr. Pines.

When Art answered Steve told him who he was and then said, "I am sitting here with Rick Spears who just told me that he could not be on TV for me because of a conflict of interest. I want to say up front that I see your point and totally agree with you, as does Rick. The reason for my call is to see if legally and ethically we could devise a plan that would be beneficial to all of us. Would you be willing to take a few moments for me to propose such a plan?"

Art replied, "If it is both legal and ethical and will benefit us all, I am willing to listen."

"First of all, I want to tell you that our broadcasts are not only nationwide, but reach most foreign countries. I can tell you that thousands of responses came in from all over the world regarding Rick's presentation. I would like to have him do a series of half hour shows, and I would like to ask you to be a co-sponsor. While I am sure that your magazine has a very good and wide distribution, not every one reads magazines. If you were a co-sponsor, your magazine would be advertised on TV and with the appearance and excellent delivery of Rick your profits would increase accordingly. Do you think there is merit to this idea Art?"

Art hesitated a minute and then said, "Yes I do Steve. It will take time to work it all out, but I know enough about it now that I will be willing to sit down with you and our respective attorneys to consider it further. I would ask you to provide to me, as I will to you, more information about demographic information on your viewers."

Steve said, "I will certainly do that, and I thank you for being understanding. I will ask my secretary to call your secretary to set up a time, place and date that is mutually agreeable."

They said good bye and hung up.

Rick said, "I am impressed. Now I know how a real businessman works. There are a few things that we need to go over Steve. How many sessions do you envision, where will they be filmed, do you have a preference on the type of stories, and how much will I be paid?"

Steve said, "The type of stories and the number will be a matter for the sponsors and yourself to figure out. Tentatively I have been thinking of one half hour per week of the type stories you have been writing for Art. They would be filmed in my studios here in your home town. As to pay, again, the co-sponsors would have a say, but I would imagine that it would be somewhere near twenty-five hundred dollars per session. As before, your clothing, armament and dog would remain the same. Incidentally, I believe that you could do two sessions in a day, one before lunch and one after lunch. I feel that I am on a roll, so after you leave I will call your publisher Ted, to see if he will be a co-sponsor also?"

They talked for a bit more, Rick thanked him. They shook hands and Rick left.

CHAPTER XXVI

Rick had been elated last evening about the meeting with Steve and the resolution with Art. It had been moderated somewhat today by the realization that he was to meet with Gail this evening. He called Gail to confirm that this evening was ok and to get the time of meeting, and to decide where to meet. Gail suggested that they meet at seven p.m. at her place. There was no mention of dinner.

Rick caught up on mail and worked on new articles for the magazine. He spent time with Bart and took him for a ride in the Cherokee. While riding he saw a dog park near his home that was new since he had been home last. He parked and took Bart in. It was divided for large dogs on one side and small dogs on the other. In the large side they found a Doberman, a German Shepherd, and a Standard Poodle. There were also a number of mixed breed dogs. Rick told Bart to be good and crossed his fingers. Several dogs came to check Bart out, but there was no trouble. Bart didn't socialize with the other dogs but instead walked by Rick's side as he walked around the park.

By the time that they got home, it was nearly five p.m. Rick fed Bart and made a sandwich for himself before he showered and changed clothes. Since they weren't going anywhere he dressed casually. The time went by and he got in the Porsche and went to see Gail.

Gail met him at the door with a hug and offered him a drink. He asked for a scotch on the rocks. Gail called out that he should have a seat. She brought his drink and one for herself.

Rick thanked her and then said, "I want you to know that I have always loved you and have always enjoyed our being together. Regardless of what you decide I will always be your friend and you can call on me at any time that you feel I may be of some help."

Gail said, "Thank you. I feel the same way, but I need to hear what you have come up with."

"Gail this year looks like it will be busier than the last. I have talks to give at clubs, articles to research and then write for the magazine, and it looks like I will be doing a series of TV shows. And of course I will be going back to Alaska in the spring. We can probably see each other more than once a week and you could go with me on a trip that I need to make now and then. Would that be helpful?"

"Not really Rick. As I mentioned before, I do not want to date a number of men anymore. I have been asked to marry a man that I have been dating. He is a bank corporate executive. He will be able to give to me the security and companionship that I need. I will now tell him that I accept."

Rick and Gail stood up. Rick gave her a hug, congratulating her, and wished her well. They said goodbye and Rick left.

As he drove off he wiped a tear from his cheek. Gail had meant more to him than either of them had realized. She was an important part of his family. And now she was gone. He had known that she had separation anxiety when he was gone, and she had dated other men to fill the void. The fear she had of being alone, he now had. He admired her for facing up to the situation in a logical way. He would have to do the same. He noted how different this year was compared to last year. Last year this time she had invited him to dinner on a Friday evening, cooked a first rate dinner, and invited him to stay for the weekend.

Friday came and he was to meet Jean at six p.m. for dinner. During the day he was catching up on articles, and mail, but he kept coming back to the meeting with Gail. He knew that he would have to review his goals and consider if he should modify them. His goal had always been to lead a carefree life as a bachelor. He now saw the danger in continuing that lifestyle. With a change he could not see the way clear to avoid someone getting hurt. He saw that he had several choices. First, continue what he had been doing and let the chips fall where they may. Second, decide if he wanted to marry either Jean or Mary and then go for it. Or, three, if he didn't want to marry Jean or Mary, start over. This time choosing a woman who met his specifications of a perfect wife.

He picked Jean up and said he had an idea. They could go to the grocery store, pick up what they would like to make for dinner and then go to his place to prepare it. He explained that he thought they would have fun working together on a project that they had not tried before.

Jean asked what they would get.

Rick said that they could get whatever she wanted. She agreed, but Rick could tell that there was some doubt in her mind as to whether this was a good idea. On the way to the store he asked her if she would like fish, a steak or chicken.

Her answer was noncommittal so Rick said, "Let's just look around and see what looks good to you."

At the store they looked around and she finally decided on Grouper. The fish was already prepared for cooking.

Rick asked what she would like to go with it. She chose rice and asparagus. He asked about dessert and she chose cherry pie and vanilla ice cream. Rick paid for the items and took them to the car.

Rick said, "I like the choices that you made. How would you like the fish to be cooked?"

Jean replied, "I am not sure what would be best. I'll be glad to go along with whatever you decide."

At home Rick got them some white wine. He said, "Would you prepare the rice while I take care of the fish and the asparagus?"

"Really Rick, I'm not much of a cook, but if you give me the directions, I'll cook the rice."

Rick said, "That's fine. First you need to heat water in a pot."

Rick helped her with the rice and took care of the fish and the asparagus. He poured another glass of wine and they ate the dinner. She said it was very good, and it looked quite easy the way Rick had made it. She said that she ate all of her meals out except for breakfast.

After dessert and coffee Rick asked what she would like to do. Jean replied that she would like to go dancing. Rick was agreeable so they went and had a great time. Spectators always watched Jean dance. She looked like an adult Barbie Doll, and was an excellent dancer. Later, he took her home. She invited him to come in for a night cap. He accepted. They hugged and kissed. Jean invited him to stay over for the weekend. He accepted, but said that he would have to leave by noon Saturday to prepare for his meeting with the publisher of his book.

On Saturday he returned home. On the way he thought, 'I didn't realize that I was always buying our meals at a restaurant, and that she had never invited me to her place for a meal. Perhaps there is more about her that I need to know. So she's not a good cook, but she is a competent career woman. We both like the outdoors, she is beautiful, and I love her.'

Rick really didn't need all of the weekend to prepare for the meetings, but he needed time to absorb all that was happening with his relationships.

In addition to the meeting with Ted, the producer, he needed to give two talks to clubs for the sports magazine. One was in Indiana. He could do that on the way to see Ted. The other one was in Virginia. He could give that talk after seeing Ted.

Arrangements were made for the club appearances and for the airplane tickets. He would be leaving Monday afternoon and making his talk to the Indiana club at their six p.m. dinner meeting. His talk was well received, and he stayed overnight before his flight the next morning to meet with Ted.

Rick arrived at Ted's office. The receptionist told him that he was expected, and that he should go right in. He knocked, and then entered. Ted got up from his desk and with a big smile and a firm hand shake welcomed Rick.

"Rick, your book and the things we have in mind for you will make you a rich man. Sales of your book are booming. There have been some changes from what you and I talked about before. I had envisioned having you make the same TV appearance, perhaps once a month. Each appearance would be in a different large city. Since then an even better plan has developed. I will join the sports magazine and the sporting good supplier as a co-sponsor of a series of one half hour TV presentations that you will make each week. Art Pines has already discussed this with you I believe. You will need to work out the details with Art and Steve."

"That sounds interesting. I would like to have some details."

"It looks like you will be able to make two shows per day, once a week. That way you will gradually build up a reserve of shows."

"What will I be paid?"

"The figure of twenty five hundred per show came up, but I believe that since we have three sponsors, we might be able to do a little better. I will talk with the others and see what I can do for you. I am going to ask Art and Steve to take care of the other details. Let's go to lunch and we can talk some more."

At lunch they talked about the book sales. Ted said that he was considering changing the description of the author on the back side of the cover to include information about Rick's heroics in Alaska. He said that he would show it to Rick before the change was made.

After lunch they said goodbye. Ted returned to his office. Rick got a cab to the airport. He made the talk in Virginia and then flew back to North Dakota.

When he had picked Bart up from the kennel they went home, and he unpacked. Then on an impulse he called Mary. Fortunately she was at home. He told her about his trip and his meetings. She told him about her recent events.

Then he asked, "Mary, would you consider coming to visit with me for a few days? It is still a long time until I return to Alaska and I miss you."

Mary replied, "I would love to visit you if I can get the time off from work. It would be interesting to see where you live. It would be so different from the environment you live in while in Alaska. I will check when I go to work tomorrow and will call you back."

Rick gave her the details regarding the airport and said that if she was able to come, he would pick her up. They talked some more and then said good bye.

Mary called back the next day. She was excited and said that she could visit for three days for a long weekend, in two weeks. Rick was delighted. She gave Rick the Delta flight number, the inclusive dates and ETA. She didn't have time to talk further since she was at work, but said she looked forward to her trip. Rick thanked her and they said goodbye.

CHAPTER XXVII

Rick called Art to set up a meeting. Art told him that he would call him back. Art then asked his secretary to set up a conference call to Steve, Mark, the sports equipment sponsor, and Ted. The call was placed. Art explained the date and time that he proposed for the joint meeting in Art's office. They all agreed, however, Ted would not be there in person, but would be participating by phone. Art called Rick and told him the date and time the co-sponsors would meet with Rick.

Rick said, "That will be fine."

"We will all meet together to decide on general terms. Steve and Mark will then leave and you and I will talk about specific stories that you will present. Ted had called me and had a few ideas that we will discuss also. Do you have any questions that we should discuss now?"

"No, it looks like the four of you have worked out the hard part. I look forward to seeing you all in two days. I do want to tell you that the talks in Indiana and Virginia went well. Hopeful you will get some positive feedback from those clubs."

"I have already been called and the response was very good in both instances. Keep up the good work."

They talked a bit more and then said goodbye.

Rick called Jean and they decided to go skiing on the weekend.

The co-sponsors met at Art's office. Ted was on the speaker phone. Art said that the meeting would be recorded. Ted had talked with the other co-sponsors previously regarding Rick's fee. The three of them had decided that he would get three thousand dollars for each show that was presented by Rick on TV. He would be able to film two shows per week. He was to wear the same clothing that he did in the first show. The armament and the dog would also be as before. Fishing and other sports equipment would be added as appropriate. The first filming would take place in two weeks. There would be commercials at the beginning, the middle, and end of each show. Each sponsor would have their product featured in each commercial. All three sponsors had the right to preview and approve or disapprove of any aspect of each show.

Art asked Steve, Mark and Rick if they had anything to add, or any questions. None of them had anything to add or any questions, and stated that for the record.

Art then asked, "Are we all in agreement on the terms that were presented at this meeting?"

All agreed. They all shook hands. Art told them that they would each receive a copy of the recording of the meeting. He suggested that they have a follow-up meeting after the first two shows had been aired. This was agreed to by all. Steve and Mark congratulated Rick and then said goodbye, and then left. Ted also congratulated Rick and then said goodbye. The phone was hung up, and the recorder was shut off.

Art and Rick began to discuss talks that Rick might give. Art had kept the record of responses from Rick's previous articles. He suggested that they start with articles from five or six years ago, selecting those with the most favorable reader responses. Rick had kept each of the issues from when he first started, so it was just a matter of matching the results with his issues. Art said that Rick would be able to modify the former articles as he saw fit.

Rick took the reader response data. He thanked Art for his support and left.

He immediately went home and began to review the articles and the reader response data. He quickly found four articles from when he first started that had good reviews. He remembered them well. He had not only written the articles, he had lived the incidents depicted in the stories. Now his task was to revise them, making changes that would make them more appealing for a verbal presentation. Knowing the stories as he did and having years of experience writing and telling stories, the work came easily to him. He spent the rest of the day on the computer preparing each story for TV. He considered what he had done as a first draft. Waiting a day or two and then rereading what he had done would help him to refine each story.

The next day was spent catching up on grocery shopping and other items.

To review the four stories that he had selected, he recorded each presentation, including a break for commercial time. He then played it back to find out how the viewing audience would hear it. Gestures and facial expressions would happen automatically. Minor corrections were made to each story. Since the shows would air in the winter, he decided to have more hunting than fishing stories for the first couple of months. This schedule could be reversed in the summer months.

He felt that he was well prepared.

CHAPTER XXVIII

It was Saturday morning. Rick got Bart, and his skis. They got in the Cherokee and went to pick up Jean. Jean was ready and put her skis in the back, saying hello to them both, and petting Bart. It was a beautiful day and they were glad to get outside. Snow had fallen during the night. Everything looked so clean. They drove to the location where they would leave the SUV and begin their cross country skiing. Bart accompanied them. It was good to get the muscles moving and the blood flowing. The temperature was below freezing, but with their clothing and activity they would be warm. Jean challenged Rick to a race of about one hundred yards to a large tree. Rick accepted and they were off. First Jean was ahead, and then Rick. It went back and forth. They pronounced it a draw. They were laughing and saying that the other one had cheated.

They sat on a log to rest and talk.

Rick said to Jean, "Did you ever think about getting married and changing your lifestyle?

Jean said, "You know me better than that. We are so much alike. We were both married to other people briefly and it didn't work out. You have your career and I have mine. I love the company I work for and its products. I love the status that I have. I am pretty much my own boss. I get to travel, which I love. A different city, and different peopled each month would suit me fine. I don't like housework, I don't want to look after someone's socks, and I don't like to cook. No, just like you, I have a wonderful situation just as it is. I wouldn't change a thing."

"What do you see happening once you retire?"

"Well, I have fifteen years in now with Jeep, and I intend to retire from there. I am only thirty nine years old. There is a long time before I am sixty two. Who knows, maybe when I retire some millionaire will marry me and we'll go on a world cruise. That wouldn't be so bad. There would be no housekeeping or cooking, and he could throw away the socks with holes in them. In addition, I could dance every night. Jean summarized her way of life. I am a career girl, an outdoor girl, and a party girl."

Rick said, "I like your positive, straight forward attitude. You are right. There is much that is similar in our life styles. We both are strongly attached to our work. We both like to travel, and we both like the independence of being our own boss."

They continued skiing for about an hour and then, after a brief rest, went back to the SUV.

Rick asked Jean if she was interested in getting some lunch. She said that she was. He asked her if she would like to prepare it. She laughed and hit him on the arm. They both laughed about it. He took them to a drive thru where they ordered food to go. He ordered a hamburger for Bart. They found an empty table that they could sit at and ate their lunch.

When Rick took her home she invited him to come in and to stay over. He accepted and they enjoyed each other.

Back at home, Rick thought to himself that he had learned some things. First, she didn't want to get married. Second, she would not make a good homemaker. He wondered if he would make a good husband. He loved his current life style, but he was getting older. It was a dilemma. On a lighter note, he laughed to himself about Jean's idea of marrying a millionaire and going on a world cruise. Perhaps he could marry a millionairess and go on a world cruise also. What an outside of the box idea.

CHAPTER XXIX

R ick wore his Alaska clothing. He took his armament and Bart to the studio. The stage was set up, and the two presentations went well without a hitch. That evening he received congratulations from the sponsors. There was a hitch however. The sports equipment co-sponsor did not like the advertising of his products or the visual presentation of his products on the one show. The show would not be aired until the changes were made. Rick would not be paid until then.

The next day Rick drove to the airport and waited for Mary to arrive. As Mary came out of the gate Rick saw her, but she didn't seem to see him. He was quite close to her when he called to her and for a moment she didn't recognize him.

"Rick," she said, "I didn't recognize you. You look so different in that beautiful suit. You look more like a lawyer or the president of a bank. In Alaska, your rugged appearance makes it seem that is where you belong. Now it seems that you belong here in a business setting."

"At least you know who I am, and the important thing is that you are here. I am so glad to see you."

They hugged and kissed. He took her luggage and they went to the car.

"What a beautiful car!" exclaimed Mary, "I have never ridden in a Porsche."

Rick said, "It is my biggest extravagance, and my pride and joy. I'll take you first to my house, and then when we are ready we will go to dinner. How was your flight?"

"The flight was smooth, and your invitation was well timed in that I needed a break, and a change of pace. Mom and Dad send their best wishes to you. I am so glad to be here to see you."

"I couldn't wait to see you arrive. Yesterday I had two shows filmed for television so I am now free to enjoy being with you. I have a modest house and it is all that I need considering the fact that I am away from home a great deal of time."

They arrived at the house. Rick took her luggage to the spare bedroom while she became reacquainted with Bart. Mary excused herself to freshen up while Rick poured them some wine and put some cheese and crackers out.

When Mary returned they embraced and toasted their reunion with the wine. Rick took her for a quick tour of the house. When she saw his office she said, "So this is where "Wilderness" was written."

"Yes, I have all of my files here from the first time I wrote an article that sold."

"It is a nice comfortable house, and as much as anyone might need."

They had their wine and cheese and talked. It was almost time to go to dinner so they fed Bart and took him for a walk, while they held hands.

With Bart back home, they went to a favorite restaurant of Rick's. The waiter knew Rick and showed them to a choice table. Rick chose a wine. Mary ordered turkey and Rick ordered lobster. They enjoyed the wine while waiting for the dinner. Rick told her of his "conflict of interest" error and how it was corrected. He described the co-sponsors and said that he was lucky to have such good men to work with.

Mary enjoyed the dinner and then asked if Rick would dance with her. As they danced Rick realized that the spark was still there. He held her close and they continued to dance. Mary was not as professional a dancer as Jean, but that didn't matter. Rick thoroughly enjoyed it.

They returned home and went to the living room. Mary brought him up to date on Alaska events and mentioned that her dad was slowing down a bit. Rick asked if he was ok and she said that he was. It was just that he was getting older. She said that her mother, Jane, was fine.

They cuddled up on the couch. They hugged and kissed and talked. Later, Mary said that she was tired from the flight and would like to go to bed. Rick had shown her to her room and asked if there was anything that she needed. She replied that all was ok. They kissed good night and Mary went to bed.

Rick took Bart for a walk and then turned in for the night.

In the morning Rick got up and quietly took Bart out for a walk.

Upon his return he found Mary in the kitchen making coffee. He hugged and kissed her. She asked if she could make breakfast. Rick was pleased and showed her where the breakfast items were. He asked what she wanted. She chose cereal and he asked for the same. He got some fruit out also. Rick said that he was thinking of some outdoor activity this morning, and mentioned walking, running, or skiing as some possibilities. Mary said that a nice long walk would be just the thing. After eating they took Bart along and began walking.

Mary remarked, "At work I am on my feet all day. I am certain that during the eight hours I cover a number of miles. Perhaps I should get a pedometer. Of course, it is not one continuous walk as we are doing, but is a start and stop, and then start again kind of walk. Here I have scenery to look at. I am enjoying this walk."

Rick asked, "Have you ever thought about making a major change in your life, like moving to a warm climate, or taking up a different type of work, or getting married again?"

Mary replied, "That is a major type of question that will get me thinking. I have thought of all of those things, but acting on them is something else. One gets in a comfortable rut. I suppose I need some external motivation to seriously consider acting on any of those that you mentioned."

"I enjoyed your answer to my difficult question. It showed a flexibility and serious thinking. Most people that I know are in that comfortable rut that you mention, and lack the confidence to even think of an alternative. Personally, I like the challenges that change presents. Going to Alaska, gold mining, hunting the Grizzly, and then going on television provide for me a few of the many opportunities that are available during this time of my life. I have in the back of my mind the idea that a warm climate may be in my future. I am glad that we can discuss topics beyond superficial items."

"I like your idea of living in a warm climate."

They continued their walk and threw items for Bart to chase. He wasn't too great about returning them but he liked to chase them.

They returned home. After lunch they played some board games.

Rick received a call from Steve, the TV executive. Steve said that they were going to give extra advertising ov sports equipment in a future show. This would resolve the problem, and Rick would be paid.

Rick thanked him and they said goodbye.

Rick said, "I would like to have your opinion on an idea that I have for dinner. This would be a joint venture that I believe could be fun. I will mention a food item. Then you mention one. Then it would be my turn again, and so forth. We would pick up the items at the store and then come back to make a dinner out of them. What do you think?"

"I like it, it seems like fun. What is your first item?"

"My first item is Swiss cheese. What is yours?"

Mary said, "I'll choose jumbo shrimp. You are next."

"I'll choose French bread,"

"And for my last item I will choose cocktail sauce,"

Rick said, "What do you suggest that we make with these things?"

"I would like to have shrimp cocktail, and I assume that you would be thinking of Swiss fondue. It sounds good to me."

"What would you like to drink with it?"

"I like the idea of beer with it."

They got in the car and went shopping.

Rick said, "I want the Swiss cheese and bread but I don't know how to make it."

"There is a kit that we need to get. The store will have it, and I will make it for you."

They went shopping and then returned home.

About six o'clock Mary said, "Let's go and make that fantastic dinner."

"Tell me what to do and I'll get to it."

"You take care of the shrimp and I will take care of the cheese and bread."

Rick said, "This is so much more fun working together than making dinner alone."

He deveined the shrimp and removed the tails. He set it aside till the last minute. He got out the cocktail sauce and the beer. In the meantime Mary was heating the Swiss cheese and cutting the bread into cubes. Rick came up behind her, gave her a hug and a kiss on the neck.

She turned around and kissed him.

"The cheese is almost ready. I believe you can start the shrimp."

He heated the shrimp, and then put some good music on. In no time they were eating and laughing about the dripping cheese.

Mary said, "I haven't enjoyed a fun filled joint meal like this ever before. It is a first, and I will remember it."

After dinner Rick fed Bart and then they took him for a walk.

Upon returning home Rick put some good music on. They talked about good books that they had read, Mary mentioned movies that she had liked. She talked about her parents and said that she thought they should be thinking about retiring before too long. She felt that deciding what to do with the Post would be a big problem. They talked about a number of items, pausing to hug and kiss and whisper sweet nothings.

It was getting late, Rick stood up, held out his hand, which she took, and they went to bed.

In the morning love was still in the air.

When Rick asked what she would like to do she said, "It doesn't matter as long as we are together."

They hugged and enjoyed the start of a new day.

Rick suggested that they take a ride to show Mary what the town was like. He got the SUV out. Bart went along and they drove by the Mall, the library and the hospital. He showed her where the TV station was. They went in and he introduced Mary to Steve.

Steve said to Mary, "Be sure to watch his shows, they will get great reviews."

They drove into the country side and Mary saw that it was a very pretty area. She asked about the winter temperatures, and Rick said that it was about as cold as the area around his cabin when he was there, but he didn't stay for the worst of the winter.

They went to a fast food drive-in restaurant. They ordered what they wanted, and Rick ordered a hamburger without the bun, tomatoes, etc. for Bart. They sat at an outdoor table.

Mary said, "This is the life. We're on a lovely vacation."

The next twenty four hours went by so quickly for them. The time came, and Rick took Mary to the airport. They had grown to know each other well in the three days. Their parting was emotionally difficult for both of them. They expressed their love and then she boarded the plane.

As Rick drove away he thought to himself, I now know her well enough to know that I love her. Hopefully, circumstances will not keep me from taking the necessary time to decide between Mary and Jean.

CHAPTER XXX

The next day Rick reviewed the next two presentations for TV that he had already prepared. He read them first and then listened to the recording that he had made. They would be filmed the next day. Then he selected the stories for the following four shows.

He first read them over and reread the reader comments and ratings. Minor changes were made to better appeal to a viewing and listening audience. He then recorded each story. It was then set aside for further review in a day or two.

In the morning he dressed for the filming, gathered his armament and Bart and went to the TV station. The stage was set. He made one presentation in the morning, and one after lunch. Steve told him that it went well.

The next time he saw Jean they went to dinner and then went dancing. They both enjoyed being together again.

Rick asked her if she ever wanted to someday move to a warm climate.

"Yes, if everything else remained the same, particularly my job and my relationships. I could not move just for a warm climate."

"I liked your answer. I liked the fact that you took the whole situation into consideration."

"Speaking of jobs, they just informed me that I have an appointment to go to corporate headquarters in Detroit. They were vague as to why I would be going, but I gather it was more of an invitation rather than a required trip."

"Perhaps they will give you an award of some kind."

"I have been getting some extra pats on the back recently. I guess I will find out soon."

They received the usual applause and approving comments regarding their dancing and appearance.

He took her home and stayed overnight. They loved each other and Rick's decision was no closer to being made.

Each week he had his stories filmed and prepared new ones. He saw Jean each week, and spoke to Mary on the phone. He realized that time was going by and he would soon need to prepare for his trip to Alaska.

Jean made her trip to Detroit and met with the top people. They took her on a tour, introduced her to many executives and took her to a classy restaurant. In the end they said they were impressed with the work she was doing and would like to ask her to consider moving to corporate headquarters in Detroit. She thanked them and said that she would need to think about it. They said the job was hers if she wanted it and that she could take a reasonable amount of time to decide.

When they next met Jean told Rick about the trip and the offer of a new position. She asked Rick what he thought.

"Very soon I will be going to Alaska. If I were staying here I would not want to see you go. But, in view of my leaving, I cannot advise you not to leave. What factors need to be considered in your best interest? In Detroit you will gain some career advantage in moving up the ladder. Depending on the cost of living there and the amount of the pay increase you may gain a monetary advantage. One question that I would ask you is: Does the idea of moving to Detroit fill you with a happy excitement, or a feeling of dread?"

"I have a happy excitement in that my work has been so well recognized. The idea of a promotion is great. But I also feel a dread about losing the relationships that I have. My relationship with you Rick is especially important to me. So, I have a dilemma. I am not concerned about the change from North Dakota to Michigan, or the change in the job duties. I know that the territory that I would be working would be much larger than what I have now. I would like that challenge."

He told her that he could relate to her dilemma. He didn't mention that he was going through a relationship dilemma of which she was a major part. He had not solved his dilemma and did not see a way to help solve hers.

They enjoyed the evening together, but their relationship problems were always on their minds. Two weeks went by. Rick continued his

TV work, and saw Jean each week. She had not given an answer to corporate.

Rick called Joel just to talk and see what was new at the Trading Post. Joel was glad to hear from him and said that Mary was ill. She had picked up some kind of a bug in the hospital. She had stayed home for a week but her fever was increasing. She was admitted to the hospital as a patient. Joel said that he was not sure that going back where she had picked up the problem was a good idea. Rick asked for her room phone number and said that he would call her immediately. They talked briefly and then said good bye.

Rick called Mary. He said, "I hear that you are goofing off. How are you doing?"

Mary replied that she was weak and tired, and had a temperature. She said that they were taking very good care of her. Rick said that he wondered why he had not been able to talk to her when he had called the last time. He asked if there was anything that he could do to help her. She said that all that could be done was being done. They talked a bit more. He told her he loved her and would be calling again soon. He wished her well. Mary said she loved him too. They said goodbye.

Rick ordered flowers, with a card to be sent to her.

Jean called and said that she needed to talk with Rick right away. "I got a call from Corporate. They asked if I had made a decision and I said that I had not. They gave me till Friday, which is tomorrow, to decide. I need your help."

Rick drove over and said to her. "I can't tell you what to do, but in reviewing facts about your job, perhaps you can come to a decision. For example, you said that your territory would be expanded. Is that a fact?"

"Yes it is."

"Would your current territory be included in your new territory?"

"Yes, it would."

"Well then, since you will still be coming here now and then you could still see me and your other friends sometimes. It seems to me that you may not have to give up your current relationships, while you acquire new ones."

"That is just the help that I needed, Rick. I love you."

"I love you too Jean. You know, that whatever plans we make there is a bit of fate in life."

Jean hugged him and said, "Would you mind if I called them right now?"

"Of course not, go ahead, I wish you luck."

Jean called and was told to arrive at Corporate two weeks from this coming Monday.

Jean threw her arms around Rick and said, "Now I have that happy excitement. Thank you for helping me. Let's go out and celebrate."

They did.

During the next two weeks Jean packed her personal items and arranged for a mover to pack the rest and to pick it all up as soon as she found a condo or apartment that suited her. She arranged for her cleaning lady to come in once the furniture was moved out. She continued to perform her regular work assignments.

Rick asked Steve if he could have an extra day of filming since he would be going soon. He wanted to have the extra stories filmed due to his proposed long absence. Steve gave him the extra filming time.

Rick called Mary. He found that she was not doing well. She sounded very weak and could not talk more than a few words. Rick wished her well. He told her that he loved her and that he would call again soon. Rick immediately called Joel. After the usual greetings, Rick said that he had just called Mary and that she seemed to be very weak, and that she had difficulty talking.

"Yes, she is not doing well. This is dragging on too long and she is getting weaker. I don't know what can be done. Jane and I are going to the hospital to talk with her doctor in a few minutes. I will call you to bring you up to date when we return home."

Rick thanked him and said he would look forward to getting the update.

Several hours later Joel called. He reported that the doctor had placed Mary in Intensive Care.

"She will have constant nursing care. Battling the infection is the big issue now. She is not doing well."

Rick replied, "Thanks for bringing me up to date. I too, wish that there was something that I could do to be of help. My time here is getting short. I need to finish up a few more shows for TV and then I will be getting ready to be on my way. When you see Mary, please give her my best and tell her I'll be seeing her soon."

The next two weeks went by quickly. Rick spent a great deal of time on the shows, but helped Jean when he could. He also called Joel every other day to hear how Mary was responding in Intensive Care. The reports were not good.

Rick picked Jean up on the Saturday morning before she was to leave. He had invited her to stay with him until he took her to the airport. Jean had her personal items that she intended to take to Detroit with her.

They enjoyed each other's company on this last weekend. Mary, however, was always on his mind. They went to dinner, took long walks and talked about the new adventures that each of them would have. Saturday evening they went dancing. It was most enjoyable.

On Sunday Rick called Joel. Mary's condition had not changed. Rick said that he would be preparing to leave during the next week and would stop at the Trading Post. Perhaps while there, he could go with them to see Mary. Joel said he would look forward to seeing him.

On Sunday Rick took Jean to the airport. He told her that he knew she would do very well. He asked her to call him on his cell phone to let him know how she was doing. They embraced and kissed and said they loved each other. Jean cried but Rick kissed the tears away. And then she was gone.

Rick drove home alone. Now he was worried about both of the women he loved

When he got home he immediately began preparation for the long drive to Alaska. A priority on his list was to take stories that he would need to prepare for the time when those already filmed had been shown. He also took along a voice recorder. He made a list of thing he would need to buy including a good supply of dog food. He also needed basic food staples for himself. The cabin was empty in that respect. He took the SUV in for a checkup. He went to the bank, got some cash and arranged to invest the excess funds from his checking account. He was surprised to see that it was quite a large amount. He had postponed that investment for a long time. He took Bart to the Vet for a check-up and the usual shots. And then, almost forgotten was his appointment with his Internist. He received, as did Bart, a clean bill of health. Each day he packed a little more. And each day he thought of something else that needed to be done. He arranged to have the electric turned off. He would turn the water off also. During all of this he communicated with Joel. He could not talk with Mary. He did his shopping and completed his packing. The flatbed trailer was hitched to the SUV and loaded. They were ready. Bart was excited knowing that he would be going along. Rick locked up the house. They got in the car and began their trip to Alaska.

CHAPTER XXXI

On the way Rick received a call on his cell phone from Jean. She had found a nice apartment and had called the moving company to bring her furniture. They were all treating her well and she was happy with the large pay increase. Rick told her that he was on the way to Alaska and would call her soon after he arrived. They said they loved each other and said goodbye.

Rick parked in his usual place by the front of the Trading Post. Bart ran around happily before they went into the store. Joel was there to give them a big greeting. He was smiling from ear to ear.

He announced, "I have good news. Mary has had a turn for the better. She is now out of Intensive Care and is in a regular room. We just came from the hospital and you can go back to see her in the morning with us."

Rick was elated at the news and said, "I would like to take something to her."

Jane came into the room and greeted Rick with a hug.

She said, "I heard what you said Rick about bringing something to Mary. I can tell you that what she wants most is to see you."

"I know that both of you must have been worried until you were almost sick yourselves. I hurried to get here as fast as I could, but the filming for the TV shows delayed me."

Jane told them that it was almost dinner time and suggested that they wash up. Joel told Rick to use the room he had used before and then to join him in the living room. Rick took his things to his room and then washed up.

Rick told Joel that he was so happy about Mary's recovery.

Joel said, "It has been over a month of hell. She has lost weight.

I don't want her to go back to nursing. I believe that she will remain sensitive and susceptible to a repeat of the problem."

Rick remarked, "She is still a young woman. Do you believe she would be willing to do as you suggest?"

"She is eligible to retire. She started at the hospital when she was seventeen. She is thirty nine now. She got a really bad scare and I hope that she will listen to reason."

Jane called them to dinner. Joel said grace with an extra request for Mary's return to good health. Joel poured wine for all and toasted the return of Rick.

Joel asked if Rick had any interesting experiences while he was gone.

"Except for some dinners with friends it was mostly work. The TV shows took a great deal of time. Of course, it was worth it. By the way, one of the shows will be on tomorrow afternoon on channel 204."

Jane said, "Perhaps we could get it on Mary's TV and she could see it."

"What happened here, other than Mary's illness?"

Joel said that he had seen Pete and Al recently and that they had a hard time finding work."

Rick said, "I can use them on the cabin. I first need to ask for your help in selecting kitchen cabinets, a sink, and lamps. Could you help me with this?"

Jane replied, "I would love it. Let us spend time with Mary tomorrow and we'll help you the next day."

Rick thanked them, and remarked about the excellent meal.

After dinner they went to the living room. Rick called Pete and asked if he and Al could help him with the cabin? Pete was delighted to hear from him and said he was sure Al would be glad to work with him. He asked when they would start. Rick explained that it would be as soon as he could have kitchen cabinets and a few other things delivered. He said that he would call Pete very soon. Pete thanked him and they said good bye.

Rick asked how they have both been except for the strain of Mary's illness.

Jane replied, "Mary wants us to think about retiring. We may be a bit slower than we were twenty years ago, but we are in good health. At least that is what the doctors say."

"Well, that is great. I too got a clean bill of health from my doctor.

I have it in the back of my mind though, that I would like, at some point, to live in a warm climate, maybe Florida, Hawaii, Arizona, or some tropical island."

Joel said, "That sounds good to me. Sometimes the cold weather affects my joints. That is when I slow down. I am glad that winter is over."

They watched the news on the TV for a bit and then Rick excused himself to bring in some things from the car. Bart went with him and ran around while Rick brought things in. Upon returning to the living room Rick said that he was tired from the trip and said that he would like to go to bed. They all said goodnight.

Joel knocked on Rick's door at six thirty in the morning. He told Rick that they would be leaving at eight. It was about a two and a half hour drive to get to the hospital. Breakfast would be ready at seven a.m.

Rick said, "I'll be there pronto."

At breakfast Joel said, "Your car is hitched to the trailer and loaded with gear, so we will take our car."

Rick took Bart for a final walk, then took him back into the house and told him to guard.

When they reached town Rick asked Joel to stop for a minute while he got something for Mary. It turned out to be a box of chocolates.

"I hope that they will not prevent her from eating this."

Jane asked Rick what his schedule was for the summer.

He replied, "I want to get some work done on the cabin. We can start mining again in about a week, if that is ok with you. Also, I will need to return to North Dakota to film some stories for TV and to write some new stories for the sports magazine. That trip should be in roughly two months. I plan to return after that work is done."

They arrived at the hospital and immediately went to see Mary. She was sitting up in bed and Rick thought that, although she looked a bit thin, she looked beautiful.

"Mary," he exclaimed, "you look beautiful. Is it alright if I hug you?"

She said, "Yes, I feel better and I won't break."

Jane and Joel hugged her too. They gave her a kiss.

Rick gave her the candy and said, "I hope they will let you eat this."

Mary remarked, "They better not try to take it."

Mary told Rick how glad she was to see him. She asked how his TV work was going.

He replied, "It is going well, and this afternoon at two pm, one of the shows will be on TV. I hope we will be able to get the channel for you to see it."

Joel said, "Let me see if I can get the channel now." He did, and it came in perfectly.

Jane told Mary that they would be going to lunch soon, but would return for the two p.m. show.

Rick explained his schedule to Mary, and asked her to visit him when she was well enough. He also told her about the shopping he needed to do the next day.

A nurse told them that their time was up. They hugged Mary and said they would see her in the afternoon.

Joel took them to a deli that he had found and they had a leisurely lunch.

Jane said, "I will ask the doctor, when I see him, how long Mary must remain in the hospital, and what her recovery time will be after that."

When they returned to the hospital, Jane found the doctor.

He said, "She should stay in the hospital for three days to a week. We'll see how she progresses. Then she could go home and have complete rest for a week or two. We have to see each day how she is doing. We don't want to exert her."

A few minutes before two they went to Mary's room. Joel turned on the TV to channel two zero four, and the show began. There was Rick on the set with his dog and armament. There was a nice camping scene in the background. Rick told his story. There were cheers and applause from the audience. Mary and her parents said that it was a great story and was well delivered. Rick thanked them.

The nurse came in and asked them to leave. They all hugged and kissed Mary, and reluctantly said goodbye.

The next morning Rick drew a drawing of the kitchen. It showed doorways, the windows, and the location of the freezer and the stove. Dimensions of all were included.

Joel decided to stay at the store since he had spent so much time at the hospital.

Jane drove them to the store. She asked for help and was assigned a sales person who was knowledgeable regarding cabinets. Jane explained that Rick wanted cabinets and counter tops that would blend with a log cabin.

Rick trusted Jane's judgment and approved what she and the sales consultant suggested. Jane also picked out a sink and additional lamps for the living room. Rick approved the order and asked that it be delivered as soon as possible. Rick thanked Jane for her help and they returned home.

That evening Rick took them out to dinner. Joel drove.

Back home they talked about Mary, Rick's TV work, the cabin work and the mining. Joel said he would be ready to begin mining again in four or five days. He said he would call Rick. In the meantime he would order the excavator. The new perforated metal top for the sluice box had arrived and Joel had cut it to fit.

After more talking they called it a night.

In the morning they said goodbye and Rick and Bart drove up the trail.

CHAPTER XXXII

As Rick drove up the trail he noticed that it had grown up a bit. He made a mental note to have Pete and Al work on it. He saw the river ahead, and as he drove closer he saw ten or more black bears in the water fishing for salmon.

He stopped a number of times to remove limbs from the trail. He had to drive around large ones requiring a chain saw. Otherwise, it was uneventful.

Parking in front of the cabin they got out. Bart immediately uttered a low growl and the hairs on his back stood straight up. Rick got his rifle and he and Bart went around the side of the cabin. In the back Rick saw what Bart was upset about. It was a carcass of what may have been an Elk or a deer. It was half eaten. Rick didn't know what had killed it, but when he got close he saw grizzly hairs. He looked carefully around at the woods but didn't see a bear. He knew that once a grizzly had a kill it became territorial. He also realized that the 30-06 wasn't adequate to kill a grizzly. It would be necessary to carry his powerful revolver when he was outside. They continued around the cabin without incident.

Rick put his holster and revolver on before moving supplies to the cabin or to the garage. Inside the cabin it all seemed to be as he had left it

He put the SUV and the trailer in the garage. Nothing in the garage had been disturbed.

It was lunch time and he ate a sandwich that Jane had sent along for him. He gave a biscuit to Bart. He walked through the cabin making notes of items to be done, while he stowed the items he had brought in.

When he had finished he sat in the living room and relaxed. He first called the Brothers to let them know that he was back. He invited them to visit. They were glad to hear from him and said they would see him soon. He then called Jean and told her of the item awaiting them in the backyard and that a grizzly was probably going to be a problem. Jean said that all was going well. She liked her new job and would probably be working briefly in her old territory in a month or so. She said that she was glad that she didn't have to be afraid of the grizzly. They said they loved each other and agreed to keep in touch. Rick called Pete and told him that he and Al could come out anytime now. If the cabinets have not arrived they could work clearing the trail.

Later he took his fishing gear and went to the river to get his dinner. It had been quite a while since he had fresh salmon and so at the start of the salmon season he was ready to indulge. While he fished he knew that Bart would be guarding his back. He caught a nice fish. It was more than he and Bart could eat at one sitting, so he threw it back. He fished again until he caught a smaller one. He removed the head, tail and gutted it at the riverside.

After a delicious meal, which Bart shared, they relaxed in the living room. He looked forward to having his new lamps. After dark he could hear noises behind the cabin. There were some snorting and loud chewing noises. He was not going out at night to check out a grizzly bear. Bart of course heard the noises. He was agitated and kept moving around growling. Rick called him, petted him and told him that they would check it out in the morning. Rick reviewed various options that he had. He did not want to shoot the bear. It was not cold enough to freeze the meat and it would just rot. He might be able to scare the bear away, but this was not likely considering that the bear had his food there. He decided to wait till morning and see if an idea formed while he was sleeping.

After breakfast he took his firearms and went to see if the bear was still there. He left Bart in the cabin. He went to the side of the cabin and saw the bear lying beside the kill. He returned to the cabin. He felt like a prisoner. He knew that the bear could run up to thirty five miles an hour, and that he would attack if his food supply was threatened. He decided to wait for the bear's departure before going out again. He had a good view from the dining room window. He decided to try an experiment. When he saw the bear leave, he got a big hook from the rafters and attached a rope to it. He armed himself and then went outside. He left Bart in the cabin. He carefully examined the woods for signs of the bear and saw none. Then he attached the hook to the rib section of the kill and pulled it about one hundred yards into the woods. He then went to the outhouse and partially filled a jar with urine. He took the jar to the edge of the woods and sprinkled drops across the edge of the woods. Rick was hoping to confine the bear to the woods. He knew that wolves and other animals marked their territory in this way. It remained to be seen if his experiment would work for him. He cleaned up the area where the kill had been and tossed it over his newly marked line.

He decided to go to the mine to check water levels in the lake and the pond. He took his rifle, his revolver and his knife. They walked to the split tree and headed east. The trail definitely needed to be cleared. He cleared what he could with his knife, but a chain saw was needed. They proceeded onto the lake. It was higher than it had been when they left. Water was not running from the lake to the pond. The trough needed to be deepened. He did not see strange tracks and nothing seemed to be amiss.

They returned to the cabin. The bear was not in view.

Rick called Joel and told him of the bear incident. Then he told him of the need to clear the trail and to dig the trough from the lake to the pond.

Joel asked him to be careful around the grizzly. He said that he had ordered the excavator. Also, Mary was improving and thought she might be able to go home either tomorrow or the next day. Joel said that he would bring Mary to the Post to recuperate rather than to her apartment. He would not be able to work on the mine until he had brought her home.

"That is a good idea. The mining can wait. I'll dig out the trough in the meantime."

He told Joel that he had contacted Pete and that Pete and his brother Al would probably be out tomorrow, he would get them started on the trail work.

Pete and Al arrived early in the morning. Rick invited them into the cabin. After the greetings Rick told them about the bear. He said that until the bear leaves they should sleep in his spare bed room. He also told them that the immediate priority was to clear the trail to the lake. The truck with the excavator had been ordered and would probably arrive today. Rick said that they would have plenty of time to talk in the evening but asked them to get started on the trail right away. They agreed and told Rick that they had removed the large trees from the trail on the way to his cabin. They took their tools and went up the trail.

It was mid-afternoon when Rick heard the truck towing the excavator. He hoped that the trail was clear. He decided to begin work on the trough in the morning.

Rick walked to the dining room and saw the bear sniffing the ground where the kill had been. His experiment had not worked. Hopefully the bear would follow the scent to the kill. In the meantime, he was still a prisoner. Now what could he do? Eventually the bear would eat the rest of the kill. Would he leave then? One thing was certain. He couldn't go to the back yard while the bear was there. What a dilemma.

Rick heard the truck heading home.

Pete and Al returned about five p.m. Pete told Rick that the trail had been cleared enough for the excavator to be brought to the lake, but it would take more work for Joel's pick-up to get through without difficulty.

Rick thanked them and told them the rest of the story about the bear and his failed experiment. He said he knew they must be hungry and that he would get salmon for dinner. They of course would eat with him.

Rick said, "I'm willing to wait a day or two until the bear finishes the kill and moves on. In the meantime we will always have to be armed when going outside, and never go out back. You can use the port-a-potty in the house."

Pete asked about Rick's work in North Dakota and Rick told them about his TV shows. Rick asked how things were going for them. They replied that it had been a slow season.

Rick showed them the plan for the cabinets, sink and counter tops that the store had made up for him. It showed the location of each item. Rick asked if they believed that they could make the installation. Pete replied that it would not be a problem. Rick told them to start on the kitchen when the trail was clear enough for Joel's truck.

Pete and Al were tired and went to bed.

In the morning Rick provided breakfast and the Brothers went back to working on the trail.

Rick got his armament and he and Bart went out to go to the garage. As they approached the garage they heard a noise from the other side. Bart's hair stood on end and he uttered a low growel. The grizzly appeared. Bart roared and attacked the bear. Rick yelled for him to come but it was too late. The bear saw Bart coming and with his great paw scooped Bart up and threw him about twenty feet. Bart yelped and then fell with a thud and lay still. Rick was temporarily paralyzed by the scene. He had forgotten to get his gun ready. He grabbed for his revolver and fired at the attacking bear. "Click". He had not released the safety. With trembling hands he released it and fired twice, and the bear was on him. Its claws were raking his back while pulling him to his open jaws. His teeth punctured Rick's head as they both fell. Rick laid there waiting for the jaws to crush his skull. He waited, but nothing happened. The bear was still, with his open jaws around Rick's head. Rick believed that the bear was dead. He tried to move his head back out of the bear's jaws, but the bear's fangs held his head like a vice. He could smell the bear's foul breath. He pulled his right arm out from under the bear, and then with both hands tried to get his head out of the bear's jaws. This was painful. Little by little he made some progress, but at the expense of creating even greater wounds from the bears teeth. At last he was free, but he was loosing a great deal of blood from his back and his head. He thought of Bart and saw him lying there. He crawled to him. Bart was barely breathing and he too was bleeding.

Rick took his cell phone and called Joel. The phone rang but there was no answer. Rick recalled that Joel was probably picking Mary up.

Rick called the Brothers and Phil answered.

"Phil this is Rick. I need your help. I had a run in with the grizzly and I am hurt. Can you help me?"

Phil said. "Where are you?"

"I am at the cabin."

"We will be in our truck on the way to you in five minutes."

Rick cradled Bart in his arms. He massaged the dog hoping to stimulate his breathing and to get him to wake up. But nothing seemed to work.

The Brothers arrived and ran to him.

"Come Rick, we have to get you to a doctor."

They helped Rick to the truck. George put Bart on the floor in the back.

Rick said, "I'm getting blood all over your truck."

Then he passed out.

"The nearest doctor is about fifty-five miles south of here. We better hurry. I don't see how we can stop the bleeding." said George.

South of the Trading Post they saw a cop car and asked for an escort to the nearest doctor. The officer put on his emergency lights and roared off with the pick-up following.

They carried Rick into the doctor's office and the nurse took them to a room and put Rick on the table.

"The doctor will come in a minute. I'll get his shirt off."

The doctor came in and asked what had happened. They said it was a grizzly attack. They were told to wait outside.

Phil said, "Let's go see how Bart is doing."

Bart still laid there with very shallow breathing.

George said, "I am going back in to see where there is a Vet. I'll be right back."

He returned a minute or two later and said, "Let's go, I know where one is."

They carried Bart in and told them he had been hit by a grizzly. He was taken into a room and put on the table.

The Vet said, "I'll take some x-rays while he is immobile to see if anything is broken."

Later, the Vet returned to talk to them in the waiting room.

"Nothing is broken, but he has had a concussion. We will have to give him some time. I will medicate him. You can call back in an hour or two."

"Let's go back to see how Rick is doing." they both said at once.

Rick was awake. He had been medicated and bandaged. Nothing was broken.

He was conscious, and said, "I feel like hell. Where is Bart?"

Phil said, "We took him to a Vet. Nothing is broken, but he has a concussion and has not awakened. We are supposed to call to see how he is doing in an hour or two."

George called the Vet and was told that Bart was starting to wake up. The nurse said that they could pick him up.

The doctor came in to talk to Rick. He said, "I took x-rays of your head and back. There is a small skull fracture, but I am particularly concerned about the possibility of an infection. The claws of a bear are filthy and the wounds on your back are deep. Also, the head wounds are very deep and of great concern. I had to use over seventy stitches.

You have lost a lot of blood and are very weak. You will need to come back here in four days to check for infection and to get new bandages. I don't want you to stoop or pick up anything heavier than a knife, fork, or spoon. The injuries that you have sustained are nothing to be casual about. Heed my words. Here are the medications that you will need to take. The directions are on the envelope. You may go home now, but the important word is REST. Go to bed. Good luck."

They picked Bart up and although he was groggy, he wagged his tail and gave Rick a kiss. Phil called Joel.

Joel answered and Phil said, "Rick got beaten up by a grizzly. We took him to a doctor and we are on our way to take him home."

Joel interrupted and said, "Don't take him home. Bring him here. We will take care of him."

Phil said, "OK, we will be there in about forty five minutes."

They arrived at the Trading Post and Joel, Jane and Mary came outside to meet them.

Mary saw Rick and said, "Oh my God, Rick, I am so sorry."

Joel and Jane welcomed Rick and said, "You are staying with us while you recuperate."

Phil lifted Bart out of the truck and said, "Here is another injured warrior."

George helped Rick walk into the house. They seated Rick comfortably, with Bart at his feet.

Joel said, "Are you well enough to tell us what happened Rick?"

Rick said, "Yes. He told them the complete story beginning with Bart's alerting him to the problem, and ending with calling Joel, who was picking up Mary, and then the Brothers. And that is the story."

Jane exclaimed, "What a terrible frightening experience. It is a wonder that you are alive."

Phil added, "We got him in the truck, and Bart in the back. Rick was bleeding pretty good, and then he passed out. We took him to the doctor, and Bart to the Vet. Rick is to go back in four days for a check-up and new bandages. The doctor is concerned about infection from the deep wounds. He needed over seventy stitches."

Rick exclaimed, "Bart and I are here among friends. We're alive and the grizzly is dead. By the way, Phil and George help yourselves to any of the meat that you want, and tell Pete and Al, and my friends at the Native Village that they can have the rest. I would like to have the hide and head though for my living room. Joel knows a good taxidermist who did the hide last time."

George said, "Thanks, and we'll save the head and hide for you.

Rick said, "Pete and Al are doing some work for me and were on the trail when all of this happened. Would you please bring them up to date and tell Pete to continue as he and I had discussed before all of this."

George replied, "No problem. We will have to be going home now. It is good to know that it all turned from a potential disaster to a victory."

Rick said, "You know, I don't feel too bad. You have Mary to take care of. I think I can manage at the cabin.

Jane and Mary both said, "No, you are not well enough. You must stay here."

Rick said, "I didn't want to burden you with my problem, but thanks."

He thanked Phil and George. They all said goodbye, and the Brothers left.

Mary spoke to Joel and Jane, "We have to get him to bed. He is very weak and could pass out at any time."

Joel and Jane got on each side of him and took him to the room he usually used.

Mary tagged along.

She offered, "He will need a snack and something to drink."

Jane said, "I have some orange juice and a sweet roll. That should give him a bit of energy."

Joel said, "You look like a partially wrapped mummy, but you are going to be ok Rick. If there is anything that needs to be done with Pete and Al, or if there is anything else, just tell me and I will take care of it."

Rick thanked him.

Mary said, "We have to get him into bed."

They did, and told him to rest. They left Bart with him and went to the kitchen. Jane got the juice and roll for him.

Jane told Mary, "Now, young lady, it is time for you to sit. I will get some juice for you also. Now that Rick has been taken care of, we are going to take care of you."

On the trail the Brothers stopped at Rick's cabin to get some choice meat. They cut out the heart and liver. Further up the trail they found Pete and Al. They told them of the grizzly attack and that Rick said they should take what meat they wanted. They also told them that the Native Village men would also be invited to take meat.

George dropped Phil off at their place with the meat and then drove to the Native Village to tell them the story and to invite them to accept Rick's invitation to get some fresh meat. The men were delighted and made preparations to leave for Rick's cabin.

In the morning Mary took Rick's pills to him. She asked how he felt and he said, "I am doing fine."

He didn't tell her that he had difficulty sleeping and that he really needed a good pain pill.

She said, "There is bound to be some pain, and I am certain that finding a way to rest your head on the pillow comfortably was a problem. This medication will help you. Let me take your temperature. It is still a little high, but that is to be expected. You just stay where you are and you will have breakfast served in bed. One of us will be back soon."

Rick said to himself, 'I can't put anything over on her.'

Joel came in and asked how Rick was doing.

He was a bit more candid with Joel, and said, "I am hanging in there, but I was glad when Mary brought the pain pills in. I couldn't find a comfortable place to put my head on the pillow without putting presure on an injury."

"You are going to be weak for a little while. Let me help you get to the bathroom."

"Thanks. That is one good idea."

When they returned, Rick was glad to get back in bed.

Jane and Mary came into his room. Jane had the breakfast tray.

She said, "Joel, help him to sit up."

Rick had not lost his appetite and thanked them.

He said, "This is better than a first class hotel, and the staff is superb."

Mary and Jane excused themselves.

Joel stayed, and pulled up a chair. Rick, I have done some thinking, and if you will not mind, I will tell you about it while you are eating."

Rick paused after a bite, and said, "No problem, go right ahead."

"These two incidents, first, of Mary getting seriously ill, and then you are hurt and almost killed, make me realized how tenuous our lives and situations are. This is especially true when we are in a wilderness setting. I would like to do as you suggested before you left last time, and put the mine up for sale. As you said, we can continue to work it one day a week in the meantime. I also am going to consider Mary's idea of Jane and I retiring. You and I have become close friends, and any suggestions that you have regarding these items that I mentioned will be welcome."

"The items sound good to me Joel. Let us start with the easy one, and place an ad for the sale of the mine.

"Let me get paper and a pen so that I can write down the details."

He returned in a few minutes and said, "Fire away with what we need to have in the ad. I believe you suggested that we list it for a million."

Rick added, "Let us make it a million two. That way we will have room to negotiate. Also, mention that it is a proven mine with records. Ask for responses from qualified principals only. Have them reply to a box number rather than to your address or to a phone number. When we receive responses, we can send a fact sheet to those that look good. The fact sheet could list a phone number to call, the general location and anything else that we chose to include. We could also answer any questions that they had."

"Those items sound good Rick. I will get busy and write an ad and will place it in the paper. But wait, which paper should we use?"

"I suggest that you look on the Internet for gold mining publications. Perhaps one will pop up that seems just right. If one doesn't, I would suggest the Wall Street Journal."

Joel left to write the ad.

Jane came in to get Rick's tray.

Rick asked, "Would someone take Bart out for a brief walk please?"

"Certainly. Should he be on a lead, or left to run free?"

"Let him run free, but he should be called back in about ten minutes.

Mary came into the room with Bart. Bart went over to Rick's bed and put his head next to Rick to be petted.

Mary said, "After ten minutes I called him and he came right back. He headed right for your room when we came in."

"If you have time, please have a seat. We haven't had much time to talk. First, how do you feel?"

"I am still somewhat weak, but the fever is gone. I don't have any pain. I will need to have a checkup by a doctor. I have been thinking that I could go along with you when you have your bandages changed and have that doctor see how I am doing. In the meantime Mom and Dad won't let me do a thing, so I am getting the rest that I need."

"Well, it looks like things are looking up for both of us. The pills that you gave to me this morning did help. I hope that the doctor will let me get back to work. There is so much to do, and I will need to go back to North Dakota in about two months. One of the stories will be about this latest grizzly attack."

"Dad doesn't want me to go back to nursing. He believes that I will be susceptible to another of the same problems, and will become sick again. I am eligible for retirement, but I don't know what to do."

"Is there a time limit as to when you must return to work if in fact you decide to continue working?"

"That would be a medical decision. I am now a patient. When it has been determined that I am well, I will be expected to go back to work. It could be a week or more. We will know more when I see a doctor."

"Is there any way to find out what the probability of a repeat of the problem would be?"

"I will ask the doctor. I don't know how else to get the answer to that question. If the doctor said the chance of a repetition is minimal, Dad would still be concerned. I don't want him to have to worry. On the other hand it is a bit early for me to retire."

"For the time being it looks like we both need to wait before making any decisions. While waiting we are resting and getting better. We also can spend time with each other, and that is an unexpected benefit."

Joel came into the room to talk about the ad. Mary excused herself.

"I found two good leads on the Internet. They both have similar ads to what we want. Which one do you prefer?"

"You are right, they both look good. Let's try one for a month. If that one doesn't produce anything we can put an ad in the other one for a month. Choose which ever one you wish."

"Ok, here is the ad that I wrote. You can compare it with the ones from the internet. What do you think?"

"That is a great ad. It should create some interest."

Jane came in and said to them, "It will be time for lunch in thirty minutes, more or less. Rick, you stay where you are. We will bring your lunch to you. Joel, I need your help in the kitchen."

In a few minutes Joel came back and said, "Some friends have come to see you."

The friends were the Brothers.

Phil and George greeted Rick. They told him that they and Pete and Al, and the men from the Native Village had taken the meat they wanted. They all said to thank you.

George told Rick, "We brought the hide and head with us and gave it to Joel when we came in. How are you doing?"

"I am making progress, and before you know it I'll be up and around. What are you fellows up to?"

"We are going to pick up a few things from Joel and then head on back. We're glad you are doing well and will see you again soon."

They said goodbye and left.

Rick petted Bart. He realized that he had a lot to be thankful for. First, he was alive. Second he, a loner, was being well taken care of by good friends, and his lovely Mary. He also had the Brothers as good friends, and a good relationship with the Native Village. He thought, 'perhaps I should stop thinking of myself as a loner.'

Before long Jane came in with his lunch tray. Mary came in with her tray.

Jane said, "You two go ahead and eat. Joel and I have some things to do. See you later."

As they ate, Mary asked, "How much more are you planning to do on the cabin?"

"I do not have a whole plan. As I have the time and the help from Pete and Al, I will have work done. Right now they are working on the kitchen cabinets. I believe that almost anything I have done will increase the value of the property. I always have the question to answer as to whether it will just be a summer vacation cabin or something more. I could put in a plumbing system for running water, a propane refrigerator, and a propane stove. If I planned to use it year around I would add insulation, and probably a cork floor. In the meantime it will be one project at a time."

"I understand what you are saying. As for me, I love the location; the beautiful view of the river, the small beach on the other side. The beautiful trees and the mountain rising in the background are so appealing. The river itself is beautiful, and abundant fish are just a stone throw away. Add the canoeing, and hunting and you have a complete vacation hide a way. I love it."

"I know that you have been in nursing since high school. Have you ever felt that you were missing something else, or something else that you wanted to do?"

"I never thought that I would want another kind of work. There are things that I missed due to my work. I always wanted a dog but didn't think it would be fair to the dog considering my hours. I would have preferred a small house rather than an apartment, but maintenance would be a problem. I would have preferred a more rural setting, but security and transportation would also be a problem. I know that you are trying to help me figure out my options with your questions. Thank you."

Jane came in and told them that it was time for both of them to rest until dinner time. Jane took Rick's tray and Mary took hers. They said that they would see each other later.

Just before dinner time Joel came in to assist Rick to the bathroom.

After washing up Rick said, "I would like to eat in the dining room with you all. I do feel somewhat better."

Joel said, "We can give it a try, but Jane may veto the idea."

They went to the dining room and Rick sat down. Jane remarked, "I am glad that you are feeling better."

They had a lively discussion during dinner. Rick said thanks for a splendid meal. Jane then asked Joel to escort Rick to his room. Rick was glad to be in bed resting again.

Mary came in to talk with Rick. Jane would not let Mary help with the dishes. And Joel was recruited to help in her place. They talked for a while, but Mary saw that Rick needed to sleep. She gave him a kiss and said that she would be back.

Later they all came in to say good night. Mary said that she would let Bart out, and then would bring him back to Rick. Upon their return Mary and Rick kissed and said goodnight.

During the next two days Jane kept close reigns on Mary and Rick. They had their rest periods on schedule, and were not permitted to exert themselves. Both of them began to feel better as they grew in strength.

They were up early the next day to go to see the doctor. All four of them went and Bart went along also.

Rick saw the doctor first. Mary went with him, while Joel and Jane sat in the waiting room. Rick introduced Mary and asked that the doctor see her after he had talked with him.

The doctor said, "The nurse took your temperature and it is now normal. Now that she has removed the bandages I can see that you are healing well. Thanks to your excellent physical condition, your down time will be significantly reduced. I would like to see you one more time. If all is well, you will be able to resume normal activities."

"While the nurse bandages him, you can tell me about your problem Mary."

Mary related the history of the last month. She told him what her work was, and where she worked.

"I have two basic questions. First, am I well enough to go back to work? And second, what is the probability that I will come down once again with the same problem while working?"

The doctor called the nurse to take her weight and temperature as well as blood pressure and pulse rate.

The doctor asked what her normal weight was, as well as her normal blood pressure. He examined her and had her walk down the hall and back.

He said, "You are obviously improving. You are a bit underweight. There is not a temperature problem. You are still somewhat weak. You still need rest, good food and time. I will give to you the same advice that I gave to Rick. Come back in one week. I believe that you will be feeling better then, but we will have to wait to find out. As to whether you may have a repeat of the problem. It could happen. We do not have good studies to rely on. Good luck to both of you."

They all went to the car. They both told Joel and Jane what the findings were.

Rick said, "In summary, we are both still weak, but we are improving. We will need to come back to see the doctor in one week."

They took Bart to the Vet. While they waited, Joel said, "Mary and Rick, I am glad that you both are coming along so well."

Jane added, "They have both cooperated so well. I know it was difficult for them to just rest, but hopefully there is just one more week to go."

Rick was called to take Bart in to be examined. Mary went along. The tech said that there was no temperature problem and that the heart beat was normal. The Vet examined Bart and said that he had made a great recovery. He suggested reduced activity for one week. Mary laughed and stated that all three of them had one week of rest coming up.

Back in the car Rick suggested that since they were in town that they find a deli and he would treat them to lunch. They all agreed.

When they returned to the Post, Jane issued orders for Rick and Mary to take a nap until dinner time. She let Bart run for ten minutes. He came when called and immediately went to be with Rick.

While waiting to see the doctor again, the week passed very much like the last week with Jane keeping close touch with her patients and enforcing rest periods. They were getting stronger.

"They left early in the morning to go to the doctor. This time Bart was left at home and told to guard.

Rick and Mary went in to see the nurse who gave them the usual tests, and removed Rick's shirt and his bandages.

The doctor came in and after greeting them said, "Rick let us check you out first. How do you feel?"

"I feel well, and I would like to get back to work."

"All of your vital signs are good. Your injuries are healing nicely. There is no sign of an infection. I believe that you are good to go. It would be helpful if you would take it easy this next week. It is important not to do more than what your body tells you is ok. Do you have any questions?"

"Do I still need bandages?"

"No, and good luck."

"Now Mary, how do you feel?

"I feel better. Each day I am stronger."

"Your vital signs are good, and you have gained one and one half pounds. You need to add another two or three pounds. How far do you believe that you could walk without being tired?"

"I would say at least one half mile, maybe more."

"I have worked in the ER as you have and know how physically demanding it is. I don't believe that you are ready to go back simply because of the physical demands. In addition, you know as well as I do that all kinds of germs are circulating there from all kinds of people with all kinds of diseases. I can't tell you not to return because of the germs, but I can tell you not to ignore their presence either. You are not yet up to par. There are three things that I will suggest: Rest, eat more, and have moderate exercise. You can come back to see me at any time. I am not making an appointment for you. Just call if you find the need. Do you have any questions?"

"No, but thank you."

They picked up Joel and Jane and went to the car.

Rick summarized what the doctor had told him, and Mary summarized what he had told her.

Jane said, "Thanks for the summaries. I must say that I am relieved about what the doctor found. Both of you have made good progress and the doctor laid out a specific plan for both of you. He didn't beat around the bush, but told you straight out what you need to do."

Joel added, "I too am pleased. We know where it all stands. So often one comes away from such a meeting with doubts about what was found and what to do."

Mary said, "Now that I have his report I can begin to plan as I follow his instructions to get stronger."

Rick said, "We are leaving the doctor on a positive note. I believe that I will leave for my cabin tomorrow. I would like to take you all to dinner tonight. Would that be ok with you?"

Jane immediately replied, "Yes, not only is it ok, it is great. I won't have to cook."

Joel and Mary echoed the ok.

When they arrived at the Post it was lunch time.

Mary announced, "In keeping with the doctor's orders for moderate exercise, I will make lunch. Mom, you can have a seat."

Jane said, "That is great. I get two bonus meals today."

Joel asked Rick to join him in the living room.

Rick asked, "Would it be ok with you if we hold off one week before we start digging in the mine?"

"Yes, I had that in the back of my mind when you gave us the doctor's report. Who knows, we may even have a reply to our ad by then."

"That would be good," replied Rick, "but it takes time to get the ad in the next issue, and then for someone with the proper qualifications to see, and then reply to, the ad. Then the publication has to send a message to us by mail. Unless the system is circumvented in some way, I do not expect a reply for about two months."

"What are your plans Rick?"

"I will see what progress has been made on the kitchen. Towards the end of the week I will go to the lake and dig out the trough between the lake and the pond. Mostly though, I plan to take it easy. I will write the grizzly attack story for the magazine."

Joel stated, "I have attached the new perforated metal top to the sluice box and it fits perfectly. I can't wait to see if it helps us filter out more gold."

Mary called them to lunch.

After lunch Rick decided to take Bart for a walk. Mary went with them.

Mary held his hand as they walked and said, "I don't want you to go."

"I understand Mary, but I have work that I must attend to. But wait, why don't you come with me? Your dad will be coming out to work the mine with me, and you can go back with him if you have had enough of the wilderness life."

"That is a great idea. I need to talk with you and get your advice about the option I have of retiring."

"It occurs to me, Rick stated, that we will need to go to the store for groceries. Perhaps we could do that after dinner."

They returned to the Post, and Mary told her parents of her decision to visit with Rick.

Jane asked Rick and Mary to take a nap before dinner time.

Joel drove them to dinner which they all enjoyed.

Rick and Mary shopped together as did Joel and Jane. Rick and Mary concentrated on getting nourishing foods that would help Mary gain weight. Rick was also interested in getting basics like milk, bread, eggs and bacon. He also picked up a few bottles of wine.

They returned to the Post. Rick gave them a bottle of wine that he knew they liked. They congregated in the living room and enjoyed talking about the prospective mine sale, health issues, Rick's plans and other interesting items.

Later, Rick told them that he would take Bart out and then he would pack before going to bed.

Mary stated that she was going to pack also.

Upon his return from the dog walk Rick said good night to all. He and Mary kissed and then went to pack.

After breakfast they packed the car. Rick expressed his thanks for their good care of him. They all said good bye and Rick, Mary and Bart went up the trail.

CHAPTER XXXIII

When they arrived at the cabin they saw the tents of Pete and Al. Once the bear was dead they had obviously moved out of the cabin.

Pete and Al came out of the cabin when they heard the car drive up. Greetings were made all around. Pete asked Rick how he felt, and added that Rick looked good. Rick replied that he was to take it easy this week, and that he should be ok after that. Al asked how Mary was doing and the echoed Rick's remarks regarding how well she looked.

Rick said, "Before we unpack, let us take a look at the kitchen."

As they walked into the kitchen, Pete told them that the counter tops and the sink were next to be installed.

Mary said, "They look nice. They blend in with the log siding."

"They are a darned site better than the empty boxes that I used for cabinets in the original cabin. You have done a good job. Thank you. We are going to unpack now. Continue as if we were not here."

As they took things into the cabin Rick mentioned to Mary that he had bought bacon, eggs and milk; forgetting that he did not have refrigeration.

Mary said, "We will use the milk and bacon up soon enough. The eggs will be ok without refrigeration for a while. Would you like to have bacon and eggs for lunch, with a glass of milk?"

"That sounds good to me. We will have bread, but no toast."

Rick continued to bring things in and commented, "It appears that Pete and Al washed the bed sheets after they used them. Good for them."

"I will need to have something to do in addition to resting and playing, so, if it is alright with you, I will be the chief cook and bottle washer. I don't know if you noticed, but since you don't have running water I bought a good quantity of paper plates and bowls, and plastic knives, forks and spoons."

"That sounds great; I can burn the paper plates. But there is one condition to your generous offer. The condition is that you take at least one nap each day."

"OK"

He brought the remaining items in while Mary made lunch.

Rick told the Brothers that he and Mary were going to have some lunch in the dining room and invited them to bring their lunch in there also if they wished. He added that they would be on their own at dinner time.

Pete and Al declined saying that they wanted to finish this particular piece of counter top before eating.

Mary and Rick brought their lunch and sat at the dining room table.

Mary said, "I wonder how they dried the sheets. I'll have to ask them.

After lunch they took a walk by the river. Bart went along; chasing sticks now and then.

Rick told Mary, "Taking a walk with you along the river is so much more enjoyable than walking alone."

"It makes all the difference to me also. I love being here with you."

Mary took her nap after the walk.

Rick wrote his first draft of the grizzly article for the magazine.

Pete and Al had finished work for the evening and went to their tents.

The counter tops were in. The sink remained to be installed.

Mary prepared dinner, but asked Rick to help with a few miner things in addition to carrying items to the dining room.

During dinner Mary asked Rick if he would share his thoughts regarding her retirement option.

"What I will say are just thoughts. I will not be the least offended if you decide to do something entirely different. I don't believe that you could go wrong by retiring. It might be best to officially retire near the end of your sick leave. During this period of time you can consider what you want to do. Retiring does not necessarily mean that you have to stop working, or even stop nursing. Being a nurse in a doctor's office for example, working day time hours Monday through Friday might be a possibility. Or, you could work in the store with your dad. Or, you might want to take an extended vacation. You have certainly earned a vacation. I am inclined to agree with your dad. I would be concerned if you went back to ER nursing."

"Thank you. You came up with some interesting alternatives. I had not thought of helping my dad, and working in nursing Monday through Friday in daylight hours sounds great. What made you suggest working with dad?"

If he decides to retire there will be a need for facts and figures. For example he will probably want to sell the Trading Post. A complete inventory with a value set on each item would be necessary. Also, his books would have to be up to date showing profits, probably for the past five or so years. The property would need to be appraised by a commercial realtor. There would be a lot of work to be done."

Mary commented, "Working with my dad is appealing. I wonder if he would see it as helpful, or as interference in his business. I will have to think about that."

"You have time to think about all of this. There may be other options also."

Later they took another walk by the river. On the way back they saw Pete and Al sitting outside of their tents with a fire burning. They stopped to talk with them.

Mary asked them, "I saw that you washed the bed sheets. How did you dry them?"

Al replied, "We hung a clothes line up out back. They were dry in no time with the nice breeze that we had."

Pete asked Rick, "Would you tell us about the run in with the bear?"

Rick told them the whole story. He started with Bart's reaction when they first arrived at the cabin, and finished with the Brothers taking him to the doctor.

Al said, "I truly believe that you have nine lives. I am sure that you almost didn't make it this time, but in the end you did."

"Yes, I was extremely lucky."

They talked some more and then said good night.

Rick and Mary sat in the living room talking. Mary had cuddled up beside him.

Mary said, "I am leaning towards helping dad if he will let me, but I have not made a decision. I still like working in the ER."

"I suggest that each day you imagine working on one of the options. Be as detailed in your thinking as possible. Imagine your physical surroundings. Try to avoid thinking of other options until the next day. Think of the pros and cons. See how you feel about the option at the end of the day."

They talked so more and then took Bart for a final walk before going to bed.

In the morning Rick took Bart for a walk. When he returned breakfast was ready. Once again they enjoyed the bacon and eggs. Shortly after breakfast Pete and Al arrived.

Pete asked, "What will we do about a water supply for the sink, and what about the water draining out of the sink?"

"Someday may have a consistent water supply. For now, I plan to have a five gallon plastic jug to supply water to the sink, and a five gallon bucket underneath to catch the draining water. When the top jug is near empty we will know it is time to empty the bucket outside. It will still be somewhat primitive, but an improvement over stooping over the wash tub."

Pete asked, "After the sink, do you have an assignment for us?"

"Yes," "I believe the cabin has settled some since last year. I would like for you to give the outside a good going over. Check the caulking around the logs, and around the windows. Check the roof. Bring everything up to par. Also, make the same survey on the garage. When that is done, I would like for you to get a cord of wood, cut to stove length, and stacked on the side of the cabin. I would like to have an over-hang to protect the wood from rain and snow."

"We'll get right to it."

Rick called Joel and told him that all was well here and that Pete and Al were doing good work. He told Joel that Mary was ok.

Joel said that the taxidermist had taken the bear hide and would let him know when it was finished. Joel had placed the ad for the gold mine sale and was looking forward to some replies.

They agreed to talk again soon.

During the next couple of days they hunted small game and fished.

On the next day they went to the lake, using the SUV to avoid the need for Mary to overtax herself.

Rick got in the excavator and re-dug the trough from the lake to the pond. The water began to run to the pond. Rick waited to see if the trough was deep enough for the lake to drain sufficiently.

They walked to the waterfall. Mary looked to see if she could find shiny pieces of gold. Unfortunately she didn't see any.

They set up chairs that they had brought and had lunch that Mary had prepared.

Mary commented, "This is such a pretty scene with the waterfall. I love to hear the water sounds as it falls over the edge, and then gurgles down the stream to the lake. Today I am concentrating on the option of continuing my work in the ER. We'll see how I feel about it at the end of the day."

"Your work in nursing requires a great deal of objectivity. I am certain that in the end you will make the right decision."

After lunch Rick called the Brothers. George answered. Rick told him that Mary was visiting him and that they were spending the day at the lake. George invited them to come to visit. Rick said they could come out tomorrow, about mid-morning, if that would be ok. George said that he would look forward to seeing them.

Rick went back to the lake, checking to see that the water was draining properly into the pond from the lake. It was running well. They returned to the cabin.

Mary took her nap.

He went to the kitchen and saw that the sink had been installed. He needed to purchase the five gallon containers. The cabinets counter tops, and the sink looked really good.

He found Pete and Al at the rear of the cabin. They were re-caulking logs.

"How does everything on the outside look to you?"

Pete responded, "We haven't found any major problem. We are bringing it back to where it was originally. In some cases it will be better than it was to begin with. We are almost finished with the caulking. The roof will be next."

"When you finish the caulking, take a fifteen or twenty minute break. Mary is taking a nap, and the noise from the roof would disturb her."

Rick thanked them for their good work and went inside the cabin. He called Joel and asked him to order the five gallon containers.

Rick sat down and reread his article for the magazine. He made a few minor changes and put it in an envelope. He included a note, asking Mary to mail it when she went to the Trading Post. Mary came out of the bedroom. She stretched and yawned. She said that she felt refreshed. Rick excused himself to tell Pete that he could begin work on the roof.

Rick asked Mary what she wanted or dinner. She replied that they had another meal or two left from their shopping, but that she would like fresh salmon this evening.

Rick got his fishing gear together. They went to the river. Bart was happy to go with them. Mary asked if she could catch the fish. Rick agreed. He was pleased that she could be a part of his outdoor life.

Mary caught a fish and prepared it for dinner. Pete and Al were invited to join them. Mary said that she would like to eat dinner at the outdoor table, and asked Rick to make a fire near there. Rick made the fire while Mary prepared the food.

Before long the fire was crackling. Mary gave baking potatoes, wrapped in aluminum foil to Rick to put by the fire to bake. She carried the paper plates and utensils. She asked how long the baking would take. He told her it would be about an hour and a half. She said that was fine, and asked Rick to come into the kitchen in about fifteen minutes. When he came in she gave him a covered bowl to take to the picnic table. She carried a jar.

When they got to the table she said, "Surprise, we have shrimp cocktail as an appetizer."

They were all hungry and excited. Shrimp cocktail was not usually on the menu. Al asked how she had managed to keep the shrimp without refrigeration.

She replied, "I had a small cooler and some dry ice."

All of them complimented her on her good idea. They talked a while and then Mary went back to the kitchen. Later she called for help in carrying food to the table. The fire had died down a bit, and the fish in a frying pan was placed on the fire. In a few minutes, the potatoes were removed, and then the fish. They were not talking now, but thoroughly enjoying their food. Then gradually they began to talk.

Mary excused herself, and when she returned she surprised them with marshmallows to be toasted over the fire. Al got sticks to put the marshmallows on. A good time was had by all. It was now dusk, and the fascinating fire held their attention. They talked and told stories before putting the fire out and going in for the night. They thanked Mary for a delicious meal and a fine time.

Tomorrow would be an exciting and busy day. Rick thanked Mary for the excellent and surprise filled dinner. They went to bed early.

CHAPTER XXXIV

Rick and Bart took their morning walk. When they returned Mary said, "Breakfast is almost ready. Today I am going to imagine that I am working in nursing, Monday through Friday, with no evening or night duty. It feels good already. I have worked for so many years working weekends, evening and nights.

During breakast Rick exclaimed, "I can see that you are going to enjoy your imaginary day. When we finish eating, I am going to see if I can get some salmon for the Brothers."

He collected his gear and went fishing. Bart was by his side. Before too long he had two nice fish. He cleaned them at the riverside, and placed them in a plastic bag.

Mary was waiting for him. He got his armament and put the salmon in his knapsack. They got in the SUV, with Bart in the back, and drove to see the Brothers.

"You met the Brothers at the Post, but this will be the first time to see their property. They have so much going on. There is the fur trapping; their chickens, their produce, and they also sell fire wood."

Mary asked, "Why didn't you buy the firewood from them rather than having Pete and Al cut it?

"Pete and Al need the money. Your dad told me that they are having a hard time this year."

Soon they reached their destination. The dogs came out baying when they heard the car. The Brothers then came out to greet them.

Phil and George greeted them, and said they were pleased that Mary was able to come along. Rick gave them the salmon and they went into the cabin.

Mary said, "Oh, I like your living room and that beautiful fireplace."

Phil offered, "Let me take you on a little tour Mary."

George and Rick tagged along. Phil continued, "Here is our greenhouse."

Mary exclaimed, "I see that you are growing a lot of vegetables."

"We sell some of it. We also can quite a bit for winter. This is our storage room."

Marry commented, "This almost looks like the shelves of a grocery store."

Phil took them outside to see the chickens and the firewood.

Mary remarked, "I understand now that when one lives here all year, there are many things that need to be done without a grocery store just down the street."

They returned to the living room. George asked Rick, "How do you feel?"

"I feel much better. I have taken it easy this week as the doctor suggested. Only the scars remain to remind me of the bear."

Phil said, "Your freezer worked well last winter. I don't know how we got along without it all these years."

Rick said, "Mary is recuperating also."

Phil asked, "How are you feeling Mary, and are you going to go back to the hospital to work?"

"I am feeling somewhat better, but I am not yet up to par. As to going back to the ER, I have not decided. I am thinking about my options. One of them would be working in a doctor's office. That position would eliminate weekend, evening and night duty. I will need to make my mind up pretty soon."

George asked Rick if they were going to work the mine this year. Rick replied that they would be starting in two or three more days. They had rented the excavator.

Phil announced that it was almost time for lunch and excused himself.

Rick asked George how the Native Village men had reacted to having grizzly meat. George said that they were very happy to get fresh meat. They even took the bones.

Phil called them to lunch. It was a hearty vegetable stew with rabbit meat.

After lunch they talked, but soon Rick said that they would have to leave. He invited them to come to visit him.

George said, "I'm sorry that you need to leave, but we will visit you soon."

Phil said, "We have some fresh vegetables for you."

Rick and Mary thanked them. Rick called Bart and they returned to the cabin.

When they had unloaded the car, Rick put it in the garage.

Mary said, "Thank you for leaving the Brothers somewhat early. I was getting tired. I am ready for my nap."

Rick called Joel to see when he would be coming out to work the mine.

Joel said, "I will be out the day after tomorrow. It will probably be about nine a.m."

Rick told him about the visit to the lake and the digging of the trough. He also mentioned visiting the Brothers. Joel asked how Mary was doing.

"She is taking a nap right now, but she is doing well. She cooked a dinner the other evening. She caught a salmon, cooked it over a fire and surprised us with shrimp cocktail as an appetizer. She also gave us marshmallows that we toasted over the fire. Pete and Al were with us for the dinner. She made it a fun dinner. We all enjoyed it."

Joel said, "I'm glad that it is going so well."

They chatted some more and then said good bye.

After her nap, Mary came out and told Rick that she had a dream about her new nursing position. She said that she liked it.

Rick told her that Joel would be out to work the mine the day after tomorrow.

Mary exclaimed, "So soon?"

The rest of the day passed without a significant event.

The next day Mary imagined herself working with her dad at the Post. She thought of living there or in the town south of the Post. She took it on face value that Joel would want her help, otherwise she wouldn't be there. She certainly enjoyed being with them when she visited, but wondered how it would be if the work extended into weeks, and then months. It was impossible to know how soon the Post would sell, or even if Joel would sell it. She couldn't imagine him retiring and still living there, but if the merchandise was sold, perhaps he might continue to live there. She tried to put these questions out of her mind and to concentrate on imagining working with her dad.

This day passed as did the others with Rick and Mary enjoying each other's company.

CHAPTER XXXV

It was the last day before Joel came to work the mine, and it was the last day for Rick and Mary to be together. She would be leaving with Joel.

Mary said that she would be imagining being on an extended vacation today.

Rick said to Mary, "Let us have a fun day today. What kind of things would you like to do?"

Mary replied, "What we have been doing has been fun. Today I would like to go for a canoe ride, and I would also like to see the Native Village."

Rick said, "Then that is what we will do. After breakfast I will get the canoe and other gear out and ready. First, I will take Bart out."

"Breakfast will be ready when you return."

Mary gave them a large breakfast since Rick did not know if they would be eating at the Native Village.

He got his armament, life jackets and took the canoe to the river.

"I have a new motor and a new canoe Mary. I will not have to paddle today."

The canoe was launched. Mary got in the bow, Bart was in the middle and Rick was in the stern.

As they went north Mary admired the scenery and called attention to each small animal or bird that she saw.

She said to herself, 'I believe that I am now in real life experiencing and extended vacation.' As long as I am with Rick it is the perfect option.'

They arrived at the Native Village and beached the canoe. Children and dogs came running out. Some children went to tell the adults of the visitors. The dogs remembered Bart and backed down after a brief bluff. The elders came to see who the visitors were. When they saw that it was Rick they welcomed him. Rick introduced Mary as his friend. She was welcomed also.

The elders asked Rick and Mary to join them in the large hut. The hut was large and circular. It had a thatched roof. In the center was a fire. Mats were placed in a circle around the fire. The elders sat in the first row around the fire and invited Rick and Mary to sit beside them. Other natives began to come in and to sit on the other circular rows of mats.

When the seats were filled the Chief addressed the group. "We are honored today to have our hero Rick to join us as we break bread. Rick saved our daughter, Dawn, from a kidnapper. He also gave us the bear meat. He is one of us. We have welcomed him as a member of our village."

The natives clapped their hands and called Rick "brother."

Native women brought in bowls of food, serving Rick, Mary, and the elders first, and finally the remainder of the group.

As they ate, the medicine man asked Rick to tell the story of how he killed the grizzly. Rick told the entire story as he had told others. The natives cheered, and called out "Rick! Rick! Rick!"

The Chief asked if there was anything that they could do to help Rick. He replied that there was nothing, but Rick said that he was honored to be their friend.

After eating, the crowd dispersed, but Dawn's father came to see Rick. The words were few, but he shook Rick's hand and wished him well. Rick asked how Dawn was. Dawn's father smiled and said that she had a man. They shook hands, and said good bye.

They launched the canoe waving at the natives, and headed south in the river.

Mary said, "What a welcome! I am so glad that I asked to see the Native Village. I will never forget how they honored you."

Rick said, "We are friends and we help each other. They helped build my cabin."

When they returned to the cabin Rick beached the canoe and then helped Mary get out. Bart bounded up out of the canoe and ran around happily. Rick brought the canoe up by the garage. He removed the gear and stowed it.

Pete and Al were stacking wood alongside the cabin. The overhang had already been built.

Rick asked how they were doing. Pete said we will probably finish the cord in an hour or two.

Rick said, "That is good. Call me when you have finished."

Rick went into the cabin and took paper and a pencil to the dining room table. He proceeded to draw a sketch of a dock that he wanted them to build by the river.

Pete knocked on the door. Rick met him and asked them to come with him to the river.

Rick asked, "Have you ever built a dock?"

Pete answered in the affirmative.

"Here is a sketch of a dock that I would like for you to build. This will be for the canoe. The sides of the canoe will be about ten inches above the water line when it is empty. The dock should be about fourteen inches above the water line. The dock should be about four feet deep and about twenty four feet long. Since some may be on the dock without shoes, we want to make certain there are no splinters. You have worked enough for today, so just make a list of what you need that we don't already have and we will get it. I imagine that the pilings will need to go pretty deep in order to give the dock enough stability. I would like to have a cleat at each end, and on the river side of the dock. You probably will have some suggestions or questions after you study the plans".

Pete took the plan.

Rick told them that he would be working on the mine tomorrow, but would meet with Pete and Al the first thing after breakfast.

That evening Mary made the dinner. Rick helped her carry things in and helped in cleaning up afterwards.

After dinner they took Bart for a walk and then returned to the living room. Rick asked Mary how she felt. She replied that she felt stronger each day, but she had a bit more to go before she was back to her usual healthy self. Mary snuggled up beside him on the couch.

Rick said, "I know your dad is coming tomorrow. We will be working on the mine. You may come along if you wish, but there are no facilities."

Mary replied, "I will stay here. I will need my afternoon nap, and there are things that I can do here. I called Mom and told her that I would make lunch for you two."

"It has been so pleasant to have you here. I hate to see you go."

"I don't want to go, but I have made a decision to retire. During this next week I will submit my resignation and file for retirement."

"Congratulations! I was hoping that it would come out this way. I am relieved that you will not be working in the ER. Have you determined which options appeal to you?"

"Yes, my first option will hopefully be a short term one. It will be helping Dad if he decides to sell the Post, and if he wants me to help him. I will talk with him to see what his desires are after I resign and apply for retirement. I am not ready to talk about the second option."

"All that you have said sounds good and makes sense. There is certainly no hurry to make all decisions now. If I can help you in any way, just ask."

They talked a while, then took Bart for a walk and went to bed.

CHAPTER XXXVI

After breakfast Pete knocked at the door. Rick went out to hear what Pete had come up with regarding the dock.

Pete said, "We will need finished boards for the top of the dock. We will need two pilings. The wood that we have is not suitable for those two items. We also need large nails and the cleats. If you wish, I can call the hardware and ask for them to be delivered. There is one thing that I believe you should take into consideration. The dock will be fine until we have ice on the river. It will move the dock regardless of how deep the pilings are or how high above the waterline the top of the dock is. It will be especially bad in the spring when the ice begins to melt, and the ice begins to move. I believe that each spring a rebuild will be necessary."

Rick responded, "I am glad that I have you to rely on. Please order what you think we need and have it delivered. They may call me to verify the order. While I am working on the mine do whatever you can to prepare for the dock work. I will see you this evening when I return."

They said goodbye for now.

Rick returned to the cabin and gave Mary the envelope to be mailed to the magazine. It contained the story of the grizzly attack.

Mary was making lunch for Rick and Joel.

Rick came up behind Mary. He put his arms around her and kissed her neck. She turned around and put her arms around him.

Both said, "I love you," at the same time.

They heard Joel drive up and went out to meet him. The men shook hands and Mary and Joel embraced.

Rick said, "I'll get things out of the shed."

He also got his armament, and Mary gave him the lunch.

They drove off up the trail with Bart in the back.

Joel exclaimed, "Mary looks better. I believe being in the outdoors with you was helpful to her."

"She tells me that she is feeling better each day, but is still not up to par."

Joel said, "It will be good to be outside and mining again. Thanks for digging out the trough. That will save us time today."

Rick told Joel about their canoe ride to the Native Village.

"Mary called us and told us all about it. That canoe ride and the visit with the natives will be a highlight for Mary."

They arrived at the lake. The water in the lake had receded sufficiently for them to take the excavator down by the water do dig. They unloaded the sluice box with its new metal top. Rick got the generator and the hose ready. In a few minutes they were ready to start. Joel took the first shift on the excavator. Several hours later Joel stopped. They climbed out of the lake bed and sat on the bed of the truck to have their lunch.

Joel said, "I would like to get your thoughts regarding my retirement."

"The way you worded your request implies that you have decided to retire. I will make my comments based on that assumption."

"I have a few questions that you may wish to consider. First, do you envision selling the Post, or only the merchandise? Second, do you have an idea as to when you might wish to retire? Third, without giving me the answer, ask yourself if you have sufficient funds to retire already, or do you need to rely on proceeds of the sale of the real property, or of the merchandise? I assume that you already receive social security payments. Fourth, do you have plans as to where you would wish to live if you sell the property? You may already know the answers to my questions. If that is the case you may tell me any, or all, of the answers that you wish. I will be glad to discuss it all with you."

Joel replied, "Thanks for your thoughts. I need to think about those questions before we talk again. Let's talk further the next time you visit at the Post."

Rick took charge of the excavator and worked for several more hours, and then shut down the machine.

They began the process of separating the gold as they had done many times before. They got about two ounces of gold. The new top on the sluice box had not made a difference in the amount of gold.

Joel told Rick, "The next time we will probably get down to the gravel layer where we were before. I believe we will get more gold then."

Joel recorded the data in his journal and told Rick that the amount would be placed in their account tomorrow.

They packed up their gear and drove to the cabin. Joel came in for a few minutes while Mary got her things ready.

Mary and Rick hugged and kissed. It was a difficult parting.

Joel and Mary drove to the Post.

Pete and Al told Rick that the order had been placed. The hardware store asked that Rick called them to confirm the order. Rick called and Ok'd the charges.

"They tell me that it will be delivered tomorrow. Prepare as well as you can for the delivery and begin work tomorrow. I'll see you then."

The next day the materials arrived and the dock work began.

During the next week Joel and Rick worked mining one day. Rick called Mary and said that he would like to take her to dinner.

Mary said, "I would love to. When will you come down?"

Rick said that he could be there about ten a.m. tomorrow. Mary said that she looked forward to it. After they talked, Rick asked to speak with Joel.

Joel said hello, and Rick said, "I will come down tomorrow about ten a.m. I will take Mary out to dinner, but I thought that you might want to talk about retirement sometime during the day."

"Yes, and good timing. Jane and I discussed retirement in general and your questions specifically. I look forward to your visit."

CHAPTER XXXVII

Rick told Pete that he was going to the Trading Post, and that he would be back sometime tomorrow.

He arrived at the Post and let Bart run before going into the store. Joel greeted him, offered him a seat and a cup of coffee.

"Pete and Al are building a dock for my canoe."

"I hope you know that the ice gets really thick and when it moves, the dock may be damaged."

"Yes, Pete explained that to me. We will find out next spring."

"We have time before lunch to discuss retirement. Is that ok with you?"

"Yes, that is fine."

Joel called Jane on the intercom. "Rick has arrived, we are going to talk about retirement and I would like to ask both of you to join us in the living room."

When they all were seated in the room Joel said, "I asked Rick for his thoughts about our retirement. He gave them to me and we are here now for me to tell him what Jane and I have decided. I wanted all of us to have the same information."

"As I mentioned we have discussed things and here is what we came up with. We would prefer to sell the property and the merchandise. I don't know how long that would take, but our retirement would start when that is completed. Financially, I believe that we have saved enough, and we do get social security payments, to retire without considering what the property and the gold mine sales would bring. Now, the last question that you asked regarding where we wished to live is a question mark. We would like a warmer climate, but where specifically, we do not know. Now Rick what do you think the next step should be?"

"I believe that your project is a bit like a painting project. There is a lot of preparation before one begins to paint, and there will be a lot of preparation before you can sell. I believe that the first order of business will be to inventory all of your merchandise, and determine a value on each item. Your books would probably be next. They would need to show clearly the profit or loss for at least the last five years. Property wise, anything that needs to be fixed, or if the appearance needs to be improved, should be done. Then, an appraisal of the property by a commercial realtor should be done. The agent will assess the best usage of the property and will give you suggestions for improvement as well as to determine a value.

Now, you can't do all of this alone. It would take too long. You will need to have someone working side by side with you in taking the inventory, assigning value and recording each item. You may have to hire people to make repairs or to enhance the exterior appearance with plantings, and so forth. Further down the line, after some of these things have been done, a realtor needs to list, and sell the property. Please remember, I am not a professional in this area. These are merely my best thoughts at the moment. If there is anything that I can do to help you, just call on me."

"Wow," Joel said, "already I feel overwhelmed thinking of how much needs to be done."

Jane said, "We all can help in some way. I will volunteer to take charge of appearance type improvements inside and outside, including hiring people to do what needs to be done in this area."

Mary said, "I am willing to volunteer to help you Dad with the inventory and with the books."

Joel remarked, "Thank you both. I feel better already."

Mary said, "I haven't told Rick yet, but I have resigned by phone. I have also applied by phone for retirement. I need to go to the hospital to personally sign for each of these items. I will need to go there in the next day or two. Dad, I want to know if you want me to help with the inventory and books. I will need to know what to do about my apartment."

"Yes," said Joel. "That is a generous offer. It will take a lot of time. I would very much appreciate it if you would help me on that project. Have you thought about what you would like to do with your apartment?"

"Yes, I will give it up. If it is alright with you I will live here until the work is completed."

Jane approved, "That will be fine. We love having you with us."

Joel remarked, "Since it is the beginning of summer, most of the trappers have already brought their furs in. It won't get busy again until all sorts of people come in for supplies for the winter. That will give us time to get a lot of this work done."

Jane said, "Thank you Rick, you got us started. Now let us get some lunch. Mary will you help me?"

"Yes, but I need to hug Rick first," and she did.

Joel said, "Thanks Rick. That was a big help. Let us go wash up."

Rick told him, "I'll take Bart out first, and then I will be right with you."

As they ate lunch Rick commented to Mary, "You will have a big job with moving out of your apartment. Have you thought how you will handle that?"

Mary said, "Not entirely. I believe that I will need to put my furniture in storage. First, I need to determine what I will need to bring to the Post with me."

Jane offered, "I will help you pack up what you need to bring here. The movers can then load and store your furniture."

Rick offered, "My SUV can hold quite a bit more than a regular car. If you wish, you could use the SUV, and I could use your car until you get back."

"Thanks Rick. That would be a big help."

Joel commented, "We are moving right along on lining up our projects."

After lunch Rick and Mary took Bart for a long walk.

"I am glad that you will be coming back to the Post. Do you think that Jane might go with you now when you are going to sign the papers and sort out your belongings right away, or do you see other things that need to be done first?"

"I don't know. I will have to talk with Mother about when she would like to help me."

After their walk, Mary took her usual afternoon nap.

That evening Rick and Mary went to a nice restaurant for dinner.

"I was very fond of you before you visited me at the cabin. At the cabin I noticed how easy going you were, and how you seemed to fit in with the wilderness life, and with me. I love you Mary, and I will miss you while you are at your apartment."

"Thank you Rick, I feel the same way as you do about us. You can count on my returning as soon as it is possible."

After dinner Mary requested some slow music and then they danced.

When they returned to the Post, they all sat in the living room.

Mary asked Jane, "When would you prefer to come to help me pack my things?"

"I can make it almost any time. I can go with you now when you go to sign the papers, or I can come later if you have things that you want to do first."

"Then let us do it now and get it over with."

Talk continued until Rick stated that he would take Bart for a walk and then would go to bed.

In the morning they had breakfast. Rick gathered his things, and Mary and Jane gathered theirs. They all hugged and said goodbye. Then Rick drove up the trail in Mary's car, and Mary drove to her apartment in the SUV. Joel stood alone waving goodbye.

CHAPTER XXXVIII

Rick entered his cabin just as his cell phone rang. Jean was on the phone.

She said to Rick, "I haven't heard from you for a while. I will be in my old territory next week. How about joining me here? I will be in town for three days."

"Jean, it is good to hear from you. I am scheduled to go to my home in five or six weeks from now. Unfortunately, I am not able to go there to meet you now. How are things going for you?"

"Things are going well. I love my new position, and I am making good friends. How are you getting along?"

"All is well here also. I have TV shows each week, and when I return to North Dakota I will be filming new shows. In addition, I need to prepare some stories for the sports magazine. Here, I am working to improve my cabin and to work at the gold mine."

They talked about a number of topics, said that they missed each other and said goodbye.

Rick thought to himself, "Things are getting serious between Mary and me. At some point it will come to a head and I will need to make a decision."

Pete and Al showed Rick how the dock was coming along. It looked good and Pete thought that they would finish it sometime today.

The dock was finished. Rick told them that he appreciated the good work that they did.

He said, "Pete you have handled everything very well, and you have done it all in my absence. In addition to the pay we agreed upon, I am giving you a bonus. I do not have another project for you at the present time, and you have worked a long time without a break. Now is your time to relax."

Pete and Al thanked him and said that they would be glad to work for him again. They gathered up their tents and tools. They all said goodbye and left.

Two days later Mary called Rick.

"We will be leaving for the Post tomorrow afternoon. Will you be able to come down then?"

"Yes, Mary, I can't wait to see you. I will help you unpack."

Rick arrived at the Post first. Joel greeted him and said, "Mary and Jane are on the way. Your five gallon containers came in. Let's put them in your car before we forget them."

"The dock is finished and I had to send Pete and Al home. I didn't have another project for them. I hope that they will be ok."

"You have done a lot for them. You can't keep them on the payroll indefinitely. I am sure that something will come up for them. Oh, here come the girls."

Hugs and kisses mingled with smiles and hellos. Bart joined in the greetings with a wagging tail and happy barks. While the men carried things into the house, the women sorted and stored the items. Rick remembered to move the jugs from Mary's car to his SUV.

When the unpacking was completed Jane said, "It is dinner time. What shall we do?"

Rick offered, "Let us go out to dinner. It is my treat."

Everyone agreed with this offer.

During dinner Mary explained, "It was quite a job packing things. I didn't know how much I had accumulated. I either gave, or threw away quite a bit. The movers came this morning. A woman that I knew began cleaning even before the movers left. Mother located a storage place near here. We met the mover there and they unloaded the furniture into the storage room. Now that I am moved, I will be ready to start on our project."

That evening they played some card games and then sat in the living room talking. Mary snuggled up beside Rick, and he put his arm around her.

"I signed the papers of resignation, and for starting my retirement. I said goodbye to my co-workers. It was difficult leaving them, but I know that it was the right thing to do."

Joel said to Rick, "We are scheduled to work on the mine the day after tomorrow. Is that ok with you?"

"Yes, I will be ready. By the way, has any mail come in regarding the sale of the mine?"

"I got so busy that I didn't look at the mail today. Let me check that out."

When he returned he said, "There is something here. It is from someone who works for the publication where the ad was placed. He wants to know the location and a name and a phone number to call. He says that he has mining experience."

Rick suggested, "Let us tell him that it is near the Trading Post. You can give him my name and phone number if you wish."

"I will get the reply ready. It will be in the mail in the morning. I am glad that we got at least one reply". I want to tell you, Rick, about a man that lives about twenty or so miles west of here. He lives with his wife, and their teen age boy. His brother and his wife have a separate cabin. I am not sure if they have children. He keeps cattle for his meat. You might find it interesting to talk with him. His name is Willard, but he goes by Will."

Rick thanked Joel and got the directions and Will's full name and phone number. Rick thought, "That's a possible article for the magazine."

Rick called Will and arranged to see him the next day.

Later Rick took Bart for a walk. Mary went with him.

Mary took Rick's arm and said, "I am here now and we can see each other more often."

Rick suggested, "Perhaps you could come to the cabin when your dad comes out to dig in the mine, and stay a couple of days. I don't think you will have to work on your project seven days a week."

"That sounds like a possibility, and then you could take me back to the Post."

"In any event Mary, I am happy that you are here and that we can be together. I love you."

In the morning Rick drove to meet with Will.

Will was a pleasant man about Rick's age. He introduced his wife Betty, and son Terry. The boy was about thirteen years old.

Will said, "I am glad to meet you. I have heard about your grizzly adventures. My brother, Mark, is riding herd with the cattle. Come in the cabin and we can talk."

Rick told them that he wrote articles for a sports magazine and explained that he had not been to a cattle ranch before.

"Would you mind telling me about your ranch? It might be that I could write an article about it. Would that be ok with you?"

"If we could have a copy of the article I would be glad to tell you about our ranch."

Will's wife Betty interrupted with coffee and cookies.

Rick said, "Thank you Betty. Will, you would certainly get a copy."

Will continued," We have about one hundred acres. I didn't care much for fur trapping, or depending on shooting a deer for meat. I have a small herd of cattle. Each year one is butchered for our meat for the winter. My brother takes care of the herd, protecting it from bears and wolves. He rides his horse and is always armed with a rifle and a pistol. We have to raise the winter feed for the cattle. This involves machinery and fuel expense. We try to repair the breakdowns as much as we can. Some years we lose one or two cattle to the bears and wolves. Like all of us who live isolated in a remote area, it is marginal financially. One of our biggest problems is to raise the cash to pay the taxes. We love the independence."

"Would you take me on a tour of your ranch? I would like to take some photos if you don't mind."

"Sure, that is fine."

Outside Rick saw the corral and the barns. He also saw machinery, but no cattle.

"The cattle are brought to the barns and the corral in the winter. They graze free range in the summer. While Mark is riding herd, I am working to produce a vegetable crop for us, and hay for the cattle. Let us go in my truck to see the rest of the ranch."

Rick had been taking pictures, and continued to do so as they drove. Finally they saw cattle in the distance and there was Mark on his horse. Will introduced them.

"We drove quite a distance. Are we still on your land?"

"No, the cattle go where the grass is good, and they have access to water. We don't know who owns this land."

"Do you stay out here at night?"

"I always have my tent with me. If a bear or wolf has been nosing around, I stay out here. Otherwise, I go home shortly after dusk."

"What do you do if a bear or a wolf is nosing around?"

"I try to scare them off by yelling or shooting the gun in the air. The last resort is to kill them."

Will told Mark, "Rick may write an article about the ranch so we are driving around while he takes pictures. We will be getting back to the cabin now."

"It was nice meeting you Mark. Good luck."

They returned to the cabin. Rick thanked them for their hospitality. He told them that if the article was published that he would see that they got a copy. They all said goodbye and Rick drove to his cabin.

In the morning Rick took the water containers into the cabin. While it was fresh in his mind he wrote the article on the cattle ranch. When the photos were added, it would be a good article.

Rick and Bart walked around the cabin and then went to look at the dock again. Pete and Al certainly did good work. Everything on the outside looked great. He thought that when Mark Hamilton, the person interested in the mine, called that he would invite him here to talk before going to the mine site.

Tomorrow Joel would be coming to work at the mine. Today with the article written he could relax.

In the afternoon he took his small game rifle and went to the woods to see if he could find a squirrel, a rabbit, or a Ptarmigan for dinner.

As he walked deeper into the woods he saw vultures flying in a circle some distance ahead. He was now several miles from his cabin. As he approached, the birds took flight. He found the remains of an animal. It was impossible to know what kind of an animal it had been. The vultures were doing a good job of cleaning up.

He continued his hunt and finally settled for a large rabbit.

After dinner he and Bart sat at the picnic table and admired the scenery. It had been a nice laid back restful day.

Mary called that evening and asked if she could come to visit next week when they would be mining. She had already started on her project and wanted to continue. She indicated that sometimes she did better working on the figures alone. Rick assured her that would be fine and that he would look forward to seeing her next week.

Joel arrived the next morning at about eight thirty.

"Before I forget to tell you, your bear hide will be ready next week. I will bring it to you the next time I come up."

They loaded up the truck and drove to the lake.

Joel remarked, "It would be nice to get more response to our ad, but in the meantime I enjoy the outdoor work. In addition, our bank account keeps growing."

"I feel the same way. I don't mind working the mine one day a week. In fact, I could work an additional day or two now that the cabin project is finished for the time being. If I planned to stay the winter I would have plenty of work to do. I was just wondering, would it make sense to hire someone like Pete to help me mine one or two days a week, in addition to you and me working one day per week?"

"That is something to think about. Even though we paid him, we would still have a good net profit per day to add to our account," Joel replied.

Joel took the first shift with the excavator. They ate their lunch by the waterfall, enjoying the view and the sound of the water.

After lunch Rick took his turn. The results were much the same as last week. Joel recorded the data, and said he would put the money in the account tomorrow.

On the way back to the cabin Joel said, "It is fine with me if you want to hire Pete to help you one or two days per week. Since you are providing your labor, and teaching him, I will pay what you negotiate to pay him."

Rick told Joel what he had paid Pete per day of work. That amount was acceptable to Joel.

Joel dropped Rick off at the cabin and continued on to the Post.

That evening Rick thought about working a day or two on the mine. He was pretty much out of projects and he may as well be working and making money. Either Pete or Al would be good workers, but since Pete had been his first contact, he decided to call Pete first.

He and Bart took their late evening walk and then went to bed.

The next morning Rick called Pete, "Good morning Pete, this is Rick. I have a new project that will take a day or two each week. Would you be interested?"

"I would like to work with you again, but I have just agreed to start another project."

Rick replied, "That is ok Pete, do you think that Al might be interested?"

"I believe he might be Rick." Pete gave Al's phone number to Rick.

"Thanks Pete. I will give Al a call."

Al was eager to work. He asked if Al had experience with an excavator.

Al said, "I have lots of excavator experience."

"That's just what I need. He told him what the daily pay would be. That was satisfactory to Al. They agreed to work the two days each week before Rick would work with Joel.

CHAPTER XXXIX

Later that day Mark Hamilton called. He introduced himself as did Rick. Mark asked for specific directions.

Rick said, "I would like to ask you to come to my cabin, which is on the way to the mine. My partner will join us. We can answer each other's questions first and then we will give you a tour of the mine. If that is satisfactory to you I will give you the directions to my cabin."

"That is fine with me. I can join you the day after tomorrow."

Rick gave him the directions, and asked him to call to confirm his arrival on the morning of the appointment.

All was agreeable. They talked briefly and then said goodbye.

Rick called Joel and told him of the discussion and the scheduled meeting.

Joel said, "I will come out early in the morning. I will bring my truck with our gear and records to show to Mark. This is going to be interesting and fun. I am looking forward to the meeting. I will see you then."

Joel arrived early at Rick's cabin. Rick got his gear out of the garage and put it in the truck. Joel brought his books into the cabin.

Mark called and said that he was by the Trading Post and was on his way to the cabin.

Rick and Joel went outside to meet Mark. Mark pulled up in his Cadillac. He and another man got out.

Rick introduced himself and Joel. He said, "Welcome, I am Rick and this is Joel, we are partners."

"I am Mark Hamilton, and this is Jim, one of my foremen."

Rick invited them into the cabin. They sat at the dining room table.

Rick explained, "Joel owns and runs the Trading Post, and I am a writer for a sports magazine. We are not professional miners and we use homemade equipment except for the excavator, generator and pump."

Mark asked, "Are you Rick Spears?

Rick said that he was.

Mark said, "I read your articles every month. They are very good."

Rick thanked him.

Mark told them, "I am on the board of the publication that you used to advertise your mine. I own several mines, and Jim is one of my foremen. I have been looking for a small mine"

Joel remarked, "Rick discovered the mine and invited me to be his partner. We worked the mine one day each week for about three hours. Rick did all the digging by hand. We then decided to rent an excavator and increased our digging to six hours each day that we worked. You will probably get a laugh after you see our homemade sluice box. It works, but it is nothing like a professional factory made box. We have kept records each time we have worked. The records include the date, amount of gold found, and the gold value on that date. You are welcome to review our records."

Joel handed the journal to Mark. Mark took his time and reviewed the data. He remarked, "It looks like you tried several sites before settling on the lake."

Rick replied, "It was at the waterfall that I first saw evidence of gold. We dug there and then moved to the lake. We have not been back to dig at the falls, nor the stream that runs to the lake. I feel sure that there is more gold there."

Mark stated, "This is interesting. You got a good amount of gold considering the time you spent digging. Let us go look at the site."

Rick said, "Because of the ground clearance, I will drive my SUV. Mark, you can ride with me, and Jim can ride with Joel."

Rick got the SUV out. Mark got in the front and Bart got in the back. They parked first by the waterfall and got out.

Mark said, "This is a pretty scene."

Rick said, "Let me show you the water source." He took them to the gushing spring.

Mark commented, "That is coming out with a lot of pressure."

They then looked at the falls and walked to the lake.

Jim said, "I see that you had to lower the lake water in order to dig."

Joel said, "I am going to bring my truck down here."

Mark remarked, "Yes, this is very interesting. It is difficult to see however that you were able to get that much gold in such a short time."

Rick asked, "How much time are you able to spend with us today?"

Mark replied, "I am willing to spend several hours if the time spent would be productive."

Rick said, "Let us dig for a few hours and show you the results. Would that be helpful to you?"

"Yes, it would, and we can help."

Joel offered, "I will run the excavator."

Jim said, "Show me what you normally do, and I will pitch in."

Joel started the excavator and helped Rick set up the generator, pump and hose. Joel began digging and Rick used the hose. After watching the operation Jim relieved Rick.

Mark exclaimed, "That is a nice sluice box, and your system is pretty efficient. Have you dug up any gravel yet?"

Rick stated that they had just started to reach gravel at the end of the last season. In the spring a lot of dirt had washed over it. He felt that they might reach the gravel today.

Mark asked, "I have heard about some grizzly stories in this area. Were you involved in those encounters?"

Rick said that he was. He asked Mark, "Have you seen the ad in the sports magazine regarding hunting and fishing stories on TV?"

Mark said that he had seen the ad but had not tuned into them.

Rick explained, "I have a half hour show each week with those stories. The ad lists the time and channel. You may find it to be interesting."

A few hours later Joel shut off the excavator and he and Rick washed the gold off the mats. They got about an ounce and a quarter of gold.

Joel said, "I barely got to the gravel area. Another three hours and we would probably do better."

Mark responded, "I think that you did great. You have proven to me that your records are true."

Jim remarked, "It has been a longtime since I have done this work by hand, but their methods and their equipment work."

Mark told them, "Thank you, I will need to go now. I have a lot to think about. I will keep in touch with you."

Rick said, I will drive them to the cabin, Joel, and then I will be back and we can finish up the last three hours."

At the cabin Rick dropped them off. They shook hands and said goodbye.

Rick drove back to the lake.

Joel asked, "What do you think Rick?"

"He seemed to be interested. I don't know whether the mine is big enough for them to bother with. He said he would keep in touch."

Mark asked Jim, "How does it look to you?"

Jim replied, "It is a small mine but it does appear to be profitable."

"How would you go about it, Jim?"

"I would take everything out of the lake that I could get and then I would work the waterfall and then the stream bed."

Mark told Jim, "I am going to work up a projection of the data they gave me. Then, figuring modern equipment, I will see if it is worthwhile bothering with it. I really liked the cabin and the cabin site."

Rick and Joe worked for another three hours finally reaching the gravel. They got another ounce and one quarter of gold. Joel recorded the data.

Rick told Joel, "Al and I will start on Tuesday of next week. We will also work on Wednesday. Then you and I will dig on Thursday. Mary said that she would come out with you. Also, I am looking forward to seeing my bear hide."

They drove separately, and Joel continued on to the Post.

CHAPTER XL

Rick and Al worked well together for two days. Al handled the excavator, and Rick handled the generator, pump and the hose. Their results were similar to what Rick and Joel got the previous week.

Joel and Mary arrived the next day. Rick and Mary hugged. Rick said that he was glad that she was here. He helped her take her things into the cabin.

Joel said, "I have something for you. Here is the bear hide. I think that he did a great job."

"Yes, look at that snarl and those fangs. That is how he looked when he charged me. Let me place it on the living room floor."

Mary remarked, "It looks great, and it is the right size for the room."

Rick asked Joel to put the amount for the taxidermist on his running bill.

Rick told Joel, "I'll get my gear and put it, and the dog, in the back."

He said to Mary, "Do you want to go with us, or are you going to stay here?"

"I want to go with you. It is so beautiful there. I brought lunch for all of us."

"I hoped that you would go with us but was concerned that you would be bored."

They drove to the lake and parked. They unloaded their gear and found that Mary had brought three folding chairs along.

Joel took the first turn on the excavator as usual.

Mary took her chair up by the waterfall. Bart went back and forth to be near Rick and then to be near Mary.

Lunch time came and they sat in their chairs by the falls while they ate.

"Mary and I are making good progress on the inventory. I don't see how I could do it without her."

"It is a great help that you kept invoices as you received the merchandise. Now we just need to match the invoice to the actual item, add the mark-up and record it."

"I love the site of the cabin by the woods and the river, but this site is also beautiful, and I love to hear the water fall."

Rick exclaimed, "I took pictures of all of this as it was in its natural state. I could see that someday it might all be mined."

Rick took over on the excavator. In about an hour he told Joel, "I am beginning to get gravel."

"We will have to watch the weight that we put on the sluice box. The gravel will be heavier, and we may need to add supports under the sluice box."

They continued, but watched for signs of stress. Rick finished the shift without a problem.

Rick said, "I'll bring along some materials to support the box next week."

Their results improved by nearly a quarter of an ounce. Joel recorded the data, and again said that the money would be in their account tomorrow. Now that Rick and Al were also working, their bank account would grow rapidly.

They gathered up their gear and drove to the cabin. Rick and Mary took their things in. Rick gave Joel the vials from the work he and Al had done. Joel recorded that data. Joel drove on to the Trading Post.

Rick and Mary went into the cabin and flew to each other's arms. They were so happy to be together for the next two days.

Rick asked, "How are you feeling? I know that you were not fully recuperated when I saw you last."

"It has taken a long time. I believe that I will be up to par in another week. I don't have to pamper myself though. I merely have to pace myself and not over do. I rested quite a bit by the waterfall."

"That sounds good. You are still welcome to take a nap at any time.

"I brought some things along for dinner, and if it is alright with you, I will make dinner including catching a fish."

"I like your idea. I certainly won't turn down a meal that you prepare. I will get the fishing gear for you."

They went to the river and Mary proceeded to cast.

Rick asked, "Would you like for me to make a fire outside, or would you rather cook, and eat indoors?"

"I liked the fire and eating outside last time. Let us have a repeat of that."

Rick made the fire. Mary caught a fish and cleaned it herself. Rick brought some white wine to the table.

In no time at all, they were eating and enjoying the fire and being together. Later, they toasted their marshmallows over the flames.

Before dusk they took a long walk by the river, strolling hand in hand. Bart accompanied them. Rick had his armament with him but this evening was without signs of danger. Mary loved the river and the view of the trees and the mountain.

When they returned Rick rekindled the fire and they sat, as the sky darkened, watching the flickering flames, and the shining stars. As they sat, with Rick's arm around her, the flames were replaced with embers. Finally the fire was out. They walked to the cabin and went to bed.

In the morning, Rick took Bart for a walk while Mary made breakfast. On his walk, Rick thought to himself, "If this is what marriage is like, I think I prefer it to being a bachelor. I love them both, but Mary would make my cabin or house a home."

Rick returned to find a breakfast of bacon, eggs and biscuits waiting for him.

He kissed Mary and thanked her. Then they had the delicious breakfast.

"Would you like to go canoeing again, swim in the river, or hike up the mountain, or do you have something else that you would like to do?"

"Hiking up the mountain would be a bit too much for me today I believe. You know that I like the canoe so I will vote for that. What would you like to do?"

"A canoe ride would suit me just fine. We could go south this time for a change of scenery."

Rick got the canoe, life jackets and a jug of water and took them to the dock.

"This is the first that I have seen the dock. It is beautiful. This way the boat will stay cleaner since we won't have to go in the mud and water to get in."

Mary got in the bow, then Bart, and finally Rick got in the stern. The engine started immediately and Rick shoved off going down stream.

He noticed that the current was quite strong. The engine and rudder were needed to keep the canoe on track. This was going to be a fast ride.

They saw a deer on the mountain side of the river. Mary was thrilled when she saw the fawn with it. She had her camera and took their picture. On the cabin side they could see the trail. They enjoyed the scenery and told each other about each interesting bird or animal that they saw.

Then, Rick heard the sounds of rapids. He had not come this way in the canoe before. Before he knew it they were in the rapids. They were going faster and Rick had to decide quickly which side of the river to be on. He called to Mary to hang on. He dodged rocks and whirlpools. It took only a few minutes to get through it, but it seemed to be much longer. He asked Mary if she was ok, and got an affirmative response. They continued downstream, but Rick knew that on the way back that they would have to carry the canoe around the rapids.

Looking ahead Rick sighted the feeding area of the bears. There were at least a dozen in the river. Mary had not seen the bears before and asked Rick if he was going to turn around. Rick did turn around and now using the engine proceeded north.

Just before reaching the rapids he beached the canoe on the trail side. He asked Mary to carry the life jackets and the water jug. He took the motor off of the canoe and then with one hand on each side of the upturned canoe he lifted and swung it over his shoulder. Off they went to the other side of the rapids. Rick put the canoe down and returned downstream to get the engine.

He took the canoe to the edge of the river, attached the engine and had Mary and Bart get in. He started the engine and they returned to his dock. Rick put the canoe and other gear in the garage.

They sat at the picnic table.

"I loved the canoe ride. Even though the rapids were scary and I was a bit afraid, I knew that you could handle the situation."

"Thank you Mary. The rapids surprised me. I had never noticed them from the trail. Did you get some good pictures?"

"Yes, the one of the deer and the fawn was the best of the wildlife. I have some of the birds. I also have some other ones including you carrying the canoe over your shoulders. That was a heavy load."

That evening they drove to town. Rick took her to a nice restaurant for dinner, and they danced afterwards until Mary became tired. Rick drove them to his cabin.

On the way to the cabin, Mary thought to herself. 'This is a sample of my preferred option, and I love it.'

It was late when they arrived at the cabin. Rick told Mary, "I have become very fond of you, and I love you. Tomorrow I will need to take you home and I will miss you."

Mary replied, "I feel as you do. Perhaps you could stay overnight at the Post to extend our time together."

"That is a good idea if it would not inconvenience Joel and Jane."

Mary took her phone and called. Jane answered. Mary said, "Hi Mom, Rick will be bringing me back tomorrow afternoon. Would it be a problem if he stayed overnight?"

"Of course not, he is like one of the family."

"Thanks Mom, I will see you in the afternoon tomorrow."

"There we have some extra time."

There day had been a busy one and they were tired. Rick took Bart for a walk and they all went to bed.

In the morning Rick received a call on his cell phone. "Rick, this is Mark Hamilton. How are things going for you?"

"They are going well Mark. How are things with you?"

"I have been mulling over your mine and would like to meet with you and Joel again. Would you have some time in the next week that we could get together?"

"It looks like Thursday would be a good time, but I will need to touch base with Joel first."

"That sounds fine Rick. Try for about ten a.m. and get back to me after you talk with Joel."

"I will do that Mark, thanks for calling."

They said good bye.

Rick called Joel. Joel was agreeable since he was scheduled to go to the mine that morning anyhow.

Rick called Mark and left a message confirming the Thursday morning meeting.

After lunch Rick drove to the Post. He helped carry Mary's things in.

Joel greeted them and said we got another person interested in the mine. "I received his letter in the mail just before you arrived. I will send to him the same information that I sent to Mark, if that is ok with you."

"Yes, that is good news. The more that reply the better our odds are."

"Let us sit down and talk a bit. Do you think that Mark is coming to make an offer?"

"I doubt it. He probably has more questions. Let us take a few minutes to think about the questions that he might ask us so that we will be prepared."

"Good idea. He might ask us to confirm our ownership of the land and to confirm our claim to the mine."

"Yes, I think those are good items. I just happened to think about the trail leading from the split tree to the lake. Did we ever check out who owned that land? Just imagine if someone does own it and denied us access to the mine. We would be in a heap of trouble."

Joel said, "I don't believe we ever did check that out. I'll get the realtor to check it out right now."

Joel called the realtor and said, "This is Joel. You handled the sale of the lake property for Rick and I some time ago."

"Yes, I recall that."

"There is a trail leading to the lake property from the main trail beginning at the split tree. I would like to know who owns that land, whether it is for sale or not, and if so, what is the price."

"I will check it out and call you back as soon as I know something."

Joel said thank you and they said goodbye.

Rick remarked, "That is a good start. What else might he be asking?

"We gave him all the information about the results of our digging. Joel asked, "Do you think he would want to ask about terms of financing?"

"I don't believe he would do that Joel unless he was making an offer with it. My immediate reaction would be to say no to financing."

"I can't think of anything else. He wouldn't be interested in our equipment."

Rick commented, "The most important information is what you have asked the realtor to get. Let us just put the question on the back burner until he calls you back."

Jane and Mary came into the store. Jane welcomed Rick with a hug.

She said, "It is about a half hour until dinner time, is wine being served here?"

Joel answered, "Let us meet in the living room, and wine will be served. Shall it be red or white wine?

Jane replied, "Tonight it should be red wine. See you in the living room."

Rick received a call from the sports magazine.

"Rick, I need for you to speak to a hunting club in Chicago in three weeks. Can you make it?"

"That will be cutting it short, but I believe that I can make it."

"Call me to confirm within the next week. Your TV shows are great, and I have picked up more subscribers to the magazine as a result. By the way, I need some new articles."

"The articles have been written. It just remains for my photographer to put it together."

"Take care Rick, I will see you soon."

They said goodbye.

In the living room Joel poured the wine.

"The sports magazine called. I am to give a talk to a hunting club in Chicago in three weeks. The time has gone so quickly. While I am there I will need to have TV shows filmed, make that talk, and write new stories for the magazine. I will be busy."

After an enjoyable dinner they went to the living room and talked.

Rick received a phone call. George was on the line saying to Rick, "We have been meaning to visit you before this, but we got busy. Would it be alright if we came to visit you tomorrow?"

"That would be great. I am at the Trading Post now, but will be back in my cabin by nine a.m. I am looking forward to seeing you."

They talked some and then said good bye.

Rick said, "It is getting late, and I will take Bart for a walk. Will you accompany me Mary?"

"Of course." She took his arm and they went out. It was a beautiful night, full of stars and a bright moon. Bart bounded on ahead.

Rick thanked Mary for inviting him to spend the evening and overnight at the Post to extend their time together.

Mary said that she hated to see him leave. Since Mark was coming to Rick's cabin on Thursday, she would not be going to Rick's until the following week. Before they went back in, they embraced and kissed and said that they loved each other.

Rick said good night to Joel and Jane and retired for the night.

At breakfast Joel said that he would call Rick as soon as he heard from the realtor. After breakfast Rick packed his things in the SUV. He thanked them all. Hugged the women, shook hands with Joel, and said good bye.

CHAPTER XLI

They arrived at the cabin without incident. Rick took his things into the cabin.

Phil and George drove up. Greetings were made and the Brothers brought vegetables and a carton of eggs to Rick.

They went in the cabin. Phil said, "That bear hide is beautiful. Look at those fangs and those claws."

"I too believe that he did a great job."

George added, "The taxidermist makes him look so natural."

"Pete and Al did some work for me in the kitchen. Come take a look. Jane helped me pick out the cupboards and countertops and sink. Pete and Al installed them."

George said, "I like the way it all blends in with the log siding."

They went back to the living room and sat.

Rick told them, "Joel and I are advertising to sell the lake property with the mine. We are in no hurry and we will continue to mine it each week."

Phil said, "Do you mind telling us what prompted you to do that?"

"We will sell only if we can make a good profit. In the meantime Joel and I work it one day each week and Al and I work it two additional days a week."

George commented, "Rick, there is always something new going on with you. At least this news is less traumatic than what you gave us regarding the grizzly attack last time."

"I also need to tell you that I will be going back to North Dakota in two weeks. I will be filming shows again, and giving a talk in Chicago in three weeks."

"Yes, as I mentioned, there is always something new going on with Rick," exclaimed George.

"We have time to stay a while, but we will have to leave about mid-afternoon," said Phil.

"I went to see a cattle ranch about twenty miles west of the Trading Post. I have written an article about it that you will see coming up before too long in the sports magazine."

Rick asked, "Would you like to take some salmon home with you?"

"We are always ready for fresh salmon," replied George.

"It is just about lunch time, let me catch one fish that we can have for lunch, and after lunch I can catch more for you to take home. First, I want to start a small fire, and we will cook the salmon there."

Rick started a fire where he had made one for Mary.

He got his fishing gear. They all went to the river.

"Pete and Al built this dock for me."

"They did a really nice job," remarked Phil.

Rick began fishing and soon brought up a medium size salmon. He cleaned the fish at the river side. They ate at the picnic table using paper plates that Mary had brought.

They talked about a number of topics and invited Rick to visit them.

Rick told them that he would not be able to visit until he returned from North Dakota.

After lunch Rick asked how much salmon they would like to have.

Phil answered, "We would like to have several, however without refrigeration we had better take only one."

They returned to the river. Rick told them, "I don't need to have all the fun. Would either of you like to catch your fish?"

George replied, "Thanks, I'll try for one."

He fished for a while but didn't have any luck. Phil took a turn, and on the second cast got a nice salmon.

Phil commented, "It is all in the touch, and I got it."

George said, "Yes, touched in the head."

Phil cleaned the fish. Rick gave him a plastic bag to put it in.

They talked a little more and the Brothers said goodbye. Rick thanked them again for helping him after the grizzly attack, and said goodbye.

After they left Rick got busy on his articles for the magazine and for his TV show.

Joel called and told Rick, "The land that the trail leading to the lake property is for sale. It is a twenty acre parcel. They want twenty five thousand for it. It is similar to your property in that it goes to, and into, the river. The river frontage is about four hundred feet.

Rick commented, "If we don't buy it we will have difficulty selling the mine. What do you think?"

"That twenty five thousand will cut deeply into our profit. We could always continue mining it as we are now doing. We are making good money. But, doing that would change my plans for retirement."

"I think that we should buy it. That is a reasonable price for water front property, and for the peace of mind that assures that no one can prevent us from using the trail and our mine. As long as the land is land bound without access, it will be a problem for anyone who owns the mine. Also, we don't want to foul up your retirement."

"You are right. Retirement and peace of mind are more important than twelve and one half thousand. Shall I tell the realtor to buy it?"

"I believe so. We do need more information about the boundaries. For example, where is the trail in relation to the sides of the property? We need to see it represented on a map showing boundary lines, the location of the lake property and the location of the trail. Both of our names need to be on the deed. I believe that we have sufficient funds to buy it immediately?"

"Yes, I can write a check to cover the entire amount, but I will get the map information for us to see first."

"I am ready and willing to buy; providing the map looks good. I will come to the Post to see it as soon as the realtor can produce it."

"I'll get on it right away."

They said goodbye.

Rick and Al worked the mine the next day. Joel called and said that the realtor would arrive at five p.m.

Rick replied that they were finishing up and that he would be there by five.

Rick arrived just as the realtor arrived. They looked at the map. The trail was very near the north side of the property. This property adjoined the lake property.

Joel stated, "This looks good to me. How do you feel about it?"

"It looks good to me also, let us go for it."

Joel wrote the check and gave it to the realtor. "I would like for this transaction to be completed tomorrow if that is possible," said Joel to the realtor.

"I will do my best. I will call you as soon as I know."

The realtor left and Jane and Mary entered the room.

"Have you completed your business meeting?" asked Jane.

"Yes and I need to have a drink."

Rick said, "I second that," as he hugged Mary.

Mary asked, "Can you tell me what that was all about?"

Joel answered, "We just offered to buy another property adjacent to the lake property."

Rick added, "It was necessary in order to provide a legal right a way to the lake property."

Jane told them to wash up for dinner.

At dinner Joel poured the wine and toasted their proposed purchase.

After dinner Rick and Mary took a walk with Bart. They talked, hugged and kissed, and then Rick said goodbye to all and left.

The next morning Rick and Al worked on the mine. About noon time Joel called Rick and said that the sale had been signed by the current owner. As soon as the deed was recorded they would be the new owners. Rick and Al completed the day and said goodbye.

Joel arrived on the next day which was Thursday, about nine thirty. He brought all of his mining gear and his journal.

Rick got each of them a cup of coffee while they waited for Mark.

Mark arrived promptly at ten a.m. This time he was by himself.

They all greeted each other and Rick invited him to the living room.

"Would you like a cup of coffee Mark?"

"No thanks, Rick. I had a nice breakfast not too long ago."

Mark told them, "I am interested in your mine. The way that you mine it is good, and is profitable for you. I would be interested in generating a greater volume which requires modern equipment. You fellows probably don't pay yourselves a salary for what you do, and you rent your excavator, so you do not have a large overhead. I am interested in your mine, but considering those differences in our methods of operation, I can't justify the price that you are asking. Before we talk more about price, tell me about the right of way that you have to reach the property."

Rick replied, "We own the land that the trail is on, as a separate piece of property."

Mark asked, "Would that land be included in the sale of the mine property?"

Rick answered, "It could be, but for an additional price. Mark, we realize that you would need legal access to the lake property. We are willing to work with you, either by selling you more land or negotiating a right of way. This can be worked out. The problem we need to address first is the price. We are pretty firm about that. Your projections are probably more accurate than ours, but we believe that the purchase price could be recovered in one year or less."

"I have a figure in mind of eight hundred thousand with a guaranteed right of way included."

Rick replied, "We are close enough to continue negotiating Mark. I will tell you that we have now reached gravel. The gold produced is up one quarter of an ounce for three hours of work."

Mark responded, "We all have a lot to think about. Let us let it simmer a bit. Either one of us can call the other when we have new thoughts, or new information to offer."

They stood up, shook hands and said goodbye.

Joel asked Rick, "What do you think?"

"It looks like a good start to me Joel."

They got in the truck and went to the lake. The results were good, two and one half ounces of gold. Joel recorded the data and said that the money would be in their account in the morning.

Joel dropped Rick off at the cabin. Rick brought the vials that he and Al had collected and brought them to Joel. Joel recorded the data and then continued on to the Post.

Rick had dinner and continued working on his articles until time to take Bart for a last walk before going to bed.

CHAPTER XLII

In the morning Rick took Bart for a walk before breakfast. As he ate, he realized that it was Friday. Next week would be his last week before going to North Dakota.

He called Mary. "I just realized that next week is my last week before I need to go. I was wondering if, when you come out on Thursday, you could stay with me until I leave on the following Monday. I would take you to the Post on Sunday and stay overnight."

"That sounds good to me. I just hate to see you go. How long will you be gone?"

"It could be as short as two weeks, but could easily take longer. In the meantime I have much to do here to prepare for the filming and other tasks. For those reasons I probably won't be able to see you until next Thursday."

"We will work around your schedule. Dad and I are making good progress with the inventory, and Mother is doing a lot to make the place more appealing."

They talked a little more and then said good bye.

Rick got busy on his articles.

Midmorning he received a call. "This is Stewart James. I am responding to your ad. Can you give mre more information?"

"My name is Rick Spears. I am a partner in the mine. My partner and I work it ourselves. My partner and I will be glad to meet with you. Can you tell me something about yourself and your mining experience?"

"I am thirty years of age, but I have ten years of experience working mines for other people. I know most of what there is to know about gold mining. I have saved my money and now I want to be the owner of my own mine."

"Well Stewart, you sound like an enterprising young man. I would like to invite you to meet with my partner and me at my cabin. It is on the way to the mine. We can answer each others questions and then go to see the mine site. Would that be alright with you?"

"Yes, when can we meet?"

"Stewart I would like to suggest that we meet at ten a.m. nest Thursday morning. Would that fit in with your schedule?"

"Yes, I know that you are near the Trading Post, but I need specific directions."

Rick gave him the directions, and after talking a bit more they said goodbye.

Rick called Joel and told him of their meeting.

He then returned to his articles and his talk preparation. This work continued, on and off, until Wednesday when Al arrived.

They worked the mine for the next two days and had results similar to those of last week. They reinforced the sluice box supports due to the increased load of the gravel and some larger rocks.

Rick paid Al and said that he would contact him when he returned. They said goodbye, and Al left.

In the morning Joel arrived with Mary, his truck and gear.

Rick greeted them. He hugged and kissed Mary and shook Joel's hand. They took Mary's things in. Rick offered them coffee.

"Mary, Joel and I will be interviewing a man who is interested in buying the mine. After talking here we will be going to the lake. Would you like to come along or would you prefer to stay here?"

"I will go with you since you will be there most of the day."

They heard Stewart drive up after Bart had sounded the alert.

Rick and Joel welcomed Stewart. He was accompanied by his wife, Alice.

Introductions were made all around. Stewart told them, "When we find our mine, Alice and I will work it together. We will be partners as you and Joel are."

"Let's sit around the dining room table to talk. Joel and I work the mine together as you two will. We are not professional miners. Joel owns and runs the Trading Post, and I am a writer for a sports magazine. Our mining is done on a part time basis. We have a small proven mine, and we have the records to show that what we will tell you is factual. I know that you have told us of your mining experience. My first question is, do you have the funds to buy our mine?"

"We have saved our money over the past ten years. We have an excellent credit rating. We believe that we can get financing if the productivity of the mine can be verified."

"My second question is, do you have equipment, or do you intend to rent it or buy it?"

"Since we have been working for mine owners, we do not have our own equipment. We plan to make what we can and to rent the rest."

"That is pretty much what we did Stewart. We made the sluice box. At first, Rick did all the digging by hand. Later we rented an excavator. We did buy a generator, a pump and a few other things. We can show our home made equipment to you when we go to the mine site."

Stewart asked, "Can you verify your productivity to us?"

Joel answered, "We first worked three hours a day until we rented the excavator. We then began working six hours a day, one day per week. We are now getting about one and one quarter ounces of gold for each three hours worked. Here is our journal from the first time we mined up to and including last week."

Stewart took his time looking, with Alice, at the journal.

Stewart exclaimed, "If it can be verified that this data is accurate, you have done very well."

Rick said, "We can verify all that we have told, and shown to you. Let's go to the site. We can talk more there. The ground clearance on the trail is not too good. Would you like to ride with us or do you prefer to use your vehicle?"

"I have a pick-up, and the ground clearance is good. We will drive in it."

Mary got their lunch. Bart got in the back of Joel's truck, Joel drove and Mary and Rick sat alongside.

They parked by the lake. Rick took them on a tour of the spring, the waterfall, the stream and the lake and pond.

Alice remarked, "This is a beautiful scene. I particularly like the waterfall."

Stewart commented, "That is a good size for the excavator, and I see that the pond is doing its job in draining water from the lake so that you can dig."

Joel said, "If you like what you see so far, we will dig for a few hours and prove to you that our journal figures are accurate."

"That would be great, and I can help."

They unloaded and set up the sluice box, the generator, pump and hose.

Stewart exclaimed, "That is one nice sluice box. It is pretty much what I intend to build."

Joel started the excavator and Rick took charge of the generator, pump and hose.

After seeing the procedures Stewart and Alice relieved Rick. Within a few minutes Alice took over and Stewart joined Rick.

Stewart remarked, "This is great. This is exactly what we want to do."

Joel stopped the excavator after three hours. He and Rick washed out the mats and found that they had a bit over one and one quarter ounces of gold.

Stewart said, "That is amazing. You did verify in front of us exactly what you told us."

Rick explained, "We are into gravel as you have seen, and we are beginning to get some rock. Stewart, have you seen enough and heard enough to know if you are interested in buying our mine?"

"Let Alice and I take a walk up by the water fall and talk it over. We will be back in a short time."

Joel asked Rick, "What do you think?"

"I would love to see them get it if they can afford it. That is the big question."

After about ten minutes they returned.

Stewart told them, "We would like to buy your mine. You realize that we will need to get financing. Of course if you would care to finance us we are prepared to go ahead."

Rick answered, "I am glad that you like our mine and operation and would like to buy it. We are not in a position to finance it for you. You know that our asking price is one million, two. Do you wish to make an offer?"

Stewart answered, "If you will finance us at a rate that we can afford, we will offer one million, with two hundred and fifty thousand down. We can produce a cashier's check in that amount. If we need to find financing elsewhere, our offer will depend somewhat on the terms that we can get."

Rick stated, "I like what you have said. Personally, I would like to see you get the mine. We all have a lot to think about. I have one more question for you. You realize that winter starts in about two months and mining is stopped in the winter. Where would you live until winter starts, and where would you live once it was too cold and snowy to work the mine?"

"We have camped in a tent at many a site. We will do that until winter shuts us down. We both have jobs for the winter about forty miles south of here. We have an apartment there. We would be camping again in the spring until we can afford to build a cabin for ourselves on the mine site."

"I admire your spirit. In my work writing adventure stories I too have spent many nights over a long period camping in a tent. Since you are getting financing, would you give us the ok to have your credit checked?"

"Yes, we will send you a note with our permission."

"I wish you good luck and look forward to hearing from you in the near future."

They all shook hands and said goodbye.

Joel remarked, "What a nice couple, I hope that they can get the mine."

Mary said, "Let's go up by the waterfall to have lunch. Would you bring the folding chairs? Mine is already up there, I will bring the lunch."

"They are nice kids, but they didn't ask about the right of way. If a note comes in from them addressed to me Joel please open it. With the note, do you believe that your bank would get the credit check done?"

"I am sure that they would."

Mary commented, "Alice is a hard worker. When I shook hands with her I could feel her strength. Her hands were hardened like a man's hand used to outdoor work."

"We could think about financing them. Earlier, I said that I was against it, but we would be pretty safe. With twenty five percent down, a good credit check, and a contract giving us everything back in the event of a default, we wouldn't have to worry too much. What do you think Joel?"

"Well, neither of us needs all of the money at once. One hundred and twenty five thousand each sounds real good for a start. I will talk it over with Jane."

After lunch they worked another three hours and Joel recorded the take for the day which was slightly over two and one half ounces. They packed up and drove to the cabin. Rick gave Joel the vials that he and AL had produced. It was recorded and Joel drove to the Post.

Now Mary and Rick had their time together. Mary started off however with a nap.

Mary came out in about twenty minutes. She told Rick that she had brought dinner along, and began to get it ready.

Rick came up behind her. He put his arms around her and kissed her neck. She turned around and hugged and kissed him.

"I am so glad that you are here."

Mary said she was glad also.

That evening they ate in the dining room. Mary said that she liked how it looked.

After dinner Rick fed Bart. They took him for a walk by the river, enjoying the scenery and being with each other.

Back in the cabin they sat together in the living room. They talked and hugged and kissed.

Rick said, "I have been enjoying these several days together."

"We will have to enjoy this time. It will give us something to remember while you are in North Dakota."

It had been a busy day. Before too long they took Bart for a walk and went to bed.

Rick took Bart for his early morning walk. As he returned he noted the scent of bacon frying. He and Bart entered the cabin to see Mary cooking breakfast.

Rick carried items to the dining room table.

"Mary, this is a real pleasure having breakfast waiting when I return from walking Bart. It is especially good when bacon and eggs are included. Thank you."

Mary said, "It is my pleasure."

As they took back items to the kitchen Rick's phone rang.

"Rick, this is Mark. I have an idea and I would like to come to see you."

"Mark, I would like to see you, but I have company now, and I am so busy preparing to go to North Dakota. Could we discuss it on the phone?"

"Rick, this is important. I have an idea about buying your mine, but there is more to it. I really need to see you."

"Mark, let me tell you first, that we have an offer of a million."

"Well, that is great, but it doesn't negate our need to talk even if just briefly in person. I can be at your cabin in an hour."

"You are very persuasive Mark. Come on out. I look forward to seeing you."

"I am on my way."

Rick told Mary, "I am sorry. I was not able to put his visit off."

"It is no problem Rick. I may even take Bart for a walk."

Mark drove up and Rick was at the doorway to meet him. They shook hands and Rick invited him to come in.

Rick said, "Let us sit here in the living room."

Mark asked, "Is this the bear that attacked you?"

"Yes Mark, sometime I will tell you all about it."

"Rick I want to buy your mine, but I would like to have something else to go with it. It is your cabin."

"I haven't put my cabin up for sale."

"I know, but combining it with the mine would be a plus for me. What kind of a price would you think would be reasonable for the cabin?"

"I hadn't thought about it. If I had to throw out a figure I would say one hundred and seventy five thousand. But, you know, I have not said that I would sell it."

"Very well, here is what I will offer: One million for the mine property including the claim, the mine, and legal right of way access. In addition, the furnished cabin for one hundred and fifty thousand dollars. This will be a cash transaction to be completed upon your return from North Dakota, within a two month time period from the date we sign the contract."

"Mark, you have completely taken me by surprise. I had no idea that you were interested in the cabin. I have built this cabin pretty much by myself with some help from friends. I didn't know whether to keep it for a summer cabin or to finish it off for year round living."

"Here is another option for you Rick. My word is good and I will stand by it. I would like to have your answer though before you leave so that we can get the contract drawn up."

"I am pretty much speechless Mark. Of course I will need to talk it over with Joel."

"That is fine Rick. Thank you for seeing me when you were so busy."

They shook hands and Mark left.

Mary and Bart returned from their walk and Rick told her what had happened.

Mary asked, "What will you do?"

"I don't know. I will need to talk it over with your folks."

Rick picked up his phone and called Joel. Joel answered and Rick said, "Mark came out to see me. I need to talk with you and Jane. Would it be ok if we came to see you right now?"

"Certainly, Rick, come on down."

They arrived at the Post. Rick parked and they walked in. They went to the living room where Rick told them what Mark had said.

Joel asked, "How do you feel about selling your cabin?"

Rick answered, "At first, I was shocked and totally against it. Then I reconsidered. With you two selling the Post and thinking of moving to a warmer climate it seemed like a reasonable idea to consider."

Joel asked, "What do you think changed his mind regarding the price of the mine?"

"Two things, first, I told him that we had an offer for a million. Second, his corporation will buy both properties, thus he doesn't personally have to pay anything for the use of the cabin. This is a big personal financial bonus of one hundred and fifty thousand to him."

Jane asked, "How did you arrive at the price for your cabin?"

"I just pulled the price of one hundred and seventy five thousand out of the air. He countered with one fifty."

Mary commented, "I am not a part of this but I do have comments. First, Mark's offer sounds very good. Not only is the amount good, but it is a clean deal with no concerns about financing. Second, what about the kids?"

Joel said, "That is a good question. We will have to sleep on these options."

Rick said, "By the way Joel, we may as well send the excavator back. I will be gone for two or three weeks, and who knows if it will be needed again."

Jane remarked, "Let's take a break from this heavy thinking and get some lunch. Will you help me Mary?"

"Of course I will."

After lunch Rick and Mary said goodbye and drove up the trail.

Rick said, "One item would remain from the sale to Mark. It would be the property that we bought to insure a legal right of way. That legal right of way will be needed for Mark, but the property will still be owned by Joel and me to do with as we choose."

Mary asked, "What could you do with it?"

"We could build a cabin, or sell the property."

When they arrived at the cabin, Mary took a nap and Rick resumed work on his articles. When Mary got up from her nap she let Rick continue with his work. When it came close to dinner time she began preparing dinner.

Before long the good aroma of dinner reached Rick. He put aside his work and joined Mary in the kitchen. As usual he put his arms around her and kissed her. She turned around hugged and kissed him.

Rick commented, "That good aroma drew me to your arms. I love you."

Mary said, "I am preparing the last of what I brought along for dinner tonight."

Rick told her, "I love your cooking."

After dinner they walked along the river, holding hands as they walked and talked. One item that was off the list to discuss was the mine sale. That was being held until tomorrow.

When they returned they sat together in the living room. They spent the evening in their usual way by talking, hugging and kissing.

It had been an emotionally trying day so it was not long before they went to bed.

After breakfast in the morning Rick called Joel. "Have you made a decision Joel? I am in favor of selling to Mark, but I am concerned about the kids."

"I agree with you Joel. I thought of how we could help Stewart and Alice. After our sale with Mark has been completed we can give our sluice box and other equipment to them. How does that sound to you?"

"Excellent idea Rick, I would feel good about doing that."

"We will need to have a sales contract prepared. Do you believe that the realtor that we have been working with could do that?"

"I don't know why not. He is familiar with all the property that is involved. He handled all the sale transactions on each of the properties."

"Since I heard directly from Mark what he wants in the contract, I will call the realtor and give the details to him. Would that be alright with you?"

"Absolutely, go ahead."

Rick called the realtor. He gave him the details and read off the name of Mark's corporation from the card that Mark had given to him. Rick wanted a down payment of twenty percent for each property at signing. He reminded him to include both his and Joel's names as the sellers of the mine property, and only Rick's name on his property. He told him that he wanted to have the contract ready for signing by all parties tomorrow at the Trading Post. Closing was to be within two months of tomorrow's date. He asked to be called when the contract was completed. He also suggested that if a witness would be needed that the realtor should bring one along.

They said goodbye and hung up.

Rick began to work on his articles and to polish the talk that he was to give to a club.

Just before noon the realtor called. He read the contract to Rick. Rick made certain that all that Mark wanted was in the contract, including the legal right away, the claim to the mine and the furnished cabin and property. The price for the mine property was to be one million dollars, payable to Joel and Rick. The price of Rick's cabin and property was to be one hundred and fifty thousand dollars payable to Rick.

Rick asked for the signing to be done at the Trading Post at four p.m. today. He said that he would contact the buyer and Joel.

Rick called Mark and reported, "I have taken steps to have a contract drawn up with the details just as you wanted. The realtor will be glad to read the entire document to you if you will call him. I have asked that a twenty percent down payment be included at signing of each sales contract. We are due to meet at the Trading Post at four p.m. today for the signing. If changes are made after you call the realtor, please call me. You have the card that I gave to you from the realtor. Is that ok with you?"

"Yes it is. Thank you for acting so promptly. I know that you have a very tight schedule."

"Thank you, Mark, now that I have had time to absorb all that you had to say, I feel very good about what we are doing. I look forward to seeing you at four p.m. this afternoon."

They said goodbye.

Rick called Joel and gave him the details. Joel was pleased and said that the dining room would be ready for the signing.

At four p.m. they met. The realtor brought a witness. The realtor was a notary. Mark and Rick and Joel each took their time in reading the contract. No corrections needed to be made. The contract was signed by the three principals, and witnessed and notarized. The down payment checks were given to the realtor to be held in escrow. The realtor and the witness said goodbye. Joel brought forth a bottle of champagne and they toasted to their proposed sale.

Jane and Mary were invited to join them for a glass of champagne.

They all laughed, talked and congratulated each other. Then they said goodbye and Mark left.

Rick offered, "Let us all go out to dinner to celebrate our signing."

They did, and had a great time.

CHAPTER XLIII

It was their last day together before Rick needed to leave. He had told Mary that he would work on his articles until noon. The afternoon and evening would be theirs.

After breakfast he worked, and by noon felt that he was well prepared.

During lunch Rick asked what Mary would like to do for the rest of the day.

"I enjoy walking and canoeing. I would like to walk to the lake once more and have one more canoe ride. This time, could we canoe to the north and avoid the rapids?"

"Of course, let's walk first, and then you can rest while we are canoeing. By the way, how are you feeling today?"

"I feel better each day. We will see how the body holds up with our outdoor activities today."

Rick got his armament and his knapsack. In the knapsack he had a bottle of water, some snacks and a biscuit for Bart. He also had a blanket.

Mary was ready and they set out up the trail. At the split tree they headed east and followed the trail to the lake. As they walked along he thought to himself,

'Are Joel and I going to be responsible to maintain the trail in its current condition?'

He had not thought to put something in the contract regarding that point. He didn't think that any mining would be done before next spring. If necessary he could get Pete and/or Al to take care of it.

They walked to the spring, and then to the waterfall. They walked the length of the stream and around the lake. Upon returning to the waterfall Mary looked for shiny objects but didn't find any.

Rick put the blanket down and they sat on it. Mary loved the waterfall. She had brought her camera and took some pictures.

"Do you think that we could come back here sometimes after the sale is completed?"

"I would have to get permission from Mark first, but I doubt if he would object."

After resting, Rick brought out his snacks and water. As they ate, Bart came by and was given his biscuit.

Mary said that she was ready and they walked back to the cabin. Rick replenished his supply of snacks and water. He got the canoe, life jackets, and motor out, and took them to the dock. They got in and motored north. They soon got to the split tree.

Rick speculated, "That would be a nice site for a cabin with a dock, south of the trail to the lake."

"Are you thinking of doing that?"

"No. The possibility just occurred to me as we passed by. At the moment, I am thinking that it would be best to put that property up for sale."

They saw an elk, which was unusual. There were many birds, some rabbits and squirrels.

Mary took pictures, talking and laughing about the beautiful animals.

They continued north for a time, and then Rick steered to the side of the river. He tied the canoe to a branch and got the snacks and water out of his knapsack. As they ate they watched for birds and other animals.

He untied the line. They turned south and drifted lazily down the river.

Mary exclaimed, "I love this canoeing, and being with you. I also like a slow laid back kind of day without the pressures of work."

"I am enjoying it too. If you were not with me, I would need to have a task to accomplish. You help me to really relax."

They returned to the cabin.

Rick asked Mary how she felt.

"I feel good. The walk got me moving, and the canoeing got me rested. I am ready to go again."

"Where shall we go?"

"Let us walk south along the river. I want to get as much exposure to this place as possible in the little time that we have left."

"That is fine with me. I have grown to love this location. It will be difficult to leave, but there will be a new adventure waiting for us just after the closing. How much longer do you think it will take to complete the inventory?"

"It is difficult to say. There are so many little things. They take as much time as a big item like a chain saw. My guess would be a week or maybe two. Mom is making good progress also."

Before they got to the bears feeding area, they stopped to rest. Rick put the blanket on the ground. They sat and munched on the snacks and had a drink of water. Then they returned to the cabin. Mary took a nap.

Rick walked in, and around, the cabin looking to see if anything more needed to be done. He thought to himself, 'I would like to take the bear hide. I hope Mark doesn't consider that to be a furnished item.'

Mary came out from her nap. She stretched and smiled. "I feel good," she said.

"We have been quite active today, and you are feeling good. It looks like you have totally recuperated."

Rick then suggested, "Since it will be our last dinner here, at least until I return; what would you think of a salmon dinner cooked outside?"

"That has become one of my favorite meals. I will prepare the vegetables if you will get the fish."

"That sounds like a good deal to me. It won't take long for me to catch and clean a fish. Please tell me ten or fifteen minutes before we need to begin cooking the fish. In the meantime, I will make a fire. Is there anything that you need help with?"

"No, it will be ok. It is still a little early to eat so take your time. I will let you know fifteen minutes in advance."

Rick got his fire wood and placed it in the usual spot. He waited to light it until he was called.

In about one half hour Mary gave him the green light to get started. He lit the fire, then took his gear and began to fish. He liked to fish from the dock. He threw two fish back before he caught a smaller one. It was cleaned at riverside.

They ate at the picnic table, using the paper plates. Rick knew that it would be quite a while before he had fresh salmon. He paid attention to the delightful flavor of the fish and vegetables. Mary still had marshmallows left. They toasted them over the fire. It was an excellent dinner, and one that neither of them could have enjoyed this way, by themselves.

Rick fed Bart and they walked along the river. They returned to the table and enjoyed the view. As dusk came the fire turned to embers. It grew dark and the stars appeared. They enjoyed the beauty and finally went indoors

They sat in the living room close together. Each realized that by tomorrow this time Rick would be in North Dakota. Although Rick had parted many times before, from his other girlfriends, this was different. He felt a deeper love for Mary. It was late, and they went to bed.

CHAPTER XLIV

They packed the car and drove to the Trading Post. It was midmorning on Sunday.

Joel and Jane greeted them and took Mary's things into her room. Jane helped her to put things away.

Joel and Rick went into the store. Joel got coffee for them and they sat to talk.

"How is the inventory coming along Joel?"

"It is going along quite well. I believe that another two weeks will be needed on the inventory. I have been working on the books while Mary was with you. That may take another week."

"That sounds good. I suppose that you have cut back on ordering new merchandise."

"Yes, I have also sent notes to my regular customers to let me know specifically what they will need for the winter. I haven't had any replies yet. Of course, those without mail delivery will not let me know before they come in."

"It looks like this would be a good time to sign up with a realtor to list your property and merchandise for sale."

"You had mentioned using a commercial agent. I don't know one personally, but I know of two companies that sell commercial properties. I will give both of them a call and see which one I like. You are right, now is the time to contact them."

"Commercial real estate usually takes longer than residential real estate to sell. We were just very lucky in being able to find buyers by ourselves for the mine. Do you have any idea what your property is worth?"

"Not really. I have five acres and some of it fronts on the river. I get mail, Fed X and UPS delivery. I also have TV and phone service. The major stores deliver to me. In the house I have bathrooms, running water, a fireplace, and central heat. Some of these are unusual this far north. I don't even know what to guess about the value."

"Well Joel, the realtor will get data for you showing what other similar properties are asking, and what similar properties have sold for in the past. The difficulty will be in finding similar properties. My guess would be in the neighborhood of at least three hundred thousand for the property. You will know more about the merchandise value once you have completed the inventory. You probably will not be able to get retail value for the merchandise since you plan to sell it as a package. I suggest that it will be helpful to get a total of your costs for the merchandise as well as a total, including your markup. That way you will know what is the minimum you need to get in order to at least break even."

Jane and Mary came in and said that lunch would be ready in about one half hour.

Mary sat on the floor and Bart immediately went to her. Bart wagged and kissed her face when she hugged him. They had formed a close bond.

Rick asked Jane, "I know that you have been working to improve the appearance of the cabin and property, would you give me a tour?"

"Of course Rick. Thanks for asking."

She went through the house pointing out items that replaced old ones, carpets that had been cleaned, floral decorations that had been added, and many other touches that made the cabin more appealing. Then they went outside. She pointed out new plantings of shrubs and flowers. She also had all woodwork around the windows repainted, as well as the Trading Post sign. New gravel had been brought to the driveway.

Rick told her, "Those are excellent improvements. I am certain that it will make a difference."

Jane thanked him and said that it was time for lunch.

That afternoon Rick made a few calls, letting friends and business associates know that he was returning to North Dakota. He called his photographer and arranged to meet in two days to finish work on his articles. He called the sports magazine and arranged an appointment for the following day.

He called the Brothers to say goodbye. They offered to keep an eye on his cabin.

Joel and Jane, and Rick and Mary played cards as they talked.

Rick suggested, "Let's talk about where each of us might want to go, or do, once the properties have been sold."

Mary said, "I have never traveled, and I would like to see new places for a while. I would like to be in a warm climate and, near the water. It doesn't matter if it is a lake or a river, or a bay. I want to canoe and swim."

Joel offered his dream, "I too want to be in a warm climate. Some time spent visiting various places might help me to decide on a location. As I get older, I want to be near to doctors, a hospital and grocery stores."

Jane commented, "I like what both of you have said. If I could combine them it would meet all of my dreams."

Rick said, "I too like a combination of what all of you have said. I would like to continue writing stories. I am not sure about continuing TV work. Although it pays well, it is taking a good deal of time and limiting my ability to go where and when I wish. I need to think about that. I don't believe that I am ready to settle down to one place at this time."

They went out to dinner. When they returned Rick and Mary went for a walk. The summer weather was perfect. It was a beautiful night. As they walked hand in hand they were quiet for quite a while; each thinking that this was their last evening together for perhaps several weeks.

Finally Rick broke the silence, "I love you Mary. I will miss you. I will call you when I can. Things have gone well for us, and for your folks. When I return we will need to talk and make our plans. We will be busy, but I believe that all will be well."

"I feel sad about your leaving, but I too believe that all will be well. Dad and I will be busy working on the inventory. I will look forward to your calling me when you can. I love you."

Later they returned to the cabin. Everyone said goodnight and they all went to bed.

Rick packed his things in the SUV. The parting was difficult. Mary cried but Rick told her that he would call and return close to three weeks. Rick wished for Joel's success in finding a good realtor and then a buyer. With hugs and kisses goodbyes were said and Rick drove to North Dakota.

CHAPTER XLV

Upon arriving at his home, he worked with the photographer and finalized his articles. He called Art, the editor of the sports magazine, and asked to have a conference call with the sponsors and Steve, the TV producer on the next day when he met with Art.

Art welcomed Rick. Rick handed over six stories. At one story each month, Rick would have time to do what he had in mind.

The conference call was placed.

After greetings Rick explained to the sponsors, "I have very much enjoyed making the shows, and working with you. Events have changed my goals, and I would like to discontinue the once weekly shows in the near future. I am selling my property in Alaska, as well as my gold mine. I have enjoyed the Alaskan adventure immensely. I want to begin a new adventure, and the TV shows restrict my other interests. You all have been great to work with and I value your friendship. I have prepared a dozen shows for filming. I have two or three weeks, at the most, to film them. These shows, if Steve can give me filming time, will give you time to find a replacement or what ever you wish to do. I want to continue writing stories. I simply need a more flexible time schedule."

They all expressed their disappointment. Ted, the book publisher asked to have a private talk with Rick. They all said that the shows had been a success and profitable to them. Rick agreed to call Ted later in the day. Art said that he would set up a conference call to all of them in a day or so after they had time to consider what they would like to do. They all said goodbye and the call was ended.

Rick told Art that he wanted to write stories for the sports magazine. He asked for some flexibility in topics and said that he might wish to visit exotic locations outside of the US.

Art responded, Rick, you do great work and as long as you have an article for me once a month I will give you the flexibility.

"I do not have a list of new topics or locations. If some of them require more time or special transportation, will you consider taking care of the additional expenses Art?"

"Rick, I like your word, 'consider'. Of course on each individual story I will consider the value of the story and the expense. I do not envision reimbursing you for a trip to Africa for a single story, but I will work with you."

Steve called and Art handed the phone to Rick.

"Rick, I will do my best to give you two days a week for filming. You should be able to film all twelve episodes within your three week period. You may start tomorrow morning if you wish."

"Thanks Steve, I will see you in the morning."

Art and Rick went to lunch. Art told him that he had read the grizzly attack article that Rick had sent to him. He said that it was a real winner.

Rick said, "You will find an article about a cattle ranch in Alaska. It is an example of what I meant by needing some flexibility in topics. The cattle ranch is not technically a sports topic."

"I will read that article with interest. I will pay particular attention to what you have pointed out."

They continued their conversation during lunch and then said goodbye.

Rick called Jean and told her that he was at home and would be here for a few weeks. He asked if there was a possibility that they could have dinner together one evening.

Jean said, "Just by coincidence, I will be in town for one day only next week. It will be next Wednesday."

"Please call me to confirm when and at what hotel I can come to ick you up."

Jean said she would and that she loved him. They said goodbye.

Rick went home and called Mary.

"Mary, I am just calling to let you know that I arrived without a problem, and met with the sports magazine editor. I also talked with the sponsors and told them I was ending the TV shows in the near future."

"I am certain that they understood, but were sorry to hear that you were not going to continue. We all miss you, and I love you."

After talking a bit more they said goodbye.

Rick reviewed the two stories that he would be filming tomorrow.

He and Bart went to the dog park to give Bart some exercise. On the way home he stopped at a deli and picked up items for dinner.

Rick fed Bart, and then himself before taking Bart for a long walk. As they walked, Rick thought to himself, 'That was a big change that I made with the sponsors, but nothing ventured, nothing gained. I still have the sports magazine account and the pending sales in Alaska.'

That evening Rick called Ted.

Ted told Rick, "I was sorry to hear about your change of plans, but I am certain that all will work out well. Your book sales are booming. I wanted to suggest to you Rick that you consider writing a new book. With the success of WILDERNESS, you will have immediate acceptance of the new book."

"Thank you, Ted. At this time so much is going on, I need to take time to finish up the filming and the property sales. Then I need to get my bearings and set my new course. I know the direction that I want to take, but I will need to fill in the details as soon as I catch up with the current affairs."

"I understand, and will be here to help you when I can."

Shortly, they said goodbye.

In the next two weeks Rick completed filming of eight episodes.

The next day Jean called and told him where she was staying. He agreed to meet her at six p.m.

Rick picked her up. They kissed, and said that they loved each other. They went to a restaurant that they had been to before. The each had a drink and ordered dinner. Rick told her what had happened in Alaska and what he had decided regarding the TV shows. Jean told Rick about her job and her new friends.

After eating they ordered coffee and dessert.

Rick explained to Jean, "I am making a number of changes. I have told you of the sales in Alaska. That adventure is now almost completed. I have also told you of the change in my TV shows. Now I need to tell you Jean, that I love you and I want to be your friend always. If you ever need my help, just let me know. Our relationship will change however. From now on it will be platonic. I will love you as a brother if you will let me. I am going to ask a girl that I met in Alaska to marry me. I do not know what her answer will be but I want to be candid with you and to let you know what is going on."

"I don't know what to say. We have been as close as a man and a woman could be for several years. I thought that you wanted to remain a bachelor."

"That is true Jean. It was always my intention to remain single, but I had a change of heart."

"Take me to the motel Rick."

He took her to the motel and escorted her to the door. He put his arm around her, but she pulled away, and crying went in and shut the door.

Rick called through the door, "Jean, I am sorry."

There was no response and Rick left.

Rick was upset too, not that he would have said something different, but that she was upset.

He went home.

Later she called, "Rick, I am sorry that I didn't handle that better. I love you, and I will accept your friendship as a brother."

"Thank you Jean. I love you too. Call me if you need my help in any way."

They said goodbye. Rick was relieved.

Rick called Joel and suggested, "I have one more week to go here Joel. Would you see if you could set the closing up for the following week please?"

Joel replied, "Yes, I will do that. How are things going with you?"

"They are going as planned. I have filmed eight shows. I will be done after four more next week. I told them that I would not do additional shows."

"I got a good realtor after interviewing two of them. He was not able to get sales data on Trading Posts or similar stores for a period of up to five years ago. He thought as you did that the cabin and the five acres should be listed for at least three hundred thousand. We set it at three hundred and fifteen thousand. He suggested that I try to return some merchandise to the manufacturer for the wholesale price that I paid. Do you have any suggestions?"

"You might advertise a clearance sale. Even if you just get a bit more than the wholesale price you won't have to pay to ship the merchandise back. Your regular customers may want to stock up for the right price."

"Good idea, I will give it a try. I believe that I will send a sales flyer to everyone within my sales area."

They talked some more and then Rick asked to talk with Mary. Mary and Rick talked and then said goodnight.

The next week Rick filmed four more shows. Steve told him that they were very good. He wished Rick well and they said goodbye.

He talked with his attorney and had the prenup prepared.

Rick packed his SUV and hooked up his flatbed trailer. He and Bart got in and drove to Alaska.

CHAPTER XLVI

Rick arrived at the Trading Post. He and Bart got out. Bart ran around happily. Joel had heard the car and came out to meet him. They shook hands. They were happy to be with each other. Rick called Bart and they went in the store.

Joel told Rick, "I sent out the flyers and got some sales that I wouldn't have had without it. The inventory has been completed and the books are ready for review. No one has come to see the property as yet, but we are prepared for their arrival. Let's go talk with our ladies."

They found Jane and Mary in the kitchen preparing dinner. Smiles, hugs and kisses were shared and happiness enveloped the room.

Mary said, "I am so glad that you are back, Rick. Tell us about your last three weeks."

The main item is that I have completed my filming, and they have shows to run for the next twelve weeks. I told them that I would not do any more filming. I handed in six articles, and at one a month I have free time off coming up. I will continue to write stories for the magazine. I feel relieved that all that work has been completed."

Jane told Rick, "Your timing is perfect. We will have dinner in thirty to forty five minutes. You have time to wash up and then have a glass of wine. This time it will be white wine."

After washing up Rick joined Joel in the living room. Joel gave him a glass of wine and offered him a seat.

Rick commented, "It is good to be back. It is also good to get out of that car. Those hours of driving are tiring."

Mary came in, and Joel poured her a glass of wine.

Rick asked Mary, "I have been thinking that I need to clear out my garage. Would you go along with me tomorrow?"

"Of course, I will pack a lunch for us."

"Good, I have the trailer to load with the canoe and other items I plan to take to North Dakota."

Jane came in and Joel poured her wine.

Joel told Rick, "I called the realtor and Mark. Closing will be at the title office three days from now at ten a.m. It looks like all the details have been taken care of."

Rick suggested to Joel, "When we go to closing, would we be able to stop by the bank and close out our account?"

"Good idea. We can ask them to give us each a cashier's check for half of the balance."

They all helped bring food items to the dining room table. Joel refilled their wine glasses and said grace. Fresh salmon that Joel and Mary had caught this morning was for dinner.

Rick said, "I haven't had fresh salmon since I left here and I am looking forward to this fine meal."

After enjoying their meal, they all carried the remains to the kitchen. When the kitchen was back to normal they adjourned to the living room.

Rick asked, "When closing is completed I will no longer have a cabin. May I stay with you for a few days until I firm up my plan of action?"

"Of course, you don't even need to ask,"

"Thank you. When your property has been sold, I believe you indicated that you might like to visit warm locations to find a place that you might settle in."

"Yes. We are thinking of Arizona, and then Florida, as the first two choices."

"Have you decided what to do with your furniture?"

"Some of it we want to sell. We will be downsizing regardless of where we settle."

Jane added, "We have a problem however in that the furniture that we have, is not new. It is heavy, cold weather type furniture. It may not really be suitable for a beach side cottage in Florida."

Mary suggested, "Storing and shipping furniture is expensive, and probably is a pain in the neck. I would like to suggest that you sell all but prized personal possessions, and once you find where you wish to settle, buy exactly what you want."

Jane said, "I knew that you had a good head on your shoulders. I like your idea. What do you think Joel?"

"It has merit. We wouldn't have to decide what will be appropriate at a location that we haven't even seen. What we would get in terms of dollars for it would not matter. We have had the use of it all these years. We could even give some to charity."

Rick suggested, "The furniture might be used as a negotiating tool, to get the price you want when you have a buyer for your property."

Later Rick and Mary took Bart for a walk. They walked with arms interlocked, enjoying being with each other.

Rick said, "I can't wait for the closing to be completed. I loved that place, but now that I have made the decision to sell, I would like to get it over and move on to other things."

"Do you know what the other things are?"

"Not completely. Once the closing is completed I will get things moving. Tomorrow will be a day of preparation. Although I will be clearing out the garage, I do not want to forget the grizzly rug."

They assured each other of their love, and returned to the cabin.

"You know, my sale prices will apply to you also Rick. If there is anything that is in the inventory that you want let us put it aside."

Rick said, "Thanks. When we get back from my cabin let us go through the store to see if anything is there that I will need."

It was getting late. They all said goodnight and went to bed.

After breakfast the next day, they went to the cabin. Rick opened the garage and began bringing out the canoe, outboard engine, pump and generator. There was also fishing gear, including the gill net. His wood working tools and other miscellaneous items were brought out last. Mary swept the floor as Rick finished loading the trailer. The garage was locked and they turned their attention to the cabin.

The first thing to be removed was the grizzly rug. Mary asked about the kitchen items. Rick replied that he was only going to take personal items. He found shaving gear in the bathroom and clothing items in the bedroom. These few items were taken to the SUV. The rest was left for Mark.

Mary asked if they could visit the lake and waterfall once more.

Rick said, "We can, but we will have to walk. I don't know how clear the trail is, and with the trailer attached, I don't want to have to back up."

Mary said, "I'm ready to go if you are."

Rick locked the SUV, and with Bart leading the way, they made their way to the lake. It was all so quiet and serene. They sat by the waterfall, and listened to the splash and the gurgle of water. They had their photos from other times, but it was good to be there in person.

After a while they returned to the cabin.

Mary said, "I'm getting hungry. Do you think that we could stay here and go to the Post tomorrow?"

"We can do that, but the only food that we have are crackers. We need to either catch a fish or I would need to find some kind of small game."

Mary said, "Let me catch and cook the fish, you take care of the fire and the crackers."

Good idea, it gives us one more evening to enjoy this place while it is still mine."

Mary said, "I will call Mom to let her know our plans.

Rick got the fire started while Mary fished. He liked the idea of staying here another night.

Mary threw large fish back as Rick had done. When she caught a smaller one she cleaned it and prepared it for cooking.

Rick had brought a cast iron skillet out for her. He pushed most of the wood off to the side, leaving a place for the skillet over embers.

They enjoyed the dinner. They would never have fresher and tastier fish. They didn't have marshmallows, but it didn't matter. All that really mattered was that they were together.

Bart had a nice piece of salmon for his dinner.

They walked by the river holding hands and singing together. When they returned the skillet was cool enough. They cleaned it and returned it to the kitchen.

Sitting at the picnic table they watched it get dark and the stars came out. To them, it was the kind of romantic evening that they would remember. It began to get chilly and they went indoors and sat on the couch. They hugged, kissed and murmured sweet nothings. It was time to go to bed.

CHAPTER XLVII

In the morning they drove to the Trading Post. Joel and Jane greeted them and asked if they had breakfast. Mary told them that they had not, since there was no food left in Rick's cabin. Rick told them about the nice sea food dinner that Mary had prepared last night.

Jane said, "We slept in, and we haven't had breakfast either. Come in and we will take care of that. Mary, will you help me?"

"Of course Mom, I am on my way."

Joel said to Rick, "Stewart called last evening and asked if we would finance him. I don't believe that he was able to find financing himself."

"What did you tell him?"

"I told him that we already had a contract, but if it fell through that we would contact him."

"That was good. I brought along the generator, pump and hose. I would like to leave them with you for Stewart after our closing is completed."

"Good, let us unload them right now from your trailer. We will put it by the sluice box."

Jane called, "Breakfast is ready, come and get it."

Joel said, "We better wait until after breakfast to unload."

It was a beautiful breakfast, just what Rick would have ordered.

Jane commented, "Mary has your number Rick. She told me what you would want to eat."

"She certainly does, and I love her for it."

After breakfast Joel and Rick unloaded the items for Stewart and Alice. They then walked through the store looking for items that Rick might want. Rick found a cooler that he could take on hunting and fishing trips that could be plugged into the cigarette lighter of his car.

It could be set to either keep items cool or warm. He also found sun glasses for Mary. He called her and asked her to pick the color.

Joel and Rick puttered around the store the rest of the morning until about noon, when Seth walked in the store. He was the mining expert that Joel and Rick had talked to about managing their mine.

They all exchanged greetings.

Seth said, "I got your flyer about your sale. Why are you having the sale?"

"Well Seth, Jane and I are planning to retire. I felt that it was a good idea to do some downsizing."

Seth said, "Is that all there is to it, some downsizing?"

"Not quite, I also plan to sell the Trading Post."

"Well, finally you speak up. I hate it when people beat around the bush."

"Sorry Seth, I didn't mean to hold back."

"How much do you want for the Post?"

"I am asking three hundred and fifteen thousand."

"What about the merchandise?"

"I can give you a good deal of—"

Seth interrupted. "There you go again, beating around the bush. How much do you want for the stock?

"Seth, I will let you have it for one hundred thousand. That is the wholesale value"

"Finally I got an answer."

"Are you interested in buying the Post, Seth?"

"I didn't walk up here just for the exercise. Let us see how good a salesman you are. Show me around and convince me that I should buy it."

"I will be glad to Seth. Let's start here in the store. First, I need to tell you that I draw my customers from a seventy-five mile radius. I have made a profit every year except one over the last ten years. In the store I have hardware, clothing, nonperishable food, fishing and hunting gear, and miscellaneous items like suntan lotion and mosquito spray. The fur trappers come here in the spring to sell their furs, and then they come in the fall to get their supplies. It is forty miles to get to a store from here, so this is where they come. The Native Village has about sixty people and they get their supplies from me. Do you have any questions about the store?"

"Joel, you're speaking my language now. My questions will come later when I examine your inventory list and your books. Show the cabin to me. Say Rick, you are looking good. What are you doing hanging around Joel?"

"We have been friends and mining partners for some years now."

"Good for you. I hear that Krazy Joe was sententensed to twenty years."

Rick said, "I'm real glad to hear it."

Joel said, "Let's go this way. I want you to say hello to my wife and daughter. Seth, this is my wife Jane and this is my daughter Mary."

"I am pleased to meet you", said Seth.

"Jane, please join us, Seth is interested in buying the Trading Post. I have shown him the store. Would you conduct the tour of the cabin?"

"Seth, this cabin is somewhat unusual in that it has all of the conveniences of a house in the city. Let's walk through and I will tell you about it as we walk. This is the living room. The grizzly is one that Rick shot. We have a nice fireplace, but you do not have to depend on it for heat. We have central heating. We have three bathrooms, all have running water. We have this large master bedroom, and three others including, a bunkroom that we let buyers use when it is too far for them to get home before dark. Everything is in good working order. Do you have any questions?"

"No, thank you. That was a good tour."

Joel said, "Let's go outside. I have a three car garage and a large shed for storing outdoor type merchandise. There are five acres to the property. There is no mortgage on it. The river front is about five hundred feet. There is a dock. The fishing is good. The exterior of the cabin, including the roof has been examined. No problems were found. The wood around the windows has been repainted as has the Trading Post sign. New gravel has been placed on the driveway. Do you have any questions?"

"Joel, once you get started you do a bang-up job. I don't have any questions about the physical property, but I want to know about financing."

"The property is listed with a realtor. He can tell you all about financing possibilities. I can have him call you or I can give his phone number to you. Which would you prefer?"

"I see you have your phone with you. Call him right now and ask him to come over here."

Joel called and said, "This is Joel. I have a man here who is interested in buying the Trading Post. He would like for you to come over here now to advise him on financing."

"I will be there in twenty minutes."

"He will be her in twenty minutes. Would you like to look outside some more, or would you like to come in for a cup of coffee?"

"I will take you up on the coffee."

They went into the store and Seth looked around while Joel made fresh coffee.

Rick asked Seth, "Do you know Phil and George? They have a fairly big operation just north of where our mine is."

"No, I don't know them."

"They trap furs for a living. They bring their furs here to sell them. I have been to their place and went with them when they were trapping. It is an interesting business."

Joel had the coffee ready and gave them both a cup. By the time they finished the coffee, the realtor arrived.

Joel said, "Rick and I will let you two talk. We will be in the kitchen when you are ready to talk with me again."

In the kitchen, Joel asked, "What do you think?"

"He is a straight forward man. If he says that he is interested, I would believe him."

Fifteen minutes later the realtor knocked on the kitchen door. He said, "Seth is ready to leave."

Joel and Rick went back into the store.

Joel said, "Thank you for coming Seth. If you have any questions or want to see anything again I will be happy to see you."

Seth said, "Thank you fellows, goodbye."

As Seth drove away Joel asked the realtor, "What do you think about him as a possible buyer?

"He is a straight forward talking man. He is interested I believe. He wants to think about it. If he comes back he will want to know more about the inventory and profit or loss information from your books. I believe that he has the cash for a good down payment. He will want to be certain that the income will give him a profit after the expenses. I have his phone number and he has mine. I will keep in touch."

He left.

They went back into the store. Jane and Mary came to find out what happened.

Joel said, "He is interested and will think about it."

Jane asked Rick, "What do you think about the possibilities that he will buy?"

Rick replied, "It is difficult to tell. He is not one to waste your time without being interested. What bothers me about figuring him out is that he does not seem like the type that would enjoy this kind of work. He is not in any way a sales type. Mining, engineering and supervising outdoor men is the type of work that I see him enjoying. His customers would know that they are dealing with an honest man. But many would be turned off by his abrupt manner. There is something more that is going on here that we don't know about. We will have to wait and see."

Joel commented, "Rick, I believe you are absolutely on target."

It was midmorning on the day before closing on the mine property and on Rick's property.

Rick's phone rang. It was the realtor. He reported, "Rick, early this morning I conducted the customary "walk through" of both properties. Mark was satisfied on all counts. All systems are on go for the closing at the title office tomorrow morning at ten a.m."

Rick replied, "Well done, thank you. We will see you tomorrow."

Joel's phone rang. It was the commercial realtor. "Joel, Seth wants to come to your place tomorrow at two p.m."

"Can you tell me any more than I knew when you left here last time?"

"Not really, he holds the cards close to his vest. I do believe that he would not waste your time. I gave him the finance information that he asked for. He will probably want to know more about the inventory and see if he can make a profit after paying expenses."

"Do the figures add up to you in away that shows he would make a profit?"

"It is pretty close Joel. We will have to wait to see how it looks to him."

Joel thanked him and said that he looked forward to seeing them tomorrow afternoon.

Rick and Joel shared what they had learned from the phone calls.

Joel mentioned to Rick, "We are going to be busy tomorrow. I would like to ask you to be in on the discussion with Seth. I have a hunch that this will be a difficult one."

"We are in this together. Of course I will be with you. I would like for us all, including Mark if he is willing, to celebrate tomorrow night at a nice restaurant. Would that be ok with you?"

"Sure thing, we will have a lot to celebrate."

"There is one more thing. I would like to ask Mary to marry me. My former girlfriends are no longer in the picture except as just friends. I also want you to know that I will ask Mary to sign a prenup. You may be aware that I have quite a bit of money, and I do not want that to influence her decision. May I have your blessings?"

"Of course. It has been a hope of Jane and I that this day would come. There is no one that I would rather have in the family than you."

"Thank you. Please don't say anything yet. I plan to take her to dinner the day after closing and ask her then."

After lunch they all sat in the living room. It seemed that the mine and Rick's property would close without a problem. The discussion therefore focused on the Trading Post and Seth.

Joel explained, "It appears that there will not be much room for profit for Seth considering the price we are asking and his finance costs and other expenses. We may have to back off a little if we want to make a deal with him."

Rick asked, "Is there any other way that you could reduce the inventory?"

"The flyer helped. The wholesalers will not take the merchandise back at what I paid for the items. My customers will not be coming to get supplies for another month or so. I do not see a way to further reduce inventory."

"One way or another it will all work out for the best. We will need to see what Seth has in mind." said Rick.

Rick called Mark, "Mark, this is Rick how are things going?"

"All is well. I checked the properties out this morning and everything looks good."

"Mark, I was wondering if you would have time to help us celebrate our closings tomorrow night at dinner."

"That is a great idea. Let's bring our ladies along as well. I know of a really great restaurant. We can discuss it and other options at closing."

"That is great. I look forward to seeing you in the morning."

They said goodbye.

Rick reported, "Mark likes the idea of dinner tomorrow night. He will bring his wife. He has in mind a really nice restaurant. We had better dress up for this dinner."

Jane commented, "Oh, good. It is so seldom that we get to dress up. We will have fun with this Mary."

Later they took Bart for a walk and then went to bed.

CHAPTER XLVIII

At last it was closing day. Rick took Bart for a walk. It was a beautiful day, and Rick was excited. When he returned, Mary had prepared breakfast. He came up behind her, put his arms around her and kissed her. Mary turned around and kissed him back.

At breakfast, Jane and Mary were excited for Joel and Rick. The gamble of buying the land and mining it had paid off.

Rick commented, "We must remember that we still own the land where the trail leads to the lake. Someday, we will need to decide what to do with it."

Joel responded, "So much is going on today that my mind will not cope with another item that is not already on the adgenda."

Rick told them, "I negotiated the fee for the realtor with him. He wanted six percent. I pointed out that he did not find the buyer, we did. Due to the size of the transaction he would get quite a bit in any event. He agreed on a three percent fee."

Joel commented, "That saved us quite a bit of money."

They got ready and drove to the title office. Mark and the realtor were there. The title company officer conducted the meeting.

The title officer said, "This will not take very long since it is a cash transaction. It will be mainly a signing of documents. We will deal with the lake mining property first."

All signing was completed and Rick and Joel each received a check for half of the purchase price, minus half of the relator fee and other minor charges.

Rick's property was next. Documents were signed. Rick received his check, less expenses. The keys were turned oveer to Mark.

The meeting ended. They all shook hands. Mark told Rick and Joel about the restaurant that he recommended. They agreed to meet there at six p.m. They shook hands again and departed.

On the way back they stopped at the bank and cancelled their joint business account. They each took away a cashier's check for half of the final balance.

Rick commented, "We are pulling in the dough today."

Lunch was ready when they returned to the cabin.

Joel laughed, and held up his checks. He said, "We are rich, thanks to Rick's finding those shiny little things by the waterfall and inviting me to be his partner. Thanks partner."

"You are welcome, and I got nice checks too."

As they ate lunch, Joel said to Mary, "I would like for you to join us when we talk with Seth regarding the inventory and the books. You have been with me all along on this and I will appreciate your help."

"I will be glad to Dad."

Seth arrived and brought someone along with him. The realtor, Sam arrived also.

Seth said, "This is my son Bill. If we are able to work things out, he will be handling the Trading Post. I will back him up, but other than helping him with the negotiations, I will not be involved except financially."

Greetings were made all around. Bill was outgoing, and told them about himself.

"I have been a fur trapper and a trader further north. I have wanted to be closer geographically to my dad. I had been in sales previously. I am forty five years old and look at this as a good opportunity for me if it should prove to be profitable. Before we look at the store, would it be possible for me to have a tour of the cabin and the property?"

Joel said, "Of course. My wife will give you a tour."

They left the store and Joel introduced Bill to Jane.

Jane said, "I am glad to meet you Bill, let me show you the cabin first, then we will go outside."

Jane gave him all the details of the cabin and the property. She showed the river frontage and the dock to him as well as pointing out the improvements that had been made. They then returned to the store.

Seth said, "Bill and I want to take another look at the inventory."

Joel and Mary showed them the inventory list along with the wholesale and marked up prices.

Bill commented, "We need to work the costs down somewhat in order to produce a profit after expenses. I am wondering how much of your stock is older than say five years. I saw a baby crib and a stroller. Do you know how long you have had them Joel?"

Mary replied, "I have the invoice information here. They are five years old."

"That is the sort of thing that would be helpful Mary. If we could identify all the stock that is five years old or older, we can see what the value of that list would be."

Mary replied, "Give me a little time and I will see if I can produce a list."

Bill said, "Thank you Mary. If I can help, just call me."

Seth and Bill walked through the store looking at the inventory items.

Mary came back to them in twenty minutes with a list of items. They were mostly small items, but they totaled about ten thousand dollars.

Bill said, "Thank you Mary. If you will excuse us I would like to talk with my Dad."

Joel, Mary and Rick withdrew and shut the door. In about five minutes Bill knocked on the door. They returned to the store.

Bill stated, "We have talked it over and told the realtor what we can handle. He will tell you what we have in mind."

The realtor said, "They want your property, but they need to make a profit. Here is their proposal; they will offer two hundred and seventy five thousand for the property. They will ask that the price for the inventory be reduced by ten thousand because of the old stock. They have financing approved for the amounts that I have related to you."

Rick asked, "If the sellers agreed, when would the buyers be in a position to close?"

Seth replied, "The bank will want to meet with the sellers to verify inventory and earnings. If that could be done promptly, closing could be within thirty days."

Rick asked the realtor, "If an agreement can be negotiated, will the buyers be able to provide a substantial binder at agreement signing?"

The realtor, Seth and Bill all said yes.

Joel said, "We will need to talk this over. We will get back to you by phone later today. Thank you for coming. We are glad to meet you Bill."

They all said goodbye and the three of them left.

They went to the living room.

Joel said, "You had Seth figured out pretty good Rick. I would like each of you to tell me what you think that we should do."

Jane replied, "Sell it for what they ask. We need to retire."

Mary offered, "My vote is to sell also."

Rick said, "There are no other offers. There are things that you can do, and others that you can consider. One of the things that you can do is to negotiate a three percent fee with the realtor. Another thing that you can consider is to offer your furniture and furnishings at some dollar value, instead of a reduction of either the sales price or the inventory. One other item that is important is the down payment. It must be substantial. You will be taking the property off the market. You cannot risk losing the time. You will need to have the contract indicate that the down payment is nonrefundable, once the bank has approved the loan. You might ask for closing to be within thirty days after the loan has been approved."

"Wow Rick, I am glad that you are on my side," said Joel, "What amount would you say would be substantial?"

"I would ask for thirty thousand."

Joel asked Jane, "What do you think the furniture and furnishings are worth?

Jane answered, "Perhaps only five thousand as used furniture. I imagine that it would be difficult to find a buyer at any price unless they were going to live here and didn't already have furniture."

Joel asked, "Do you have an opinion regarding the furniture Rick?"

"I believe that Jane is correct. I would not let the furniture be a problem for the sale. It would be worthwhile to ask the realtor to ask Bill if he would be interested."

Joel said, "I will make some notes as to what you all have said and then I will call Sam. Rick, please stay nearby in the event that he has a question we have not discussed."

Joel called and made each point to the realtor. The realtor said that he would call him back.

Later the realtor called back. Bill offered three thousand for the furniture and furnishings. Joel agreed.

Still later Sam called again. The other items that Joel had asked for were approved. Sam agreed to the three percent fee. A contract would be drawn up and delivered to Joel and Jane tomorrow.

Jane stated, "Now that that is done. Let us remember that we are due at the restaurant at six p.m. It is now five p.m."

They arrived at the restaurant at six p.m.

Mark met them just inside the door. He said, "I reserved a room for us, please follow me. He introduced his wife, Joan. Joel introduced Jane, Mary and Rick. Joan, Mary and Jane immediately found a friendship among themselves. Joan was about half way age-wise between Jane and Mary. They all related so well.

Mark explained, "I own a portion of this restaurant, so we can stay as long as we want. Please have whatever you want. This dinner celebration is on me."

Everyone thanked him.

The waiters came in with champagne, and finger food.

After they were seated, Joan said to Rick, "I have heard that you had an encounter with a bear. Please tell us about it."

"Actually, I had two grizzly bear encounters. I don't want to bore you all, so I will just touch on the highlights of each."

Rick told them of each incident.

Mark said, "My word man, you are brave."

Joan remarked, "I know what you say is true, but I didn't know that one had to take such dangerous chances to get food to eat."

Mark and Joan expressed their amazement that he survived the injuries in the second incident

Rick said, "Let's lighten up and toast to our successful closings, and to our friendship."

They all lifted their glasses in the toast.

The waiters entered and took their orders. Their glasses were refilled and the conversation flourished.

After dinner Rick took Mark outside for a few minutes. Rick said, "Tomorrow I am going to ask Mary to marry me. If she accepts, would you permit us to be married in front of the cabin?"

Mark replied, "Of course. I want to have photos taken on the property anyhow. I will have the photographer cover your wedding as well."

"Thank you, Mark. I would like to invite you and Joan to the wedding."

"I certainly appreciate that. Let me know the details if it all turns out as you anticipate."

"Will do."

They returned to the room. Conversation continued. Later they all thanked Mark and Joan and said goodbye.

CHAPTER XLVIX

After breakfast Joel called the bank and made an appointment for ten a.m. to verify the inventory and records of profit and loss. Joel asked Rick and Mary to go with him.

They arrived at ten in the morning, and the banker greeted them. He knew Joel, and was introduced to Mary and Rick.

The banker said, "I need to see a summary of your inventory in terms of dollars. I also need to review your books to verify that sufficient profit has been made to justify the loan."

Rick and Mary guided the banker over the documents. Within fifteen minutes the banker was satisfied.

He said, "You have confirmed what Seth, Bill and Sam have told me. I do not see any problems. Thank you for coming in so promptly. It is good to see you again Joel, and good to meet you Mary and Rick."

They returned home, pleased at the banker's report.

They had lunch and then Rick said to Mary, "I would like to take you to a dress up dinner tonight. Would that be ok with you?"

Mary said, "I would love to go to a dress up dinner with you tonight, thank you."

Jane said, "I am marking thirty days from today as the last possible date for closing on my calendar."

Rick offered, "Someone will come out to survey the property and someone else will come out to appraise its value. I am certain that all will come out well, but you need to know that those things, as well as the loan approval, need to be done before closing.

They talked until four thirty and then Mary excused herself to get ready for dinner.

Rick took Bart for a walk and then he showered and changed to a suit.

Mary was ready about five thirty and they all said that she looked beautiful.

Joel offered the use of his car since Rick's still had the trailer hooked up.

Rick chose a restaurant that they both liked. He asked for a quiet corner table that had some privacy from most of the patrons. There was soft music and Mary said that it was most romantic.

Rick ordered a nice wine. They ordered dinner and talked while they ate their appetizers. The meals arrived. Rick had ordered a steak, and Mary ordered lobster.

They enjoyed the food and the wine. They had dessert and then they danced. After dancing Rick ordered champagne.

Rick said, "Mary, I want to talk very seriously with you. I would like to ask you to marry me, but before I do, I want to be very candid with you, to let you know what you would be getting if you said yes."

"Before I came to Alaska, and until just recently I had two girlfriends that I loved. We were as close as most married people are, except that the relationship was part time. One decided that she wanted to be married, and I did not. She married another person. The other one I loved also, as I did the first one. Last week I told her that I was going to ask you to marry me, but I didn't know what the answer would be. I came to Alaska to live in the wilderness and to write a book. That has been done, but in the process I had a marvelous adventure and found three gems. The first was gold, the second was your parents and finally I found the third gem. It was you. I did not start out to find the three gems. I want to continue to have adventures, and I don't know where they will lead me; or if they will be successful. But, I am not ready to find a nice little house with a wife and a recliner and live the rest of my life that way."

"Financially, I am secure, as your folks are, and as you are. Now, you have your savings that you told me were ample. In time you will have Social Security, and someday you will inherit your parent's fortune which will probably be in excess of a million dollars. If you decide to marry me I would want a "prenup". We would not want for money. It is my intention to continue to write stories. I don't know where they would take me, but I would want you to be with me always. Do you have any questions Mary?"

"No Rick."

Rick got down on one knee and asked Mary, "Will you marry me?"

"Yes Rick. I love you and I will marry you and be by your side to the end of the earth."

They embraced and kissed. Rick put a diamond ring on her finger.

"Thank you, Rick. It is so beautiful."

They had champagne, and then danced again before driving to the Post.

Mary and Rick met Joel and Jane in the living room.

Mary said, "Rick asked me to marry him and I said yes. Look what he gave to me."

Jane and Joel stood. They hugged each of them and said the ring was beautiful.

Joel said, "Wait I will get champagne."

When he returned he toasted them and said, "Welcome to the family officially. You have been a member of our family for a long time, but it is now official"

Jane asked, "When will you be married, and where will it be, and will it be formal or casual, and what about invitations?"

"Rick and I will need to talk about those things, but we will talk with you about the details as soon as we decide."

Joel remarked, "I couldn't be happier about this. We have been hoping that this might happen."

They drank the champagne and talked until they all were tired and went to bed.

CHAPTER L

In the morning Rick asked Mary to go for a walk with him so that they could talk.

Mary suggested, "Let's go down by the river. There is a bench there that we can sit on."

That sounded good to Rick.

As they walked out Mary said to Jane, "We are going down by the river to make some plans. We will be back soon."

Rick told Mary, "The wedding will be as you want it to be. I might make a suggestion, but I want you to have exactly what you want. Money is no object. If you want something, you may have it. I do have one request. I would hope that we could get married as soon as possible. I would like for us to get started on our own. Do you have an idea where you would like the wedding to be held?'

"I guess we could have it here. I really don't know."

"Mary, remember what my question was. Where would you *like* to be married?"

"That is a problem Rick. If you still owned the cabin, I would like for it to be in the front of the cabin."

"That, we can take care of. It will be at the front of the cabin."

"Would you like to have a minister to perform the ceremony?"

"Mom and Dad know a minister that they like. I would like him to marry us."

"I don't believe there will be any problem in getting him. Do you want to have formal or informal dress?"

"In front of the cabin I believe that informal would be best."

"Do you have in mind a list of people that you would like to invite?

"I have two girl friends from the ER, and I would like to invite Mark and Joan. I may think of others later."

Rick suggested, "I would like to invite the Brothers, Pete and Al, and any at the Native Village that would like to attend."

"That sounds fine to me. I will talk with Mom about invitations, and things like food and drink."

"Let me know anyway that I can help."

"On a different subject, "If you wish we can go to your storage unit and pick up anything that you want to take with you. My house in North Dakota will be our headquarters, and anything that you wish to keep we can take there."

"I made an inventory of what I stored. By looking at the list I can see what I need."

Do you have any idea where you would like to go for our honeymoon?"

"Yes, I would love to go to Hawaii."

"Then, Hawaii it will be."

"You will be handling the wedding. Do you want me to tell you what I have in mind for our adventure after the honeymoon?"

"You are letting me have the wedding that I want, and the honeymoon in Hawaii. I love that. I don't know anything about arranging an adventure or about finances. I would ask you to take care of those two things. I would like to be surprised. Whatever you decide I know will be in my best interest, and I will love it. I do have a question about my furniture which is in storage. Will I need to continue to store it? Will we need it somewhere, sometime?"

"If there is any furniture that you like that could replace mine, we could take it and make the change. Other than that, I believe that rather than pay storage and moving fees, we can buy what we want if we decide to settle down somewhere other than North Dakota. By the way, you will be free to modify my house, or change furniture or whatever you want."

"Thank you, Rick. I believe that I would like to talk to Mom about all of this, and then go to the storage place tomorrow for a preliminary look."

"Let's use your car tomorrow rather than borrowing your Dad's car again?"

"Of course."

They returned to the cabin. Mary sought out Jane, and Rick teamed up with Joel.

Rick briefed Joel, and Mary briefed Jane.

Joel remarked, "If the two ER girls need to get off at the same time that might become a problem."

"The main thing is that Mary gets what she wants. We can't have a repeat if it doesn't come off as planned. I like her idea of going to Hawaii for our honeymoon. We will go to North Dakota after the wedding, and then fly to Hawaii from there. North Dakota will be our home base. You may use it at any time if we are there or not."

"Thanks. I have never been there."

The next day Rick and Mary drove to the storage facility. Mary took only a few things.

Mary said, "I don't believe that it is worth shipping this to your house, and we don't have the time to sell it. I suppose that we will have to give it to "Goodwill.""

Rick suggested, "I wonder if Stewart and Alice could either use it or sell it?"

"That would be fine with me."

"I will give them a call this evening. We have the mining equipment to give to them also."

Rick reminded Joel that they needed to call Stewart and Alice. He also told him about Mary's furniture.

Joel gave Stewart's phone number to Rick. Rick called and left a message for them.

Later, Rick's phone rang. It was Stewart.

"Stewart, we sold the mine, but we would like to give to you and Alice our mining equipment."

"That would be great. Thank you. When should we pick it up?"

"You can come out now, or some time later. It is up to you."

"We can come now. Where are the items?"

"We are at the Trading Post, and the equipment is here also."

"Thank you, we are on our way."

Stewart and Alice took the gear, and the storage unit and contents was transferred to them.

Plans had been made for the wedding. Invitations were made primarily by phone. A caterer had been hired. Tables and chairs were brought in. The minister had agreed to marry them. The wedding day arrived. Mark had brought his wife Joan and his photographers. Pete and Al as well as the Brothers were there. The Native Village had responded by bringing what appeared to be the whole tribe, except for their children, and their baby sitters. Mary's ER friends, Terry and Ruth arrived just in time. Joel had hired a group of musicians. There was a violinist, a bass fiddle player, a drummer and a vocalist. The air was filled with happy sounds of laughter, and music. The weather was perfect with a temperature of about seventy degrees. The sun was shining. The ladies all looked beautiful. Rick, Mark, Joel and the minister all wore suits. The other men wore their customary Alaska clothing.

Rick had asked the Brothers to act together as his best man. The ring had been made from some of the nuggets that Rick had first found at the waterfall.

The loud speaker asked for quiet, and Joel escorted Mary to the front of the cabin where the minister was standing, while the musicians played.

To the minister's questions Mary and Rick said "I do."

The Brothers gave the plain gold ring to Rick. He placed it on Mary's finger. The minister then pronounced them married. He invited Rick to kiss the bride. He did, and the audience applauded and cheered. Congratulations were made. Joel, Jane, Mary and Rick happily hugged. Rick and Mary spoke with each person and thanked them for coming.

Rick and Mary thanked Mark and Joan for the use of the site for the wedding, and for the photographer. Mark told them that photos would be sent to them in care of the Trading Post.

Tables were set up. The group of almost a hundred people sat. A large table at the front was set up for Rick and Mary, Joel and Jane, the Brothers, Pete and Al, Ruth and Terry, Mark and Joan, the minister, and the Chief of the Native Village.

The caterers served the food while the music played.

Rick was asked to speak. "My wonderful adventure in Alaska would not have been possible without your help and friendship. As I leave, I take along, my wife, the friendship of Joel and Jane, and the bonds that have formed between you and me. I will always be grateful and will remember each of you. Thank you."

After eating, Joel and Jane drew Rick and Mary aside. They gave them a wedding present of a check for ten thousand dollars. It was to be used for their honeymoon. Rick attempted to decline the generous gift, but Joel and Jane insisted.

The good bye with Joel and Jane was very emotional. "We will see you after the honeymoon. Please take good care of Bart."

Mark approached Rick one more time. He said, "You and I relate well together. Let this meeting not be our last. We may have further business, or just enjoy our friendship."

"I am with you friend. We will keep in touch."

After saying goodbye, Rick and Mary drove off on their honeymoon and to the next adventure.

ALASKA
The End